FALLIN' TIDES

ALSO BY TORI FORD

(Writing as Victoria Scott)

The Collector

The Liberator

The Warrior

Fire & Flood

Salt & Stone

Titans

Hear the Wolves

Violet Grenade

We Told Six Lies

FALLIN' TIDES

TORI FORD

White Rock Books

Content Notice: *Fallin' Tides* contains depictions of alcoholism, family estrangement, military death (off page), strong language, and explicit sex.

ISBN: 979-8-9958-3720-6

Ebook ISBN: 979-8-9958-3720-6

Cover illustration by Austin Drake

Cover design by Jet Purdie

For my grandmother, Jo Ford, the most vivacious, glamorous woman who ever lived. I will set pages on fire in your name.

HOLLY RIVER
HOLLY HALL
HOLLY HALL
Clover Patch Market
HUMBLE PIES
MAGNOLIA ANTIQUES
HUMBLE PIE
MAGNOLIA ANTIQUES
CLOVER PATCH MARKET
STAGE COACH INN
GAZEBO
MOONBEAM CREAMERY
STAGE COACH INN
STAGECOACH INN
MOONBEAM CREAMERY

MUG SHOTS
Mug Shots
BLESSINGS BARN
HOLIDAY TREE
PARDON MY GARDEN
BUTTERMILK CAFE
ALICE'S HOUSE
COMMUNITY GARDEN

AUGUST

1
ALICE

IN HOLLY RIVER, autumn arrives the first day of August, temperature be damned. The residents stand determinedly on their front porches, hands resting on hips, eyes cast toward the blazing sun, and collectively decide that summer is over. Regardless of whether the pool floats are still inflated. Never mind that their A/C units wheeze from exertion.

Summer is out.

Fall is in.

No one accepts this fact faster than Maggie, who insists we must bid farewell to one season and welcome the next with ceremonial lemon drop martinis. And that I have fifteen minutes to get my rear end to her place.

I rush down the stairs, the steps groaning like bullfrogs beneath my feet. Through the stairwell window, the street is a cornucopia of orange and burgundy, and Mrs. Devonshire, my neighbor, is wrestling a life-size scarecrow into a rocking chair. School isn't back in session for another week, and yet all of Holly River is already huffing pumpkin spice.

But for a small town whose economy runs on tourism, creating a perpetual holiday environment makes perfect sense.

Grabbing the feed from the mudroom, I head outside to where my girls are scavenging for beetles and earthworms. Pickles, an Easter Egger with a deluded sense of superiority, pecks my ankle the moment I step into the grass.

"Calm down, you little piranha." I smile at her unapologetic audacity, wondering if she could spare a smidge.

As I scatter the grain, Dixie and Mabel join the fray, their feathers catching the fading sunlight. In East Texas, our Sinclair name is synonymous with HVACs. Specifically, the industrial-grade cooling systems required for broiler warehouses. My parents spent thirty years ensuring that twenty thousand chickens at a time didn't turn into rotisseries prematurely. With that feat came the assumption that their children would one day take the company reins.

Four months ago, my family moved to Louisiana to expand the business, expecting I'd follow suit the moment I tossed my Texas A&M graduation cap and packed the remaining furniture in our home. Except every time I contemplate leaving the house I grew up in, a cold knot of anxiety forms in my chest. I should be sitting in the Sinclair Systems new Shreveport office right now, talking ductwork and ventilation.

Instead, I've parked myself in Holly River, hiding sketches and dreaming about things that don't involve cubic footage of a broiler warehouse. I've been back here since June, and so far my biggest accomplishment is teaching Mabel how to jump for a grape. I have plans—big, terrifying, will probably, definitely fail plans. But summoning the courage to actually take the leap has proven insurmountable. But I'll get there.

I think.

My phone vibrates, and I pull it from my pocket, laughing when I see the text from Maggie.

> If you aren't here in five minutes, I'm telling everyone your middle name is Pervis. Get moving, Sinclair!

Dashing back inside, I throw on a pair of high-waisted jeans, a cream silk camisole, and my favorite pale-blue cowboy boots. Then I dart for the front door, stopping in the foyer for one indulgent moment. The wall here is high, damask wallpaper faded. If it were gone, sunlight would pour across the space, bathing the room in a golden hue each afternoon. In my sketchbook, I planned it so that local art would hang...*right there*. I can see it so clearly in my mind. It's a dangerous daydream I'm harboring, one that keeps me anchored to a house that's no longer meant to be mine.

On my way to Maggie's, I pass Mug Shots, the smell of coffee and nutmeg wafting through the open window, and The Buttermilk Cafe, the diner where I spend my mornings slinging hash browns and grits. Further down is the Stagecoach Inn, a gazebo, and a wine and cheese shop that sells the most divine raspberry jam.

The layout of Holly River is dictated by the water. The town was built in a crescent along the riverbank, and even now, as the sun begins its flamboyant descent, the air holds that familiar earthy smell I love. I can hear the low rush of the current against the stone embankments behind the main strip. It's the steady heartbeat in a town whose months are measured in holidays, festivals, and homecoming parades.

When I arrive, Maggie is already locking the front door of her flower shop, Pardon My Garden, wearing a pink eyelet dress and combat boots.

"Look at you." Maggie's eyebrows waggle as she catches sight of me. "You actually left the chickens. I was worried you'd start a cult and crown yourself queen."

"Pickles is the queen," I laugh. "I'm just the handmaid."

"Well, the handmaid looks hot tonight." Maggie hooks her arm through mine and steers me down the sidewalk toward the riverfront. "June is battling a new recipe and existential dread, so we'll need to be persuasive."

As we walk, we pass shop after shop with windows dressed in faux-foliage. Even Mr. Hernandez is stapling maple leaf garland to his hardware store awning as the streetlights flicker on.

"The Fall Festival's in November." I gesture to a display of cornstalks outside the pharmacy. "And it's only August. Do we really need a three-month head start?"

"Uh, yeah. It's the biggest night of the year. People have to practice their decorating. It's like the Olympics, but with more burlap." Maggie bumps my hip. "Besides, you love it. We may have just started hanging out this summer, but I know a holiday junkie when I see one."

I shake my head, but I can't stop the smile that sweeps across my face.

"I knew it!" she exclaims. "I have a nose for these things.

That's what people always say about me. They say, 'That Maggie can spot a holi-whore anywhere. And also, she's *really* hot.'"

I nod. "They do say that."

"I know! It's absurd how much people talk about me. *I* should be the queen of your cult. I could usurp that...that bearded one..."

"Pickles," I supply.

Maggie snaps. "Pickles."

We reach Humble Pie, and June emerges, an ethereal, flour-dusted goddess. She usually rivals Maggie's artistic energy, but tonight she's dispirited. June presses her back against the glass door and groans. "I can't go. I've forgotten how to bake and I'll be bankrupt by month's end."

I grab the woman's shoulders, forcing her to meet my eye. "Don't you dare doubt your talent, June. I have erotic fantasies about your quiche. Not a single, solitary Texas soul could bake the way you can. You could make a literal dirt pie and I'd eat it."

June brightens. "Oh, I used to love making those! Maybe I'll make one tomorrow. Extra gummy worms! But wait, adults won't buy a dirt pie unless it's for kids. Which is a shame because it tastes heavenly." June holds up a finger. "I'll make it a *surprise* pie. Only three available. Can't open it until you're home. People'll go nuts."

"Yeah, seems like your creative well is entirely dry," Maggie deadpans.

"I suppose I could go for a drink," June wavers. "But no more than three. Or four."

Our trio complete, we make our way closer to the river and reach Holly Hall, a local institution and sprawling wooden structure that's survived three floods, two fires, and at least one fistfight involving a mechanical bull. As we push through the doors, we're greeted by Garth Brooks crooning over old speakers and a dance floor packed with shuffling boots and weather-beaten cowboy hats.

"To the bar!" June shouts over the music.

I place our order, and after the chilled glasses arrive, Maggie hands out our drinks. "To the end of a perfect summer, and the continuation of an epic—nay, *legendary*—friendship." Maggie and June clink their glasses against my own, lemon drop froth sloshing over sugar-crusted rims. I bring the drink to my lips and sip, relishing the tartness on my tongue.

"Could use more mint." June leans over the bar top, reaching for the garnishes. Dalton, the owner of Holly Hall and June's childhood best friend, slaps at her hands with his rag. "June, I swear to God, if you don't get out of my shit. You are a *customer.*"

"A customer with superior taste buds." June pops another mint leaf into each of our glasses and nods in approval after sampling it. "You love me," she fires at Dalton with a wink, and then turns toward the dance floor.

I glance around the room, a wave of nostalgia hitting me. When I was younger, my brother and I would chase each other around the gravel parking lot while our parents slow-danced to Shania Twain's "You're Still The One." This place has barely changed over the years. The same wooden beams cross the ceiling, and the same stage awaits local touring bands. There isn't an act tonight, but when there is, you get a straight shot of them playing while standing in the bathroom line. Some things are just built exactly right.

"We should dance," I say.

Maggie scrunches up her nose. "God, no. We don't dance sober. We sit our beautiful behinds on these benches and rate the cowboys' asses."

When I give Maggie my best pleading face, she sighs. "Give me 'til the bottom of this glass and then I'll hump your leg on the dance floor all you want."

"Deal!"

One hour of dancing bleeds into two, and then three. The initial rush of the martinis, followed by draft beer, leaves me with a satisfying kind of exhaustion. Outside, the river fog has likely rolled in, blanketing the town in damp coolness, but inside the Hall, the heat is rising. It's nearly eleven when I check my phone. My feet are throbbing, and the music is starting to vibrate behind my eyes.

"I think I'm calling it, guys," I yell so that Maggie can hear me over the fiddle solo ripping through the air. "I've got a glamorous day of refilling coffee tomorrow."

"No! Not yet," Maggie protests, grabbing my wrist. "You can't leave before the slow songs start. Just one more dance, Alice. For the sake of our youth."

I look to June for backup, who gives a sympathetic shrug. "I'm making cinnamon-sugar doughnuts in the morning. Come by the shop before work and I'll give you one on the house. But only if you stay."

I sigh, feeling the siren's call of my bed, but I've only been out with Maggie a handful of times, and June even fewer. It's been a welcome change having friends in Holly River. Friends that feel like they could become permanent fixtures in my life, which is all I ever wanted.

"Fine," I relent. "One more. Then I am walking straight into the river and floating home."

I stand up, stretching my back, and a guy in a tan pearl-snap shirt approaches our table. He's a bit older, with a kind smile and even kinder eyes. He asks me to dance, and I accept, mostly because June is making a *go* expression at me.

He's a good dancer—he knows when to lead and when to spin—but as we move through the two-step, my mind is miles away. I'm thinking about the sketches again. I'm thinking about what kind of lumber I'd need and realizing I know nothing about lumber or what lumber even means. I'm also thinking about the historical romance I'm reading and wishing I could return to those tragically conflicted characters and their lush world.

Across the room, I spot Maggie and June watching me. Maggie catches my eye and, with the subtlety of an earthquake, begins thrusting her hips against the table.

I burst out laughing, nearly stepping on the man's toes.

"Something funny?" He smiles down at me.

"Just my friend." I shake my head. "Sorry."

Suddenly, there's a commotion near the bar. A chair scrapes loudly against the floor, followed by glass shattering. The dancing slows. People crane their necks to get a better glimpse.

"Sounds like a fight," the man holding me mutters. He releases my hand, drawn by the irresistible spectacle of two grown men throttling one another.

The crowd shifts, and now I can see what the crowd does.

I spot a man's broad back, stretching the seams of a dark t-shirt. He's nearly a head taller than anyone surrounding him, and he has a handful of another man's shirt gathered in his fist. The other guy is shouting something incoherent, but the bigger man doesn't respond. He simply shoves the guy away as if bored by the interaction. He shakes his head, points a commanding finger toward the exit, and watches as the troublemaker retreats.

When he turns, my breath hitches.

Because it's *him.*

It's Colt Mitchell.

The boy who made me feel like more than a tennis player. The boy who told me to keep dreaming and was more of a brother to me than Grant was half the time. My parents' honorary second son who practically lived with us for three years before joining the military.

He's older now, his jawline stronger, with shadows beneath his dark eyes. But it's definitely him. I think of the letters I wrote him over the eight years he's been gone. And the few he wrote back.

I hesitate, my feet rooted to the floor. But then his gaze sweeps the room and locks onto mine. His eyes widen. His body goes rigid. And before I even realize it, I'm moving, cutting through the crowd, drawn toward him with magnetic force.

"Colt!" I cry.

He barely has time to brace himself before I launch myself into his arms.

2
COLT

I HAVEN'T STEPPED foot inside this shed since I was sixteen, and the smell certainly hasn't improved. A layer of dirt and pollen covers every tool, including rusted lawn equipment I've never seen operational. Grabbing a shovel, I nudge a pile of dried leaves, ensuring a copperhead isn't sleeping inside, but nothing stirs. My eyes fall on my old man's buzz saw and I give it an awkward pat like it might have the answer for this mess. But it's been silent since my dad left.

That shithead took off in the middle of the night and left behind my mother, his two sons, and a broken-down truck. He didn't even leave a note. Just a half-finished birdhouse he'd promised to build for my birthday and a stack of unpaid bills where a father should be.

I run my hand over the worktable, and my fingers come away filthy. Brushing them off on my jeans, I bend down to inspect the table saw. Despite the neglect, she might have a little life left in her. I continue maneuvering around the cramped space, examining what else might be of use back at Camp Inwood.

I'm not a carpenter yet, but I will be soon enough, especially under Gunnery Sergeant Taylor, now retired, but you wouldn't know it the way he maintains his tools. That man treats plywood with more respect than church folk do their pastor. And he's been generous enough to teach me what he knows, like how to join a dovetail and how to plane and sand oak until it feels like silk.

But my dad taught me the basics long before that. He taught me how to swing a hammer so I wouldn't ruin my wrist. He taught me how to respect the grain of the wood. And then he taught me how to leave.

Two years later, my brother, Warren, followed suit. The day he graduated high school, he packed a bag and hit the road before the ceremony even ended. I was fourteen, standing on the porch, watching his taillights fade. I don't think he even looked back, and I don't blame him. Not anymore.

I glance toward my mom's place, at the rotted siding and grimy windows. Its mere existence is a weight in my chest. I think it has been since I was old enough to realize home wasn't safe. After all, I'm the one who stayed to manage my mother.

Eventually, though, I found my way through that front door too. I traded in secondhand clothes for a combat utility uniform and joined the Marines. Suppose I figured the soil from a half dozen different countries might wash the Holly River silt off my boots. But shit happened, as it always does, and now I'm here again.

The shed doors screech as I yank them shut and turn

toward the house, gravel crunching underfoot. The bank says this one-point-five acres of weeds belongs to me and Warren now. And since Warren is off finding himself in Oregon and hasn't answered my texts in months, it's become my responsibility to sell it.

I should have done exactly that directly after the funeral. But I couldn't stay then. The thought of Mom dying here alone filled me with guilt so paralyzing I felt immobilized by it. It didn't make sense to me, grieving someone who made my life miserable. So I returned to Camp Inwood the moment her casket was lowered into the ground, as if I could somehow outrun the fact that she was gone.

But now, despite being determined to avoid this place, I've found myself back here.

And the reason why is folded inside my wallet.

The air is stale inside the house, the curtains drawn tight. Despite the limited light, I can still see and smell the dust, and I know without looking that every sink and shower is crawling with mold. It's a dump, just like I remember.

The hallway floorboards creak under my weight. I've put on thirty pounds of muscle since I last lived here, and sometimes I feel alien inside my own skin, especially in this house. Pushing open the door to my childhood bedroom, I pause. It's exactly the same—faded posters of classic cars, a mattress without a headboard, and a busted beanbag my dad plucked off someone's curb.

I sit on the edge of the twin-sized bed as if it's someone else's, and then lay back, my head hitting the flattened pillow. My feet hang off the end, and for some reason, that makes me smile. I like the idea of not fitting here anymore. And then, just as quickly, the smile fades. Because I know that's not the way I should feel.

My eyes flick to the open sea bag squatting near the bed. It's the only thing I brought with me from base. A stack of envelopes peeks out from inside, their edges worn from being handled.

Reaching down, I pull one out. The paper is velvet-soft, the handwriting feminine. I don't need to read the words to know what they say—I've memorized them over eight years and three deployments.

I read a few lines anyway. A tentative smile tugs at the corner of my mouth. Then I catch myself and tuck the letter back into the bag.

My phone buzzes, vibrating against my thigh.

I fish it out and see a photo from Dalton.

Dalton was a fellow linebacker back when I lived to hit people under stadium lights. We weren't best friends, but we were brothers in the way only a locker room can forge. Now, he owns Holly Hall, the only bar in town worth its salt. He's sent a picture of a beer sitting on a mahogany bar top. There's an empty stool in front of it.

It's a clear invitation, and I'm grateful for it. Hell, I'd accept it if I didn't have a mountain of paperwork I needed to get through.

I stand and head for the kitchen. The sun is dipping below the treeline, casting the room into shadows. I reach for the light switch and flip it. Nothing happens.

"Dammit," I mutter.

I forgot that I called the utility company and had it turned off after the funeral. The water's off too, then.

Walking to the window, I yank the flimsy curtain aside. Then I collapse into a chair at our wobbly kitchen table and open the folder the realtor sent over. There are disclosures to sign, titles to transfer, and a dozen different ways for the state to take a cut of whatever pittance this place sells for.

I'm twenty-seven, but looking at these papers, I feel eighty. My back aches from the drive down, and my head is heavy with the kind of exhaustion sleep doesn't fix. I start on the forms, my pen scratching against the paper in the dim light.

I work for a couple of hours, checking comps online to see which nearby listings the realtor is referring to. I'm using the flashlight on my phone to see, propping it against a salt shaker. It's pathetic. A grown man sitting in the dark, trying to sign away his meager inheritance by the light of a cell phone.

It's near midnight when my phone buzzes again. Dalton has sent another photo. This time, there's a shot glass sitting next to the beer.

I huff a laugh. Dalton always was a persistent bastard.

Standing, I shove the paperwork back into the folder, grab my wallet from the counter, and make for the door. I've made enough progress for one night, and a beer sounds like exactly what I need.

The walk to Holly Hall takes me through the center of town. As I walk, my eyes dart to every shop I pass. Even though most are closed, I still find myself looking for her. I know where she lives, or rather where she used to live. I could walk the three blocks over and check if her car's in the driveway. Or if the light is on in her bedroom window.

But I haven't worked up the nerve. When I came back

for the funeral, I didn't tell anyone I was coming into town, not even Grant. Even though it's a small town, it's big enough to hide in when you make it your mission, and that's exactly what I did. The last thing I wanted was to broadcast my mom's passing, because then the same people who'd gossiped about her *habits* would've asked me how I felt. How I was doing. I couldn't handle the hypocrisy.

As I pass the town square, I notice everything is already decorated for the festival that'll happen in November. People here live for festivals. They spend all year planning bake-offs and parades and town-wide picnics. It's a bubble of manufactured cheer that I liked as a kid. Now, it feels like people desperate for a diversion.

I know one person in particular who loves it though. She even made her own costumes when we were kids, though her parents disapproved of her spending time on such endeavors. She used to drag me to the apple cider stand and make me drink the stuff until I was sick. Just the thought of her excitement lifts my spirits. Makes me feel something other than numbness.

But then I remember that's all ancient history. Being in the military has given me a new perspective, and it goes like this—people are shit and evil exists. And no amount of decorating can disguise that truth.

I reach Holly Hall and head inside. The music hits me first, followed by the smell of fried chicken and cheap beer. A country song blasts through the speakers as couples scoot across the dance floor. Near the bar, people laugh and smile, talking over one another with such merriment that I want to turn around and walk right back out.

Dalton spots me and grins, teeth white against his

beard. He comes around his bar just enough for us to do that awkward bro-clap—part handshake, part hug.

"Look what the cat dragged in." Dalton slides the beer and shot glass toward me. "Thought you might have crawled into a hole and died."

"Close enough," I mutter.

I take the shot of tequila, feeling it burn all the way down. I follow it with a long pull of beer.

"How's the house?" Dalton crosses his arms.

"Falling down," I reply. "Needs more work than it's worth. Thanks for setting me up with the realtor."

"Everything in this town needs more work than it's worth, Colt. That's the charm." He grins.

I grunt and turn my stool around to face the room. It's late, and the music has shifted to something slower, though not at all quieter.

I'm halfway through my drink when I spot a guy, mid-thirties, leaning over a woman at the end of the bar. She's angling away, her face tight with discomfort. I try to ignore the military instinct to step in and help, and focus on my beer instead.

But then the guy grabs her upper arm, yanking her off the barstool. She stumbles, sending a glass crashing to the floor. Dalton sees it and waves frantically at someone near the back, pointing at the guy. He's signaling for the bouncer, a kid barely old enough to vote.

I sigh, getting to my feet. "Damn it."

The man is still shouting at the woman, his fingers digging into her arm, when I reach him. I snatch his wrist, twisting until he breaks his grip on her. Then I shoulder him away. The man stumbles before finding his footing.

"The hell do you think you're doing?" He sizes me up, taking in the fact that I'm six-foot-three, two-twenty. This makes him pause.

I grab his shirt, yanking him close enough to hear. "You're leaving."

"Let go of me," he slurs, trying to fight me off. "Fucking psycho!"

I lean closer. "If I ever see you lay a hand on a woman again, I'll break your wrist. And then your arm."

I point toward the entrance and shove him in that direction. "Go."

He trips, nearly hitting a table, and then scrambles for the exit. "You're lucky I don't kick your ass!" he yells over his shoulder.

That gets a laugh out of me, because really, the dude can barely walk. I watch until he disappears through the door and then glance in Dalton's direction. He gives a thumbs up as he sweeps the broken glass.

The music is still blasting, but the chatter has died down. When I turn to the dance floor, I realize that people are gawking. Immediately, I'm hit with a familiar twist of unease. The one that demands I find a corner, or a bottle, to disappear into.

I'm about to return to the bar when someone steps aside to let a server through. And I see her.

My heart stops.

At first, my brain sees only the past. That eleven-year-old with the ponytail and the paperbacks who used to follow me and her brother around. My best friend's little sister. The girl whose home and life I intruded upon.

The same girl who wrote me all those letters.

But then someone crosses in front of her, and the illusion shatters. And I recognize then that she's not what I remember. She's grown up. She's a *woman*. And that fact seems somehow more unbelievable than anything else I've encountered these past eight years.

Alice.

Her eyes are wide, fixed on me with an expression of pure, unadulterated shock.

I'm instantly hit with a wave of shame.

She starts moving. Quickly. She swims through the crowd toward me and I brace myself. Because she may yell. She may demand to know why I didn't answer her letters after everything her family did for me.

But instead, she launches herself at me.

Her arms wrap around my waist, and her face buries into my chest.

I stand frozen, my hands hovering in the air, unsure where to place them. But then, the warmth of her hits me, and with it comes every good memory I have of Holly River.

I wrap my arms around her, tucking my face into her hair, and pull her so tightly I'm afraid I might actually hurt her. For one unsullied moment, the last fifteen years of my life—the deadbeat dad, the deployments, the funeral—it all just... fades away.

My lips find her ear. "Hey, kid."

Alice releases me suddenly, taking a sharp backward step. I notice the flush in her face, though whether it's from the heat or something else, I'm not sure.

"I'm sorry," she mumbles. "I'm so sorry. I've got to go."

"Alice," I call out.

But she's already barreling toward the front door. I start after her, because I just sent a drunk asshole out there and the thought of her running into him shoots panic through me.

A woman I recognize from years ago—Maggie?—throws up a stiff hand in front of me. "We've got her," she snaps. And then she and another woman all disappear through the exit.

And I'm left standing there, feeling like I just lost Alice Sinclair all over again.

3
BEFORE

I CLUTCHED THE THIRD-PLACE RIBBON, disappointed because I knew I was supposed to be. The plastic medal—adorned with only a cheap sticker—swung in a pendulum as I walked toward our car, a constant reminder that while I wasn't the worst ten-year-old to pick up a tennis racket, I certainly wasn't the best either.

I slumped into the passenger seat of our SUV, the leather sticking to my sweaty thighs. The car smelled like industrial-strength sunscreen and the banana I ate between matches. Outside, the sun was setting, making the world shine in a way that felt far too cheerful for my mood.

"You should be proud, Alice." Mom's hands gripped the wheel. She didn't look at me as she navigated the parking lot of angry parents and exhausted players. "Third place is progress."

I flicked the ribbon. "It's basically a participation trophy."

Mom sighed. "It doesn't matter what place you got.

Not yet. What matters is that your footwork has vastly improved since last month. However," she paused, and that pause carried the weight of countless group classes and private lessons. "We need to carve out time for that backhand. You're still slicing when you should be driving through. You're not returning with topspin. Especially on cross-court shots."

And there it was.

I leaned my head against the glass window. My calf was twitching, and my elbow ached from overuse, but I still had the drive-home lecture to survive.

"I know, Mom. I was tired."

"Fatigue is just a lack of preparation," she replied.

My parents met at Vanderbilt, both scholarship athletes with a shared love for small towns and big ambitions. They had their heads squarely on their shoulders at all times, unlike Grant and I who—according to them—didn't know how easy we had it and might very well watch our heads roll off from lack of use.

As we neared town, I let the window down and breathed in the smell of the river. The rushing wind made it feel cool outside, even though spring in Holly River was already hot enough to fry eggs on asphalt.

The gazebo was wrapped in colorful artificial flowers, and every window box along the square was planted with real ones in preparation for Easter. The sight made me smile despite today's results. Soon, all the little kids would race through that same gazebo searching for what the Bunny brought, and Sarah-Beth and I would walk around watching them and eating frosted sugar cookies from the bakery, because we were *way* too old for the Easter Bunny.

Mom rolled up the window, and my smile vanished.

"It's making my ears ring," she explained.

I sighed and shoved an arm into my backpack, my fingers searching for the dog-eared copy of *The Cowboy Alchemist*. I needed magic. I needed lassos. I needed a world where nobody cared about the velocity of a yellow felt ball. Inside the pages of a book, there were no expectations. No disappointing looks. There was a life vastly different from my own, one where character flaws were celebrated instead of criticized.

But as my fingers closed around the paperback, Mom held out her phone, wiggling it.

"Actually, jelly bean, watch this instead," she said. "I filmed your last match. It'll be helpful to see your backhand for yourself."

I gritted my teeth and tapped the play button. My own ponytailed silhouette stood at the baseline, looking small and perpetually late to the ball. Watching myself play, my cheeks burned with shame. Every technical flaw, every mistake, was suddenly glaring.

"Can I please just read?" My voice shook.

Mom frowned, reaching over to pat my leg. "Just watch it, Alice. You're going to have to outwork the competition, and that means watching while everyone else is reading."

Wonderful. A metaphor and a veiled insult in one.

Outwork the competition was code for: *you don't have natural talent*.

By the time we pulled into our alleyway, I was over tennis and beyond starving. My stomach gave a cavernous growl that sounded like a tectonic plate shift (I learned about that in science!).

When I glimpsed Dad's truck in the driveway, I shot upright. "Did Dad make dinner?"

"He said he was picking something up." Mom turned off the engine.

Best thing I'd heard all day.

I unbuckled, grabbed my tennis bag, and sprinted for the front door. When I burst inside, the scent of grease and salt nearly buckled my knees.

"Oh, my god, that smells so good." I headed toward the kitchen, dropping my bag. "Mom told me you—"

I froze.

Dad was leaning over the granite island, shoving fries into his mouth. My older brother, Grant, was slumped at the kitchen table, wearing a grass-stained football jersey and stretching out his hamstring with an obnoxious groan.

But it was the third person who stopped me mid-stride.

Sitting next to Grant was a boy I'd never seen before. He was older than me—my brother's age, I figured—with shaggy, dark blonde hair that fell over his forehead, and brown eyes that appeared startled by my entrance. He was wearing a high school practice jersey, same as Grant.

When our eyes met, he didn't look away. Instead, he gave a small smile that made me suddenly very aware that my hair was a frizzy mess being held back by a sweaty pink headband.

Grant barely even looked up. He just flipped a limp hand in my general direction. "My sister. The dork."

"I'm not a dork," I snapped, though my heart wasn't in it. My eyes were darting between the greasy white paper bags that littered the table. "Where's mine?"

Dad tipped his head back, still chewing. "Your brother

invited a friend over. And I didn't know what time y'all'd be back."

"So you gave him my dinner?" My voice went so high it cracked.

"I can make you a grilled cheese or something." Dad reached for his drink, pointing the straw at me like a conductor's baton. "You should talk to Colt. He'd be a good influence on both of you."

I glared at Colt. He was looking down at his lap, his ears turning a faint shade of pink.

"You kids don't know what real work looks like," Dad continued, launching into his favorite monologue while scratching his beard. "Colt here spent his whole summer working on one of our client's farms before two-a-days started. That kind of work ethic translates to the field. *And* the court," he added as Mom walked in behind me, dropping her keys on the counter.

I didn't catch the rest of the sermon on manual labor. I was too busy staring daggers at the good influence squatting in *my* chair, eating *my* dinner. Colt seemed to feel the heat of my gaze. He shifted, his chair creaking, and grabbed the box sitting in front of him. There were four nuggets left, growing cold in a bed of crumbs.

I snatched my tennis bag off the floor, ready to storm into my room, but stopped when I heard the boy speak. "Hey, kid. You can have the rest." I turned to find him standing up halfway, holding out the box to me. "I'm done."

I looked at the nuggets. Then I looked at him. Then I looked at Grant, who was currently seeing how many fries he could fit in his mouth at once.

The indignity was too much. I was third-place Alice. I

was no-topspin Alice. And now, I was pity-nugget Alice, which maybe I deserved. Trophy Kid was probably at their favorite restaurant right now, a still-warm cheeseburger and fries presented to them on bended knee and a silver serving dish.

"I don't want your leftovers," I hissed.

"Alice, don't be rude," Mom warned from the sink.

I spun away from the boy's consolation prize and marched down the hallway. I didn't stop until I'd closed my bedroom door behind me, barely restraining myself from slamming it because that'd only earn me another lecture.

Flopping face-down onto my bed, I groaned. Behind me, my room was a graveyard of *potential*. There were trophies on the shelf—mostly from camps I'd attended, nothing won. There were posters of professional players mid-swing, their form perfect, their wrists locked in the exact position Mom wanted. In the corner, my desk was buried under an avalanche of library books and smooth river stones I'd painted to look like monsters.

I rolled onto my back and stared at the ceiling. Then I reached for a basket nestled in my nightstand that held resin figurines I'd collected since kindergarten. I'd been awarded one each time I did my homework unprompted, but they'd quickly become repetitive. Now, I had eight or more replicas of each animal, though the colors and sizes varied slightly.

I started organizing them into groups. The ducks—white and yellow both—gathered near my knee, the elephants next to the opposite one. When I placed the rabbits halfway between the other two, I decided maybe *all* the animals were traveling somewhere. I began rearranging them into one long line, and then my hand stilled, imagining what my parents would say if they caught me doing this instead of checking my homework.

In my head, I could hear Mom's voice: *If you don't brush up the back of the ball...*

And then Dad's: *Colt is disciplined. He isn't afraid to put in the work...*

Most annoyingly, I saw Colt's face. That shy smile. The way he'd offered me his dinner like I was an orphan in my own home.

I swept the animals back into the basket, picturing them begging for more playtime as I tucked them away. Instead of caving to their tiny demands, I rolled off the bed and trudged to my desk. After shoving hand-painted rock monsters aside, I grabbed my math folder.

If I couldn't have topspin, I'd at least have this algebra worksheet completed well before its due date. I sat down, stomach rumbling with hunger, and began to work. Somewhere in the distance, I heard the boy laughing and gripped my pencil so tightly it nearly broke.

4
COLT

I SWING THE MALLET, the crack of wood hitting wood echoing through the loblolly pines. The fence post sinks another satisfying inch into the red clay. My hands, calloused from eight years in the Corps, sting with the vibration of each strike. Already, I'm sweating through my shirt, the fabric clinging to my back in the August heat.

I stop, wiping the salt from my eyes with the back of a work glove. This fence is a piece of shit. Half the rails are rotting, and the wire is rusted through where deer pushed their way into the makeshift garden—one of Mom's many temporary hobbies, each lasting as long as her sobriety.

I don't know why I'm even bothering. Within weeks, some family or developer looking for a fixer-upper will own this one-point-five acreage, and they'll probably tear the whole damn fence down anyway. But repairing the perimeter feels cathartic, like maybe there's one thing I can set right again.

Leaning against the post, I pull from a lukewarm gallon

of water. Then I rip off my gloves and stare down at my hands.

I can still feel her.

In my head, Alice had remained thirteen or fourteen years old with braces. She was the little girl who sprinted down the river dock barefoot before curling her body into a tiny cannonball. But the Alice walking toward me last night was no child.

She was wearing a top that draped over curves I had no business noticing. Her hair was pulled back in one of those buns that could be let down in seconds, and her eyes—those wide, blue eyes—were locked on mine. She looked happy. Genuinely, heartbreakingly happy to see me.

And I stood there like an idiot when she hugged me. Until my brain caught up with what was happening. Then I'd wrapped my arms around her, pulling her flush against me.

And that was the mistake.

Because when I held her, I felt the press of her breasts against my chest, the narrowness of her waist, the heat of her breath against my skin. My body—which apparently has zero loyalty to my best friend—instantly reacts to the memory.

"Absolutely the fuck not," I mutter. Shoving my hands back into the gloves, I pick up the next rail and slide it into the notches, determined not to think about her. Or the way she felt.

Dalton mentioned that she's been working at the diner. I wonder, for the tenth time today, if she's there now. She seemed upset last night. It'd only be right to check on her.

I drop the tools where I stand and start walking.

Ten minutes down a blacktop road, the oaks and pines give way to boutiques, antique shops, and an ice cream stand where children chase each other, sticky-faced and laughing. Overhead, the sky stretches wide and blue the way only a Texas sky does.

The scent of the river carries on the breeze. It's a muddy, earthy smell that's always grounded me. I can't remember how long it's been since I took a swim, but Grant, Alice, and I used to spend every Sunday at the bend, jumping off the cypress knees until our skin wrinkled and we raced back home for fried chicken.

I reach the diner—The Buttermilk Cafe.

I walk past it.

When I get to the end of the block, I stare at a window display of knitted scarves and fall leaves, then turn around and walk back. I do this twice more, approaching the front door only to bypass it. My heart is thundering against my ribs in a way I haven't felt since I was on point in a hot zone.

But I can't return to working on the fence until I see her. I need to know she's okay.

I push the door open. Overhead, a bell jingles so loudly that I wince. Anyone in the tristate area now knows I've entered The Buttermilk Cafe.

The air smells of bacon, maple syrup, and burnt coffee. My eyes immediately sweep the restaurant, searching for her, but she's nowhere in sight. The diner is packed with the lunch crowd, so I slide into a vinyl booth in the corner, trying to make myself small, which is comedic given my frame.

"Afternoon. What can I get you?"

A girl who looks like she should be in a high school

geometry class instead of a waitress apron stands over me. Her name tag reads *Suzanne*. She's got a wad of bubblegum in her mouth and a look of rehearsed exhaustion on her face.

"Coffee. And..." I glance down at the menu. "Two eggs, over easy. Grits. Bacon." I pause, my gaze darting to the pancake section. "Couple of pancakes."

"Anyone else joining you?"

"Nope, just me. Thanks." I hand her the menu, and she flits away. I scan the room again. Through the kitchen pass-through window, Frank—a man who's owned this place for as long as I can remember—argues with the cook. I spot a group of ladies drinking from red plastic cups and sharing a plate of fries, and a few tables down, I see two boys—one older and one younger—that immediately remind me of Warren.

My food arrives quickly, and I dig in, glancing up every few seconds, pretending like it doesn't matter who I see. The counter is lined with butts on barstools, cowboy hats resting nearby. Between every third patron is an arrangement of orange and yellow flowers protruding from a miniature pumpkin, undoubtedly purchased from the florist next door.

The stuff is inescapable. I have no doubt its purpose is to instill a sense of festivity and drive sales of—I check the chalkboard—pumpkin pancakes and apple pie French toast. And yet, the militant fall decorating happening across this entire town makes me feel hollow inside.

"Listen," a voice booms from the kitchen. "I know meat. Hear me? I know what I'm talkin' about."

Frank has a way of both overenunciating every word

that starts with a 'wh'—as if attempting the sound for the first time—and adding a drawl to any others. His lips move aggressively with every 'who, what' and 'where.'

The massive, horizontal man rounds the corner, throwing a rag over his shoulder. He stops shy of the counter and puts his hands on his hips, inspecting the crowd the same way I did. When he spots me, a thinking line forms between his eyes. And then he grins as his mind connects the dots. He tosses the rag onto a nearby table and makes his way across the room.

Frank stops when his belly presses against the edge of my table. He points at me. "I remember you. You're that military boy."

I smile. "I think there's more than one of us in this town."

"You come back for your mama's funeral?"

My breath catches at the question. "How'd you know—?"

"Me and hers was friends. She was a beautiful woman, that one. *Real* beautiful."

Horror grips me as I realize what he's getting at. I try to focus on my eggs, slicing them so that the yolk runs yellow across the plate.

Frank drops his substantial weight into the booth across from me, and I lean back, my fork stilling. He puts his forearms on the table. "Lotta' beautiful women in this town. I need to get out of this restaurant. I'm practically chained to it, you know. I need to spread my wings." He lowers his voice, but not by much. "And my seed."

"Jesus," I mutter.

Frank produces a pack of Marlboro Golds, taps it

against his palm until one protrudes, and then yanks it out with his teeth. He lets it dangle there at the corner of his lips as he says, "Doctor says I gotta cut down on nicotine, so I traded out my Reds for these Golds."

"I don't think—"

"Hey," he interrupts, shoving his heavy frame backward against the booth. The woman sitting on the opposite side throws a startled look over her shoulder. He points at me with the cigarette now, tucking the pack away. "That brother of yours doing alright? Where'd he end up anyhow?"

My eyes drop to my plate. "He's in Oregon."

Frank whistles. "Long way from Texas. What's he doing out there?"

"Uh, he's with a team of—"

I trail off when an older woman walks by and Frank practically breaks his neck watching her cross to the far side of the restaurant. When he catches her eye, he cocks his head in greeting. She purses her lips and sits down, smoothing her dress beneath her.

And then she returns his smile, just barely.

Frank guffaws and turns back to me. "Goddamn, women just get hotter and hotter as they age. They get that life experience in 'em and they just don't want our shit no more and that makes me want to crawl on all fours and bark like a dog, know what I mean?"

"Frank," I say.

Frank slaps the table. "Well, go on then, tell me what your brother's up to."

I breathe in, losing a fighting battle against laughing.

"He's in Oregon. He's been a firefighter for several years now."

Frank nods thoughtfully and digs a lighter out of his shirt pocket. "Mm-hmm, mm-hmm. Both of you boys became men of the cloth. I like that. It's fitting."

"I think that's...a religious thing."

"What is?"

"Man of the cloth. It's about, like, ministers and pastors."

Frank flicks the grinder on his lighter and leans in. He sucks on his cigarette and then blows smoke out of the corner of his mouth while shaking his head. "No," he says. "No, I don't think so."

The waitress materializes beside our table, appearing stricken. "Excuse me, Frank. There's..." She glances around wildly, as if willing someone to save her. She softens her voice. "There's no smoking in here."

Frank scrunches up his face. "Says who, Suzanne?"

The girl's eyes widen. "Y...you do."

"These. Fuckin'. Rules." Frank shakes his head, looking at me like I'll back him up.

"Frank," I say. "Give her a break." I look at the girl. "He's putting it out."

"Like hell I am."

I take the cigarette from him and, after considering where to put it, I drop it in my coffee.

"Goddammit, Colt. I'm not getting you another one!" Frank schootches over—the vinyl creaking beneath him—and then rises to his feet. He looks at Suzanne and jabs a thumb over his shoulder. "Grab him another coffee, will you?"

He points at me. "But only because you're a vet. Otherwise, I'd kick your ass." Frank thinks deeply for a second. "You think I could kick your ass?"

"Definitely," I say, biting into a piece of bacon.

Frank sniffs the air and spins toward the kitchen. "What did I say about putting it on the grill?" he hollers, already headed in that direction.

It's only when he moves that I see her.

Alice comes out of the kitchen with three plates balanced on her arms. Before I can stop myself, a smile forms.

She's wearing a simple white t-shirt and jeans, a dark green apron tied around her waist. She's moving through the chaos of the lunch rush with a grace that seems almost balletic. She beams at an older man, laughing at something he says as she refills his water. She looks happy. She looks capable.

She looks like she belongs here, in this sunshine-filled room with these jovial people who clearly adore her.

I should get up. I should leave cash on the table and disappear back into the pines. My brain is screaming at me to get the hell out and leave her to her serene life.

But I can't move.

The letter in my wallet roots me in place.

5
ALICE

I SEE Colt and instantly I'm smiling. I don't think about how humiliated I am that I threw myself into his arms last night. All I think is:

He's here!

I refill a customer's coffee before setting down the pot. Then I move toward Colt, wiping my hands on my apron as I go. Under the fluorescent lights, with the sun shining through the windows, I can see more clearly how he's changed.

The boy who once hung his head is gone. In his place sits a man with broad shoulders and a face that's traded adolescent uncertainty for quiet confidence. His dark blonde hair is buzzed into a military cut that highlights the intensity of his gaze. He's sitting with his back perfectly straight, squared to the world.

"Hey," I say, smiling so widely it hurts.

"Hey," Colt responds. "I, uh, I didn't know you worked here."

I glance around the restaurant, gesturing vaguely at the

wood-paneled walls and broken jukebox. "Oh, yeah. Just for a couple of months." Twelve inches from the ceiling, a toy train rattles along a miniature track, making loops around the room. I adored watching it as a kid, and still do. "I'm the lead specialist in caffeine distribution and...pie management."

He smiles softly at that, and my heart sings. It's always been satisfying to get a smile out of Colt Mitchell.

An awkward silence descends, and my mind immediately rewinds to last night. The Hall. The hug. And then me, practically sprinting away.

"Is it good?" I ask quickly, nodding toward his half-eaten breakfast plate. "You still like eggs, I see. Not as good as I make 'em though, huh? If you don't like them, I could get you something else—"

"No," he interrupts, his voice gentle. "They're... It's perfect." He pauses, leaning forward onto his forearms. "Listen, Alice—"

"Sinclair!"

Frank, my boss, marches over. "The delivery truck is here. And Luke just called in *sick*." At the last word, Frank mimes drinking. "Damn kid doesn't know how to hold his liquor. Or lie, for that matter. I need you to unload it. Suzanne will cover your tables."

Frank jabs a thick arm toward the kitchen and booms, "I saw that, Suzanne!" He shakes his head and walks away, muttering, "Fuckin' Suzanne."

I turn back to Colt, frowning, feeling like I might consider quitting if it meant staying here, with him, for just one moment longer. "Sorry, I've got to run."

Colt shoots to his feet, producing a twenty from his wallet and tossing it on the table. "I'll help you."

My eyes widen as he stands. *Was he always this tall?* "Oh, you don't have to do that." I glance in Frank's direction. "I'm not even sure you're allowed to."

Colt smiles again, just a small thing. "I'm not worried about Frank."

He motions to go ahead, indicating he'll follow.

I shrug, secretly delighted, and turn on my heel. We walk to the back of The Buttermilk Cafe where a white truck idles in the alleyway, its back doors flung wide to reveal towers of cardboard boxes and crates. We get started, working in a rhythm that feels surprisingly natural. I grab the lighter stuff —the napkins, the plastic cutlery, the bread—while Colt lunges for the heavy crates of canned goods and milk.

Every few seconds, his eyes flick to the alleyway, and then the sky, as if searching for something. "You don't do this at night, do you?" he finally asks, frowning. "There aren't any streetlights."

A warm sensation spreads through my chest. "No. We never unload at night."

Colt nods to that, visibly relaxing. "So," he continues, hoisting a crate of whipped cream. "How's Grant?"

"He's okay," I reply, dodging a rogue puddle. "He's in Shreveport with my parents. They're trying to expand into Louisiana."

Colt stops mid-lift. "The chicken thing?"

"The chicken thing," I confirm. "And Warren?"

"Also good. He's in Oregon now."

Still working as a firefighter, I suspect. Colt mentioned

that in one of his early letters. But since I haven't heard from him in three years, I can't be sure.

We move back and forth, the silence between us filled by the thud of boxes hitting the metal dolly. I can't help but notice the way the muscles in his arms and back flex as he works. His skin glistens with a light sheen of sweat, and his forearms are peppered with dirt, as if he were working outdoors before arriving at the diner. I suddenly remember how his arms felt around me last night. Strong, firm. Like my legs could've given out beneath me and I'd still be standing. Watching him work, I find myself chewing my lip, imagining his hands—

Stop. Oh, my god. No.

He's practically family.

"Are you staying at your mom's place?" I ask, firmly extracting my mind from the gutter.

"No." He sets a box down a touch harder than necessary. "I'm at the Stagecoach Inn."

"The Stagecoach?" His mom has always been a touchy subject, of course. But if he'd needed a place to stay... Had I known he was in town... "Is your mom not... Is she doing okay?"

"She's dead."

The ground falls out from under me. How could I not have known? How could someone in my *family* not have known? It makes me question the three years he spent basically living with us.

Colt is trying awfully hard to pretend this is simply factual information he's sharing, but I catch the grief he attempts to conceal.

"It was about six months ago," he adds shortly. He

doesn't look at me. "So the power and water are off at the house. I'm selling it, so there's no need to turn them back on."

"Colt," I say gently.

He keeps working, avoiding my gaze. "Doctor said it looked like she was trying to quit cold turkey." He shakes his head. "I told her before that she couldn't do it that way. She should have called me, or seen the doctor. It's her own fault." Colt sounds detached from what he's saying. But I know better.

I move toward him cautiously, abandoning the crates. Reaching out, I wrap my hand around his forearm and keep it there. I *want* to keep it there.

"I'm so sorry, Colt," I murmur. "But listen, she was *trying.*" I tip my head so that he's forced to meet my eyes. When he does, I offer a sad smile. "Maybe she felt like she needed to do it on her own. It's kind of admirable, you know? She died...fighting."

Colt winces like he's pained by what I just said, but then his eyes are tracing the lines of my face and his lips are parting. And he says, quietly, "You always look at the world in perfect lighting, Alice. I envy that." Colt takes an almost indiscernible step closer, and my skin burns at the proximity. "What are you really doing here?"

The question steals the breath from my lungs.

And I want to answer him.

I want to tell the entire world what I want to do. What I *intend* to do. But the words catch in my throat, replaced by the echo of my father's voice:

You focus too much on what's possible instead of what's

likely. You gotta be realistic, Alice, or you're going to face more days like today.

Colt is watching me too intently, his face mere inches away, and it suddenly feels hard to think because I'm not sure anyone has ever looked at me the way he's looking at me now. It's like he wants to unravel every thought in my mind, turning each one over in the light before tucking them into his breast pocket for safekeeping. I wet my lips to speak, to say *something*, but before I can respond, the back doors of the cafe clatter open.

"What the hell are you two doing out here?" Frank bellows, stepping onto the loading dock. "Would you care to return to your tables at some point?"

"Easy, Frank," Colt says.

"Easy?" Frank echoes. "You want me to take it easy? Well, I'd love to, Colt, but I've got four tables demanding their checks and a guy at the bar asking for a cheeseburger with no grease. You know how to make a greaseless burger, Colt, because I sure as hell don't. Alice!"

I smile and walk toward my boss, who is the epitome of *no bite*. "I'm coming." I lift up on tiptoes and kiss his cheek.

A smile flickers across Frank's face, erased just as quickly. "Go on then."

Before I disappear inside, I turn back to Colt, my heart still thundering. "We're going to the Hall tomorrow night around seven," I offer gingerly, "if you want to meet us there."

Colt looks at the truck and nods slowly. "Yeah, maybe."

I give Colt one last glance, memorizing the way he looks now—all these years later—and then hurry back inside.

6
ALICE

AFTER MY SHIFT, I head next door to Maggie's shop. I find her outside, decorating the Texas redbud that grows between The Buttermilk Cafe and Pardon My Garden. Right now, it's glossy green, but soon the leaves will morph into vibrant shades of orange and yellow.

But the real showstopper is in the spring, when magenta flowers erupt from the branches.

Maggie is currently standing on a ladder, wearing a white sundress and grappling with a faux pumpkin, which dangles by an invisible string. As I watch, she tosses the pumpkin over a lower limb. It catches, and she proceeds to tie the string off.

She's owned Pardon My Garden for five years, carrying on the previous owner's tradition to decorate this tree with each passing holiday and season. When I first returned to Holly River, I'd made a point to drive by on my way into town and was delighted to find inflated beach balls and hot pink flamingos hanging from the branches. The tree was also wrapped in pink twinkling lights—every last branch—

and inspired June to open an (adult) pink lemonade pop-up on Friday afternoons.

Which is how June and I met: over margarita glasses and beneath plastic flamingos.

To avoid startling Maggie, I make a wide circle and wave both arms. When she spots me, she yanks her headphones down around her neck. Even several feet away, I can hear the classical music blasting—something frantic and violin-heavy.

She climbs down the ladder. “Hey there, Forrest Gump. You run from any other men today?”

“Not today.” I follow her toward the shop doors. “But there’s still time yet.”

A spool of fishing wire is working its way out of her back pocket, so I grab it as we make our way inside.

“Watch it.” She halts, shooting me a look over her shoulder. “Don’t make any moves you won’t follow through on.”

I laugh and shake my head as she drops three pumpkins onto her counter with a clatter. “I’ve only got...” She silently counts the dozen or so pumpkins in the immediate vicinity. “Thirty thousand more to go.”

I flop down in the rolling chair behind the counter. The scent of lilies and damp moss hits me, a welcome relief from the smell of frying oil. Maggie picks up a pair of rose strippers and starts attacking stems like they owe her money.

“So,” she says without looking up, “he’s back.”

"He’s back," I echo, heaving a sigh.

“And you ran from him.”

I nod. “That I did.”

“You say you wrote him letters for how many years?”

Maggie looks at me with those sharp green eyes, softened by freckles that appear hand-placed in their beauty. Her appearance straddles the line between seraphic and sultry, but right now, I can't even meet her gaze.

"The whole time he was gone."

Maggie stops stripping and glances in my direction. "Which was...?"

"Eight years?" I say in a question, even though it's a hard fact.

"Damn, girl." Maggie resumes her work. "You thirsty."

I collapse forward onto the counter. "I wasn't *thirsty*. He was my... friend."

Maggie points at me with a freshly shorn rose. "He was your brother's friend." She tosses the rose onto the counter in front of me, and I roll the stem between my fingers.

"He felt like a brother to me," I admit quietly. "I missed him when he was gone."

To this, Maggie doesn't reply. When she speaks again, her voice is softer. "When did he stop responding?"

I blow air out from between pursed lips. "Years ago. When I was in college."

Maggie nods and then gets up to mess with the speaker on a high shelf. Soon, the sound of calming strings fills the air. "I liked him in school. I told you we were in the same grade. Maybe *liked* is a strong word. We ran in different circles, but he seemed nice enough. Your brother, on the other hand, was and *is* a moron." Maggie hops up on the counter. "No offense."

"None taken. He once put his mouth over a lit sparkler on the Fourth of July." I place the rose stem between my teeth like they do in the movies.

Maggie's face opens in alarm, and she yanks it from my mouth. "Oof. Don't do that. If you're going to serenade me, do it without swallowing pesticides." She tosses the rose in with the others, then she looks at me, her mouth pulling into a smirk.

"He looked hot last night, huh?" Maggie raises her eyebrows.

I smile and shrug.

Maggie throws her head back and laughs. "Oh, my god, you want to screw your brother's best friend."

"I didn't say—"

Maggie's face scrunches up into one of mock disgust. "And you just said Colt was like a *brother* to you."

"Maggie!"

"How many times you beat it last night thinking about him?"

I shake my head. "I'm gonna leave."

Maggie scoffs. "Yeah, right. We're on your favorite subject. You know, this is because of all those romance books you read. How many have you read this year? All of them?"

I glance out the front window, partially obscured by chalk calligraphy, and catch sight of a mom walking past with her son. The little boy is holding an armful of back-to-school supplies and struggling to keep up. The sight makes me wistful.

"He came by the diner today," I admit sheepishly, knowing she'll find out soon anyway. Around here, news travels faster than the weather changes.

Maggie's eyes practically explode from her head. "He *did*?"

My face falls. "Yeah. He told me his mom passed away. And that he came back to sell her place."

"Shit." Maggie glances at the fall blooms waiting patiently in black buckets, and then at the freezer near the back. Finally, she looks at me. "He had to have known you worked there."

"I don't know. Maybe." I chew my lip. "I invited him to the Hall tomorrow night. Hope that's okay."

"Course. Dalton always intrudes anyway. Might as well add another sweaty, disgusting, muscly...chisel-jawed...meat stick to the mix."

"*Meat stick*? Really?"

"It's bullshit he didn't write you back. What else was he doing?" Maggie does air quotes and makes a dismissive face. "Being at war? Defending our country?"

"Trying to stay alive?" I add, playing along.

Maggie scoffs. "Be a man, am I right? Learn how to multitask."

I glance down at my hands, thinking about his mom again. What else has happened in his life that I don't know about? And should I even concern myself if he doesn't care enough to tell me?

"Hey," Maggie says, her smile fading. "I don't forgive him. He's a dick for not responding."

I drop my head to the side. "No, he's not."

"Yeah, he is." She gets up and begins dropping pumpkins into a storage bin. "Want to help me decorate the tree?"

I hop up, seizing the opportunity to take my mind off Colt. "Hard yes."

Maggie tosses me a pumpkin, her eyes darting to the Fall Festival poster plastered above her flower buckets.

"Have you heard anything about the festival? If we don't get enough tourists, half the shops on this street will be boarded up by Christmas. The Fourth of July carnival last month? Only a *fraction* of my usual sales."

"First meeting's in a few days," I remind her. "I'll be there. I promise."

Maggie stops and looks at me for a long moment, appearing far more serious than I've seen her in the past. "You got a plan to stay here until then?"

My heart clenches. I think about lying to her, because admitting that, *yes*, I do have a plan... It feels like committing to it. And commitment comes with an expectation of action. And results. But Maggie looks at me like she needs a friend just as much as I do, and so I tell her the truth. "I got a plan," I admit quietly.

Maggie nods. "Good. That's good. You're the only person I know who looks at a weed and sees a wildflower, Alice. This town needs that right now. So you take that plan and you make it happen. Understand?"

I make a face that says I'm touched by the sentiment, because I am, and her eyes widen in alarm.

"Don't even think about it." Maggie takes an exaggerated backward step.

I catch her by the elbow before she can escape and pull her into a hug, squeezing her as tightly as I can with a plastic pumpkin still wedged under my arm.

"Get off me, hornball," she groans.

But I hold on for a beat longer, soaking in her encouraging words, letting them seep beneath my skin. When I release her, she marches straight for the front door, shaking her arms out like she's dislodging cooties. I laugh watching her go, but the spark she lit doesn't quite go out. It stays there, a fragile, glowing coal in the corner of my mind, right next to the image of Colt sitting in Booth Four, looking like a man who finally knows exactly who he is.

I wish I could say the same for myself.

7
BEFORE

THE COTTON-BALL CLOUDS had severely tested my patience, but the scene was finally perfect. I pressed the tiny switch at the top of the shoebox, and the interior flooded with a warm, battery-powered glow. Through the peephole I'd cut into the front, a scene from *The Outsiders* glowed to life. Three weeks of obsessive crafting culminated in the best school project I'd ever completed. Even my parents had seemed pleased with my dedication.

"Alice, we gotta go," Mom said from my doorway. "We've got to stop by Colt's on the way."

"What? Mom, no. We'll be late," I protested, getting to my feet and gathering my project. "Why do we have to do that now?"

Mom glanced down the hallway and then at her watch. "Because he needs a form signed for football, and if he doesn't get it done today, he won't be able to play next year. Come on, let's move."

"Why doesn't he drive himself?" I grumbled as I jogged

down the stairs, backpack flopping against my back. "He's *sixteen.*"

Mom froze a few steps from the bottom and lowered her voice. "And you're eleven. That's old enough to understand that not everyone has the privileges we do. It's a ten-minute detour. Enough."

I huffed, because it felt like Colt was *everywhere* lately. He was at our breakfast table, he was in the passenger seat of our car, and he was the hot topic of conversation at dinner. It felt like we'd adopted a stray teenager, and I was the only one who found his constant presence obnoxious.

When I reached the dining room, there he was, yet again. Colt was hunched over a history textbook, and Grant was next to him, actually writing in his notebook instead of bouncing a Nerf ball against the wall.

That was the magic trick that'd earned Colt a permanent invite. In the six months since he'd started hanging around, he'd managed to do what my parents never could: get Grant to care about school.

Dad walked over and delivered a slap to Grant's back, and then shook his shoulders. "Keep this up, and you'll have scouts on our doorstep. Just gotta stay locked in, buddy, just like you have been."

"Colt, time to go." Mom jingled her keys. "Eddie, you'll meet us there?"

"Right behind you." Dad peered over Grant's shoulder. "He's got...six questions left."

Colt stood up immediately, the ever-obedient, well-mannered third child. "Yes, ma'am. Thank you."

I rolled my eyes.

We piled into the sedan—me in the back with my

project on my lap, Mom driving, and Colt in the seat next to me. I dropped my backpack between us, ensuring Colt didn't get too close. It was awkward enough that he chose the back when he could've easily ridden up front with Mom.

I peeked through the peephole to ensure everything looked okay with my model.

"And your book report is finished, too?" Mom asked.

My head popped up. "Yeah, it's done."

Mom pressed her lips together, and I knew exactly why. The teacher had only assigned the class a written book report. But I'd wanted to do something special. To show my parents that *I* was focusing, too. But also because thinking through all the individual elements of the diorama had been exhilarating.

I could already imagine the look on Mrs. Clark's face when she saw it.

"Can I see?" Colt asked quietly.

"It's not finished," I lied. I didn't want his big hands anywhere near it. But then I saw Mom watching me in the rearview mirror, her eyebrows raised in a warning. I sighed and tilted the box toward him. "Don't touch anything."

Colt leaned over, squinting through the peephole. A small, surprised laugh escaped him. "Whoa. That's awesome. Look at the clouds." He paused, his eye still pressed to the cardboard. "I like the little guy in the red and white shirt. He looks tough. He'd be a good linebacker."

I pulled the box away. "He's a character from the book. It's not about *football*."

"Alice, be nice," Mom warned.

I opened my mouth to point out that I *was* being nice

by letting him look. And that Colt was the one who'd made my own project, and everything else for that matter, about *him*. But instead, I snapped my mouth shut and turned toward my window.

We drove toward the edge of Holly River, past the cheerful brick houses with their immaculate lawns and plastic Santas. Then, we turned down a gravel road I didn't recognize. The trees grew more congested—tall, spindly pines that blocked the late afternoon sun. We stopped in front of a house that made my stomach drop.

It was small, the paint peeling, the windows dark. The wooden porch sagged in the middle, and a crooked fence surrounded an overgrown yard. The place looked like every haunted house I'd seen in movies. It was unfathomable (vocabulary word from *The Outsiders*) that Colt lived here.

"I'll just be a second." Colt practically fell out of the car and jogged toward the front door.

"Is this where he lives?" I whispered, my grip tightening around my diorama.

Mom sighed. "Yes, baby. And it's more than many people have."

I stared at the house. I couldn't imagine living there. I'd be scared to even close my eyes at night. My gaze caught on a broken window, shoddily covered with cardboard and tape. *Was that Colt's room?*

It must be freezing at night.

The front door of the house swung open with a violent bang. Colt came out first, his face harder than I'd seen it before, holding a crumpled piece of paper. Right behind him, a woman stumbled onto the porch. Her hair was frizzy, unbrushed, and her blouse was unevenly buttoned. Even from the car, I could see that her face was flushed red.

"You think you're better?" she screamed at him. "Running off with those people? You come back here, Colt!"

She was swaying, her movements uncoordinated. She reached for his arm, but Colt dodged her, keeping his head down. "Don't you walk away from me!" She chased him down the steps, but on the last one, her foot caught on something. She tripped, stumbling over a cracked ceramic pot, and hit the gravel hard.

"Mom!" I cried.

Mom threw open her car door.

Colt dropped his paper and rushed to the woman's side. "Mom! Are you okay? Are you hurt?"

The woman shoved Colt, a violent push that sent him reeling. She scrambled to her feet, clothing streaked with dirt, and resumed screaming. This time, using words I wasn't allowed to say.

Colt scooped up his paper and raced for the car. Mom met him halfway, grabbed his arms, and said things to him I couldn't hear. Colt shook his head vehemently. She nodded and they barreled toward our vehicle. With Colt's mom hollering at them both, Colt dove into the back seat, his chest heaving.

Mom got in next and locked the doors. "Should I call someone? Do you think she needs—" I craned my neck and saw Colt's mom storm inside, slamming the door in a way that would've had me grounded for a month.

"No." Colt cut her off, his voice firmer than I'd ever heard it. He turned fully toward his window. "Please. Just go."

Mom didn't argue. She backed out of the driveway so fast gravel sprayed against the undercarriage.

I sat in the back, gripping my project like a lifeline through the suffocating silence. I felt sick. Like I'd seen something I wasn't supposed to see.

Colt remained turned toward his window, arms crossed tightly over his chest. There was a chasm of space between us now as he huddled against the door.

"I'm so sorry, Colt," Mom said softly after a few minutes. She reached back, trying to pat him, but her fingers barely brushed his jacket. He didn't move. "Did you... did you get it signed?"

Colt nodded, but he didn't look at her.

I glanced down at my project. The perfect world I'd built inside the box felt small and stupid. A hot, prickling sensation burned behind my eyes as shame filled my body. The weight of what I just saw, of what I just learned, hit me full force. My throat tightened with emotion, and I sniffed, fighting back tears. I thought about all the times I'd complained about Colt being at our house. How annoyed I was when he'd taken a third helping of lasagna and stayed over for the fifth night in a row, intruding upon family time my parents normally held sacred. I'd made it obvious I didn't want him around then. I'd treated him like an intruder when he was only trying to escape *that.*

A tear slipped down my cheek, and I quickly brushed it away. When I glanced over at Colt, he was still curled against the door, forehead pressed to the glass. I wanted to apologize—to make him *feel* better—but I didn't know how.

I looked at my project, and an idea formed.

I reached through the bottom access flap of the box, feeling around until my fingers closed around the plastic figurine with the red and white striped shirt. I pulled it free, dried glue snapping off.

Then I stretched my arm between us, holding it out to Colt.

He didn't notice at first. He was still staring out at the passing trees. I nudged his arm with the toy. He glanced at it from the corner of his eye, then quickly looked away. His face looked red and blotchy, and the sight of it made my heart ache.

I waited a beat, then laid the little man on the seat between us, pushing it right up against his thigh.

A few minutes later, as we neared the school parking lot, Colt's hand moved. Without turning his head, without letting anyone see his face, he reached down and closed his fingers around the small plastic figurine.

8
COLT

I LOOK up at the towering white columns of the Greek Revival, the cornices catching the final, bleeding rays of sunset. A half-dozen pumpkins dot the front porch steps, and a wreath of burnt-orange leaves hangs from the door. It looks like a woman planning to stay awhile, but she said her family moved to Shreveport. If they're there, why is she here?

It feels like I should walk right in. Find my chair at the table. Flop down on the twin bed Alice's parents moved into Grant's room for me. But it's been over eight years since I left this place, and suddenly I wonder if the things I longed for while stationed thousands of miles away will still be there.

I take a breath and knock.

When the door swings open, the air in my lungs stills. Alice stands there, her blue eyes widening in shock. For a second, she's frozen. Then, she breaks into a slow, dazzling smile that makes my pulse kick. She looks every bit the woman she is now—wearing a red dress with well-worn cowboy boots, brunette hair spilling over her shoulders.

"Well, well, look who finally returned home."

I lean against the doorframe, letting a playful drawl take the edge off my nerves. "The sun is settin', and I figured a lady shouldn't have to walk alone in the dark. So, I'm volunteering my services as an escort."

She laughs, a bright sound that echoes through the foyer, and steps back to let me in. "An escort, huh? How chivalrous of you." Right before I enter, she kicks her boot out, eyes sparking with mischievousness. "Of course, you could be feigning chivalry only to become a villain once you step inside."

My mouth quirks upward. I wasn't sure what to expect tonight. Whether we'd still be awkward around one another, or if we'd quickly move past the reacquainting period. She's just given me an opening to seize the latter.

I step closer. "I guess you'll have to trust that you weren't living with a wolf in sheep's clothing for three years."

She laughs, her head falling back. My eyes slide down her throat, the sound of her laughter soothing something inside me. "Oh, I always knew you were a wolf." She removes her boot and makes way for me again. "I tried to warn my parents."

"That you did. Smart girl." I remove my hat and step inside. My smile falters the moment I take in the once-familiar space. The unadorned hallway feels cavernous, and the corner sofa is gone. In fact, about half the furniture has vanished.

"Alice?" I turn back to her with a furrowed brow.

"I'm, uh... I'm selling the place." She opens her hands and then drops them, a bittersweet glint in her eyes. "I guess we both need a realtor."

The news sends an unexpected pang straight to my heart, but I have no right to feel that way, not when I'm leaving soon too.

My gaze travels toward the grand staircase. I know the layout of this house as well as my own, but the silence upstairs feels different now.

"I'm staying in my parents' room," she explains, following my line of sight. "Well, I guess it's not really theirs anymore. It's mine." She looks back at me. "Do you want to see upstairs? Grant's old room?" She swallows, and my eyes lock on hers. "Or mine?"

My heart thuds against my ribs. Years ago, Alice was a sweet, daydreaming kid I wanted to protect from the world and, somctimes, even from her own parents. Now, Alice is a woman in a red dress, standing in a half-empty house, and she just invited me to her bedroom.

I clear my throat, wavering between playfulness and something I hardly understand. "Alice." My voice drops an octave. "You'd invite a wolf upstairs?"

Alice's smile falters and—I may imagine it—but her eyes seem to drop to my mouth for a beat. But then, just as swiftly, she gives my ribs a nudge. "Oh, please. You're no wolf. I've watched you eat Jell-O pudding cups, Colt."

Alice grabs her blue jean jacket and makes for the front door.

"Uh, I've been to war," I say.

Alice laughs harder, closing the door behind us. "Yeah, right."

"I shot a gun. Many times."

Alice pats my arm as we make our way to the street. "Sure you did."

I laugh hard. The sound is foreign to my ears, but it feels better than I'm willing to admit. Shaking my head, I look at Alice. "You're different now."

She meets my gaze and smiles softly. "You, too." She narrows her eyes and tilts her head, as if searching for something. "But also, the same."

I nod to that. "Yeah."

~

WE WALK INSIDE THE HALL, and I nod at Dalton as Alice scours the room. When she spots two women she recognizes, she grabs my hand and leads me toward the table. My eyes dart to where her hand disappears inside mine.

She holds it naturally, like this has happened a hundred times before. I wrap my fingers more fully around hers as a warm, comforting feeling swims through my veins. I can't stop staring at our clasped hands, willing the moment to stretch for some unfathomable reason, but the second we reach the table, she lets go.

"This is Maggie." Alice points to a vaguely familiar redhead. "I think you two were in the same grade in school."

I offer Maggie a hand, and she shakes it with pursed lips. "Uh, huh," she mutters.

Okay. So that one hates me.

"And this is June." Alice nods to another woman, whom I recognize as the town baker. I bought a cherry pie from her when I was down for my mom's funeral. Warren and I ate it on the kitchen table with two forks, forcing ourselves to swap the few pleasant memories of our mother. We'd lasted ten, maybe fifteen minutes before the reminiscing turned into an argument and Warren hurled his fork across the room.

June and I shake hands, and the four of us sit. Instead of diving into our past and how Alice and I know each other, June carries on chatting as she was, making me feel more at ease and not like a fourth wheel. For that, I vow to buy everything in her shop.

"I was just telling Maggie about this guy who came into my store today," June explains.

Maggie brings a glass of white wine to her lips, glaring at me over the rim.

"He buys a cake from me," June continues. "German chocolate."

Alice moans, her head falling back, and my cock twitches at the sound.

Fucking hell.

"And then, not an hour later, he brings it back, a quarter of the cake missing, and asks if he can exchange it for a different one. Said it was... dry." June closes her eyes on the last word, as if this part of the story is too painful to bear.

"He did *not*," Alice gasps.

"Bastard," Maggie tuts.

Alice leans forward and grabs June's hands. "You have never made a dry pastry in your entire life."

June nods quickly, pouting. "Except for my shortbread cookies."

"Except for those," Alice agrees.

"I've had your pie," I offer.

Three heads swing in my direction, and I really, *really* wish I hadn't spoken. Clearing my throat, I add, "It was incredible. I've never eaten anything that good. I still, uh..."

Stop talking, Colt.

"Still what?" June's eyes are wide and eager.

"Think about it. I still think about it."

June's face scrunches, and at first I think I've freaked her out. But then she and Alice are going, "Aww," and June is saying, "I like him. Alice, I like him."

"He's easy to like." Alice shrugs, and my eyes shoot to her.

Maggie, I note, is not so easily won over.

"Someone order a hangover?" Dalton approaches, setting down beer bottles before slapping me on the back. "On the house."

I reach for my wallet, but Dalton stops me. "What did I just say?" Dalton points at me, while looking at the women. "I don't see you three trying to pay me. Look at Mr. Manners over here. Be more like him. *Learn* from him. Adopt his ways."

Alice twists off the cap and brings the bottle to her lips. Right before she drinks, she says, "Colt? No... Colt's a wolf."

I tip my head, a playful warning in my eyes, enjoying her teasing far too much.

She smiles around the bottle as she drinks.

"I believe it," Maggie deadpans.

Alice is about to respond when a man approaches the table, his eyes fixed on June. Removing his cowboy hat, he says, "I mean no disrespect, but if you're not spoken for, ma'am, would you care to dance?"

June looks taken aback, but quickly recovers. "Sure. I'd love to."

She rises, and I glance at Dalton to ask if he wants to sit, but he's watching every step June takes like the two of them are about to torch the Hall.

"You know him?" I keep my voice low.

Dalton shakes his head, his eyes still on June.

"Are you and her—?"

Alice catches my eye and shakes her head vigorously.

Dalton glances down, suddenly remembering our existence. "No," he says with a face that implies the question is ludicrous. "She's my friend though. I'm just keeping an eye..." He trails off. "Why aren't y'all drinking?" he booms. "Want me to take them back?"

Everyone snatches their bottle.

When I set the beer back down, I realize I have two choices—sit here under Maggie's scrutinizing glare, or find a method—a very appealing method—to escape the situation.

I stand, summoning the courage to offer Alice my hand.

Her face opens with surprise, but she swiftly rises to her feet and slips her small hand into mine. *Back where it belongs*, my mind adds. I lead her to the floor, shaking off the thought, as Blake Shelton blares from the speakers. Glancing around, I see that even Dalton hasn't escaped the fall madness.

The wooden beams overhead are wrapped with faux

maple leaves, and strings of Edison bulbs glow like embers. Atop the scuffed whiskey-barrel cocktail tables, small pumpkins and tea candles sit atop burlap.

Though the manufactured cheer grates like sandpaper against my skin, I understand the financial appeal to local businesses. But for some people, like Alice, it's simply about the enjoyment that comes from celebrating and decorating.

I guide Alice's hand to my shoulder before wrapping my arm around her waist. Pulling her a little closer than necessary, we begin two-stepping across the floor.

"You like this stuff, huh?" I ask when I notice her staring up at the garland.

"I do." She nods energetically. "You remember when we'd pick out a pumpkin from the patch?"

I huff a laugh, shaking my head. "Your mom wanted this nice family moment, but Grant always made a mockery of it."

"He'd measure every pumpkin," Alice continues. "Smell them, roll them, knock on them and pretend to listen. Mom would get so mad."

"But Grant would be like, 'Mom! Mom, this is *serious*. Why don't you care about finding the perfect pumpkin? Do you know what's riding on this?'"

Alice and I laugh together and then—in an instant—I'm flat on my stomach in the sand, heat radiating through my fatigues, my hands gripping the rifle. And then I'm right back here, holding Alice in my arms, and the difference between the two worlds is bone-rattling.

Alice seems to notice the change in my mood because she quiets. "Do you remember that little plastic toy I gave you when I was, like, eleven or twelve? It was this tiny guy from my school project. He had a red and white shirt? You probably don't—"

"I still have him."

Her eyes widen. "You do not."

When the music turns to a slow song, we adjust our pace and remain on the dance floor. "I do. You told me to keep it with me."

"You know I got a C on that project? I was *destroyed*. I thought my teacher would be, like, blown away. But the light I'd put in there went out before I could show it, and I'd spent so much time building a scene from the book that I neglected the written portion. I mean, I did the paper, but it wasn't great. My teacher was like, 'Alice, this is nice, but it wasn't the assignment.'"

Embarrassment colors Alice's face, and I want to brush it away with my thumbs.

"I always do that," she admits as our boots scuff against the floor. "I always get too deep into something that catches my interest and miss the forest for the trees."

Alice looks up at me, like she's waiting for me to concur. The vulnerability on her face wrecks me, especially because it feels like we're talking about something deeper than her fifth-grade English project.

I stop our dancing, holding her still. "Alice, that teacher was a moron. I would have given you a hundred on that thing. A hundred and *fifteen*."

Alice laughs and her head drops to her chest. I reach out and lift her chin, forcing her to meet my eyes the same way she did me yesterday.

"You attempted something big while everyone else

thought small. They did just enough, and you swung for the fence."

Alice's eyes get glassy and she smiles so widely I crack right open.

"I missed you," she says suddenly.

I open my mouth to ask why Alice ran from me the other night, but a voice rings out—

"Hey! Ya'll want another round?" I glance over and see June wiggling an empty bottle in the air.

Alice gives a thumbs up and looks at me. "I'll be right there. I'm going to use the restroom." She starts to walk away and then turns back. "Thank you, Colt."

I nod, wondering what I did. Not much. Not nearly as much as she did for me.

"Is she going to the bathroom?" June yells. "I need to go too. Alice!"

She runs off, and I turn around to meet Maggie's raised eyebrow.

"So," she says, tapping her fingers on the worn, graffitied table. "Couldn't respond to her letters, huh?"

I lower my head and a soft smile tugs at my lips, because I realize two things: one, Alice was talking about me, which I like more than I should, and two, Maggie is protective of Alice, which makes me like her instantly.

"Something funny about that?" Now Maggie is leaning in, her expression growing even more wary.

I shake my head, sobering. "No. I just appreciate that you care about her." When Maggie stares blankly at me, that eyebrow rising once again, I sigh and attempt to explain myself. "I did respond at first. Not as often as I should've, but I did. And then she went to college, and I was deployed." I grip my beer bottle, thumbnail peeling the edge of the damp label. "Alice was happy. She was...*always* happy. And the things I saw there... They weren't good things." I take a sip of beer and tap the bottle back down decisively. "Alice had a perfect life and I wasn't going to be the one to darken it."

"Are you kidding?" Maggie scoffs, furrowing her brow. "Alice wasn't happy. She was abandoned by her family and classmates. She was *alone.* It's not just you I'm angry with. I also want to throttle—"

A chill rushes across my skin, and I start shaking my head adamantly, hardly able to comprehend what she's saying. "What? No. Alice was—"

"Depressed. She was depressed, Colt. And for good reason." Maggie cranes her neck to ensure Alice isn't coming. "Her parents basically left her in favor of Grant's football schedule in Louisiana. And then there were these guys in high school who singled her out."

"The fuck?" My entire body tenses.

"I don't know exactly what happened, but it sounds like she was kind of ostracized after that."

I can barely remain seated. My muscles strain with the need to *do* something. To correct some egregious oversight. I think about the letters Alice sent. Letters bursting with cheerfulness, brimming with excitement over all the wonderful things she'd done and was looking forward to. Was she lying? Why would she do that?

"I wish I'd been there," Maggie continues. "But I only knew her as Grant's sister then and—" Maggie cuts herself off when June joins the table.

"What are y'all talking about?" June bounds over. "Where's Alice?"

"Wasn't she in the bathroom?" Alarm bells go off in my brain.

"There she is," Maggie states. And then, under the breath, she mutters, "Oh, crap."

I spin around and see a man crowding Alice.

"That's Travis," Maggie clarifies. "He's been giving her problems ever since—"

I'm already on my feet, pushing my way through the crowd. The dude is standing too close to Alice, one arm blocking her retreat. She's smiling, but it's clearly to placate him. Alice gently pushes at his arm, but he keeps it firmly in place. I grab that same arm and yank it from the wall with more force than necessary. Alice immediately moves away, and I step in front of her.

"What the hell do you think you're doing?" I snap.

Travis holds his hands up. "I was just saying hello."

I step closer, keeping my voice measured. "Looked to me like you were blocking her in. You want to try doing that to me?"

Alice takes hold of my hand. "Colt, let's just go."

Travis's eyes dart to the place where she touches me, and his eyes narrow. Then he glances at Alice.

"Don't look at her," I say evenly.

"Think about what I said," Travis says to Alice, and then he looks back at me. He smirks, raises a stiff hand to his forehead, and salutes me. "Soldier," he says, with as much sarcasm as he can muster.

I watch him walk away, my free hand flexing into a fist.

I spin around and raise my hands, nearly touching

Alice's face, but catch myself at the last second. "Are you okay? What did he say to you?"

Alice waves it off. "It was nothing. Really." She drops her head to one side, an imploring look in her eyes. But I can tell from the forced cheerfulness in her voice that it's far from nothing. "Can we just go back to the table?"

"Alice—"

"Please."

I study her a moment longer and then find myself nodding, willing to do just about anything to erase the worried look off her face. "Alright," I manage. "But Alice, if you need help with something, you tell me, yeah? You're not..." I hesitate, not wanting to say too much. "I'm here now. Okay?"

She smiles, and this time it's the one I'm accustomed to. It spreads from ear to ear and radiates joy. It fills my chest with possibility and colors the world a shade brighter. But as she strides back to the table, I can't help questioning everything I thought I knew about Alice's life.

9
ALICE

THE LIMESTONE BRICKS of the Holly River National Bank are cool against my back, which is a mercy, because the rest of me is burning with humiliation. I'm leaning against the wall outside the entrance, trying to avoid looking like a woman whose lifelong dreams were politely shredded.

I take a shaky breath, the kind that threatens to turn into a sob if I'm not careful, and stare down at my feet. I'm wearing a navy blazer, cream-colored slacks, and nude pumps I purchased on the way here. This morning, looking in the mirror, I felt like someone about to shake up this town with seismic intensity.

I'm here now.

That's what Colt said to me last night, his steady voice cutting through the uncertainty in my head. That's all it took. Three little words. And I'd stayed up until 1:00 a.m. polishing my business plan, my heart doing a tap dance. *I'm here now.* It felt like a permission slip to be brave.

To be the girl I once was.

I push off the wall and walk toward Maggie's shop, shoving the sketchbook and business plan into my tote. Mr. Grayson loved the sketches. Said the idea was precisely what Holly River needed.

The following *But* had been soul-crushing, consisting of credit scores and down payments that'd require selling three of my two kidneys. The only thing worse was the unsubtle suggestion of my parents co-signing, which I'd swiftly sidestepped. Because I wanted to build something on my own, just as they did.

I turn the corner and duck inside Pardon My Garden. The bell above the door jingles merrily, and the inviting smell hits me at once—crushed eucalyptus and the sweet, robust scent of lilies.

Maggie is in the center of her shop, knee-deep in a pile of grapevine and silk marigolds. With sleeves pushed to elbows, she wrestles a mammoth wooden archway, muttering curse words as she struggles.

"Hey!" I yell above the music.

Maggie's head snaps up, her lopsided bun flopping to one side. "Alice! Thank God. Tell me honestly—is this arch giving *Photo Op* or *Children of the Corn*?" She gestures wildly at the structure. "Roxanne still hasn't given us a directional plan for the festival. Everyone is losing their minds, and rightfully so. That woman is coasting on her mother's legacy, but legacy doesn't drive foot traffic, Alice. Legacy doesn't buy artisanal soaps and hand-poured candles."

Maggie clicks a remote, and the music softens.

I examine her work, forcing this morning's failure out of mind. Colors explode along the wooden lattice, with unexpected pops of pink amongst the orange and red. The result is breathtaking, but of course it is.

"It's perfect, and you're a genius." I sift through boxes, seeing what she has, and discover a pile of cords near the bottom. "Ooh! What if you add lights, then people can take pictures with it at night too?"

Maggie considers this, and then nods. "Hot damn, Sinclair. I think you're onto something. I'll do it after lunch though. I'm beat. And starving. You must imagine a goddess like me needs no sustenance to survive, but alas, I'm a mere mortal."

I laugh, grateful for my friend who wields humor when I need it most. "Why don't we knock it out now? I'll help. Then I can run next door and grab you lunch. I'm off today, but Peter will slip me a burger if he knows it's for you."

Maggie shakes her head. "You're a godsend, Alice. You have the biggest heart. Unlike me, who is a selfish troll-human."

I grab the lights and start wrapping the arch. "If you're a troll, Mags, then the rest of us are doomed."

Maggie grimaces. "Speaking of behaving troll-like, I'm afraid I wasn't very welcoming to Colt."

I freeze. "Maggie. No." She winces, and I groan. "Don't tell me you brought up the letters. Because that would mean he knows I've been talking about him."

"Okay, I won't tell you."

"Maggie!"

I start chasing her and she scream-laughs. "I was mad he didn't answer you."

"That wasn't your business!" I grab a sunflower and

hold it like a sword. "Talk." She shoots her arms into the air, shaking as if I really am about to cut her to pieces. It's not beyond the realm of possibility. But right when she opens her mouth to defend herself, I lower my weapon. "Actually, don't tell me. I'd rather live in ignorance."

"Ignorance is best," Maggie agrees.

She bends her knee in an exaggerated fashion, stretching the stringed lights toward me as if terrified of getting too close. I snatch the lights from her. "Get your be-hind back over there." I nod toward the arch, and she scurries over, pumping her arms.

We work in silence for a few moments before Maggie says, "You know, Colt did win some brownie points when he rescued you from Travis. Now *that* guy is a forever-douche. He's been buying every available retail space and renting them back out for way more than they're worth. And now he's after your parents' place. And your panties. He's like that guy from *It's a Wonderful Life*."

"Mr. Potter?" My shoulders tighten at the mention of Travis.

"That's it. Man, I'm on fire with the movie references today. But yeah, Travis is going to turn Holly River into Pottersville, and Roxanne is gonna step aside and just let it happen. It really should be you directing the events in this town. Roxanne only does it because her mom handed her the reins." Maggie rolls her eyes. "That's some nepotism right there."

I bark a laugh. "That's a sad use of nepotism. I don't think anyone wants that role, Maggie. Event directing in Holly River is practically a full-time job. Besides, Roxanne is great at it. You're too hard on her."

"I can think of someone who'd want the role," Maggie chances.

I busy myself with manipulating the foliage, my cheeks warming.

Maggie drops her arms to her sides, her face softening. "Alice, if you believed in yourself half as much as you believe in everyone else in Holly River, you'd be mayor."

I continue rearranging the silk flowers, doubting her assessment of my potential, the memory of Mr. Grayson's rejection fresh in my mind.

"And then you could grant me dubious favors," Maggie exclaims, "like circumventing city taxes. Or granting me special permits to install two male models at my entrance."

"Would one need special permits for that?"

"For the pornographic things that'd happen inside my shop? Most certainly."

"Is that what this tripod is for?" I nod toward the filming equipment.

"No, that's for the 'Gram, Alice. And the TikTok. I've been posting for years, and I'm finally getting some traction. Apparently, people find the sight of me swearing at a rosebush relatable." Maggie grabs her phone, holds it high, and drags me into the frame. "Smile!"

The shutter clicks, capturing my blazer and forced smile.

As Maggie examines the photo, I think about the festival plans hidden in my closet. Yet another elaborate plan that's half-finished and unexecutable because I got carried away with the vision and neglected things like budgets. And physics.

We finish Maggie's arch well enough for her to photograph it, and then I collect my things to leave. But first—

"Can I buy some flowers before I go?"

Maggie's eyebrows shoot up, her romantic-comedy-obsessed brain firing on all cylinders. "A bouquet? For what purpose? Is there a date?"

"No." A flush creeps up my neck, the thought of Colt rushing back to me. Him in his dark jeans and long-sleeve black Henley. My god, the cowboy hat. I've replayed the image of him standing on my front porch, and the warmth of his hands as we danced, a mortifying number of times. "I thought I'd go out to the cemetery. Visit Colt's mom's grave."

The teasing light in Maggie's eyes vanishes, replaced by the bleeding heart she tries so hard to hide. "You're too good for this world," she says, already moving toward the back cooler with a sense of purpose. "I'm not charging you for these. Consider it my contribution to the Saint Alice Foundation."

She starts pulling stems with practiced ease. "We'll do bronze chrysanthemums. Some of these burgundy dahlias. They're called Arabian Night. Total drama queens. And..." She considers the rest of her stock. "Orange ranunculus for a pop. Oh, and let's add dried wheat to give it a harvest feel."

As she works, I hook the leather tote over my shoulder, my proposal suddenly feeling like a child's frivolous dream. If I can't get a loan, and I won't ask my parents for help, then they're just pieces of paper. I can't believe I thought the cash I hoarded in college and a few hundred dollars earned at The Buttermilk Cafe would be enough to convince a banker.

"Here." Maggie turns around with a sensational arrangement wrapped in brown butcher paper, tied off with twine. "Tell her... tell her I said hi. And that she owes me thirty dollars for the flowers."

I take the bundle, breathing in the intoxicating aroma. "Are you sure I can't pay you?"

Maggie nods toward the arch. "You already did."

10
COLT

THE GEAR SHIFT on my '92 Ford F-150 grinds beneath my palm. It's a stubborn old beast, navy paint fading to reveal primer beneath, but it runs. If Alice's dad taught me one thing before I left for the Corps, it was that money works harder in the bank. I lean my elbow out the window, humid air rushing by, and try to ignore how my chest tightens the closer I get to the cemetery.

I haven't been here since we lowered the casket into the dirt six months ago. I was in uniform then, eyes locked on the horizon because I couldn't handle the sight of that mahogany box. I did my time in the Sandbox, saw things that no one should have to carry, and yet that six-foot hole in the ground is what did me in.

There's nothing but ugliness in this world, that's what I've learned.

Gravel crunches under my tires as I pull into the cemetery. It's a modest, quiet place, overgrown with ivy and shaded by ancient oaks borne witness to anguish and grief across the decades. I kill the engine, and the silence that follows is deafening. For a minute, I just sit there, hands gripping the steering wheel.

When I finally climb out, my knees pop like firecrackers —a souvenir from a jump in Helmand that didn't go as planned. I start walking toward the back corner, where the newer markers are. But as I round a weeping willow, I stop in my tracks.

Someone is already there.

A woman sits on a patch of grass next to my mother's headstone, legs curled up beside her. She's wearing a wide-brimmed sunhat and a yellow sundress that looks like a splash of spilled lemonade. There's a bundle of flowers resting at the base of the stone.

And she's talking. No, she's *reading*.

It's a voice I would recognize anywhere.

I stand there, paralyzed, as Alice turns a page. "Magic is always pushing and drawing and making things out of nothing," she reads softly. "Everything is made out of magic, leaves and trees, flowers and birds, badgers and foxes and squirrels and people."

I take a step forward, and a twig snaps under my boot. Alice jumps, her head whipping around.

"Colt," she breathes, her face flushing pink as she pulls the book to her chest. "I… Oh, god. I'm sorry. I didn't think anyone— I shouldn't be intruding."

She scrambles to her feet, gathering her things.

"Don't." The word comes out rougher than I intended. I clear my throat and try again. "Don't go. And please, don't apologize."

I walk closer, my heart hammering as I glance down at the grave. The flowers are fresh, the cut stems glistening at the ends. My mother's name stares back at me: Eleanor Mitchell. Beloved Mother. Those last two words are a punch to the gut.

"You were reading to her," I say.

Alice clutches a worn copy of *The Secret Garden*. "I figured she might like some company, but I didn't know what to say," she offers quietly. "So I figured..." She tilts the book.

I look away, blinking hard against the sudden burn in my eyes. I feel like a bastard. I'm her son, and I haven't said a word to the woman in years. And here's Alice, who owes my family nothing, sitting in the dirt beside her.

"She didn't deserve this." My voice strains. "This kindness. She made things difficult for everyone. You especially. I basically lived at your house because she couldn't keep it together. I intruded on your life because of her."

Alice steps toward me. She doesn't reach out, but I can feel the warmth radiating off her. My fingers twitch, desperate for that warmth. "That's why I'm here," she explains. Her voice is steady, surer than mine. "I'm thanking her for letting us have you for a little while."

I look at her, confused, and she continues gazing down at the grave. She reaches out and moves the bundle of flowers an inch higher on the stone.

"She could have forced you home," Alice elaborates. "You were underage. She could have forced you back to her house every single night. But she didn't. Somewhere in her heart, she knew you were better with us, with my parents and Grant. And so she allowed it. I think that was her way of loving you, the best she could."

The air leaves my lungs in a long, shaky exhale. It's a

perspective I never allowed myself to have. I always saw her rejection as neglect, her pushing me away as a sign she didn't care. To hear Alice call it a sacrifice rattles me to my core.

I have to turn away. I walk a few paces, staring at a distant fence line until I can breathe. I'm a Marine, for Christ's sake. I'm supposed to be made of tougher stuff. But Alice has quickly proved to be my tactical weakness, slipping past my defenses. Disarming me in a way I want to hate, but don't.

When I turn back, she's watching me with those soft, patient eyes. I need to move. I need to be anywhere but this graveyard, which brings back memories not only of Mom but of others I've lost.

"Alice," I say. "You want to go to the river?"

A smile breaks across her face, slow and infectious. She nods once. "I'd love to."

~

WE DRIVE IN SILENCE, but it's not the suffocating kind from before. The windows are down, and the smell of the changing season fills the cab. As we pull off the main road and onto the dirt track that leads to town, the scenery shifts.

The oaks are deepening into a rich, burnt umber, and the cottonwoods shiver in shades of pale gold. Even the sumacs along the bank are a startling, bloody crimson. It looks like the world is slowly catching fire.

We reach our old spot, a hidden bend where the water slows down and the limestone banks form a natural shelf.

The sun is beginning its slow descent, hanging low in the sky.

"We should swim." Alice hops out of the truck before I've even killed the lights. "The water's going to be freezing in a week. This might be the last warm day."

I climb out, leaning against the door. "We don't have suits."

She shoots me a playful look over her shoulder, reminding me of the twelve-year-old girl who used to steal my cleats just to watch me hunt for them. "Then turn around, Mitchell." She circles her finger.

My heart skips a beat. "Ali."

"Turn. Around."

I face the truck, staring at the rusted tailgate, occasionally glancing at the road to ensure no one is coming. If someone does come along and sees her half undressed, I'll handle it calmly. By blinding them.

I hear the rustle of fabric, the soft thud of her sandals hitting the grass, the slide of a zipper. My imagination goes into overdrive. I picture the curve of her breasts, the way the fading sunlight hits the small of her back.

Stop, goddamn it. That's Grant's sister.

But I don't stop. Not until she calls out from behind me.

"Okay. Your turn."

I hear a splash. When I turn, I see her head bobbing in the water, yellow dress crumpled on the bank. I strip down to my boxers, trying to hide my erection, and dive in. The water is shocking at first, a cold slap that ignites every nerve ending, but then it settles into a cool embrace.

I surface a few feet from her. She's treading water,

watching me with an unblinking gaze. She doesn't look away as I wipe the water from my eyes, and I release a surprised laugh.

"What?" she asks.

"You could have at least pretended to avert your gaze while I stripped to my underwear."

"You and Grant swam in your boxers around me all the time," she counters, splashing me.

The water surrounding us is golden, reflecting the sky. High above, the birdsong reaches a crescendo—the frantic, beautiful trill of mockingbirds and the low coo of mourning doves. The sun is nosediving now, casting long shadows across the surface of the river.

We drift for a while, the current lazy. Then we find a shallow spot where we can stand, the water to our waists. Alice reaches out and touches a scar on my shoulder, her fingers light as a dragonfly.

"Does it still hurt?" she asks.

"Only when it rains," I lie. It hurts more often than I'd like, but right now, I feel little else outside of her touch.

She looks up at me, and for a second, the air between us feels charged. I can see the droplets of water clinging to her eyelashes, the way her lips part slightly. I want to lean in. I want to see what she tastes like. I want to wrap my arms around her like I did at the Hall, but this time, feeling her bare skin beneath my hands.

I picture Grant sitting inside the darkened cabin of my truck, face twisted in disgust by what I'm imagining doing to his little sister, and I pull back.

"Remember the chicken heist?" I change the subject

abruptly, forcing my mind off the fact that I could undress Alice in under sixty seconds.

Alice's laughter echoes off the limestone. "My chickens!"

"You wanted those fluffy yellow chicks from the feed store so badly." I shake my head at the memory. "But your dad was dead-set against it."

"And you built a coop for them," she adds, looking at me with gratitude I don't deserve.

"Grant helped."

"Barely," Alice deadpans. "Even with the coop *and* Grant pestering Dad, he wouldn't budge. He even called down to ensure they didn't sell us any. Told me how they carry diseases, which, now that I think about it, was pretty disloyal of him considering poultry paid our bills."

I grin. "And so Grant stole them. Tucked them under his shirt and walked right out."

"Yeah, and you were the getaway car!"

"Was not." I try to hide my smile.

"Absolutely you were. What's more, days later, when my dad was set to return them, you said that Grant had been playing better ball since the chicks showed up." Laughter pours out of Alice. "You knew damn well that would freak my dad out. Even if he *knew* it wasn't true, he wouldn't have chanced it. But he did pay the feed store."

"Did he?"

"Of course. You know my dad." Alice swooshes her arms in the water. "I still have them, you know."

I blink. "Seriously? They're still alive?"

"Old ladies now. Pickles still bullies the other two. She's a tyrant."

We laugh together, and it's easy and effortless and foreign. After that, it's quiet for a long while, just the sound of the river moving past us and the crickets buzzing in the tall grass.

"Colt?" Alice is floating on her back now, her hair fanned out. "Let's do like we used to."

"What's that?"

"Secrets. Remember? We'd float on our backs so we didn't have to look at each other, and we'd say one thing that was true. No judgment."

I hesitate, gawking at the moonlight bouncing off her skin, the swell of her breasts inside her lace bra. I trace the dips and valleys of her waist and hips, and then roll onto my back before I do something I'll regret. The sky above has shed its vibrant colors, the first few stars blinking into existence. "Ladies first."

I can hear Alice breathing, the gentle *slap-slap* of water against her skin.

"I want to open a bookshop." Her voice is tiny, as if she can't risk saying this boldly. "In my parents' house. I want to fix it up, put in floor-to-ceiling shelves, and a big window near the front so people can read by sunlight. I've wanted it ever since I was a kid, and I want it even more now."

I turn my head in the water to look at her, but she's staring straight up at the stars. "Is that why you came back here after college?"

"Yeah," she whispers. "Everyone thinks I'm here to sell the house. But I don't want to, and I don't want to live in Shreveport either. I want to stay here and build something."

"Thank you for telling me." It's a beautiful dream. One that fits her perfectly. Alice always had a book with her, stuffed into her tennis bag, lying near her cereal bowl, laid open in her lap. I think she enjoyed the escape books gave her, because her parents had high expectations, and I think —no, I *know*—that they often came down too hard on her.

Alice would make for an enviable entrepreneur. She's creative, and though her parents might doubt this, Alice Sinclair sticks to things when they're important to her. I know, because I have eight years' worth of her letters.

"Your turn," she prompts.

I stare up at the vast, empty sky. My secret feels heavier, but also simpler. "I just want to sell the house," I concede. "I want to sell my mom's place and get the hell out of here. Everywhere I look in this town, people are celebrating. I used to kinda like that, but now it seems...empty. Makes me feel like there's something wrong with me. I mean, I always felt that way, but now it's worse."

Alice doesn't say anything at first, and I start to worry that I've admitted too much. Her confession was commendable, full of hope, and I just deflated the moment. When she speaks, though, she simply mirrors what I said. "Thank you for telling me."

We float silently for a moment longer, and then Alice lowers her voice to mimic a man's. "Did you know the tides affect the river, Colt? The water moves differently when the moon is full."

I chuckle because I know exactly who she's imitating. "Even this far from the coast?"

Alice punches her arm toward the moon. "Yes, Colt! Even this far from the coast!"

"Your dad used to use that as an excuse for why the fish weren't biting. 'Tide's wrong, boys. We ain't got a chance.'"

I turn my face to look at her. "You really want the bookstore?"

"More than anything," she admits.

"I can see it," I tell her, and I mean it. "You were always a dreamer, Alice."

She lets out a forlorn sigh, and the current pulls her a few inches further from me. "That's all it is. Just a dream."

I want to reach out and grab her hand, to tell her that dreams are the only things worth holding onto. But I'm the man who wants to run, and she's the girl who wants to plant roots, so who am I to talk?

The sun is long gone now, leaving only the silver glow of the moon on the water.

I stay on my back, floating in the dark, wondering if the tide is indeed turning, and if it's time to let it carry me somewhere new—or if, for the first time, I should try swimming against it.

11
COLT

THE MATTRESS SPRINGS groan under my weight. I've been sitting here in my room at the Stagecoach Inn for two hours, staring out at the street, thinking about what Alice admitted earlier in the river.

A bookstore.

She said it was just a dream. But the way she said it, with a dejected little sigh, had pierced my chest like shrapnel.

I stand up and pace the carpet as the sky finally breaks. A low rumble of thunder shakes the windowpane, and it starts to drizzle. The smell hits me through the cracked-open frame, the metallic scent of rain hitting hot August pavement.

Why the hell is she hesitating? If she's wanted this since childhood, and she has a college degree and family money, what's stopping her?

The answer comes swiftly: her parents. They always preached practicality over passion. Said they'd watched countless businesses in Holly River fail because the owners focused on what they *wanted* to do instead of what was *needed*.

Maggie's words echo in my mind:

Depressed. She was depressed, Colt.

I snatch my bag from the chair and dig through it until my fingers hit paper. I pull out the first letter I touch.

I check the date. Five years ago. Alice would've been a junior in high school. I was twenty-two, a corporal and a grunt still stationed at Camp Inwood, spending my days calculating trajectories for 81mm rounds and my nights wondering if I'd ever feel happy again.

I unfold the paper.

Dear Colt,

I've been thinking about what you're eating these days. Are you getting enough? I bet my mom's peach cobbler will taste so good when you get back. I've learned how to bake it myself, so now I eat it too often (which is still not enough - ha!). Oh, guess what?! I'm running for Student Council Historian! There are five other candidates, and they're all really smart, so it'll be a tough campaign (do I sound like a politician?). But why not try, right? Life is too short to sit on the sidelines. You'll appreciate the effort I just made to include a football analogy.

I also joined a book club! We're reading 'The Heart is a Lonely Hunter.' It's a bit sad, but sad things can be beautiful, don't you think? Do you ever look at the sky at night, Colt? The other day, I had the whole house to myself. I went out onto the balcony and stared straight up for hours. The stars looked like little doorways to other worlds, so bright they made my ears ring.

Look at me being literary! It's that book club. And maybe all the other books I've read over the last seventeen years. Can you believe I'm seventeen?! One more year, and I'll be old enough to vote, which I'll do of course, because people like you work hard to ensure I can. It's a very important thing you're doing, being a Marine.

Anyway, when I was looking up at the sky, I wondered if you were looking at it at the exact same time. It makes the world feel smaller, doesn't it? Like we aren't that far apart even though it might feel that way.

You know, when you return, you'll have so many stories to tell and an appreciation for simple pleasures in a way few would. You're lucky in that regard, to see the world so clearly. Watch the sunrise tomorrow. Promise me? And tell me what colors you see in your next letter.

With Love,
Alice

I refold the letter slowly. My throat feels tight, like I've swallowed a handful of red clay. Because after what Maggie said, I see things I didn't before. Like how Alice was alone and had the house to herself, and how she yearned to feel nearer to me. With painful clarity, I realize why Alice's letters read as if she were relentlessly happy when she wasn't.

For *my* sake.

Alice was struggling, dealing with her own shit, yet every word she wrote was designed to keep my head above water. She was my scout, clearing the path ahead of me when I was too blind with misery to see it myself. Even as she herself was drowning.

She did that for me. And now she's standing in a big, empty house, dismissing her own dreams like they don't matter.

"Fuck that," I mutter.

Stuffing the letter into my pocket, I grab my boots and head for the door. I don't bother with a jacket. I hit the lobby and the old guy behind the desk looks up from his crossword.

"Hey, son! I wouldn't go out there. It's coming down cats and dogs—"

I push through the heavy oak doors and step into the deluge.

The rain is coming down in sheets, making the towering trees lining the street sway. I march down the sidewalk, my boots splashing through puddles. A decorative hay bale on a porch sags, soaking up water, and a plastic pumpkin bobs along, riding a current toward a storm drain.

By the time I reach the Sinclair house on the corner, I'm

soaked to the bone. I stop at the edge of the lawn, rain blurring my vision.

The lights are on inside. Through the front window, I see her.

Alice is shoving a heavy couch across the floor, her face tight. She stops, rips a piece of art off the wall, and sets it on the ground. Her hair has escaped her ponytail, damp strands sticking to her forehead.

She disappears into the kitchen and comes back with a red spray paint can. She hesitates, then holds it erect and sprays a defiant **X** on the main wall.

She freezes, staring at the mark. Then she spins toward the window. Her eyes narrow, squinting through the glass and the rain until they lock onto mine.

Alice doesn't wait. She lunges for the front door and swings it open. "Colt?" she shouts over the storm. "What are you doing out there?"

I don't say a word.

I just stride toward her.

12
ALICE

"IT'S ALRIGHT, GIRLS," I soothe as I lock the coop door. "Just a bit of rain. Nothing you haven't seen before." My hens cluck softly in response as I sweep my hoodie over my head and dash for the back door.

Inside, the house smells like the vanilla-orange soap I used to scrub the river silt from my skin. I'm clean as a whistle, yet I can still feel Colt's hands when he helped me out of the current. And when he guided me into the passenger seat of his truck.

I had a crush on him when I was a kid, of course. Colt was attractive, he was older, and he came from a family vastly different from mine, which made him interesting.

But most importantly, he was kind to me. He asked questions about my classes and my tennis practice and made me feel like what I said mattered.

He looked at me like the kid I was, and I looked at him as an annoyance first, then as a welcome presence, and later —after he left—as an anchor.

While he was gone, I'd envisioned him as indomitable

and infallible. I'd built him up in my head to impossible heights. Because that's what I needed during that time. To believe I was communicating with someone omnipotent.

And then he returned to Holly River so much *more* than I'd ever imagined.

I lean against the kitchen counter, closing my eyes. I can see him standing in the river shallows—all hard lines and military precision, his silhouette backlit against the moonlight. He moves with a calm, erotic gravity, never hurried, never rushed. But I've also seen the fire under that steady exterior. I felt it at the Hall when Travis wouldn't take no for an answer. Colt stepped in, a wall of protective intent, and the air in the room had changed without him even raising his voice. In an instant, I knew I was unquestionably safe.

A sudden heat blooms between my thighs, deepening. Tonight in the water, I'd wanted him to touch me. The realization steals my breath, because while I missed Colt—while I often dreamed of him returning to Holly River—I wasn't expecting him to come home looking like *that*.

I can see it, Colt had said. *You were always a dreamer, Alice.*

Coming from my parents, those words were a strike—a sigh, a shake of the head, a reminder that *dreamer* was another word for *unreliable.* But Colt had said it like it was a gift. Like he was proud of that quality in me.

But dreams don't pay for renovations, I remind myself as I flop onto my sofa. The bank had been polite but firm. My management degree and business plan weren't enough to overlook my lack of collateral.

Not everyone has the luxury of dreaming, kid, Colt had said to me years ago. *Don't ever stop dreaming.*

I shoot to my feet, his words ringing in my mind, drowning out any others. I'm moving before I can talk myself out of it. After yanking my hair back into a messy ponytail, I grab a bottle of Chardonnay from the counter and uncork it. I take a long, stinging sip straight from the bottle.

Then I turn to the living room, my pulse racing.

You were always a dreamer, Alice.

I shove the heavy coffee table aside with a grunt of exertion. The rug is next. I roll it up, dust tickling my nose, and raise it into the air, letting it flop into the corner with a *thud*. My eyes fall on the wallpaper. Wallpaper I never envisioned in my bookshop.

I could put the table back, and the rug too. But once I strip—

I tear it away with a wild scream, nails digging into the faded paper. It peels off in long, satisfying strips. I hurl misshapen pieces of it over my shoulder and keep going. Next comes the artwork—one painting lifted off its hooks, then another. And another. With every action, my confidence builds. I'm a machine that's been put in motion, and I wonder if that's all I needed. To yank the pull cord and get my motor running.

Maybe I didn't need a foolproof plan.

Maybe I just needed to *begin*.

I spin toward the couch and start pushing it toward the kitchen, its legs screeching against the floorboards. I struggle with an oversized framed landscape, panting, sweat slicking my forehead, until the wall is bare.

The wall.

The one separating the den from the kitchen nook. In my mind, it's already gone, allowing the entire space to become a sun-drenched reading room. I run to the garage, my breath coming in ragged gasps. I find a lone can of red spray paint and dart back inside.

Standing before the creamy drywall, I tremble, hesitating because everything else could easily be undone. Not this.

Don't ever stop dreaming.

I press the nozzle.

A glistening red **X** bleeds across the center of the wall, marking it for demolition.

The pungent, chemical scent of the paint fills the room, making my head spin. I turn toward the front door, intent on throwing it open for fresh air.

I freeze.

A shadow stands in the rain. Tall, broad, unmistakable.

I'm moving again, pulling open the door and stepping out onto the porch.

"Colt," I yell over the downpour. "What are you doing out there?"

He walks toward me, his boots heavy on the steps, and stops directly in front of me. His intense eyes roam over my face, and he takes another determined step closer, our bodies so close they practically touch. Rainwater drips off his jawline, wets his lashes and lips. His gaze moves from my flushed face to the red X behind me. "You really want to open a bookstore?"

"Yes," I reply at once, his presence emboldening me.

"Then do it."

"It's not that easy," I admit, reality crashing back down. My shoulders slump, my bravado slipping. "I tried getting a loan. The bank said no."

"Ask your parents," he persists. I start to turn away, but he catches my hand. "Ask them. Explain the dream. Not positioned as a fantasy, Alice. Explain it so they understand."

"They'll never agree."

He lets go, thinking. I can practically see his mind racing. He scrubs a hand over his head, back and forth, then looks at me, fire blazing in his eyes. "I'll do the carpentry. For free. Tell them that."

"Colt, no. You told me you wanted to get out of here. You can't—"

"I need something to do, Alice," he interrupts, his voice dropping. "I need a project. Do you believe that? That I might need this as badly as you do?"

I look into his eyes, searching for the truth, unable to decipher him. But...I *want* it to be the truth. Because I don't want Colt to leave. I like who I am when he's beside me.

I slowly nod.

He doesn't waste a second. He grabs the phone from the kitchen and presses it into my hand. "Call them. Now."

I hesitate, staring down at the phone.

Colt wraps my fingers around it and squeezes. "Do it, Ali."

My fingers shake as I dial. When my dad picks up, the words tumble out of me in a frantic rush. I explain the layout, the vision, the shop. I'm pacing, fumbling through my pitch. My dad starts to protest, his voice loud enough that I can hear my mom in the background asking what all the shouting is about.

"Colt is here," I interject, my voice gaining strength. "He's going to do the labor for free."

Silence. Then, "Colt Mitchell? What's he doing in Holly River? Does he even know how to swing a hammer, Alice?"

I cover the receiver and look at Colt. "Can you really do this? "I mouth, motioning toward the house.

He looks at the walls, the windows. Uncertainty flashes in his eyes.

"Hell, yeah," he says resolutely.

I turn back to the phone, my business degree finally kicking in. I scramble for my tote bag, pulling out the laminated plan. I talk numbers. I talk about how a retail-friendly layout this close to town square increases resale value. I tell my dad that if I fail, he'll get his down payment back with interest because we're slashing labor costs.

I listen to him talk for a long time, nodding to the empty room. "Okay. Okay, Dad. I understand."

I hang up. Colt's hands are raised in a silent question.

A slow, wide smile breaks across my face. "They'll co-sign."

Colt lets out a whoop, and I laugh at the sudden sound.

"But," I add, "we have three months. We have to be open and turning a profit by the Fall Festival, or I agree to sell the space. Immediately."

Colt's expression turns serious. "That's a hell of a deadline."

"This is going to be really hard, Colt."

"I've done plenty of hard things." He steps in close, heat rolling off him.

"I haven't."

"Yes, you have," he says softly. He looks at me, at the excitement and worry etched on my face as I examine the house with fresh eyes.

"Hey," he says.

I look up at him.

"Let's fucking go, kid."

He raises a hand in the air, palm open.

I laugh and slap my hand against his in a high five that echoes through the house.

SEPTEMBER

13
ALICE

"LEFT, COLT! NO, MY LEFT! PIVOT!" My hands flutter as I direct Colt's progress. "If we scratch these floors, I'm gonna cry, and we both know I'm an ugly crier."

Colt is pure muscle and concentrated effort, maneuvering a gleaming table saw through my front door. The early September humidity is already doing a number on us, and we haven't even hit the hottest part of the day.

"Alice, if you don't stop moving your hands, I'm going to lose my depth perception," Colt grunts, his voice strained but teasing. He shifts his weight, his forearms tensing as he hoists the heavy equipment. His white cotton t-shirt clings to his back, outlining the broad planes of his shoulders in a way that makes my brain spin.

"Focusing! I am a beacon of focus," I promise, my attention locked on the way his muscles flex, imagining how those arms would feel wrapped around me. "Okay, three more inches toward the stairs. Now tilt it. Yes! Like that. Keep coming...and...touchdown!" I throw my arms in the air like a referee.

Colt eases the machine onto the drop cloth in what used to be the family dining room. Today, it's the staging area for my future. The heavy thud of the saw hitting the floor vibrates through the soles of my feet. I let out a shaky exhale and toss him a triumphant grin.

"See?" I wink. "Dream team."

Colt looks around the room with an appreciative nod. "It's a good piece of kit. It'll make the custom shelving go twice as fast."

He moves into the kitchen to wash his hands, and I bend down to inspect the saw, pushing random pieces as if I know what they do.

"Be right back," Colt calls over his shoulder.

I pop up to find him staring through the kitchen window as he dries his hands. He rehangs the dishtowel before disappearing into the mudroom, only to reappear on the other side of the window.

Gazing out, I realize with a pang of guilt that I never opened the coop this morning. Pickles, Mabel, and Dixie are huddled against the entrance to their run, agitated beaks dragging across the wire mesh. I'd been so preoccupied with the arrival of the carpentry tools that I forgot about my own girls.

Pickles will have my head for this transgression.

I lean against the counter, watching Colt through the glass. The sun filters through the giant bur oaks, casting long, dappled shadows across the grass and Colt's shoulders. He unlatches the coop door, and the hens burst out like shots from a cannon.

Pickles beelines for the grain Colt scatters, pecking and flapping her wings at Dixie to scare her off. Colt leans down and scoops up Dixie. She's a Barred Rock with striking black-and-white stripes, and usually, she's the most skittish of the trio. But in Colt's hold, she settles instantly. He tucks her under his arm, his large, calloused hand stroking her feathers. After murmuring a few words to her, he opens his palm, offering Dixie a private buffet.

There is something so devastatingly attractive about a man strong enough to renovate a house but gentle enough to comfort a rebuked chicken.

For a moment, I'm the happiest woman in Holly River. But then, as quickly as the warmth came, a cold shiver of reality follows. I look around my house, which is in a total state of disarray. This is the place where I grew up, the place I'm betting everything on. We have two and a half months until the Fall Festival, and the weight of *what-ifs* is crushing.

What if this town can't support a bookstore? What if I'll be out of my depth as the owner? The fear is a physical ache in my chest, a tightening of my throat that makes it hard to swallow.

Colt catches me watching him through the window and gives an easy smile—the kind of smile that says everything is under control.

It's going to work out, I think to myself.

He strides back inside. "Ready to start moving stuff?"

I tighten my ponytail. "Am I ready to embarrass you with my staggering strength? Yes. Yes, I am."

Colt shakes his head with a chuckle. "What stays?"

I point to the pieces I've lived with my whole life, the ones that will provide the cozy seating nooks for my future customers. "The velvet couch, those wingback chairs, and that coffee table. Everything else goes."

"Let's start with the end tables and lamps." Colt motions around the room. "Small stuff first to clear a path."

Over the next two hours, we move credenzas, end tables, boxes of décor, and framed artwork that hasn't seen the light of day in years. Colt is in his element, muscles tightening and releasing with every lift. His white t-shirt grows damp with sweat, becoming nearly translucent against sun-kissed skin. I watch his back flex as he carries a heavy crate toward the U-Haul, and heat pulses between my legs.

My imagination, fueled by years of reading the very books I plan to sell, takes a wild, unauthorized detour. I envision Colt dropping the crate, the sound of it hitting the floor echoing through the empty rooms. Then he strides over to me, his eyes dark with a hunger he's been hiding all morning but can no longer suppress. He grabs my waist, his large hands spanning the curve of my hips, and lifts me onto the carpentry table he just moved in.

He doesn't say a word, he just pulls my dress up around my hips. And then his hands are on his jeans. He's tearing the zipper down, freeing himself, his ravenous eyes never leaving mine. And then he does speak, kissing my neck before whispering in my ear, "Alice, spread your legs wider for me," as he positions himself between them. And when I don't immediately respond—because this is Colt Mitchell we're talking about, and I didn't know he had it in him—he takes my face in his hands, forcing me to look at him, and says, "Are you going to be a good girl for me, Alice, and do as I asked?"

"Alice? You okay? You're looking a little...pink." Colt pauses by the door with a floor lamp in each hand.

"Just the heat!" I force out, grabbing a random box to hide my shaking hands.

He sets the lamps in the U-Haul and wipes his forehead with his sleeve. I'm right behind him with the box, and what's left of my virtue. The two of us head back inside, but once we cross the threshold, Colt stops abruptly and turns to face me. He shifts his weight, looking down at his boots, then back up. "Hey, so, since we're making such good time today, I was thinking maybe tonight we could—"

"Alice! Oh, my god, look at this lighting!" The front door swings open, and Maggie strides in like she owns the place. Almost immediately, she rips out her phone and starts filming. "Dude, this place is going to *kill* on Instagram!"

"Hi, Mags," I say, trying to hide my disappointment that she's interrupted at the worst possible moment.

Maggie follows us as we grab opposite ends of the dining table and begin moving it. "Yes, exactly! Just like that. Alice, toss your ponytail to the other shoulder. Colt, off with the shirt, please."

"Maggie!" I bark a laugh, trying not to drop the table.

"Oh, sorry." Maggie places two fingers beneath the center of the table. "I gotch y'all."

We head toward the U-Haul, but right when I'm about to step off the porch stairs, I misjudge the distance and slam my shin against the railing.

"Ow!" I yelp, hopping on one leg.

Colt is there in a heartbeat. He takes the weight of the table from me and sets it down. "You okay? Let me see."

He guides me to the porch steps, his hand firm on my

arm. I sit down, clutching my shin, which is already throbbing. "I'm fine, I'm fine."

Colt ignores my protest and kneels in the dirt at my feet. He gently moves my hand away to inspect the damage. His touch is so tender that it makes my heart do a somersault. "That's going to leave a bruise. Don't move. I'll be right back."

Meanwhile, Maggie is crouched three feet away, filming. "This is gold," she whispers.

"Maggie, if you post that, I'll ban you from the shop for life."

"Too late. I already started the account." Maggie flops into the porch swing, tapping furiously at her screen.

I lean my head back against the railing. "I was going to do that this weekend."

"You were going to do a lot of things this weekend," Maggie corrects, typing away. "Including a United States Marine."

"Maggie!"

Maggie grins without looking up.

I make an everything-is-normal face when Colt returns. He dabs at my shin with a cool rag, and I try not to imagine more dirty thoughts, like his hand sliding higher up my thigh while my friend magically disappears in a puff of purple–no, pink—smoke.

"Do you want to stay for dinner?" I turn to Maggie, mostly to distract her from saying anything else incriminating. "We're almost done, and I think we've earned pizza."

"Pizza? *And* I get to stay and harass you both? In!" Maggie stands and pockets her phone.

An hour later, the U-Haul is packed and locked. We're

exhausted, covered in a fine layer of dust, and starving. Since the kitchen and dining tables are currently parked in the back of the truck, we're huddled around the kitchen bar on stools. Soon, this view into the living room will be gone. Colt is going to build a partition wall to separate the kitchen from the retail space. The thought is both exciting and a little sad, because every step toward my dream is a step away from the childhood home I remember.

I slide a plate of pepperoni pizza toward Maggie and pour three glasses of sweet tea.

"So." Maggie takes a bite of pizza. "Tell me the vision again. Books everywhere, right? Like, a hoarder-level situation?"

My excitement returns as I gaze around the rooms. "Yep. That's the idea."

"What about your parents' old office?" Maggie gestures toward the front of the house.

"Books," I say.

"The guest bedroom?"

"More books."

"Living room, dining room, den?"

"Dirty magazines," I say around a mouthful of pizza. "Just wall-to-wall smut."

Maggie slaps her hand down on the counter. "Hot damn! That's my kinda bookstore, Sinclair! I'll be your best customer."

Colt chokes on his iced tea, coughing into his napkin while we dissolve into laughter. When he finally catches his breath, his eyes meet mine over the rim of his glass. There's a warmth there, a shared past, a shared endeavor, and for a second, it's like we're alone again. Goosebumps race across my skin as his eyes drop to my mouth.

Maggie, missing nothing, catches the look. She stops mid-chew, her gaze darting between the two of us. She raises a groomed eyebrow and gives me a look that is essentially a three-page interrogation. Heat crawls up my neck, and I concentrate very hard on my pizza crust.

Suddenly, my phone buzzes on the counter. The screen shows a FaceTime request from Grant.

I look at Colt questioningly. Along with my parents, Grant has been skeptical, to say the least, about my bookstore venture.

Colt gives an encouraging nod. "Answer it. Let him see the progress."

I swipe the screen, and my brother's face fills the frame. He's wearing a crisp polo shirt, looking precisely like what he is—a successful, young businessman and vice president of Sinclair Systems.

"Hey, Black Sheep." Grant grins. "How's the demolition of our family home going? Was your childhood really that traumatic?"

"Funny." I turn the phone to show him the empty rooms. "The furniture is out, the tools are in, and I only have one minor leg injury."

"She's doing great, Grant." Colt leans into the frame.

"Hey, man! Good to see you. Blink twice if you need help," Grant jokes. "Alice, you know that place is going to be a money pit, right? Are you allergic to *making* money? Do you have a body buried in the backyard you don't want anyone knowing about? Dad is actively recruiting for a marketing position. It comes with this thing called a salary. And health insurance. Think about it."

"I'm thinking about how much I like not hearing you talk," I retort.

Maggie laughs, and Grant's eyes narrow. "Is that Maggie?" he asks.

Maggie begins waving her arms frantically and mouthing *I'm not here!*

I turn the phone around. The second the camera hits her, Maggie's entire persona shifts. "Hiii, Grant! How've you been? You look so corporate. Your collar is very... stiff."

Grant grins. "Maggie Evans. How those tits holding up? Alice, tilt the phone down."

"Jesus," Maggie groans.

"Grant!" I yell.

"Let me talk to Colt," Grant says.

I hand the phone over and watch as the two of them fall into their old rhythm. Grant hassles Colt about his time in the military, and Colt fires back with inside jokes from their football days.

While they talk, my eyes wander to the calendar I hung on the pantry door. I've already crossed out today with a big X.

The days are disappearing.

If I don't pull this off, I lose everything I care about—this house, this town, and all the people who live here. Because if I fail, what's left for me? Would I really be happy waiting tables at The Buttermilk Cafe for the rest of my life? Most Holly River locals either run their own business or work for someone who does. If I can't hack the first one,

I'm left with the latter. And Grant's right, I do need things like *income* and *dental checkups*.

As I look at Colt, laughing at something Grant said, a new fear takes root. Once the bookshelves are built, once the paint is dry and the open sign is flipped on, Colt is leaving.

And the thought of this house without him—without the sound of his soft knock on the front door each morning, or his diligent attention to the maintenance of my home, or the way he checks on me when I'm not looking, as if assuring himself I'm still in one piece... Losing all that, losing *Colt*, is almost as terrifying as the thought of losing my bookshop.

It's almost as if my dreams for my future, and Colt Mitchell, are becoming one and the same.

14
COLT

ALICE IS buoyant as we stroll down Main Street, her steps light, arms swinging. It's a beautiful day. I'll admit as much. The air smells crisp and clean without a stitch of humidity, and the sun warms our skin, not a cloud in the sky to inhibit it. I might even feel happy if we hadn't spent two weeks waiting for our building permits to get approved. Mid-September already, and we still can't move forward.

Alice is distracted by a group of elementary school kids dancing around the gazebo as their teacher calls out instructions. As music plays from a portable speaker, the kids grip a fake vine of orange, red, and yellow leaves. All at once, they spin to the left, entangling themselves, and then to the right. They shuffle backward and then forward before forming a tidy circle and skipping in the same direction.

"And now, the finale!" the teacher trumpets, throwing her hands in the air.

Each kid plucks a leaf from the vine and they toss them over their heads. The leaves rain down and Alice claps. The teacher turns, grins, and waves.

"We've got a lot of work to do before November," the woman says.

"Looks great already!" Alice responds cheerfully.

As Alice's sparkling eyes travel from an artist offering caricature drawings to a rolling ice cream cart, I think about what I told Alice about needing something. In the river, I'd explained wanting to leave Holly River, and that's still the truth. Because in the Marines, I became someone respectable, someone with value. But I'm no longer enlisted, and though I swiftly jumped into learning carpentry as a trade, returning here has reminded me of the helpless person I once was. A person people felt sorry for.

In her letters, Alice wrote what she thought I needed to hear to lift my spirits and help me. And so I'm trying to repay the favor. But maybe I'm doing myself a favor too. Because this bookshop has provided me with a new, concise mission. And the funny thing is, every day I spend working beside Alice feels a little less like hurting, and a little more like healing.

Of course, the sight of Alice's ass in those jeans could be clouding my thinking. I picture wrapping my arm around that slim waist and tugging her backward against my chest, my lips coming down on her neck. In my imagination, she'd giggle, and man, how I'd relish the sound. I'd whisper against her skin that we should forget the bakery. Forget the permits. Go home instead and—

"It's right here," Alice chirps.

"Hmm?" My eyes snap up to her face.

We reach June's Bakery just in time, because I need a distraction from these unremitting fantasies I'm having about someone who is *entirely* off-limits. The moment I push open the glass door, I'm hit with the scent of brown sugar, cinnamon, and baked bread. And in every corner of the shop are Halloween decorations. Glossy paper bats are pasted to the walls, a witch's cauldron billows dry ice, glowing ghosts squat on tables, and plastic jack-o'-lanterns dangle from the chandelier.

"She likes Halloween," Alice whispers over her shoulder.

No kidding.

"There you are!" Maggie waves frantically from a corner table, already halfway through a cup of coffee. She tips her plate to show off a pumpkin cinnamon roll the size of a hubcap. "You're going to thank me for calling you. They *just* came out of the oven."

"Oh, my god. Gimme!" Alice rushes toward the counter, her face lighting up.

I follow Alice, old hardwood floors creaking beneath my boots. Behind the display case, June is balancing a tray of cranberry muffins while reaching for a rolling pin. The muffins are dangerously close to nose-diving toward the floor.

"Morning, June." I reach over the counter to hand her the rolling pin.

"Oh, Colt! Thank you." June spins toward the dishes, nailing the rolling pin against a stray pot. "Alice, I've got y'alls rolls right here. I saved you one with pecans." June starts plating them, and I watch her movements carefully, ready to intervene if she accidentally launches one into the cauldron.

Alice reaches for her purse to pay, but I've already got my wallet out. I slide a twenty across the counter.

"Colt, I told you I'd get these." Alice pouts slightly, and goddammit if I don't want to kiss that pout right off her face.

"You can get the next round of whatever," I lie.

Alice slides into the chair across from Maggie, her expression shifting from thrilled to concerned in a matter of seconds.

"So?" Maggie senses Alice's mood change the same way I do. "How's the progress on my dirty mags?"

Alice sighs. "We're still waiting on the building permits to get approved. It's been two weeks since we submitted the request."

I grip the back of Alice's chair, my jaw tightening. I can hear the anxiety in her voice, the kind that comes from watching your dreams sit forgotten on someone else's desk. Every day we aren't swinging hammers is a day she's losing her window of opportunity, and she was on a tight deadline to begin with.

I keep worrying that I messed something up, but I checked those forms three times before submitting them. Every square inch of the floor plan, the fire egress map, the ADA compliance for the ramp... It was all there.

Alice lifts her fork, poising it over the roll. "We're headed to the city office after this to check on them. If I call them one more time, I'm afraid they'll block my number. I've tried using charm, but I'm about five minutes away from throwing a brick through a window."

"Alice Sinclair." Maggie leans back, feigning shock. "I've

never known you to be the violent type." She grins. "Do go on."

Across the room, June is working on another dish, singing to herself as she tosses sliced fruit into a cast-iron skillet. Suddenly, a blue flame leaps up from the back of her stove, licking at a pile of dish towels.

"Fire!" I bark. When June doesn't react, I vault the counter, grabbing a lid from a nearby pot and slamming it over the flaming skillet. Then I toss the smoking towels into the sink, dousing them with the sprayer.

"Uh, excuse you." June casually wipes a smudge of flour off her cheek. "We do not simply leap into a woman's kitchen."

Maggie and Alice are still sitting at the table, unmoved. In fact, Alice is mid-bite into her cinnamon roll.

"You good, Colt?" Alice's voice is muffled.

"Good?" I widen my eyes at her, then look at June, then back at the scorched towels. "The stove caught fire. The towels were on fire. This entire kitchen was ten seconds away from becoming a bonfire."

"It's just the pilot light." June shrugs before glancing at Alice. "Is he always this dramatic?"

I turn to the wall, inspecting the tangle of greasy wires behind the stove. "June, this wiring is ancient. And frayed. You need to get this checked."

"I have a system." The woman shoos me away with a wooden spoon.

"June, I'm serious. This entire place could burn down." My voice drops into the authoritative register that used to make privates jump.

But June has already returned to cooking.

I look at Alice and Maggie for backup, but Maggie is grinning now. "Oh, my god. He just used Dad Voice on June." She spins toward Alice. "Has he used that voice on you? Alice, is this guy a Marine or a fireman? Or is he both? Surely that would be too much shirtless calendar potential for one man."

Alice actually pretends to consider this, looking me up and down while I'm standing there with soot on my palms. "Surely it would," she agrees. "Holly River couldn't handle that much testosterone."

Heat crawls up my neck as the three women ogle me. "I'm not a fireman," I say, glancing back at the wires. "My brother is, though. And he'd label this a death trap."

Maggie's face lights up. "Say more immediately. Is he hot? Colt, is your brother a *hot* fireman? Explain him to me in inappropriately graphic detail."

I bark a laugh, moving a heavy prep table to get a better look at the outlet. "I don't know if he's hot, Maggie. He's my brother."

"God, I love me a firefighter." Maggie sighs dramatically and lifts her coffee. "Just out there fighting a literal wall of fire, saving my babies from an untimely death."

I crane my neck, glancing over my shoulder at her. "I didn't know you had kids, Maggie."

"I don't," she responds. "I'm talking about my wildflowers. The heat last year nearly toasted my bluebonnets. I need a man who can wield a hose."

I steal a glance at Alice to see if she's agreeing with Maggie's assessment on firefighters, but she's looking directly at me, those pretty blue eyes doing more damage to my nerves than any fire would. I smile, and she returns it.

June moves to their table, bringing Alice a cup of coffee. "Are y'all coming to the Hall the Saturday after next? There's a band coming up from Austin. Dalton says they're the best he's booked all year."

She says Dalton's name with a certain emphasis, a little lilt in her voice I pick up on. She mentions him again ten seconds later while talking about the drink specials. I catch Alice's eye and we share a knowing smile.

"I'll try to make it." Alice stands and walks her plate back to the counter. "As always, the food was orgasmic."

Fuuucking hell. My mind immediately snaps to *me* giving Alice an orgasm. To giving her one after the other as she moans my name. For once, I cut myself a break. Because really, those jeans she's wearing are criminal.

June beams. "You kids have fun. Don't let those bureaucrats get you down! Here, take Colt's for the road since he was too busy playing unnecessary hero."

"I think I managed to bypass the short for now," I tell June, taking the boxed cinnamon roll from Alice. "But please, call an electrician."

"Yeah, yeah, I will." She waves me away and turns back to her stove.

"Bye, Mags." Alice waves as we leave, and I throw Maggie a wave too, relieved that the woman seems to have given me a chance, despite our rocky start. Surprised to find that I *want* her approval, and June's approval too.

Because they're a part of Alice's world.

INSIDE THE MUNICIPAL BUILDING, we make our way to a counter and the visibly bored woman sitting behind it. She looks like she's been sitting in that exact chair since the town was founded and has no plans to move anytime soon.

"Morning, Mrs. Devonshire." Alice's voice is light but professional. "We're here to check on the permit for 402 Willow Creek. The residential-to-commercial conversion?" Alice leans over the counter and flashes a bright smile. "And may I add, that scarecrow in your yard? Spectacular."

Mrs. Devonshire peers over her spectacles, and then clicks a few keys on a computer that surely belongs in a museum. "Ah, yes. The bookshop. Let's see..." She frowns at the screen. "There doesn't seem to be a decision yet."

"Is it normal to wait this long?" I press. "It's been over two weeks."

Mrs. Devonshire looks at me and then Alice, her expression softening a fraction. "I suppose not. We usually get these turned around in five business days. But Harold isn't in as often as he used to be. He's getting on in years, you know." She sighs as if Harold's aging is an inconvenience of the highest order. "We've been using a new guy to help with the backlog. He's... Well, he's a bit stricter on standards." She looks toward the back office. "Let me see if Harold's in today. Sometimes he slips in through the back."

As Mrs. Devonshire shuffles off, the door to the inner office swings open.

My body tightens the moment I see him.

It's Travis, the asshole who hassled Alice at the Hall.

Travis strides over and leans against the counter, his eyes fixed on Alice. "Hey, Ali. Don't you look nice today." Travis smirks at her, and I immediately bristle. Because while I'm already wary of this dude, I *really* don't like hearing him call her Ali. "Can I help you with something?"

"We're here for our permits." Alice stands up straight, her posture rigid.

"Ah, right. The permits." He nods, clearly enjoying his moment of power. "I recall seeing that come across my desk. I've been helping the city council as an interim code enforcement consultant. Legally, I'm authorized to review all applications to ensure they meet the mayor's new safety initiatives."

"Unfortunately, there were quite a few errors in your paperwork." Travis cuts his eyes toward me. "Did one of y'all's contractors fill this out? Because if so, I'd be letting that person go. They clearly don't know what they're doing."

I recognize the directed shot, and the blood in my veins simmers. I spent six hours on that paperwork. I read and reread the local government code, scrutinizing every word to ensure I didn't miss a single comma.

"What's the issue?" I ask cooly, because I'll be damned if this guy elicits a reaction out of me.

Travis walks to a desk and returns with a folder. He flips it open, stabbing a finger at a page. "For starters, your plumbing schematic doesn't specify the PVC piping grade for the grease trap. And your parking plan? You didn't account for the three-foot setback from the neighboring oak tree's drip line. That's a violation of the new Green Holly ordinance."

"The grease trap?" I say, incredulous. "It's a bookshop."

"That may be, but the code requires a grease-ready

interceptor if there's a possibility of future food service." Travis's eyes are back on Alice. He frowns like he hates delivering such news. "Look, I'm just doing my job. But I'll need to examine this for another couple of weeks. I'm allotted thirty days for a commercial review, and we're talking about the safety of the town here."

"You're full of shit, Travis." My voice is dead calm.

His eyes flash. "Excuse me?"

Before he can respond, the door behind him opens. A man—Harold, presumably—walks in, followed by Mrs. Devonshire. Harold is wearing a fly-fishing vest over a flannel shirt and looks like he'd rather be anywhere else on earth.

"What's the issue?" Harold mumbles, reaching for his glasses.

"Just explaining the deficiencies in their application." Travis's tone quickly changes from patronizing to helpful subordinate.

Harold takes the folder and flips through it, eyes squinting behind thick lenses. "This the Willow Creek place?" Harold glances questioningly at Mrs. Devonshire. "That's near your house, huh?"

"Mm, hmm," Mrs. Devonshire hums. "Right across the street."

"This gonna bother the residents around there, you reckon?" Harold asks her.

Mrs. Devonshire looks over the top of her glasses at Alice. "You got a plan for parking? I don't want them parking in front of my house."

"The side street." Alice points to the forms. "It's

notated. No one faces that street so it shouldn't be an issue."

"You gonna sell them *ro-mance* novels?" Mrs. Devonshire punches the word.

Alice looks to me for help, but I just shrug, because I have no idea which genres she plans to offer. I'm just building the shelves for them. Alice glances back at Mrs. Devonshire and squares her shoulders. "Yes, ma'am. All kinds of books. Romance too."

Mrs. Devonshire smiles, satisfied. "I think a bookstore'll be a welcome change."

Harold grunts. "Well, then. Everything looks to be in order."

Travis steps forward, his face reddening. "But Harold, the grease trap ordinance—"

Harold pulls out a rubber stamp and thumps it onto an ink pad. "Travis, they're selling books, not burgers. I think it'll be alright." Harold slams the stamp onto the permit.

APPROVED.

"Thank you!" Alice squeals. "Thank you so much!"

Harold nods and promptly walks toward the rear exit, likely returning to the river to continue fishing.

I pick up the folder, but before I leave, I hold Travis's stare for a long moment. He's standing there, arms crossed, stewing on the fact that his power play was undermined. And I know, from years of gauging hostile intent, that we haven't seen the last of him yet.

The second the door clicks shut behind us, Alice hollers in victory. She jumps up and down on the sidewalk, waving the folder like a trophy. "We got it, Colt! We got it!"

And then she's throwing herself into my embrace and

I'm lifting her off her feet, my arms locked around her waist. Laughter shudders through my chest and a grin splits my face despite my best efforts. I hold her far longer than I should, feeling the warmth of her body seep into mine. When she pulls back, I notice the little dimple in her chin, the flecks of yellow in her blue, hopeful eyes.

"Yeah, kid," I say, unable to let go. "Goddamn right we did."

15
BEFORE

MY RACKET SWUNG through the air, connecting with the tennis ball in a satisfying *thunk* my coach would have praised.

You hear that, Alice? That's the sound we're gunning for every time.

But it gained me no advantage over the two boys on the opposite side of the net. Grant lunged for the ball. He didn't have proper footwork. He didn't even know how to grip a racket. But what he did have was long arms and even longer legs, and in tennis, those things mattered. He returned the ball, a weak shot that managed to float to my side.

I backed up, set my feet, and fired the ball back.

Against a single opponent, that frustration-fueled, laser-focused shot would've scored me a point. But instead, it greeted Colt's clumsy racket and that blasted ball returned to me.

I was playing two-on-one, a tactic my parents devised before leaving to check on a client's warehouse, because apparently playing against one six-foot-whatever football player wasn't challenging enough. And if I were focusing on my lessons the way I *should've* been, two non-tennis players wouldn't be an issue.

I ran for the ball, court shoes squeaking. At the last moment, I hit the ball backward over my head, abandoning all form and going on instinct alone. Grant was waiting at the net, no forehand or backhand to speak of, and yet he managed to smash the ball down. He threw his arms in the air, roaring with victory, and then pretended to beat the racket against the ground, which made absolutely no sense.

I stood there, panting, red-faced from exhaustion and heat and humiliation. I'd been playing since I was eight, and now—at age thirteen—I was getting beaten by two boys who didn't even know what a drop shot was.

Although that was the problem; they didn't resemble real players. In an actual tournament, I could tell where an opponent's ball would go based on their shoulder placement and how they'd set their feet. But with these two and their clumsy shots, the ball could go anywhere.

"You okay?" Colt asked, wiping the sweat from his forehead with his T-shirt. My eyes went briefly to his toned abdomen, and then I glanced away, fuming.

I let my racket clatter to the court and marched to the bench, grabbing my water and guzzling.

"Ah, don't be pissed," Grant called out, attempting a cartwheel and failing miserably. "The thing is, I was born first. And I took up all the athletic genes Mom and Dad had to offer." Grant stood, brushing himself off. "I just..." he mimed pulling and sucking things into himself. "Took them all in. There was nothing left for you but dork genes."

"I'm getting kind of bored," Colt announced. "Let's do something different."

"But I need to—" I began.

"Seriously," Grant groaned. "*Anything* but this."

"Let's hit with only one hand now. And only straight up." Colt glanced my way with a smile. "The ball isn't allowed to hit the ground at all."

My anger softened around the edges. "You *are* allowed to hit a ball before it bounces, actually."

Colt pointed at me. "See? It's real tennis. Let's go."

Grant swung his racket in a wild arc over his head. "Fine. Whatever." My brother tossed the ball in the air and hit it straight up, his racket flat to the court. The ball soared over the net to my side, and while normally it would've been out, I played along, chasing after it and hitting it straight up like Grant had.

The ball went wild, arcing toward the chain-link fence. Colt ran for it, yelling.

"You better get that ball, Mitchell, goddammit." Grant's voice deepened, mirroring their football coach.

The ball bounced off the fence, and Colt fumbled before hitting it. I laughed, shocked that he got it, while Grant ran for the rebound, sprinting across the court and connecting with the ball not a moment too late.

The ball soared straight up, touched the sky, and came right back down, landing on their side of the court.

Colt grabbed Grant's shirt and shook him, using the same tone Grant had moments ago. "You missed the shot, Sinclair. You want to play ball in college, boy? Then you better show me something better than that shit. And you!" Colt pointed at me. "Not bad."

We played a few more rounds of Colt's revised game, and by the end, all three of us were roaring with laughter. At one point, we all stood twelve inches from the net and just popped the ball straight up to each other in a one-two-three triangle. And the thing is, I'm not sure my coach would've called it a waste of time, because in his opinion, each time your racket touched the ball, it helped you understand the game a fraction better.

"This grows tiresome." Grant sidestepped the ball when it returned to him. "I am bored by your *sport.*" Grant did air quotes here. "It's not your fault, Alice. Football players are at the pinnacle of athletic prowess. And your little yellow ball is no match for pigskin."

"Play her one-on-one then," Colt suggested.

"Nooo," Grant groaned.

Colt flopped down on the bench, draping a sweat towel over his head. "We can't just sit here. Your parents will freak out when they get back, and then they won't take us to the river."

Grant bobbed his head side to side and moved his lips quickly, mocking Colt. "Fine! It's clear I'm the dominant one here, and I will now demonstrate my strength. Watch in awe." Grant tapped his racket against the court twice like a batter at the plate. Then he poised it on his shoulder, awaiting an invisible pitcher.

I sighed, knowing Colt was right. If my parents returned to find us messing around, they'd be pissed. And I'd get the brunt of their disappointment since it was me who was supposed to be practicing. The surprising thing is, I *did* want to practice. Just not the way they'd chosen.

I backed up to the baseline and bounced the ball,

preparing. My eyes cut to Colt and I noticed he was wearing an odd grin. He nodded subtly toward Grant and winked. I shot my gaze to Grant, watching him rock back and forth theatrically, and suddenly realized what Colt was getting at.

It was one-on-one now. And Grant hadn't seen me play in ages.

I smiled.

I bounced the ball a couple more times. "Ready?"

Grant shot straight up. "I've *been* ready. Come on!"

I served, hitting at the very top of my toss, and slammed it into the service box with everything I had. Grant ran for it, swinging, hitting only empty air, and watched the ball whiz by his head.

"Out," Grant said.

"No." Colt shook his head, laughing.

Grant huffed. "I let you have that one so you wouldn't cry all the way home. Now we play for real."

And so we did. The next half hour was a blur of my balls going exactly where I wanted them to, and Grant missing every opportunity to gain an advantage. Without another body to depend on, he became an unsuspecting victim, and I became the player I remembered I was.

After slaughtering Grant, Colt took his place, and even though I dripped sweat and my legs shook from exertion, I felt exhilarated. How long had it been since I'd played a novice? How long since I'd been reminded how far I'd come?

I beat Colt 4-0, 4-0. And by the end, even Grant became a fair-weather fan, cheering for me to cream Colt. When the match was over, I expected Colt to sulk the way I might've at a tournament. But instead, the moment the match concluded, Colt rushed over and grabbed my arms. I didn't understand what was happening until he yelled for Grant to get my legs. Together, they swung my body side to side through the air until I laughed so hard my sides ached.

My mom's sharp voice rang out. "Looks like you're working pretty hard."

Instantly, my heart was in my throat. Grant and Colt set me down, and I clambered to my feet. "Mom! We just got done. We were practicing and—"

"And she killed us both," Colt chimed in.

"That right?" my dad said, swinging the car keys around his pointer finger.

"*Killed* is a strong word," Grant grunted, already bypassing my parents and striding toward their idling SUV.

"It is," Colt agreed. "Though *obliterated* might be a better one."

Mom removed the baseball cap from her head and ran a hand through her sweat-dampened hair. She seemed tired, though not entirely displeased by what she was hearing. "Alice beat y'all two-on-one?"

My face burned. "We switched to one-on-one," I admitted, my voice too high, feigning excitement in the hopes that it would deter her disappointment.

"Hmm." Mom frowned.

"Y'all get any points on her?" Dad bent over to help Colt pack our rackets and gather the water bottles.

Colt barked a laugh. "Not a single one. She's a little machine."

"Come on!" Grant yelled out the car window. He was in the front seat, two hands gripping the steering wheel, shaking himself forward and backward.

"Not a chance, buddy," Dad called, walking toward the SUV. "Get in the back seat."

"So, can we go to the river?" I watched Mom's reaction closely. I knew her well enough to know she was irritated. Her lips pursed, and then, with a glance toward the cloudless sky, she sighed. "Yeah, y'all can go. In fact, we'll all go."

Mom squeezed my shoulder as we strode toward my dad, who was dragging a hollering Grant out of the front seat. "Good work today, kiddo."

I beamed up at her, soaking in her praise like a desert would rain.

~

THE CAR RIDE was quiet toward the river, the *whoosh* of the AC the only sound. Eventually, I reached into my tennis bag to retrieve my book. It was a hardcover, so thick it made me proud. I cracked it open and tucked the rainbow-colored bookmark into the back. If I finished it by tomorrow, I'd be in the lead for the ninth-grade summer reading challenge. I wished all competitions were this easy. And enjoyable.

Colt noticed my book and cocked his head. "That any good?"

I glanced up at him, shrugged, and then nodded.

"What's it about?"

"Nooo," Grant groaned.

"Cut it out, Grant." Dad's eyes flicked to the rearview mirror.

"She's going to talk about it for the rest of the night,"

lamented Grant. But he was wrong, because now I didn't want to say a single word about it.

I gripped the book tighter. "Just...about a boy."

I expected Colt to let it go. He didn't. Instead, he shifted in his seat, facing me more fully. "And?"

I glanced at my brother, who shook his head and pretended to hang himself.

I cleared my throat, keeping my voice soft as I continued. "It's about a boy who goes on a safari with his dad to..." I checked the back cover to ensure I got it right. "Kruger National Park in South Africa. He gets lost and sees this lion by itself."

"Why's it alone?" Colt's brow furrowed. "Don't lions usually hang out with other lions?"

I smiled, sitting up straighter. "No, it was like, rejected by its pride. It's a male lion. I guess that happens sometimes. Anyway, the lion sees the boy, and instead of attacking him, he lingers nearby, seemingly out of loneliness."

My brother pulled headphones up over his ears, so I kept talking. I explained the drought, the regional geography, and the way the boy finds water by studying birds' flight patterns.

"So what happens in the end?" Colt seemed genuinely interested. "Does the lion get his own pride, or does he stay with the boy?"

"I don't know. I haven't finished it," I admitted. "But also, there's a sequel and I couldn't find it at—"

"Come on." Grant shoved the SUV door open and spilled outside. "Last one in the river's a fart licker."

"Grant!" Mom yelled.

Colt hopped out after my brother. "Thanks for telling me about your book," he said.

And then he dashed off, racing after Grant.

I glanced down at the hardcover in my hands and smiled, warmth spreading through my chest. Slowly, I closed the book and tucked it away, suddenly more interested in getting in the river than I was in finding out the ending.

16
COLT

I DRIVE the last three-inch screw into the side gable, the drill vibrating against my palm. Satisfied that it's firmly in place, I lay the drill aside and take hold of the bookshelf, raising the eight-foot-tall beast and then sliding it until it's flat against the wall.

The bookshelf boasts character-grade white oak that shows off its knots and mineral streaks and, more importantly, will handle the high traffic Alice is hoping for. I grab the glass of iced tea she left me and take a few steps toward the open window, feeling a slight breeze rolling in off the river.

My mind wanders to the conversation Alice and I had about Travis. She explained that they dated briefly in high school, and then something happened, and she distanced herself. She didn't seem traumatized, more like embarrassed, so I hadn't pressed. Still, my eyes travel down the sidewalk and up the street out of habit, searching for anything that might come between Alice and her goal.

In her parents' old office, Alice moves quickly and efficiently. She's got a steamer in one hand and a putty knife in the other, fighting a layer of wallpaper that has more willpower to hold the line than kudzu. Today, she's wearing denim cut-off shorts, a white tank top, and pink sneakers, and I'm losing my ever-loving mind over how sexy she looks. Finding Alice Sinclair attractive was *never* supposed to happen, and I'm still trying to pretend it's a figment of my imagination—me wanting her like this.

When one tank top strap slips halfway down her shoulder, I tell myself to get back to work. But I don't. I fixate on that damn spot, where errant fabric kisses skin. I picture pushing it back up with my thumb and putting my mouth there instead, against her shoulder. And then her neck.

Alice climbs a step stool to reach higher up the wall, and my eyes trace the backs of her firm, tanned thighs. I can almost see the underside of her ass at this angle, and that's my cue to turn the fuck around.

I spin away and force myself to breathe, trying to suppress the impulse to run my hands up those legs. To scoop her off the step stool and draw her against my chest. The record player we drug downstairs is playing an old country song I recognize but don't remember the name of. Lifting the tea once more, I glance back in her direction. The air moving through the window brushes through Alice's hair, and I swear I can smell her shampoo carrying on the wind.

It's been nearly two weeks since we got the permits. Two weeks of me being in the same house as her, occupying the same space, and in that time I've decided something—

There are three Alices I've known.

There's the one I basically lived with when we were

younger. The kid who toiled to earn her parents' approval, then sought escape into her beloved books. She was funny then, and she loved her brother fiercely even though he teased her the way brothers do. The way Warren did me before he left. My last memory of young Alice is when we stood on her parents' front porch. My eyes cast sideways to the window as I recall the moment. *It was right there.* She was fourteen, and I was nineteen. She was just a kid to me, and I'd felt like an adult for several years by then, though I know now that's not the way it should've been.

When I said goodbye, a duffel bag slung over my shoulder, she'd cried. Had begged me not to go, and I'm not sure she realizes how much that destroyed me. Because Alice had felt akin to a kid sister. And I'd have leveled anyone who looked at her the wrong way.

The second Alice arrived during my deployments, when I learned how to shove my anger into my gut and harness it against a common enemy. In the military, I met people like me. People whose childhoods had been as fucked up as mine. And we found our opportunity to pay the world back for the injustices we felt we'd endured. But inflicting violence and being encouraged to hate fellow human beings was not the remedy I needed. It sharpened my depression, made it cut deeper. And the Alice I knew then—the Alice during my military days—was the only real hero I encountered, because sure as hell, she rescued me.

Her letters became my lifeline, even when I lost the will to respond. Each time one arrived, often when I needed it most, I'd imagine her on the other side of the paper, writing it, tongue pressed into her cheek like she did while reading. And in my mind, she'd be the exact same age as when I left her on that porch. I think my brain purposely concocted that vision—kept her fourteen. Because had I allowed myself to picture her at seventeen, and then nineteen, and then twenty and twenty-two, I might have felt something stronger than affection. And that couldn't happen, because she was young. And she was brimming with possibility. And she was the daughter of two people kind enough to take me in and my best friend's little sister. So even when she sent those letters, and my attachment to her grew, she was *Alice*. Untouchable.

Now, she is something different. She is bright ideas and confident smiles. And she is also thighs and hips and breasts and hair I want to touch so badly it makes my hands clench. She is the woman who stayed when everyone else left.

After I enlisted, Grant sent emails and postcards for a while, but life pulled him away. He had a football scholarship to maintain and then a family business to run, and I sure as hell understand that. Alice's parents too—I love them, despite their flaws, because they made room for me. They sent messages and care packages, especially on my birthday. But life came for them as well, and I'm certain I became a fond memory as Grant's football career, and later their business expansion, took center stage. And that's okay. It makes sense. Responsibilities directly in front of us tend to dwarf those that aren't within eyesight.

But Alice.

She remained. Every month, every year, her letters arrived. Never email. Always blue ink, white paper, her careful penmanship, and my name on the envelope. It's this last Alice, the Alice of today, that I find myself thinking of the moment I open my eyes in the morning. It's that Alice I see right before I fall asleep.

I want her. I fucking want her so badly that I physically ache when she's around. But that ache's got nothing on the agony I feel when she's *not* around. When I lie in my hotel bed at the end of every night, itching to return to her. To hear her laughter and see her smiling face just one more time before I fall asleep. My god, how I've tried to push these thoughts aside. But they are unshakable.

Alice climbs down the stairs and turns, wiping her forehead. My face burns when she meets my gaze, like she can somehow intuit what I'm thinking. Her eyes widen when she sees what looms behind me.

"Oh, my god," she gasps. "Is that the first one? It's up?!" Alice rushes over and throws her arms around the bookshelf, pressing her cheek to the wood. "They're better than I ever imagined." She turns her head and kisses the shelf, and I never anticipated being envious of a shelf, but here we are. "You're a genius!" she cries and throws her arms around me.

I pull her closer, fingertips pressing into her shoulder blades. When my cock swells from the proximity, I step backward, clearing my throat. "Want me to grab those books from the attic?"

She does a little dance across the hardwoods and I find myself laughing, because I adore this playful side of her. "I'll take that as a yes."

The attic is a furnace and smells like mothballs, but I ascend into it anyway. One by one, I open boxes to find those housing Alice's childhood books. She's decided to offer a small secondhand section and to kick off that area with her own personal library. I open the final box to ensure it's filled with books, and when I discover that it is, I dig through out of curiosity.

My hand stills on one book in particular, and I lift it, brushing off the cover. I recognize this book, but can't explain why. Turning it over, I see that it's a library book. When I flip it back, the pieces fall into place and my face splits into a grin.

I toss the book back in, grab the box, and head down. When I get back to the old living room, Alice is clearing a space on the floor. I set the box down with a *thud* and withdraw the library book. "Care to explain this?" I wiggle the book with a grin.

Alice's mouth drops open, then snaps shut as a rosy color blooms in her cheeks. "Where'd you find that?"

"Uh, in the box." I step closer, a scolding note in my voice. "This is a book from my high school library, Ms. Sinclair. I checked this out for you when I was a senior. And *you* said you turned it into your librarian who, if memory serves, said they'd get it back to the high school."

Alice presses her lips together and looks toward the ceiling as if searching for something.

"Hey, eyes on me, Sinclair." She looks at me, fighting laughter. I am thoroughly enjoying making her squirm. "Did you know I had to stay after school on a Friday and help the librarian to repay her for the missing book? And she was a terrifying woman, Alice. Truly terrifying." I squint, leveling her with an admonishing look. "Did you lie to me when you said you turned it in?"

Alice spins around and resumes gazing toward the ceiling. "Do you think we should paint up here?"

"Ali."

She points upward. "We could even wallpaper it. Some people do that."

"Alice Sinclair."

"Of course, I did just spend two hours peeling *old* wallpaper."

I seize her waist and twirl her around. She erupts with laughter and tries to run from me, but I grip her tighter, holding her firmly in place. "No. No running. Tell me right now. Did you know you still had that book?"

Alice cranes her neck, peering over my shoulder toward the large front window. I take her chin gently and force her to look at me.

"Answer me, Alice."

Her giggles quiet when our eyes meet, though she's still smiling. She tips her head back, meeting my gaze defiantly. "Yes. I knew I had it. I never even attempted returning it."

My eyes study hers, searching for an answer to a question I'm incapable of voicing. Instead, I ask the closest thing to it. "Why did you keep it?"

Her answer comes swiftly, unapologetically, the smile falling from her lips. "Because you gave it to me."

I just nod, finding it hard to breathe.

"Because you asked about the book I was reading," she continues, her blue eyes locked on mine. "And you brought me the sequel home without a word, and just left it on the counter."

My thumb slides from her chin, traveling down her neck. Alice lifts her head a touch more, making space for my hand. Slowly, my fingers wrap around her, lifting ever so slightly to brush the soft hairs at the nape of her neck.

I stop breathing entirely, every inch of my skin burning to close the distance between us and do what I haven't been able to stop thinking about. The music plays on in the background, indifferent, but I can barely hear it over the roar of adrenaline in my ears.

Alice's eyes drift to my mouth, and suddenly I'm sixteen again, and I'm standing in the living room, steps away from where I am now, and I can hear Grant talking in the kitchen, trying to keep his voice low. But it's not low enough, because I can make out that he's explaining my mom and what he saw in our fridge and asking if I can stay for a while.

I jerk my hand away and step back, sucking in air, remembering how much I needed this place and these people years ago. "Well," I say, clearing my throat. "I'm pretty sure it's a...federal crime. Stealing from a public institution." Returning to the box, I start yanking out books and putting them on the shelves, trying to resume a normal breathing pattern and forget what I almost did.

Alice comes to stand beside me, and we line up the books, handful after handful. She's close enough that her arm brushes mine when we reach into the box at the same time. There's a current in this house. The same sensation I'd feel before an enemy erupted from their hiding place. It's a sensation of knowing something big, something dangerous, is coming.

"You were always doing stuff like that," Alice says quietly, her eyes fixed on the spines she's straightening. "Lifting my spirits when my parents were being strict. Listening when no one else would. Showing me I had talent where I thought none existed." She bites her lip, and the sight causes my vision to blur. Alice puts her hand on my forearm, stilling me. "You saw me, Colt. And the memory of that attention, even while you were gone, kept me going when I felt...alone."

Something inside me snaps.

I drop the book I'm holding, grab her waist, and pin her against the very shelves I just built. Her lips part and her breath catches. I plant my hands on either side of her head, gripping the shelves, locking her in. The gold flecks in her eyes catch the light, and I can see her pulse thrumming against her neck. I lean in, my face inches from hers, my mind screaming at me to take what I want. To find out if she tastes the way I imagine. To cling onto her happiness and make it my own.

It's this last thought that stops me.

Because she is sunshine and hope and happiness. And I can still see my mom passed out on the linoleum floor and my father's abandoned clothes hanging in the closet. I can see the unread texts I sent to Warren and I can see the sand.

And the flash and the smell of burnt metal.

My team. My boys. *My fucking responsibility.*

Alice is a woman who believes the best can happen.

And I'm a man who believes I should have died alongside them.

"Colt." Alice's soft voice cuts through the noise, and I step closer, my forehead going to her shoulder. Her hands find my back and she's pulling me toward her, but I need no help with that. Alice arches into me, her breath warm against my neck. I turn my head just enough and my lips graze her skin.

I keep them there for a second. Just long enough to

think this could happen. I could be happy. I could be the man she thinks I am and share this dream alongside her. And then I'm stepping back, head hanging.

"I should get back to work," I rasp, unable to meet her gaze. Because I'm not worthy of Alice, and if she looked closely enough, she'd see that too.

She's quiet for a long time. And then, "Okay."

I nod.

We both stand there for a moment longer, and then Alice walks back into the office. I snatch my keys off the counter and bang through the front door, the sunlight blinding. Swinging the truck door open, I climb inside. Start the ignition. Back up. Head toward the lumberyard. I'll get more wood.

I'll sand more shelves.

I'll build every bookshelf in the world if it prevents me from reaching for Alice again.

17
ALICE

I'M SITTING inside Blessings Barn, a structure that's both a picturesque wedding venue and a torturously uncomfortable town hall meeting spot. The doors and windows are thrown wide open to gently swaying grass and wildflowers, and the subtle, mossy scent of the river. Overhead, twinkling lights accentuate wooden beams, and lengths of burgundy silk drape from one end of the barn to the other, crossing beneath a chandelier of antlers.

As I wait for the other attendees to arrive, I think—as I do lately—of Colt.

These last three weeks have been a blur of swinging my legs over the side of the bed the moment I wake, my body electric from the knowledge that it's *happening*. I'm chasing my dream, and I'm doing it beside someone I trust and care about.

During that same stretch of time—longer if I'm being honest—I've been consumed by thoughts of *him*. The way he arrives with two coffees each morning, wearing a smile like he's surprised to find me on the other side of the door. Or how we swap shared memories from our childhood, laughing until we can't breathe, and other memories too—ones from before we knew each other, or from the years we spent apart, as if desperate to fill in the missing pieces.

I hold the things I've learned about Colt in my mind like secret, intimate treasures. Like how he loves chilled watermelon and (unsalted) scrambled eggs. And the intensity with which he examines the world—ceaselessly looking, listening, touching. Most of all, how he loves watching birds, studying them like they hold the key to happiness. So much so that I've hung a bird feeder near the front window. He smiled when he saw it, and now he'll frequently pause mid-swing, mid-build, to look at a small winged-creature as it rifles through black oil sunflower seeds.

I've also learned that Colt is unbelievably, undeniably *sexy.*

I always thought he was handsome, but the boy I remember has been replaced by a *man*. All hard lines and broad shoulders and, my god, those dark eyes dusted by long lashes. Instantly, I'm there again. Two days ago. Me pinned against the bookshelf.

Those eyes had dropped to my mouth, heat radiating off his massive frame. And the way his biceps had flexed as he gripped the bookshelf had nearly incinerated me. I've replayed that moment in the dark, my hand slipping between my legs, fingers rubbing frantic circles as I imagine him hoisting me up against that same bookshelf.

Was he going to kiss me that day? If so, why did he stop himself? A tiny, cruel voice in the back of mind whispers that I'm not enough for Colt. He's been a Marine. He's seen the world, faced real danger, and possesses the ability to kill a person with his bare hands—hands that are now building my future.

Colt marched into that military recruitment office and, without a safety net to fall back on, took a chance on himself. What have I done other than follow my family's direction? Even starting work on my bookshop required my parents' sign-off. I wonder if I will always be Grant's little sister in Colt's eyes.

"Thank god you're here." Maggie drops down in the seat next to me, plopping her purse into her lap. "I'll need someone to hold me back if Roxanne says she doesn't have shit planned."

I throw my arms around Maggie, hugging her. "Thank *you* for being here."

Maggie looks at me more closely. "You okay?"

Before I can respond, June slides into the seat on my opposite side. She reaches into a paper bag and produces two waxed sleeves. We're already craning our necks to see what she brought when she hands them to us. "Strawberry danishes," she announces proudly. "Still warm."

"Be still my heart," I sigh, the smell of buttery pastry slowing my spiraling mind.

"Marry me, June Bug." Maggie bites into hers immediately.

A shadow falls over us, and I look up to see Frank standing directly in front of my chair. He's wearing a stained apron and a frown.

"You ready to come back to the cafe?" he asks.

I lower my pastry and offer a sympathetic smile. "Oh.

No. I'm sorry, Frank. I'm still working on getting my bookshop up and running."

"Bookshop." Frank huffs. "People don't like reading. They just liketa' *say* they do." Here he mocks some unnamed person. "Oh. Oh, have you read.... *Gone With the Wind?* No? Oh, what an *idiot.* I have."

I stare at him, slack-jawed. "Uh, well. I kinda—"

"Y'all hiring?"

"Sorry?"

"You looking for an em-ploy-ee?"

I can feel the confusion twisting my face. "Are you asking for a job, Frank?"

"You offerin'?"

"...no?"

Frank points a thick finger in my direction. "You should buy my cafe instead. People are too busy with their screens and their tik-taks to read books. But they'll sure as hell eat." He gestures to the pastries we're holding to punctuate his point. Then he looks to June and holds her stare.

June rolls her eyes and reaches into her bag for another Danish. "Here ya go, Frank."

Frank shoves half the Danish into his mouth and nods to himself. "This's good shit, Jane."

"June," she corrects.

But Frank is already walking away, taking another enormous bite. A woman carrying a newborn tries to get past Frank, but he stands unmoving, blocking the aisle and blatantly staring down her shirt.

Roxanne claps her hands at the front of the room, and all heads turn in her direction. The exacting woman stands behind a podium, an exasperated look on her face. "Alright, let's get through this so we can move on with our days."

"Hasn't even started and she's already over it," Maggie whispers. "Sounds about right."

"The Fall Festival is our biggest draw of the season, and I know local commerce depends on it being well-attended." Roxanne shuffles some papers. "Unfortunately, reservations at the inn aren't looking promising. So here's what we'll do. Each shop will offer a festival-only special—be it a themed treat, a free experience, or a sample. We'll have fliers promoting the offerings available at the inn by next Friday, and I'll also post it on our socials to drive reservations."

Maggie leans in. "Speaking of socials. Have you checked yours? People are obsessed with you and Colt." The moment Maggie finishes talking, her grin morphs into a scowl. "That's *it*, Roxanne? That's all you've got? That's the same thing we've done all year. It doesn't work!"

The room mumbles their agreement.

Roxanne purses her lips. "Then perhaps you'd like to take over the position? Do this on top of your day job?" Roxanne glances around the room, wearing an expression of annoyance and—beneath that—a shadow of hopefulness. "Anyone?" She holds the gavel out, inviting someone to take it.

Maggie nudges my ribs on one side and June bumps my shoulder on the other. They both give me *Come on* eyes. I think about my sketchbooks. The ones that hold not only plans for the bookshop, but for the town. But between the looming deadline and Colt's confusing signals, I have enough on my plate.

But the bigger reason I don't volunteer is that I worry I

couldn't pull it off. This build has shown me just how much work goes into fulfilling a vision, and that there's zero guarantee of success at the end of it.

What if I spent the town's budget on a plan that didn't work? The festival would be deemed a failure, businesses would be hurt, and the people of Holly Rivers would undoubtedly snub my shop, and for good reason.

Taking risks feels exciting, Alice, but most success lies in risk aversion.

Focus on what's in front of you.

I shake my head at my friends.

"Didn't think so," Roxanne mutters when no one speaks up. The meeting carries on for another twenty minutes with bickering breaking out about hayride routes and parking logistics. Finally, Roxanne slams her gavel down. "Meeting's adjourned." She checks her watch. "And in record time. Have your Fall Festival offerings to me by Monday morning, please."

"I've got to get back to the bakery," June says. "But I'll see you two at the Hall? The band starts at eight."

"I'll be there," Maggie confirms, checking her phone. "Alice?"

"With bells on," I respond.

We give each other quick hugs and turn to leave. My stomach is already twisting into knots thinking about tonight, and who I want to invite.

Right before I exit the barn, I notice Harold, the man who approved my permit. I start to wave hello, but stop when I realize he's moving toward my neighbor and his secretary, Ms. Devonshire. As I watch, he removes his hat with shaking hands and opens his mouth to say something to her. But Ms. Devonshire walks away without noticing him. I frown, imagining a missed opportunity for romance.

~

AS I PULL into the driveway, the sun is waving a final farewell, stretching long fingers of dying light over my porch and the few pumpkins scattered there. I take a moment to appreciate the majestic white two-story home with its wraparound porch and swing. In my mind's eye, there are people trailing in and out of the front door, chatting merrily with one another, arms filled with paperbacks. A customer sits on the swing, rocking back and forth, so absorbed in the book they're reading they hardly notice the comings and goings.

When I go inside, the house is quiet—no hammering, no circular saw screaming. I walk toward the kitchen, and that's when I see him.

Colt is standing by the sink, his back to me. He's finishing up for the day, and the universe must have a twisted sense of humor, because the man is shirtless. Tanned, taut muscles shift as he splashes water on his face, and I watch on, hypnotized. There's a faint scar near his shoulder, the same one I traced in the river, and I want to touch it again.

I want to touch all of him.

Colt turns around, wiping his face with a paper towel, and stops when he sees me. "Hey. Didn't hear you come in."

"Uh, huh," is all I can manage. My gaze is trapped on a stray water droplet racing down his pecs, on its happy little way to a six-pack. I follow its progression before my eyes stray to the waistband of his work pants.

"Meeting go okay?" His voice is a low, rumbling baritone, and I have the sudden desire to put my mouth on his throat and feel the sound as it leaves him.

"Fine. Yeah." I realize I'm staring and force my gaze back to his face. "Are you done for the day?"

"I think so. I wanted to finish the crown molding in the dining room, but it's getting dark and I don't want to mess it up. So..." He rubs the back of his neck. "I guess I'll take off and see you back here first thing?"

"Wait." The word jumps out of my mouth before I can stop it. "We're headed to the Hall. Remember that band June was talking about a while back? They're playing tonight."

Colt looks at me, and for a second I see that same flash in his eyes I spotted two days ago. His jaw clenches, and it almost seems like he's working himself up to saying no. I prepare myself to smile through the rejection, even though it'll absurdly break my heart. But instead, what comes out of his mouth is, "Yeah, that sounds great."

My heart leaps. I glance at the clock. "We're supposed to be leaving soon. You could just...shower here if you want."

Alice. What?!

Colt glances down at himself. "These clothes are pretty dirty. And I'd need a shirt."

I shrug. "Borrow something of my brother's. Or my dad's. They both have a few things in the master closet that I was supposed to donate. We can throw everything else in the wash on quick cycle."

He looks to the laundry room. "Quick cycle, huh?"

"The quickest."

He smiles and looks back at me. "Alright, then."

My heart leaps.

We head upstairs, and he moves toward Grant's shower, the one he used when he'd stay over.

"Should I just...?" he begins.

"Yeah," I chirp. "I can take them. Just drop everything on the floor."

He nods, and a few moments later, after giving him privacy, I run the clothes down to the washer, trying not to focus on the fact that Colt's boxers are somewhere in the bundle.

After starting the load, I jump into my own shower and run the water hot, watching as steam fills the small space. My mind doesn't just wander, it *vaults* to the fact that Colt Mitchell is just down the hall, undressed, water cascading over his powerful body. My brother isn't here. Nor are my parents. And we are both undressed under the same roof. If he were to just walk down the hall...

My hand moves between my legs, and I press my cheek against the cool tile as water runs in rivulets down my back. My eyes slip closed as I think about Colt. His large hands. His shirtless torso. His mouth. The way he makes me feel both seen and protected.

I bite down on my lip as I move my fingers slowly over my clit and then inside of myself.

There's a knock on the door, and I freeze, my heart in my throat.

"Alice." It's Colt—his voice deep, strained.

"I wanted to let you know I'm in your bedroom. Just

checking what's in the closet and then I'm going to move my clothes to the dryer."

My hand is frozen between my legs. "Okay," I squeak, my voice far too high.

I make out the sound of his footsteps retreating, and I fold over on myself, cringing, because that man just interrupted me masturbating to the thought of him and I am an absolute *pervert.*

After toweling off, and managing to make eye contact with myself, I focus on getting dressed, laughing because if Maggie knew this story, she would bring it up every five minutes for all of eternity.

I peek around the door to ensure Colt is gone from the bedroom, and then I pull on jeans, a long-sleeved sweater that shows a few inches of midriff, and red cowboy boots. After dressing, I dry my hair and brush it into a ponytail, carefully curling the ends. In a final touch, I apply two coats of mascara and a bright red lip, then dash toward the stairs. I'm halfway down when I catch sight of Colt.

He's leaning against the window frame, watching the last of the sunset. His cargo pants are back on, and he's paired them with a white starched shirt, the sleeves rolled to the elbow. He looks rugged and clean and devastatingly attractive.

I find myself yearning for a real date with him, one that ends with a kiss and him asking if we can do this again. But I worry Colt will never see me that way. I never expected to see *him* this way, even though he always meant a great deal to me.

When he turns, his pupils seem to dilate. But perhaps that's wishful thinking.

"You look..." he begins, then stops, shaking his head. "You look great, Alice."

When I reach the bottom of the stairs, he offers me his arm.

I take it at once, the feel of his skin against mine so soothing, so *right*, that for the first time in my life, it feels like I'm exactly where I'm meant to be.

18
COLT

I SCAN THE HALL, searching for Alice's friends. When I catch sight of them, I touch Alice's lower back and tip my head in their direction. We make our way through the press of bodies, and Maggie holds up her tumbler in greeting.

June scoots over, making space for Alice, and Dalton—who's abandoned his duties as owner for the night—nods toward a chair for me to take.

"Beer or liquor?" Dalton asks, gesturing to the drinks on the table.

"Beer. Thanks." I reach for my wallet.

"Get the fuck outta here." Dalton bats my hand away.

As the band tunes on the stage, my mind ventures back to Alice's house. To the soft moan—*was it a moan?*—I heard on the other side of the bathroom door. I nearly took that damn door off its hinges. I'd been hard instantly, and had to grip the edge of the dresser and take slow, measured breaths not to do something monumentally dumb—like ask if I could join her.

But that couldn't happen. Because a relationship, even if she were receptive to it, could jeopardize working together, which had been going so well. What if things between us soured? Or she immediately regretted doing something with me? We'd be forced to see the project through, even as the awkward tension strangled our productivity. Worst-case scenario, she kicks me out. Then what? Her loan wouldn't cover a paid carpenter.

No. I can't risk interfering with Alice's dream.

Suddenly, the house lights go down and a collective cheer erupts.

The four guys from Austin, looking like they just stepped off a bus after a three-day bender, explode into their first song. It's an upbeat alt-country track, and a burst of energy sweeps the room.

The five of us go in waves of talking and watching the band play. It's easy banter, and at one point I catch myself. Because laughing with these four people, it almost feels like this is *my* group of friends. And that I belong. Not because we're teammates, or fellow soldiers. But because we're choosing to be here with one another.

Jesus, what the hell is Alice doing to me?

The band slows, a pedal steel guitar starting a haunting intro.

A man steps out of the crowd and walks directly over to our table. He's tall, wearing a Western shirt and a Stetson that he removes as he approaches. He smiles, focused entirely on Alice.

"Excuse me, ma'am." He bows his head. "I was wondering if I might have this dance?"

Dammit.

Alice turns to look at me, a question in her eyes. I want her to turn him down. I want her to say she's already taken. But that's preposterous, because Alice isn't mine. And she shouldn't be because she's better off without me.

I tip my beer toward the man. "You should go."

The words burn leaving my mouth. I want to shove them back down my throat immediately and wipe the eager look off that man's face.

It's too dark in here to be certain, but I think hurt flashes across Alice's face, replaced swiftly by resolve. She looks at the man and beams. That smile, directed at someone else, shatters me.

"I'd *love* to." She emphasizes the word. And then her hand is in his and the twosome are moving toward the dance floor.

Dalton stares at me, barely holding back laughter. "You coulda said something."

"Fuck off," I grunt, my eyes locked on every movement Alice makes.

Dalton is still howling with laughter when another man arrives at the table and asks June to dance. His amusement is eviscerated on the spot. Now we're both tracking one particular woman and white-knuckling our beer bottles.

Maggie sighs and gets to her feet, tugging on Dalton's arm. "Come on, friend. You can't look that disappointed at your own bar. Bad for business."

As Maggie and Dalton trudge toward the dance floor, I mutter to no one that I'll get another round. But this is merely an excuse to get a better angle at where the man's hands rest on my girl. Fuck. *No*. She's not mine, I remind myself. I make a wide circle around them, trying—and failing—to be inconspicuous.

Alice catches my gaze and allows Stetson Guy to pull her a touch closer.

I'm about five feet from the bar when Travis steps between me and my view of Alice. He nods toward her, his trademark smirk plastered on his smug face. "Looks like she's enjoying herself."

Instantly, my blood boils. Because at this point I'm just looking for a reason to be pissed off. But instead of reacting, I just sigh and attempt to sidestep Travis. He puts a hand on my chest and pushes me back into place. My eyes dart to where he touched me and then back up at him.

He has my full attention now, and he's going to regret that.

"Colt," he says, almost like he's sad to deliver this information. "You know me and Alice are going to end up together, don't you? I'm an upstanding citizen, and I love this town, same as she does. And..." He pats my chest twice. "I have the financial resources to give her the comfortable life her parents did." Travis leans in a touch nearer, ensuring I hear him over the music. "And you... Well, you're just a washed-up vet." Now Travis comes close enough so that only I can hear him. "If I were you, I'd steer clear of Alice. I heard you have a tendency to get people killed." Travis steps back and laughs to himself. "Oh, I'm sorry. Slip of the tongue there. I meant a tendency to get *projects* killed. Did I say people?"

I falter, my heart thundering. He knows what happened to my men, and that it was my fault. I could have Travis squealing on his knees in the blink of an eye, and yet I'm frozen by his accusation.

My eyes dart back to the dance floor, and I spot Stetson Guy sliding his hand toward Alice's ass. She reaches back, attempting to halt the grope, but I'm already moving, Travis forgotten in an instant.

I reach them in five long strides and rip his hand off Alice, shoving him backward.

"The hell?" Stetson Guy yells over the music.

I step between him and Alice. "Go."

The man glances at Alice, and then at me. "We were just dancing. What's your problem?"

I jut my chin. "Walk. Away."

He stares at me for a long moment, as if weighing how far I'm willing to take this. Relenting, he rolls his eyes and holds his hands up in surrender. "Whatever, man." He turns and leaves, shaking his head as he vanishes into the crowd.

I look at Alice, my hands finding her shoulders. "Are you okay?"

"Yes, I'm fine, Colt." She frowns, breaking eye contact and glancing at the stage. Then she looks back at me. "I was handling that, you know."

I drop my hands from her shoulders. "I know. I'm sorry, I..."

Alice looks at me, and though it feels like I should say something else, I'm not sure what. I can't think straight around her, maybe because I want to say *so much* to her. She sighs deeply and then turns toward our table, walking toward it. I don't know what possesses me, but I reach out and grab her hand.

Her eyes meet mine, surprise coloring her cheeks.

"Dance with me, Alice," I say before I can stop myself. It's what I should have said the moment that man came to our table.

She pauses. I can feel her pulse fluttering against my thumb. She looks at my hand, then at me, considering. I'm asking for something I shouldn't, but right now, I can't summon the will to care.

A small smile tugs at the corner of her lips. "Might as well. Doesn't look like you're gonna let me dance with anyone else."

"Not anyone who touches you like that." I take Alice into my arms, pulling her close. She returns the gesture, closing the distance between us a touch more. For a brief, terrifying second, I rest my chin on top of her head. And dammit if it doesn't feel right—her, in my arms. Safe. *Mine.*

I spot Maggie at our table. She's standing up, grinning widely, her phone raised. The woman is overtly filming us.

I lean down, my lips brushing Alice's ear. "Just so you know, your friend is filming this."

Alice laughs, the sound reaching through my chest. "Well," she says, scrunching her adorable nose. "Let's give her something good then."

I pull her even tighter against me.

~

OUR BOOTS CRUNCH over the fallen leaves as we walk the final few steps to Alice's house. Before I say good-night, I head inside and check each room as Alice shakes her head, asking when's the last time I heard of a break-in in Holly River.

But construction projects attract attention because it's an easy way to steal and sell tools and copper wire. I check the back door, the side entrance, the windows on the ground floor. Everything is secure.

"Okay." I stop just inside the doorway. "Everything looks good. Tonight was fun. Thanks for inviting me. I'm sorry about that guy..." I shake my head, smiling suddenly, because I've a bit of liquid courage in me now. "No. I'm not sorry."

Alice leans a shoulder against the wall, her boots already kicked off. She smiles too. "I know you're not."

I meet her gaze. Hold it.

Her smile fades.

Mine does too.

We stand unmoving as the air between us grows heavy, charged. I clench and unclench my hands, trying to remember how to breathe. I know it's time to walk the fuck away, but I can't seem to do so.

"Goodnight," she says finally, her voice a whisper.

I nod for several seconds. Then swallow. "Goodnight, Alice."

I definitely should be opening the front door by now. And waving goodbye. But my boots are cemented to the floor and there's not a goddamn thing I can do about that.

Alice opens her arms. "Hug?"

I step into her embrace, wrapping my arms around her. I bury my head in her hair, squeezing her tighter. My heart pounds in my chest. I can feel hers too, beating like a wild thing. Every letter she's ever written me shoots through my veins at once—an injection, a *reminder*. That she never left me. That she always saw the best in me. I pull back slowly, and my brain says—

Get the hell away from her, Colt.

Go the hell home!

Her cheek slides past mine and we pause, right there, her lips an inch away from mine, both of us breathing hard. I hesitate, thinking of all the reasons I've told myself not to touch her. She's my best friend's little sister. This could complicate our work. I'm not good enough for her.

The reasons...they mean *nothing*.

I kiss her.

For a moment I'm afraid she'll jerk away, ask what the hell I'm doing. But then she's gripping me tighter, her lips moving with mine. And I fucking *lose* it. My hands find her thighs and I hoist her up. Alice gasps against my mouth, her legs locking around my waist.

I shuffle forward until her back presses against the wall. My tongue meets hers and the soft, wet sensation shoots straight to my cock. I grip her thighs harder, push myself closer, our mouths moving with blinding urgency.

I fumble toward the kitchen, tripping over a stray piece of wood, and find my footing well enough to press her against the bookshelves. Her hands rake down my back, nails digging into flesh.

More, my brain roars.

Her tongue traces the inside of my mouth, my lips, and I have half a mind to catch her jaw and demand to know where she learned that.

"Colt," she whimpers.

"I've got you, baby," I growl against her mouth, striding toward the kitchen now. With one hand, I sweep the sketches, pens, and stray mug off the counter. The porcelain crashes to the floor, and Alice giggles against my mouth.

I lay Alice down, careful, and take a moment to admire her. Her hair is fanned in a halo around her head and her face is flushed, pupils blown wide. She reaches for me, and I'm right fucking there. I spread her thighs and lean over, coming down between them, her back pressed into the granite, my weight pressed into her. Her legs encircle my waist, and this time I'm grinding against her, my cock painfully hard, aching for friction. Aching for *her.*

My hand slides up her side and cups her breast through her sweater, squeezing gently, thumb brushing over her nipple. When Alice rocks her hips upward, I drag my tongue up her neck, grinding harder against her.

"Please," she begs.

I kiss her again, tasting her like I always wanted to. My hands move to the button on her jeans, and she's already lifting her hips, giving me space to remove them. I want my mouth between her thighs, her cunt on my fucking tongue. And then I'm going to drive into her and—

I stop.

Because if I move one single muscle, it's over. I'm going to fuck Alice until I can't see straight. And then I'm going to destroy anyone who tries to touch her again.

What the hell am I doing?!

With a reserve of willpower I didn't know existed, I step back, my hands raised.

"Colt." Alice reaches for me, and I take another backward step.

"Alice, I..." I shake my head, unable to process the line I just crossed, and all the others I want to cross over and over again. "I'm... Fuck, Alice. I'm sorry. I shouldn't have..." I turn and slam my hands down on the barstool. My pulse is thundering in my ears, and Alice is still lying there—impossibly beautiful, face twisted in confusion—and my god, I just screwed this all up like I knew I would.

"I'm sorry," I repeat. I'm shaking with adrenaline and from the withdrawal from her, my body *burning* to return to hers.

Alice is starting to sit up, and I'm struggling to find the right words, and just as the silence stretches into something agonizing, a banging thunders through the house.

Our heads pivot toward the front door, and another knock comes—loud, aggressive.

I glance at Alice and she shakes her head, indicating she doesn't know who it is. It's late, and her eyes are wide with alarm.

"Wait here," I order before crossing the room. Stopping by the front window, I peer out, moving the curtain a fraction. It's dark out, but the motion sensor has kicked on, bathing the stoop in harsh floodlights.

For a second, I can't comprehend what I'm seeing.

I hang my head, disbelief washing over me.

"Shit," I mutter.

"Colt?" Alice's voice is tentative behind me. She slides off the table, buttoning her jeans. "Who is it?"

I unbolt the door and pull it open.

The man steps toward the threshold, looking at me and then Alice. He throws his arms wide, a lopsided grin plastered on his face.

"Hey, fucker," Grant says. "Miss me?"

19
ALICE

I LEAN AGAINST THE COUNTERTOP, waiting for the coffee to brew. It's cold beneath my palms, but four nights ago, this slab of granite was the hottest place in Texas. I can still feel Colt's hands on me. The way he'd laid me down carefully, then ground against me, that breathy growl in my ear that makes my skin burn to remember it.

I'd felt how hard he was. How desperately he wanted me. That fact wasn't open to interpretation. So why, then, did he pull away? Did he stop because of our past? Or because he's planning to leave in a few weeks?

The last thought twists my stomach.

I wonder if I'll ever get the answer. Not anytime soon if my brother has anything to do with it. Because for the last four days, he has been *everywhere* we are. The ultimate cockblock. A constant reminder that we only know each other because of him.

I've got you, baby.

Colt's words—words I'd imagined verbatim in my

fantasies—had rolled off his tongue and into my mouth. I'm replaying that line when Grant strides into the kitchen, hair disheveled, scratching at his chest. He looks like a bear woken mid-hibernation, none too happy about where he finds himself.

That makes two of us.

I've just poured my coffee and am about to take a sip when Grant yanks it from my hands.

"You're too kind," he mutters.

"Grant!"

"Alice," he deadpans before drinking from *my* coffee mug.

Not the one Colt and I broke the other night when we were—

I reach into the cupboard and pull out another one—a Christmas mug with Snoopy on it, because it's never too early for Christmas, especially in Holly River. Pouring myself a fresh cup, I nod toward the couch. "Are you sure we shouldn't get you a room at the inn? I really do worry about all the construction dust you're breathing in."

Grant snorts, leaning against the fridge. "I spend half my time at ranches. I'd breathe in less dust on the daily if I huffed a vacuum bag. I think I'll survive your little hobby project."

My jaw tightens, because there it is. He may pretend that he came to visit his old friend, but I know who really sent him, and why.

"It's not a hobby. It's a business." I take another sip of coffee before setting it aside and digging through the cabinets for breakfast. What I'm saying would hold more weight if what I had in here amounted to more than Cap'n

Crunch and S'mores Pop-Tarts. "And you can let Mom and Dad know that when you scurry back to Shreveport with your formal report."

Grant reaches past me to grab the Pop-Tart box. "Don't know what you're talking about."

A knock at the front door makes my heart somersault, because I recognize that efficient *one-two* rap. I hurry to the door, pulling it open to find exactly who I expected. Colt stands on the porch wearing a fitted white shirt, jeans, and a baseball cap. Behind him is June, a ray of sunshine in her yellow cardigan. She's holding a large, parchment-lined box that she lifts a few inches, acknowledging my request.

"Morning, Alice." Colt's greeting is a deep rumble that shivers through my body.

"Colt," I manage.

Colt's eyes drop to my lips before raising again. It's subtle, quick. But it broadcasts: *I remember. I'm thinking about it too.*

Colt passes by me, and when I catch the scent of soap on his freshly showered skin, my knees go weak.

"I brought reinforcements!" June exclaims as she steps inside. "And by reinforcements, I mean sugar. Lots of sugar."

Grant wanders over. "Finally. A real breakfast." He reaches into the box and grabs two cookies, shoving one into his mouth immediately.

June slaps his hand. "Alice asked me to bring these for her meeting. They're not your breakfast."

"Mmph," Grant grunts around a mouthful. "If not breakfast, why breakfast-shaped?"

June leans over the box, face contorting with confusion

as she tries to piece together his meaning. "Because they're round?"

Grant raises his fingers, counting off evidence. "Pancakes, fried eggs, doughnuts...bowls...of things."

June waves Grant's arm away when he reaches for more, but she's looking at me. "Why did you want three different types of cookies at eight in the morning? Not that I'm complaining about the business. Stop, Grant!"

I catch Colt looking at me from the main room, where he's already getting to work taping off baseboards. My face heats beneath his gaze. I pull in a steadying breath and say to June, my eyes still on Colt, "I'll explain everything when Maggie gets here."

"Speak of the devil," a voice rings out.

Maggie bursts through the front door, her arms flying up to do jazz hands.

Grant groans and moves to the couch, flopping down and yanking the blanket over his head. "It's too early."

Maggie stops in front of Grant's blanketed form and shoves her hands on her hips. Bending at the waist, she says to Grant. "It is early, isn't it? So early that if you got on the road now, you'd be to Shreveport by lunch." She claps her hands together, and Grant jerks at the sound. "Go on, boy!" Maggie's voice rings out. "Go on home. You can do it, boy! Find home!"

Maggie spots June's cookies and rushes over to grab one.

"Look what I've got here!" Maggie waves the cookie directly above where Grant's nose would be.

June and I start laughing, and from the corner of my eye, I note that even Colt is cracking a smile.

Grant throws the covers back.

"Come on," Maggie coaxes, backing up.

Grant sits straight up, perking, his eyebrows shooting up.

Maggie wiggles the cookie and then tosses it out the front door. "Go on! Get!"

"Hey," June protests, right as Grant flops back down on the couch and recovers his head.

Maggie strides over and hugs June tight. "I'll pay you back."

June laughs. "You will not."

"In flowers," Maggie finishes.

"Now that I believe." June looks at me. "Alright, we're all here, and I have to be back at the bakery by nine. What've you got?" June glances around the place. "You guys are crushing it, by the way. It's starting to look like an actual bookstore."

"It's getting there," I agree. "We've built most of the shelves, but we still need to do the electrical, replace the front window, build the counter, and..." I pause, thinking.

"Install the crown molding," Colt supplies, finishing my thought.

I point at him, grateful once again to have a partner in this, especially someone as competent as him. "Right, and that. From there, it's the fun stuff. Painting. Wallpaper. Decor." I pause, plucking one of June's cookies from the box and shaking it. "Speaking of fun stuff, I want to pitch you guys an idea."

Maggie slides onto a barstool with an *I'm all ears* face.

At the same time, in the main room, Colt nudges the couch with his boot. "Come on, man. If you're going to be here, you might as well help your sister out. Let's get these floating shelves up."

Grant grunts.

Colt pulls the blanket off him and tosses it away. "Get up."

Grant groans, but manages to get to his feet, slumping over dramatically. Colt starts walking him through the task as I turn back to Maggie and June, pouring them each a cup of coffee. After I hand their mugs over, I take a deep breath and begin.

"The thing is, I'm hoping for a favor." I pause, my eyes drifting over to Colt as he measures and then marks the brackets, preparing to screw them in. I summon his confidence and start anew. "Actually, this is a business opportunity. One I hope you'll both consider."

I look at Maggie. "Mag, I want to buy fresh flowers from you every Monday morning. I'll put one arrangement on the coffee table, and another by the register. Beside the register arrangement, I'll leave a stack of your business cards so people know where to buy them. Then, out front, I'd like a silk flower arch at the porch entrance. If you're up for it, we'll change out the flowers seasonally. The goal is to create a spot where customers take photos, and because my bookshop name will be directly behind the arch, it'll be captured in every pic." I swallow, nervous for reasons I can't articulate. "I'll pay you for all of this, obviously. And—"

Maggie grabs my hands. "Alice, say no more. You're asking to become my best customer *and* promote my work. Yes, I want to do this. Absolutely, yes. I'm going to build you a silk arch so hot you'll strip every time you see it."

I laugh, relief whooshing out of me that she's onboard.

"Good! Oh, I'm so happy. I really want the shop to have a fall feel. I've been so busy with the inside, I haven't had time to properly decorate outside." I wave toward the front. "My parents used to buy fifty or sixty pumpkins from their ranchers as a show of support. I've got like...five."

Maggie waves away the concern. "You keep focusing on the inside. Once the arch is up, your porch will become a fall mecca."

I smile gratefully and grip Maggie's forearms. "Thank you, friend." I turn my attention to June.

"June," I begin.

"Ooh, it's my turn! This is so fun!" June settles onto her barstool, her hands in a prayer position beneath her chin. "I am rapt with attention."

"From you, I'd like to buy cookies. I'm guessing two or three dozen each morning. I want to offer a promotion where if a customer purchases a book, they'll receive a free cookie. I'll purchase a toaster oven and reheat them so they're served warm in the fall and winter. One cookie per transaction, and again, we'd keep the flavors seasonal. On the counter, I'll keep a glass cookie jar and include your Humble Pie logo."

June raises her arms into the air, her head bowed and swaying side to side as if worshiping the idea. Encouraged by their excitement, I share the other idea I had. "Oh! And my favorite part. I'm going to print bookmarks with the bookshop's logo, and on the back I'll include a cute cookie illustration."

June drums her hands on the counter. "I love it!"

"You really do?" I ask, because I'd worried she wouldn't be open to me giving away her baked goods for free.

June looks at me, incredulous. "Are you kidding? I spend countless hours trying to figure out ways to sample my stuff. You just solved a problem for me. They'll buy books, eat my cookie, and then come see me when they can't stop daydreaming about it." June points at me. "You'll be buying my cookies at cost."

"No, June."

June crosses her arms through the air. "Non-negotiable."

I hesitate, and then mime spitting into my palm and holding out my hand. "It's a deal, partner."

June shakes my hand in exaggerated fashion, and then reaches into the box and hands out cookies. "You need to pick which ones you want to start with. Here, try the dark chocolate sea salt. No, wait. The brown butter maple! It's perfect for fall."

Maggie lifts her coffee cup, avoiding my eyes when she says, "I won't mention how both of these ideas are better than anything Roxanne has come up with for the festival. Sure would be nice if you shared what you're hiding in—"

June bumps Maggie's shoulder. "Give it a rest, Magpie. We just closed a business deal. Let's cheers to that."

Our three mugs clink in the kitchen, the sound ripe with possibility.

Soon after, Colt's voice echoes through the front room. "Alice, you want to tell me how much higher you want this center shelving?"

I walk over, coming to stand beside Colt. Almost immediately, the air becomes easier to breathe, almost as if any decision I make becomes undeniably correct as long as he's next to me. I point toward a spot high on the wall.

"I'm thinking six to...nine inches above the two flanking it."

Colt grabs a ladder, positions it between the two existing bookshelves, and hands me a pencil. "Mark where you want it."

I begin climbing, the pencil clenched between my teeth. Colt's hands hover near my thighs and I say a silent prayer that the ladder suddenly wobbles so he's forced to catch me.

"Hands a little closer," Maggie calls out

I glance over to see Maggie's phone out, and I can't help but laugh at her ability to turn any moment into content.

"Why are you filming my sister, creeper?" Grant asks, gazing over her shoulder at the screen.

"*Because,*" Maggie sighs, moving closer to us. "Her following is exploding. People love watching this house become a bookshop. But more than that, they like imagining what's happening between these two during the build." Maggie taps the screen and then turns the camera horizontal. "I swear, if we keep this up, it might actually translate into more foot traffic at the festival. Okay, Alice, now...fall. And Colt, you catch her."

"Come on," Colt says, though there's little conviction in his protest.

"Trust the director." Maggie rolls her wrist, motioning for us to do as instructed.

I glance down at Colt and he meets my gaze. My skin tingles imagining where his hands might grip me as I fall. He nods. "Go ahead. I've got you."

I've got you, baby.

I start down the ladder stairs, and then pretend to miss a step. My hands fumble for the frame and—because some dreams do come true—I fall, and Colt is right there. He scoops an arm beneath my legs and another beneath my arms, and then he's drawing me against his chest, striding backward on sure footing.

Morning light from the front window pours over our frames, and I gaze up at Colt, a smile forming on my lips. His grip on me is firm, fingers warm against my skin. My muscles instantly relax as a sense of safety sinks into my body. Being held by Colt—it's like lying in the sand, ocean waves washing over me, sunshine kissing my skin.

"Hi," I manage, barely able to speak.

Colt stares down at me intently and, for a moment, the fact that my two best friends and brother are in the same room with us is astoundingly insignificant.

"That's it," Maggie whispers, afraid to rupture cinematic magic. "Now...even more longing."

My fingers move up Colt's neck, nails light against his skin, and his pupils dilate as his breathing quickens.

"Gross." Grant's voice severs the moment. "They can't look at each other with longing, Maggot. They're practically siblings."

Colt's eyes hold mine for a breath longer, and then he's glancing sharply away. He carefully sets me back down and then steps away.

"Don't call me that!" Maggie barks at Grant. "You know I *hated* that. And they're not siblings, you caveman."

Maggie and Grant continue arguing as June makes her way to the front door, waving goodbye and saying she needs to open the bakery.

After trying and failing to interrupt Maggie and Grant, my eyes return to Colt, who is busying himself with the shelves once more. He seems to purposely avoid my gaze, his back forming an impenetrable wall. I open my mouth to say something, because the unspoken words between us are killing me. But in the end, I just heave a sigh and glance at the kitchen—to the evidence of progress made. To coffee mugs and cookies toasting new business between good friends.

And just beyond that, to the wall calendar, marking the passing days that will define my future. Anxiety slices through this morning's accomplishment. Because this may all be a fantasy that never materializes. Seven weeks until the Fall Festival. Seven weeks until I learn whether I've defied my parents' expectations, or proven their point.

Seven weeks until Colt puts Holly River, and me, in his rearview mirror. Again.

20
COLT

I WALK THROUGH THE HOUSE, calling Alice's name. When there's no answer, I move to the kitchen, expecting to find her pouring coffee, but she's not there either. Turning, I catch sight of her in the backyard, speaking quietly to her hens as she sprinkles feed, a galvanized bucket hooked on her arm.

I knock once on the screen door to avoid startling her and push it open, stepping outside. Alice turns and, when she spots me, her face splits into the wide smile I'm quickly becoming attached to. Seeing her out here, framed by the early morning light, brings back every memory of our kiss. It's been almost a week, and I can still feel her lips against mine. Can still hear her soft whimpers as she moved against me.

"Colt," she says. "I didn't hear you pull up."

My eyes travel to the black Australorp, the meekest of the three hens. "Yeah, I let myself in. Hope that's alright." I cough, trying to clear the mental image of Alice on her back, legs wrapped around my waist. "Where's Grant?"

Alice wipes a strand of hair from her eyes. "He went to visit a client over in Jasper." Her gaze diverts as she adds, her voice a touch higher, "Said he won't be back until tonight."

The implication hangs there, that the house is empty for the first time since we kissed. My body reacts before I can stop the mental images. I can't stay here with Grant gone. If I do, I'm going to reach for Alice again, and this time, there's no way I'll stop unless she asks me to.

I glance back at the house, then at her. "We've been making good progress," I say, sounding a little like the sergeant I used to be. "Maybe we oughta' get out of here for a while. Just to avoid burnout." I glance up, gauging her reaction, half hoping she says she has a better idea.

Alice's smile widens. "I'd like that."

~

THE RIVER UNFURLS like a ribbon through the dense cathedral of trees. We're at a spot where the current slows, though closer to the center, the water churns into frothy whitecaps. The air smells of mud and decaying sweetgum leaves, which have already started to drop.

The hardshell kayaks scuff against the truck bed as I haul them out and drag them toward the water's edge. A bright blue dragonfly darts above the reeds where I drop them. I pull a life jacket out of the first kayak and turn to Alice. "Here," I say, holding it open for her.

She glances up from the ground where she's adjusting her sneaker. "Oh, I don't need it. The water's like four feet deep here."

I wait until she stands and then take her wrist, guiding her arm through the sleeve.

"Actually, yes. I'd love a lifejacket, Colt." She laughs as I finish securing it, clicking the buckles and pulling the straps tight. I tug the jacket a few times to test it, my hands lingering a beat too long.

After I put on my own jacket, we push off from shore, sliding into the water with a *thump-splash*. Soon, the only sound is our paddles slicing through the current and a woodpecker hammering at a tree deeper in the forest. We move upstream, traveling beneath a canopy of loblollies and the occasional bald cypress, bent knees peeking out from the surface. Cicadas buzz peacefully overhead, but come late afternoon their melody will reach a fever pitch.

A hawk swoops down—a Red-shouldered, by the looks of it. I don't realize I've stopped paddling to watch it circle until Alice speaks.

"You really like birds, huh?" she says.

I start stroking again, the water swirling in eddies behind my blade. It takes me time to find my voice, because I've grown more than accustomed to keeping my thoughts inside. "When I was deployed," I venture, keeping my eyes fixed on the horizon where the river disappears into the trees. "Birds became... I don't know. A good sign." I stop paddling, letting the kayak drift. "They stop making sounds during gunfire. Their silence seemed to coincide with something going wrong, or something coming. So if I could hear them..." I shrug.

"It felt like everything was okay." Alice finishes my thought for me.

I shrug. "Wasn't a perfect science."

Alice doesn't say anything for a long time. She leans back in her kayak, paddle resting across her lap, and stares up at the vast, pale blue sky. "Why did you leave the Marines, Colt?"

The way she says it opens my ribs. There's no accusation. No demand. Not even a note of tentativeness. She asks like she's asking about my favorite meal (steak, mashed potatoes, green beans if there's any room left on the plate).

And because she asks it this way, I find myself responding in the same fashion.

"I was a section leader," I say, my eyes on the water. "I was checking the perimeter. There was a...communication breakdown. My own gunmen were mistaken for enemy fire by another unit." I force myself to breathe steady inhales and exhales through my nose. "They were killed in friendly fire. I suffered a secondary injury, but that's it." I tap my shoulder, indicating the scar she touched the last time we were in this river. "After that, I decided not to reenlist."

I don't mention the obvious. How it was my job to keep them safe. How I failed them, and was presented a Purple Heart anyway. And how the day I watched my men die was the day I realized everything, all of it, was pointless. Because after all that, after everything we'd survived—*killed by our own people?*

Alice sits up. I meet her eyes, afraid of what I'll see there. When she speaks though, it's to say, simply, "That's a terrible thing that happened." She doesn't offer the platitudes I've heard before. Like how it's not my fault, or that I did my best. Free passes that make me want to put my fist through a wall, because if my best means people dying, what does that say about me?

Instead, Alice says only, "Bad things happen. But that doesn't mean there isn't good in the world." She smiles softly. "Like your birds."

I nod, because I don't know what else to do. And because I'm thinking on what she's saying. That bad existing doesn't deplete the good. It just...sits beside it. Co-existing. We paddle on, the current picking up as the river narrows.

"What about you, Alice?" I ask, relishing the mild burn in my arms as I paddle. "What happened while I was gone?" I pause, because the last thing I want to do is put her on the spot. But I need to know. I need to know so I can ensure she remains happy. "You seemed so upbeat in your letters. But Maggie hinted that you weren't telling me everything."

Alice looks at me, a forced smile on her lips. "I *was* happy," she insists.

"Alice," I say evenly.

Alice sighs, her cheeks turning a light shade of pink. She opens her mouth to speak. Closes it. Opens it once more. "In high school, I dated Travis. I mentioned that." She brushes a hand over her life jacket, avoiding my gaze. "One day after school, I was reading a book, waiting for my mom to pick me up. Travis jerked it out of my hands and started reading the scene aloud to his friends." The pink hue in Alice's cheeks deepens. "It was a romance book. And I'd just hit a pretty explicit scene." Alice purses her lips, then shakes her head. "They were laughing really hard, and after that everyone started calling me *Dickens*, even though that made *no* sense."

Alice accentuates these last few words as if she's more upset by the literary blunder than the bullying. I can hear the pain in her voice behind the deflection though, and it makes me want to find these boys—each one of them in turn—and hurt them. Badly.

"They acted like I was some sort of pervert. And my friends distanced themselves." Alice looks at me then, nodding her understanding. "And I get that. I do. High school was..." She laughs, but it sounds hollow. "You know how it could be. But honestly, I was fine. It wasn't a big deal." Her voice grows quiet. "It's nothing compared to what you've been through."

"It *is* a big deal," I press. "Being targeted like that? And abandoned? It's fucked up." I watch her for a second, thinking through the timeline. "And your parents? They were gone a lot during this time, yeah?"

Alice turns her head, looking at a crane standing motionless in the shallows. "Yeah, but Grant needed them. He was under a lot of pressure with his scholarship."

"You needed them too." My voice is harsher than I intended, because it's not her I'm angry with. It's Travis. It's her friends, her parents even. And *me*, because I soaked up every optimistic word she offered in those letters with depression-fueled desperation. The kind that forms from homesickness, exhaustion, and watching people do vile, nightmare-inducing things to one another.

"You were too young to be left by yourself," I continue. "You were dealing with shit alone while they were cheering in the stands."

"I was happy," Alice interrupts, and even though her eyes shimmer, her chin is tilted stubbornly. "I found things to be happy about, Colt. There are *always* things to be happy about if you pay attention."

I shake my head, unable to follow this...this *naive* line of thinking.

Alice paddles in silence for a few moments, and I follow her lead, doing the same. Her voice is softer when she begins speaking again. "My dad told you about the tide impacting y'alls fishing, but did he ever tell you about tidal bores?"

I squint at her, entirely lost.

Alice stretches her hand toward the river's current. "When the tide is rising and coming in, the ocean can push a wall of water up the river. It forms a sort of tidal wave, and that wave forces the river to defy its natural, gravitational pull toward the sea and *reverse direction.*" Alice laughs at that, almost childlike in her amusement, and shakes her head. "Our whole lives, we go along thinking some things can't be changed. The sky is always blue. A bird has two wings." She smiles at the mention of birds. "And a river runs downhill. And then, one day..." Alice snaps her fingers. "Here comes a tidal bore."

I'm thinking about what she's saying, and what she's not saying, when we hit rapids—nothing life-threatening, but enough to require focus. The water turns white and choppy, spraying over the bows of our kayaks. Alice lets out a sudden laugh as she navigates a tight turn, her face lighting up from adrenaline.

"It's been a long time since I've done this," she cries out, her laughter ringing through the air.

"You're doing great." My eyes are glued to her, ensuring myself she's okay. I open my mouth to say more. To apologize for not responding to her letters. To ask about the last one I received from her.

The one currently folded in my wallet.

But the sky opens up, the humidity cleaved through by rain. It isn't a drizzle. It's a gully washer that turns the river into white noise from the sheer force of it. The temperature plummets as I yell over the downpour, "We need to get out of here. The rapids are too strong further down."

"I know," she shouts back, grinning through the water streaming down her face. "I grew up here too, remember?"

By the time we get the kayaks back to the truck and drive to her place, we're both soaked to the bone. We stand on her porch, shivering, as Alice ducks her head inside and announces that Grant's still gone.

She bites her lip, her eyes darting to my truck. "You want to...come inside?"

The rain has plastered her clothes to her body, and she's so beguiling with her wet hair and nervous smile that I desperately want to say *yes*. Because this woman is everything I'm not—hopeful, resilient, happy. And I want to put my mouth on every part of her and tell her exactly how perfect she is. And that if anyone wishes to hurt her again, they'll have to get through me first.

But I know...I *know*...that I still have a lot of healing to do, and I don't want to drag her down into the regret that darkens my mind.

With Herculean strength, I mutter, "Thanks, but I should go. Need to run to the hardware store and get those rails for the porch."

Alice's face falls in fleeting disappointment. "Okay," she says softly, and for once, Alice doesn't hide behind a smile. "I'll see you later?"

"Sure will," I promise.

I turn and stride toward my truck before I can change my mind. The second I'm in the driver's seat, I throw the truck in reverse, muttering to myself, "Drive away, Colt. Drive the fuck away." I start down the road, wipers slapping against the windshield.

It's physically painful leaving Alice behind. Every foot of distance between me and Alice with her wide, vulnerable eyes and her full lips asking, *You want to come inside?* is like a rope around my neck. By the time I reach the end of the road, the feeling is unbearable. I can't breathe. Can't think. My mind is an endless loop of:

There are always things to be happy about.

There are always things to be happy about if you pay attention.

I slam on the brakes, the tires skidding on wet asphalt. The truck fishtails slightly before coming to a dead stop. I sit there, white-knuckling the steering wheel, the engine idling in the rain.

21
BEFORE

I WATCHED through the living room window, breath fogging the glass, as Grant and Colt stood on the front porch. Beyond them, my dad's SUV idled in the driveway, exhaust clouds extinguishing as they hit cold morning air. I couldn't hear what they were saying and longed to. At least then, I might have some semblance of what to say when it was my turn.

My mom stepped up behind me, her hand rubbing soothing circles on my upper back. "I know this is hard, Alice."

"I'm fine," I clipped, my eyes glued to the boys.

Mom paused. And then, "He's scared, baby. Even if he doesn't act like it, he is. So when you get out there, do your best to just...encourage him."

I didn't want to believe that. To me, Colt was never scared. He was the one who'd climbed our oak tree, far higher than I'd dare go, to collect my kite. He was the one who'd never seemed nervous before football games and had faced down seniors when he was only a sophomore. But my mom sniffled as she pressed a kiss to my temple, and doubt crept in, uninvited.

Mom walked away, heading toward the kitchen, and I watched as Grant laughed at something Colt said. I leaned closer, trying to overhear the exchange. But then Colt and Grant were hugging, and it was like seeing my teacher at the grocery store. It didn't seem possible until I caught them, red-handed, testing the firmness of an heirloom tomato.

Grant and Colt didn't *hug*. They wrestled over cellophane-wrapped popcorn balls on Halloween. They tripped each other while going up the stairs and argued about who flew furthest off the river rope swing and sword-fought with pool noodles until they both had angry red welts.

But here they were, hugging, and Grant—who always joked when things were serious—wasn't letting go. Colt patted Grant on the back, and Grant hugged him a moment longer and then released him, stepping back. They nodded and exchanged a few more words before Grant came through the front door. He bolted for the stairs, his face turned away. I watched him go, horrified, listening until I heard the sound of his bedroom door slam.

I turned back to the window and saw Colt leaning against the railing, his head lowered. With one boot, he toed a dead leaf. His canvas duffel bag sat nearby. Mom had insisted Colt pack it with a few belongings, and then she'd added a package of Funyuns, a bottle of Gatorade, and a fifty-dollar bill, even though Dad said Colt wouldn't be able to bring much of anything in with him.

I pulled in a deep breath and forced myself to move. The cold air nipped at my cheeks as I stepped through the screen door. Colt didn't look up as the door slapped shut behind me. I studied his face then, searching for any trace of redness, and finding none. He looked older than nineteen standing there, and I felt far younger than fourteen. Hanging out with him and Grant, I'd always wished to be older. But right then, I wanted to be younger than I was. To have an excuse for delivering only shallow words and a mediocre goodbye.

My hands shook as I clutched the rectangular package.

"I got you a Christmas present," I said, my voice quiet. "I know it's not for a few more weeks. But I didn't want you to..." I bit off the thought and shoved the package toward him. "Here."

Colt finally looked up. His eyes fell on the package, and he smiled softly. Reaching out, he took the gift from my trembling fingers and then, with a sad kind of slowness, he set it on top of his duffel bag. That done, he straightened and met my gaze.

"I'll write you," I blurted out. "All the time. Real letters." I jabbed a thumb over my shoulder toward the house. "Mom got me envelopes already, and she's taking me to get stamps this weekend. I'll write you..." I glanced down, trying to find the words. Shaking my head. "The whole time."

Colt nodded slowly, his eyes falling to his boots again. Silence stretched between us, filled only by the low rumble of Dad's SUV.

"Alice," Colt said after a while. "I want to thank you for tolerating me being around so much these last few years. I know it must have been...annoying at times."

I stepped toward Colt, wanting to hug him the way Grant did. "No," I said. "It wasn't annoying. I liked you being here." I wanted to say more, but my throat was tightening, and my eyes were stinging, and I knew if I said anything else, I'd start crying. And Mom had said to be encouraging.

Colt reached out and put a hand on my shoulder. It felt warm and comforting and I didn't know what I would do if he took it away. "I want you to do me a favor, okay? I want you to...keep dreaming. Keep...reading all those books. And drawing. And painting those little rock monsters and thinking about all the big things you want to do. I know your parents want you to focus on practical stuff, and that's good too, but not everyone has the opportunity to dream and take chances. And you do, so you need to seize that opportunity."

Colt looked over his shoulder, and I followed his gaze to find my dad staring at us through the windshield. Dad tapped his watch, signaling that they needed to go.

Colt glanced back at me, and there was an urgency in his expression. He gripped my other shoulder. "You let the rest of us worry about practicality. You just keep dreaming, okay, kid? Promise me." Here, Colt's voice broke, just a fraction.

I nodded, unable to force a single word past the lump in my throat. I could feel my bottom lip quivering. Colt must have seen it, because he pulled me into a hug then, his arms wrapping around me like a warm blanket. "Thank you for being a family to me," he whispered into my hair.

I hugged him back, hard, my eyes clenching shut as the first hot tears spilled down my cheeks.

Colt released me abruptly and grabbed his duffel bag and gift and marched toward the porch steps, his boots thudding heavily. The absence of his embrace was jarring. Almost violent. Watching him go, panic flared white-hot through my body. My eyes widened and my breath came fast and the earth tilted beneath my feet.

He was leaving.

He was *really* leaving.

"No!" I cried. The word tore from my lungs as a sob broke in my chest. "No, don't go. Please don't go!" I ran after him. Colt turned at once, dropping his things and catching me when I flew into his arms.

"I've got to, kid. I'm sorry." His broken words were muffled against my shoulder.

"No!" I wailed. "Don't go. Don't leave. *Please!*" I heard the car door open and my dad calling out, telling me to let him go, his voice pained. But I only clung tighter and tighter. Humiliation burned my face and twisted my stomach, but I couldn't summon the will to care. I pulled Colt closer, and he did the same to me.

My dad's hands came down on my shoulders, hauling me backward. The second he dislodged me, Colt pivoted, snatching his things off the ground and striding toward the SUV, his movements becoming clinical, detached.

Mom came out onto the porch, her own face wet with tears. "Alice. Baby."

The moment she reached the bottom step, I turned and threw my arms around her waist, crying.

"It's okay," she soothed, her hand stroking the back of my head. "It's alright."

"But what if he doesn't come back?" I wailed into her sweater. The question cut through her composure, because with it came the fear we'd refused to address.

What if something really bad happens to Colt?

The shock of naming that fear aloud rattled me to the bone. I turned back to the car, intent on running after him again. But the SUV was already backing out of the driveway. As I stood watching, Colt raised a stiff hand—a silent, final goodbye.

My chest heaved as the car reached the end of the road. It paused for a second, blinker ticking. And then it turned the corner, tail lights disappearing behind winter-bare hedges.

And just like that, Colt Mitchell was gone.

22
ALICE

I STAND SHIVERING in my bedroom, watching as Colt backs out of the driveway. The spread of his shoulders behind the windshield, the grip of his hands on the steering wheel—they are blurred by the falling rain.

"Don't go," I whisper to the empty room.

The truck straightens, pointing down the street, and then begins its trek toward the stop sign.

"Stop," I mouth silently. "Come back."

My heart beats frantically in my chest, and suddenly I'm that broken-hearted fourteen-year-old again, watching Colt leave for boot camp in my parents' SUV. And just like then, the truck continues moving, regardless of how hard I pray for its return.

I'm dripping onto the hardwood floor, rainwater puddling at my bare feet. I turn resolutely from the window and head toward the bathroom. My teeth chatter as I flip on the hot water, old pipes groaning somewhere deep inside the house. As steam curls from the shower head, I strip, peeling off my clothes and tossing the sodden bundle into the freestanding tub. Then I step under the spray, the heat enveloping me at once.

Colt's face flashes in my mind. And then his lips. His hands. I want to touch myself to the thought of him again, just as I have every night since we kissed. But something stops me. I invited him inside. My meaning couldn't have been clearer. And he declined. I could see that he wanted to, but wanting isn't enough.

I decide, right then and there, that I must focus on the bookshop. Yes, I want Colt. I *burn* for him. But he pulled away during the one and only time we kissed, and now he's turned me down. I have to focus on what *does* require my attention, and let go of this fantasy I have of something real happening between us. Because Colt is either unwilling to cross lines given our history, or he's just not that into me. Either way, it's time to let go, even as my body craves his touch.

I'm reaching for the shampoo bottle when a soft knock sounds at the bathroom door.

"Yeah?" I call out, craning my head to listen.

When no one responds, I fumble for a towel folded above the toilet and wrap it around my body, tucking the tail between my breasts. I pad toward the bathroom door, my mind racing with who might be—

I open the door.

Colt stands on the other side, dripping wet, water running in rivulets down his throat. The look on his face leaves no room for interpretation. His eyes are determined, *hungry*. My stomach flips as I take in the size of him—his towering height and wide, muscular build filling the doorway.

Colt steps toward me, and I fall backward a step, making space for him.

My breath hitches as Colt takes yet another step and then, with his eyes locked on me, he closes the door behind him. He watches me a beat longer, as if ensuring I don't demand he leave. And then he turns just long enough to twist the lock with a soft click.

His eyes find mine once more, dropping to my lips, the towel. He tips his chin toward the shower, his gaze flicking there for a half second before returning to me. He starts walking. I back up, matching him step for step, following his lead until my shoulder blades press against the shower wall. Colt follows me into the spray fully dressed, his pupils wide, eyes locked on mine with an intensity that reminds me he's a trained soldier.

He continues moving until his chest presses into my own. Colt stares down at me for a breath, and then his lips meet mine. The kiss is slow at first, gentle, his lips warm and questioning. Then he angles his head and deepens it, tongue sliding along the seam of my lips until I'm opening for him. Heat explodes between my legs and a small moan escapes into his mouth. He answers with a low groan, one hand coming up to cup the back of my head.

His other hand slides down my spine over the soaked towel. The water pounds down on us, soaking his clothes until they cling to every ridge of muscle. Colt Mitchell kisses me like he's starving, like he waited far too long to feed himself and now he's insatiable. I cling to his shirt, fisting it in my hands to pull him closer, returning his kiss with every part of me because this is all I've wanted since the moment he returned to Holly River.

Without breaking the kiss, Colt pulls his hand down, tugging the towel free from my body. Cool air hits my skin for a heartbeat as Colt takes a half-step back. His gaze trails down my body, taking me in, and then it's back on my face. Holding my heads in his hands, his eyes bore into mine, unapologetic as a thunderstorm. And I see it then—that I was wrong about everything. That Colt has wanted this just as much as I have, and that he's not letting go this time.

Colt slides his hand slowly—agonizingly slowly—down my stomach, and my brain explodes when I grasp his intention. The pace at which his hand travels downward feels deliberate, like he's giving me time to stop him. But I'd rather die. And if he doesn't touch me there, where I need it most, I just may do so.

His fingers brush the top of my thigh, and then they're sliding between my legs. I gasp against his mouth when they brush, featherlight, over my pussy.

He explores me with unhurried patience, fingertips gliding, testing, learning exactly how I feel, savoring every shiver. I whimper at the confident drag of his fingers, and my hips jerk forward on instinct. When I open my legs wider, his middle fingertip presses more firmly on my clit, rolling in smooth, firm circles.

I reach for him, my palm sliding over the front of his jeans. His cock is hard, thick, straining against the wet fabric. Colt sucks in a sharp inhale as I grip him, stroking him through the denim. For one dizzying moment, he thrusts into my hand with a groan. And then he's capturing my wrist and pinning it against the tile above my head.

With his other hand, he keeps rubbing intoxicating circles over my clit, never breaking rhythm.

I whimper my discontent and reach for him again, but he spins me toward the shower wall in one smooth motion, pressing my front to the cool tile. My cheek rests against it, breath fogging the surface. His strong arm bands around my middle, holding me steady. The other returns to my pussy. Colt slides one thick finger inside of me, so slowly that I find myself begging. When I press back against him with a moan, he adds a second finger and increases the pace, curling them slightly. I'm overcome by the sensation, nearly incapacitated though my legs shake beneath me.

Colt's lips brush my ear, his voice low and commanding. "Move against me, Alice."

I obey, rolling my hips, chasing the friction.

"More," he growls.

I abandon any semblance of self-control. My fingers grip the shower shelf and I grind shamelessly, rubbing myself against his palm, desperate, greedy, caring nothing outside of chasing the pleasure from his touch.

"That's it," he praises. "Just like that."

His fingers hook inside of me, stroking a spot I'd never managed to find on my own. The heat of his body consumes me, pinning me against the wall in the most delicious way. His cock is pressed into my lower back, his arm locked around my middle. He works me steadily, relentlessly, until the pleasure coils so tight I'm nearly blinded by the oncoming orgasm.

Somewhere far away, over the roar in my ears, I hear Grant's voice calling my name. My body tries to freeze, but Colt's mouth is at my ear again. "Keep going, Alice," Colt demands. "I want you to come on my fingers." He kisses the shell of my ear, then my neck, open-mouthed and hot. His free hand slides up to cover my mouth—firm but gentle, muffling the sounds I can't hold back.

"Come for me, Ali," he growls. "Give it to me. Now."

I shatter. The orgasm crashes through me so violently that my vision whites out. I cry against his palm, hips jerking, thighs trembling. Colt keeps moving his fingers through every pulse, drawing out my pleasure until I'm folding in on myself, gasping, forehead resting on the shower shelf.

I sag back against him as the aftershocks fade. He eases his hand away and turns me to face him. Water streams down his face, long dark lashes spiked together. He takes my face in both hands and kisses me deeply, reverently, one thumb stroking my cheekbone. Then he steps out of the spray and hands me a fresh towel.

The fog of pleasure lifts and reality slams into me. My eyes widen, darting to the bathroom door. "Grant is downstairs," I whisper, snatching the towel from Colt and wrapping it around myself. "Your truck is down there!"

Colt glances down and to the right, thinking. Then he meets my gaze, the solution coming easily. "I'll go out the window and come in through the back."

I shake my head, keeping my voice low, hoping the running shower will drown out any sound. "It's raining. We're two stories up. You'll hurt yourself."

To this, Colt laughs, his chin dropping to his chest. He looks back up at me, cupping my cheek, thumb brushing my lower lip. "Ali. Baby. I'm a Marine." With that, he presses one last kiss to my forehead before cracking the bathroom door open, peeking out, and slipping through on silent feet. I hurry to lock the bedroom door as Colt eases the window open and deftly maneuvers out, silent as a shadow.

"Well, that's a little creepy," I mutter before rushing to pull on leggings and a sweater. I'm still twisting my hair into a wet bun as I jog down the stairs. When I reach the kitchen, Colt is already coming in through the back door, behaving as if he's been outside this entire time.

Grant stands at the counter, frowning. "What were you doing outside?"

"Making sure the chickens were in their coop," Colt replies, unruffled. "It's coming down pretty good."

Grant narrows his eyes. "You went out there shoeless?"

Colt glances to where his boots sit near the front door. He looks back at Grant. Shrugs.

Grant stares at him for a beat longer, slack-jawed. And then he shakes his head. "You're fuckin' weird, man."

I clear my throat, trying to act natural. Trying not to act, in fact, like my brother's best friend didn't just finger me in the shower. And that I'm not literally floating on air, my feet hovering twelve inches off the ground. Because Colt *came back.* And because I just had the best orgasm of my life. And because this bookshop, the bookshop that I've dreamed about for a decade, is coming together far better than I dared hope.

"What's that?" Colt tips his chin at something Grant's holding.

Grant glances down at it. "Oh. Something from the city, I think. It was taped to the front door."

Colt crosses to him in a single stride. He plucks the

paper from Grant's hand and starts reading. I step up beside him, close enough that our arms brush.

Colt scans the page, jaw tightening.

"What is it?" I ask, leaning in.

Colt meets my gaze, his eyes blazing. "It's a stop work order."

OCTOBER

23
BEFORE

I SAT in the passenger seat, duffel bag between my feet, as Mr. Sinclair backed out of the driveway. On the other side of the windshield, Alice clung to her mom, her small back quivering. She released her mom suddenly, her face wide with alarm when she spun toward the car.

Mr. Sinclair hit the street at an angle, foot firmly on the brake, and then threw the SUV into drive. I raised my hand in a final goodbye as Alice ran a few steps toward us, the pain on her face shooting doubt through me for the first time. Her mouth circled around my name, calling out, and a lump formed in my throat.

I turned to watch Alice as we drove away from 402 Willow Creek, the only place that'd ever felt like home. The only people who'd felt like family. I kept my head turned, straining my neck to watch her as long as I could while I fought to breathe. Mr. Sinclair didn't say a word. He just gripped the steering wheel, eyes fixed on the road ahead, and for that I was grateful. We turned the corner at the end of the block, and the little girl, the house—they blinked out of sight.

I looked down at my feet to the rectangular package. It was wrapped in red Christmas paper with a multicolored candy cane pattern. There wasn't a bow, and I suddenly remembered Alice asking her mom if they had any in a hushed voice. Her mom had said she hadn't bought any yet, but would next week. I hadn't given that conversation a second thought, but now it filled my chest with dread—that I wouldn't be around to overhear mundane conversations like those anymore.

So many little things would pass—small moments that seemed inconsequential but weren't—and soon I'd be someone on the outside. Someone who had to ask, *when was this?* And, *who is that?*

I lifted the package onto my lap.

"Alice give that to you?" Mr. Sinclair asked.

"Yes, sir," I mumbled, afraid to speak for fear of losing my composure.

I wanted to wait to open it. To keep a piece of home for when things got hard at Camp Inwood. But I had to face reality. The moment I arrived at boot camp, they'd strip me of my clothes, my hair, my privacy. They'd break me down and rebuild me into a new man. I'm sure some Marine recruits feared this process, but I welcomed it. Take my past and kick it to the curb. Good riddance.

Sliding my finger beneath the tape, I carefully tore it open, trying to salvage the paper for some absurd reason. I pulled it away to reveal a leather-bound photo album. On the cover, embossed in gold script, was a single word: *Family*.

I opened to the first page, and a smile touched my lips.

It was a collection of photographs. But it was also... more than that. Alice had painstakingly curated the photos to capture the last three years of my life. She must have worked on it for weeks, digging through prints and her family's phones to fill in the gaps.

There I was at my first Easter with them, looking stiff and uncomfortable in one of Grant's button-downs, a bright blue egg just visible in my closed fist. I flipped the page. The next shot was taken at the river, all of us in our bathing suits, Alice with her arms above her head like she was about to do a handstand.

Then Galveston. I remembered that trip—the first time I'd ever seen the ocean. Someone, I can't recall who, had taken a picture of me staring out at the horizon, looking small against the Gulf. My feet were in the sand, red swim trunks dry. I glanced at the opposite page and saw me and Grant sitting on rocking chairs, watermelon rinds bit between our teeth, forming ludicrous, oversized grins.

The next few shots were of me, Grant, and Dalton in our football jerseys, followed by a selfie of me sandwiched between Mr. and Mrs. Sinclair at Alice's tennis tournament.

I lingered over a photo of myself in a navy work shirt. On the pocket was the Sinclair Systems logo. I remembered the pride I'd felt wearing that shirt, seeing my name stitched on the fabric beneath the logo. But that pride had been complicated. Because Grant had left for Louisiana Tech the August following our graduation, and it was then that my situation became glaringly awkward. I was living in their son's bedroom, sharing a house with two people who weren't actually my parents. Eating their food. Sitting beside a girl who, god love her, wasn't actually my sister.

I'd just turned nineteen and needed to pave a path through my own hard work. I'd considered college, but a classroom didn't feel like the right fit. I needed to see the world, to grow into a man, and bring something to the table that was mine alone.

Before I closed the album, I returned to a particular picture. In it, Alice was sitting in a restaurant booth next to me, arms crossed, lips pressed together in frustration. That must have been when Grant and I had just started hanging out, back when she resented my constant presence. And who could've blamed her? Her parents accepted me like I was one of their own, but never put pressure to excel on me like they did her.

I laughed under my breath as I took in her little face, and then closed the album, sliding it into my duffel bag. After sitting up, I folded my arms and leaned my head against the headrest, staring out the passenger window.

Mr. Sinclair cleared his throat. "I know I've already said this, but it's an admirable thing you're doing, Colt." He shifted in his seat. "I hope you didn't think you needed to leave or...prove anything to us."

I shook my head, watching a passing fence line. "No, sir. I know I could've stayed. You guys made that clear." My voice was strained, emotion heavy in my chest. "You've done enough for me already. More than enough."

"Well." His tone shifted into one of familiar practicality. "Since you're set on this, be smart about it. Stay in the barracks as long as they'll let you. Eat on base and avoid buying a vehicle if you can. Save a few thousand, and invest the rest in a mutual fund. Have you looked into their Thrift Savings Plan?"

I nodded along, murmuring *Yes, sirs* where appropriate, but my mind was miles behind us. I was still thinking about Grant telling me not to get syphilis, and Mrs. Sinclair saying she'd kill me if I got hurt, and Alice...

I was still thinking about Alice, who gave me this gift to remind me that I have a family and people to return home to. But more than that, though this may not have been her intention, she's reminded me I have people to *fight* for.

Because the Sinclairs rescued me from the life I was living, and the future that awaited me had I remained at my mom's. But now it was time for me to take care of myself. And maybe I also hoped that by becoming a Marine, it'd finally be me doing the saving.

24
COLT

I'M double-checking the measurements for the final bookshelves and check-out counter for when I can resume work. It's not a productive use of my time considering our deadline, but there's little else I'm allowed to do. For eight years, I practiced sitting still in the midst of chaos, but the stillness that comes at the expense of Alice's dream is a different kind of animal.

It's been twelve days since Travis tacked that red slip of paper to the front door. Nearly two weeks of bureaucratic bullshit and filing appeals that disappear into a black hole at the county office. We were cited for a noise violation and unauthorized after-hours labor.

Except the only after-hours activity I've been up to is kissing Alice during stolen moments when Grant is out, which isn't nearly often enough. I'm not sure what's going to make me lose my damn mind first—Travis's insistence on sabotaging this project, or the fact that Alice and I can't seem to get past foreplay without Grant barging through the front door.

The thing is, Travis isn't just a part-time city inspector with a chip on his shoulder. He's a man with a plan, and I've spent the last twelve days stewing on that plan. My shoulders tighten when I hear him slam his car door. The man knocks once, and before Alice can hop off the kitchen counter and open it, Travis lets himself in like he owns the place.

Which is exactly what he's gunning for.

Travis removes his visor sunglasses when he steps inside, hooking them through his polo collar as fall air follows him in—cool, crisp, and smelling of pine needles. He surveys the space like he's examining a crime scene instead of the makings of a bookshop. In his grip is a clipboard, surely brought along for theatrics more than anything else.

Alice reaches his side and offers a glowing smile. "Morning, Travis. I'm glad you were able to make it. Sorry you were held up the last few times, but we're happy you're here now."

We absolutely the hell are not.

Still, I admire that Alice is able to play politician when needed. It's a smart strategy. Far smarter than the one I proposed, which is to bury him beneath the chicken coop. Grant even offered to help.

"Did you want some coffee?" Alice asks. "I just brewed some. You still drown it in vanilla creamer?"

Travis smiles down at her, and then meets my gaze, a smug look on his face, clearly enjoying that I'm here to witness Alice referencing their past. "Nah, Ali, I drink it black now. But funny that you remember that. I'm good for now, thanks." As I lean against the far wall, arms folded to keep from hitting him, Travis glances around the room. He nods toward the stairs. "You still in the last room at the end of the hall?"

I push off from the wall, arms uncrossing.

Alice laughs, but it sounds forced. "No, I've moved into the master." She clears her throat. "So, did you want to have a look around? I'm sorry about the noise complaint. Maybe it was a neighbor who mistook another sound, like a barking dog, for us working? But I swear we've adhered to construction hours."

Or maybe it was Travis who filed the anonymous report in an attempt to have Alice beholden to him or, failing that, to get this property for himself.

"That might be. But unfortunately, I've got to treat it as valid. So I'll just have a look around and be on my way." Alice steps back, allowing him to examine the work we've done. He looks far too closely at everything, and I know why.

Maggie shared with me what she'd already told Alice—that Travis has been on a quiet shopping spree across Holly River. He's snatched up every distressed property, tax-lien lot, and historic storefront he could wrangle away, slapped a coat of paint on 'em, and then rented them back out for double what they're worth. He's a vulture in a button-down, and now he's got his eye on Alice's parents' property. This house sits on an oversized corner lot, located near the creek, and is close enough to town to draw foot traffic from tourists. The man is going to try to bankrupt this project, then swoop in and 'save her' with an offer.

Travis stops at a junction in the wiring, squinting at the box like it's an IED.

"Everything is to code, Travis," I say, losing my patience

already. "I checked it. The electrician checked it. The ghost of Thomas Edison checked it. It's good."

He meets my eye, removes a pen from his pocket, and scribbles something on the clipboard. Then he shuffles toward the window, taking his time to get there. He examines the permits taped to the glass, and his mouth tugs upward in a *gotcha* grin.

"Oh, man." He frowns, though I know he's delighted. "We have a problem."

"The hell we do." I step toward him, tiring of this charade. Because I know the full story now—how Travis tried and failed to get Alice back after humiliating her in front of his friends. And how, after she refused him, he stepped aside while his friends, and several others in their high school, bullied her. And then he had the gall to pursue her each time she'd come home from college. Travis is a man with a hurt ego he rightfully earned, and I'll be damned if I let him hurt her again.

Alice's face opens with alarm, and in her eyes I see the fear that whatever he's found may finish us. Because we've only got a little over four weeks remaining until the Fall Festival, and we can't handle further delays. I'm not even sure we'll survive the two we've been dealt.

"The notice of subcontractor validation." Travis points his pen at a form that's been posted since day one. "The one outside is missing the stamp for the secondary HVAC vent installation."

I stare at him. "Are you kidding me? The vent is three feet long. It's a bathroom fan. It doesn't require a secondary validation. The primary mechanical systems are signed off."

"Now, Colt." Travis smiles patronizingly, as if I am incapable of understanding this supposed oversight, which is exactly what he's trying to communicate to Alice. "In Holly River, any modification to the ventilation system requires an exterior validation during active construction. It may be a technicality, but it's a violation all the same."

His eyes slide over the interior, as if estimating what he can list the property for once it's his. "I'm going to have to maintain the stop work order. In fact, I might have to pull the existing mechanical clearance until a full audit can be performed."

He's reaching. He's reaching so hard he's going to pull a muscle. And I've had it. I move toward him, suddenly remembering that I have military training and this guy has predatory behavior and a clipboard.

"Colt!" Alice's voice rings out. When I meet her eyes, I see the quiet calculation there, replacing the docile, appeasing woman she'd been roleplaying to Travis. She steps between us, putting her back to me, and I'm surprised by how much that hurts. And that I'm still capable of being hurt.

I storm away, turning back in time to have the air stolen from my lungs. Because Alice's small, soft hand is flat against Travis's chest. The sight of it there, on him instead of me, makes my stomach churn.

When her hand spreads, my chest tightens. I want to rip the man's heart out for being the recipient of her touch. I've felt jealousy before—seeing a kid at school with new sneakers, watching a mother hug her son, or even when a fellow Marine received a bundle of letters while I awaited the one. But I have never known the jealousy that accompanies wanting a woman only for myself. Until now. I wonder if Travis feels some measure of what I do, because his own challenging gaze is locked on mine.

"Travis." Alice's voice is pleading, almost intimate. For a beat, I imagine his name leaving her mouth some years ago. Did she once say it around a smile? "Please. Look at me."

Travis's gaze drops to her at once. "Alice, I'm just doing my job," he explains, his tough guy act dissolving in the face of her undivided attention, attention he's craved for almost a decade.

"I know you are," she says gently, her hand still on his chest. "And I know how much you care about...this town. About making sure things are done right. You've always been a determined man."

She's playing him. I know she is, but god, it hurts to watch.

"But Travis," she continues. "This bookshop, it's everything I have. It's my dream. And I'm asking you, as someone who's known me since we were kids, to give me a chance. Please. Overlook the stamp. If I fail to open this place, I'll have to sell it and leave Holly River."

Travis frowns at this news, and I know she's got him. His expression softens, and his eyes search hers with a desperate kind of longing. But he doesn't want *her*. Not really. He just can't handle the fact that he lost her. Not winning Alice back is probably the only thing this asshole has ever failed at.

Travis looks over her shoulder at me, and his face hardens again. "Fine," he relents. "I'll overlook the violation. Just this once. But Alice..." He looks back at her, his tone condescending. "If you really want this place to succeed, hire a professional. You need a partner who can actually protect your interests."

I know exactly who he believes would make for a better partner.

"I'll take that into consideration." The pleading in Alice's voice is gone as quickly as it appeared.

Travis lingers for a moment, and then nods, giving the space one final inspection before heading for the door. I start to follow him, hands balled into fists, intent on ensuring he gets into his spotless car and vanishes.

But Alice catches my arm.

"I'll walk him out." Her eyes flash in warning, but she also squeezes my hand in a way that reminds me we're on the same side.

I squeeze back, managing a stiff nod, and remain in the shop as they make their way onto the front porch, the screen door banging shut behind them. Alice slips her hands into her sundress pockets, and Travis guides his sunglasses back on. As they linger, Travis says something I can't make out, and Alice laughs politely. But I can see how empty the gesture is.

Can he?

She looks up at him, the wind catching her hair, and for a split second, the image of them standing there—looking almost like a couple—sears itself into my brain. Travis is right about one thing: he could give her the comfortable life she's used to. He's educated. He owns real estate. He has ambition, however twisted, and he reveres Holly River, to the extent that he's aiming to own a substantial slice of it.

And me? I'm a Marine with a disappointing heritage and career history. I've got a rotting house without an interested buyer and a set of rusted tools as an inheritance. Over my dead body would I allow Alice to end up with a snake like Travis, but what can I really offer her?

I watch as Travis pulls away in his car. The moment he's out of sight, Alice turns to me, two thumbs held high and a smile on her face. And it's then, in that moment, that the seed of an idea plants itself in my mind.

If she wants this bookshop, she's going to have it. And if she wants a future, then I'm going to build that too. By the time Alice has stepped back inside, the gears inside my brain are in motion, groaning and shaking off dust, because it's been a long time—perhaps never—since I allowed myself to imagine my future.

Slowly, tentatively, a plan grows roots. And it's petrifying, that plan. Because dreaming like Alice does means letting go of the resentment and guilt I've clung to all these years.

My entire life, I've focused only on the immediate challenge before me. Endure my mother's tirade. Find my next meal. Await my commander's orders. Build this bookshelf. What happens when I ask myself what I really want? What happens when I start thinking long-term? I wonder, shamefully, if I'm even capable of doing that.

25
ALICE

COLT HAS me pinned against the siding of my house, his warm hand sliding up my sweater, his mouth dragging down my neck. I'm in heaven as my fingertips trace the protruding veins in his arms and then grip the hard ridges of his abs. In the backyard, the hens cluck softly in their coop, disturbed even as we strive for absolute silence.

I lift my right leg, trying to get Colt closer to where I want him. He hooks his arm beneath my knee, tugs it upward, and steps in, grinding against my core with a groan deep in his throat. My head falls back against the side of the house.

"Colt." His name rolls off my tongue like a prayer.

Colt is a man of few words, but the way he's breathing—ragged and desperate—tells me everything I need to know. He brushes his thumb over my nipple through my lace bra and my hips buck. I don't know how much longer I can do this. I need him closer. I need him inside of me.

A sudden sound makes us both freeze. We're on the side of the house, and it's dark out, but we're still terrified that

Grant will catch us in the act. We remain still for another beat, ears straining for my brother's voice or the telltale squeak of the screen door. But nothing comes.

Colt's forehead drops onto my shoulder and he releases a groan of frustration.

"This is ridiculous," I breathe, running my fingers through the blunt hair at the nape of his neck. "Come on, Colt. Let's just go to the inn. You've got a room."

I feel his forehead shake back and forth against my shoulder. "Someone will see you go in with me." He presses a kiss to my shoulder, my neck. "By morning, everyone in Holly River will know."

And what's so wrong with that? I wonder. But then my stomach flips, because what would my parents say? Or my brother? I'm not ready to find out until I figure out where this is going.

I consider suggesting his mom's place, because at this point I'm thinking only of the ache between my legs, but then Colt lifts his head to meet my eyes, and my mouth snaps shut. "Okay," I say through a sigh. "I need to go anyway. They're waiting for me."

Colt releases my thigh and steps back. "Go on then," he says, but the words sound pained leaving him.

I turn to rush off, and he gives my butt a playful slap. I yelp, and then giggle, grabbing my purse and wine bottle from the ground. When I near the front of the house, I turn back to find Colt standing there, head bowed, drawing in a centering breath. In the light of the moon, he adjusts himself, trying to coax his erection into submission.

Colt turns his head, and when he sees me watching

him, he says in a hushed voice, "I can't get this thing gone until you're out of sight."

I do a sultry little dance and Colt lunges forward.

I squeal and race for the sidewalk, purse bouncing against my hip. Somewhere over my shoulder, I hear Grant's voice ringing out, asking where the hell we are.

~

THE WALK TO Pardon My Garden is short, red brick streets lined with oaks dropping their gold and crimson cargo. I head for the exterior stairs that lead to Maggie's second-story apartment. The railing is wrapped in twinkling orange lights, and a wreath made of glittery black maple leaves and white pumpkins hangs from her front door.

I knock, then turn to see the Texas redbud rooted between her shop and my previous place of employment. It's fully decorated now, glowing orange against the night, plastic pumpkins dangling from various branches, each jack-o'-lantern grin lit from within.

Maggie's voice reaches me through the door. "It's open!"

I step inside and am greeted by candles flickering across every surface. It looks like a scene ripped from the pages of a romance novel instead of a girls' night in. The various, strategically placed flower arrangements aren't helping matters.

"Am I about to be seduced?" I toss my purse onto a kitchen chair and reach for the wine opener. Pausing, I point to the pie on the counter with the quirk of an eyebrow.

"Sweet potato pie," June chirps.

I swoon, letting my knees go wobbly, falling back against the kitchen counter while clutching my heart.

"Get over here, you freak," Maggie orders with a laugh. "We already have glasses."

I walk toward where they sit around the coffee table, gripping the wine bottle by the neck, and stop when I spot a tan board spread out before them. "And what do we have here?"

Maggie leans her head back on the couch cushion. "June brought an Ouija board."

I immediately cross my fingers and hiss. "Witch!"

June curls her hands into claws and then flexes her fingers as if casting a spell on me.

I set the bottle down robotically, my stare going blank, voice distant. "I'm suddenly...overcome...with desire." Dropping to my knees, I hunch over Maggie, pretending to hump her.

"Getcha' some!" Maggie hollers. She rolls over, wrapping her legs around me and thrusting wildly.

"Aww," June says.

We both turn and look at her. "Aww?"

"You're in a good mood," June notes, filling our glasses.

Maggie untangles herself, sitting up and casting suspicious eyes in my direction. "Yeah. You are. I'm usually the resident perv, but you're radiating perv power. Did you finally get that Marine to report for duty? Between your thighs?"

I stiffen, because Colt and I haven't discussed whether

it's okay to tell anyone. But the flush in my skin is practically radioactive in the glow of eight thousand candles. "No?"

June points her wine glass at me. "Liar! No pie for you."

"No pie for *Colt*," Maggie clarifies. "Sounds like he's eaten plenty."

"Nothing happened!" I grab a pillow and bury my face in it.

"Uh, huh." Maggie rises to cut the pie now that it's become the hot topic of conversation. She doesn't add anything else as she navigates the kitchen, and eventually, I remove the pillow from my head because Maggie is rarely quiet. When I find her frowning, worry tugs at me.

"What?" I ask. "Say it."

Maggie shakes her head, nudging slices off the cake cutter and onto dessert plates. "No. It's nothing. Don't listen to me."

"Maggie, talk," I press.

She sighs and carries the plates back to the coffee table, handing them out. "I was just thinking..." Maggie lowers to the floor, folding her legs beneath her and leaning back against the couch. "I mean, Colt doesn't really have family outside of you guys. I wonder what happens if things go south. Especially since his mom just passed."

The bubble of euphoria I've existed in since Colt and I first kissed suddenly pops. It's something I'd considered before, but Maggie articulating it so clearly makes the topic unavoidable. If one of us hurts the other, does Colt feel like he can no longer come around? Yes—he, Grant, and my parents haven't been in touch as much lately, but they're still like family to him.

And what was with Colt not wanting me to touch him? Did that have anything to do with this? Because he seemed all too eager to touch me, but every time I tried to pleasure him in return, he turned the focus back on me.

Maggie must see the light leave my eyes, because she reaches out and squeezes my arm. "Hey. Forget what I said. You can't help who you want, and neither can he. Besides, you're my priority. Why am I even worried about Colt?" Maggie's head pops up like a dog that's detected a distant sound. Her wide eyes dart around the room. "Oh, my god. Do I like Colt now? Is he a...man friend?" Maggie feigns retching, shoulders hunched.

June shoves Maggie playfully. "Hey! Man friends are the best. They can fix things and reach things and check closets for burglars."

"Dalton is an outlier." Maggie grabs the teardrop-shaped pointer and slides it around the Ouija board. "Can men and women really be friends?" Maggie shoves the pointer violently toward *No* and nods toward the answer as if that's undeniable proof.

We laugh and place our fingertips lightly on the device and begin cycling through questions. Maggie asks if she'll ever find a man who sets her whole body on fire. The glass window on the pointer—which June declares is actually a *planchette*—displays an illustrated sun, which we take as a sure sign of Maggie's impending engulfment.

Next, June asks if she'll win the pie contest at the Fall Festival, and the planchette moves immediately to yes, which we agree with wholeheartedly, especially since June's won that contest the last four years in a row.

We ask other things:

Will June have more than two kids? Yes.

Will Maggie eventually get a bigger storefront? Maybe.

Will Grant ever stop being an idiot? Yes. (Still yes after Maggie requests a redo).

Are there aliens? Maybe.

Who does June have a crush on? D-A-L... (June threatens to take our pie away at that one).

At last, I ask a question of my own, feeling obscenely idiotic for assigning any weight to what this toy blindly spits out. And yet... "Will my bookshop be a success?" I force out. Maggie and June meet my eyes before glancing down.

The candles flicker and music plays softly in the background as the pointer whooshes softly around the board in lazy circles. Finally, it moves toward *Maybe* before thudding off the corner and onto the table.

Maggie leans over the board. "The board says..." She looks closer before her head snaps up. "That you need a soft opening for your bookshop."

June claps, and I gather that they've had this conversation already.

"What?" I cover my glass when Maggie tries to refill it for the third time.

Maggie sets the bottle down and leans back. "We think you should have a soft launch for your bookshop. Next Saturday. And that you should invite your parents so they can see what you've accomplished." Maggie wags her eyebrows. "And Colt's fireman brother."

June twists her hair into a bun. "Next weekend is only a

few days before Halloween, so we can make it Halloween-themed! I'll decorate and bring spooky treats and—" She holds up a finger when Maggie opens her mouth to speak. "—yes, apple cider doughnuts."

Maggie nods, pleased.

My stomach flips. It can't be possible that next weekend would make for a good soft launch date. But when I do the math, I realize that's a little less than two weeks before the Fall Festival.

"And," Maggie continues as if sensing my hesitation. "I've been tracking the engagement on your posts. Alice, it's moving from serious numbers to potential for media coverage. We have a few reels that may tip over a million views."

"What?" I grab her phone and look, my eyes bulging when I discover she's right. There are *four thousand* comments on the last post. *How is that even possible?*

"A soft opening would give us tons of content. And Alice? We need it. We need every opportunity we can get to drive festival attendance. For the sake of our shops, and yours."

I raise my head from the phone, and for the first time, I see genuine worry etched on my friends' faces. "You're really concerned." Guilt cuts through me that I never appreciated the gravity of the situation until now.

"You will be too once the bookstore opens." June shakes her head. "Our businesses depend on tourists and events to stay afloat."

I knew this already, but for the first time, it truly sinks in. The look in their eyes makes it impossible to turn away from. This isn't someone else's responsibility. These are *my* friends. My town. Handing Maggie's phone back, I ask,

"What do you need from me? Outside of the soft opening, which is a yes. And a very grateful yes at that."

June pumps a celebratory fist into the air as Maggie unfolds her plan—a plan I swiftly agree to, with the caveat that Colt must also agree, as it involves him.

We spend the next hour back on the board, asking increasingly preposterous questions—like which Holly River bachelor is actually a werewolf (Frank), and who would serve as our hypothetical town serial killer (Pickles)—until the wine is gone and we can't possibly eat another bite of pie.

"I should go," I say, standing up and stretching and swaying a bit, because Maggie ultimately succeeded in refilling my wine glass. "We're still playing catch-up after our *second* delay." I hold up two fingers. I'm fairly certain it's two fingers.

"Fucking Travis," Maggie groans, her head falling back.

I throw a hand in the air. "Night, witches!"

"May ye bring a handsome man to thine threshold and—"

I close the door before I can hear the rest of June's spell. The air is even colder now, and I wrap one arm around my waist, shivering as I navigate the stairs. When I reach the bottom, a familiar, broad-shouldered figure rounds the corner.

"Dalton?" I squint.

He stops, holding a white paper sack, neatly folded. "Hey, Alice. Heading home?"

"Hear, hear!" I respond with a raised finger, certain that's an appropriate usage. "What's in the bag?"

"Dinner for June," he explains. "The woman is a master

baker, but she subsists on bread and sugar alone." He glances down at the bag, lifting it a fraction. "Chicken. Mashed potatoes. Green things."

"Good man," I say, patting his arm as I pass.

"You okay to walk home?" he calls after me.

"Are *you* okay to walk home?" I fire back, and then shake my head, because that made no sense.

Dalton laughs and heads up the stairs right as Frank steps out of The Buttermilk Cafe. He lights a cigarette and, before I can bypass the diner, he points the cherry at me. "Drunk," he announces.

"Affirmative."

"Wait there," he says, and vanishes inside his restaurant. I wait obediently, swaying only slightly, until he reappears with a sleeve of French fries. Right before he hands them over, he yanks them back. "Next time, you invite me."

I salute him.

He hands me the fries, visibly amused, almost...*proud*. I resume walking, stuffing the greasy, salty goodness into my mouth, moaning because they're damn good. It takes a single moment of pleasure before my mind zips back to Colt. And then I'm smiling around the fries, practically bouncing on my toes because that man will be at my front door within a few hours.

The smile falters for a beat when Maggie's warning ricochets around my mind.

I wonder what happens if things go south?

26
COLT

THE LAST OF the day bleeds through the pines, giving me just enough light to see what I'm doing. I have the miter saw set up on sawhorses as I cut through a length of picture frame molding. My sleeves are rolled up to my elbows—a halfhearted attempt at keeping the dress shirt clean for our fake date.

The screen door to the backyard swings open and Alice steps out. When I glance up and see her, the soft evening light making her skin and hair glow, I nearly send my fingers under the blade. The whirring of the saw stops and I tug my gloves off, gawking.

"God, Alice," I manage, taking in the skirt, the knee-high boots, the little white cardigan that dips toward her cleavage. "Are you trying to kill me?"

Alice grins. "Maggie is here." She winks and slips back inside.

I dust off the front of my shirt and roll the sleeves down as I stride after her. My feet feel like lead as I head inside, because I don't want a phony date with Alice. I want a *real* one. I want to bring her flowers from her friend's shop, linger over a candlelit dinner, and then walk her home, her small hand securely in mine. Also, I want Grant out of the damn house when we return, so I can enjoy eating my dessert—the kind found between Alice's thighs.

Inside, Maggie is already filming B-roll of the bookshop. "You two need a rundown of the plan?"

Alice shakes her head, lifting the sketchbooks and manila folder she's carrying. "No, I filled Colt in. We're ready."

Maggie nods. "Okay, then. Let's give the people what they want."

Maggie walks through the front door and down to the sidewalk, and Alice and I follow along. I put my hand on the small of Alice's back and guide her to the inside of the sidewalk, taking the street side for myself. Lately, the night-mares I collected during deployment have been replaced by ones that feature terrible things happening to Alice.

I can't be too careful where she's concerned.

Maggie walks backward in front of us as we head toward Hillstone, where we'll have dinner and discuss the soft opening. Maggie is filming for marketing reasons, but this dinner will serve another purpose, because Alice came home from Maggie's place with a hangover and a head full of ideas, but we haven't discussed the details yet.

Maggie taps her screen and there's a quick chime sound. A moment later, she points the phone in our direction. "So, you two are on your way to a business dinner?"

I immediately begin to sweat as Alice jumps in, not missing a beat. "That's right," she grins. "We've decided to do a soft opening for my bookshop next weekend. And there's a lot to go over to ensure it's a success. Maggie, am I doing this right?"

Maggie removes one hand from the phone and rolls her wrist. "Perfectly, girl. Keep going."

I glance at Alice, the urge to touch her nearly impossible to resist. I want to brush my thumb over the back of her neck. I want to press a kiss to her temple. But mostly, I want to hold her hand. To assure myself that she's safe, and that I can *keep* her safe. With each passing day, it seems I worry less about who knows about us, and more about Alice not getting *everything* she wants.

"Colt." Maggie interrupts my spiraling mind. "I asked if you two were together."

I swallow, then force the lie past my lips. "No," I grunt. "Just business partners."

Maggie keeps filming, glancing over her shoulder to ensure she doesn't trip over the hay bale and pumpkin display outside the pharmacy. "And you're both single?"

Alice smiles at me quickly, a secret passing between us. My chest tightens because I hate this secret. I want to cup her face between my hands and kiss her until we can't breathe. I want to look straight into the camera and tell Maggie, tell the whole damn town, *No. She's not single. And neither am I.* But Maggie explained that Alice's followers are riveted by the *will they, won't they* tension, so I bite my tongue.

Alice glances back at the lens. "Yes, we're both single. I have too much at stake to entertain a relationship right now."

My eyes dart to her. Is that true? Or was that just for the camera? I've told myself the same thing a dozen times—that a relationship, or even messing around, could screw this up for her. But that line of thinking went by the wayside the moment I got a taste of Alice, and now I can hardly breathe when she's not around.

Maggie plunges onward. "Just one last question, one I'm sure we won't get an answer to, but your followers are dying to know. Do we have a name for the bookshop?"

Nope.

"I do, actually," Alice responds coyly.

My head snaps in her direction. "You do?"

Alice beams at me. "I do."

Maggie releases a squeal. "Ooh, the entrepreneur has been keeping secrets, folks. Well, go on then, tell the world what it is."

Alice shakes her head. "Not yet. I'm going to reveal it at the soft opening." She points at the lens and adds, "So you'll just have to hang around for a few more days."

Maggie lowers the phone, raises a free hand, and snaps her fingers while swaying her head side to side, eyes closed. "That. Was. Money."

A FEW BLOCKS DOWN, we reach Hillstone, Holly River's only upscale restaurant. Maggie, Alice, and I step inside and are greeted with white tablecloths, dark wood, and the clink of polished silverware.

Maggie wastes no time scanning the room. "I'll grab a nearby table and film a bit of you two eating and discussing plans. I won't be able to pick up what you're saying, so you're free to discuss how devastatingly attractive I am."

Maggie dashes off, and the hostess seats us at a corner booth. Alice slides in first, and I follow on the other side, the cool leather pressing against my back. Alice smiles at me, and I return it, happy to be here with her, even if it's staged.

She leans across the table, her hair falling over her shoulders. "This is weird, huh?"

I shake my head. "No. Not weird. It's good. It's smart."

When the waitress returns, we order—steak for me, salmon for her, and a bottle of red wine, which I know nothing about, but Alice claims is a good one. While we wait for the food to arrive, Alice walks me through the soft opening details. How June will bring enough Halloween-themed pastries to feed a battalion, and that Alice will help transform the space into a haunted house, which the ongoing construction—if any remains—will lend itself to.

She explains that I'll string lights along the front porch and Grant will build a backplate for the bookshop with the name she's chosen, which remains highly classified. Alice also explains that she's invited her parents, which causes me to seek out the waitress, because I could use that wine right about now.

Maggie films pieces of the conversation, occasionally sighing in frustration when waiters accidentally obscure her shot by daring to do their jobs.

Alice glances down at the sketches she's drawn for the Halloween party slash soft opening, and casually shuffles some papers around as she asks, "Do you think...maybe you'd want to invite Warren?"

The name lands like a grenade. Warren come to the soft launch? I hadn't even considered it. I can't even get him to respond to my texts about selling our mom's place. I can't imagine he'd respond to a message about something he has no part in. "Warren's still in Oregon, I think."

She presses gently. "But would you want him there?"

I sit with that question, eyes searching the table, the room, as if I might find the answer there. Eventually, I realize it doesn't matter what I think. "He'd never come."

Alice nods and graciously moves past the subject, returning to the bookshop. We open the folder she brought and sift through the sketches, budget spreadsheets, and materials lists she's created over the years, many of them recently. As she talks, pointing out things she still needs to buy and what she's heard back from vendors, I watch her face, the way she moves her hands. I study her expressions, how she smiles at the mention of certain things—like which books she plans to stock, and how she'll host a monthly book club and serve croissants from Humble Pie and coffee from Mug Shots.

She glows as she speaks about these things, and there's a confidence in her manner that I only see when she's doing this. When she's dreaming about a permanent place for all the stories and worlds and fantasies that live in her mind. I could spend all night listening to her and would be a better man for it. Because Alice isn't just a visionary, she's an inspiration. I'm practically vibrating in my chair, eager to return to work just listening to her.

"You're incredible, Alice," I blurt out, unable to keep the thought in any longer.

Alice smiles, tilting her head. "Colt..."

"No, let me say this." I shake my head, struggling to find the words. "You went out in the world and got yourself a college degree. You had an easy path to success through your parents' company, but instead you chose to chase your own dream, and you're making it look easy." I sweep my hand above the table, referencing the P&L projections and publisher discount tiers and wallpaper samples. "You're kind to every person in this town, even those who don't deserve it. You… You carried me when I needed it, Alice. And when I look at you, when I think about the kind of person you are and what you're capable of, I feel like…"

Alice leans forward expectantly. "What, Colt? What do you feel?"

Inadequate.

Unworthy.

Maggie's voice cuts in from the side. "Gah, that was great! You two were really bringing the drama there. That conversation looked *intense*. That was for me, right? For the camera?"

Alice's gaze lingers on mine for a moment longer, and then she smiles up at Maggie. "Yep. We're Grade A thespians."

"I'll say!" Maggie says, shoving her phone into her purse. She hugs Alice and then gives me an awkward shoulder pat that turns into her squeezing my bicep. "Jesus!"

"Maggie," Alice laughs.

Maggie throws up her hands in surrender and slinks off, calling over her shoulder, "You kids enjoy yourselves. See you at the meeting tomorrow!"

The rest of the dinner passes uneventfully. We eat, we listen to the pianist play, and we even order a slice of pecan pie, which Alice says I am *not* to tell June about.

When the check arrives, I pay without argument and

then walk Alice home, itching to wrap my arm around her when I notice she's cold. We've just reached the front door when Grant comes charging out, yanking on his jacket.

"Where are you going?" Alice stumbles backward out of his way.

"To see a client," Grant yells, already jogging down the sidewalk.

"Now?" Alice checks her phone. "It's almost nine."

"I'm seeing a client!" Grant hollers back, shoes slapping pavement as he disappears around the corner.

Alice and I meet each other's eyes, and the realization hits us at the same time: the house is empty. No Grant. No interruptions. We rush up the porch stairs and I shove open the door—guiding her inside—and then slam it shut, sliding the deadbolt into place. I still have my hand planted firmly against the door, as if assuring myself no one is coming through it, when I turn to look at her.

Alice takes two measured steps backward, a playful smile on her lips.

I shake my head at her retreat and crook a finger toward me.

She squeals and runs for the stairs.

I'm barreling after her before she can make it five feet. Laughter pours out of that beautiful throat as I catch her halfway up the stairs and haul her up into my arms.

"No running from me," I say.

Alice pretends to faint, holding the back of her hand to her forehead. "Please. Someone save me! I've been abducted by a barbarian."

I release a long caveman grunt at this and let my footsteps fall heavier on the stairs as I ascend them. When we reach her bedroom, I set her on her feet, wondering if we're still playing. I am up for absolutely anything this woman wants to do.

The smile dies on Alice's lips, replaced by a look I'll remember as long as I live. She walks past me, taking her time, and shuts the door. Then she clicks the lock and turns to face me, her eyes flicking to the chair in the corner.

She nods toward it. "Sit down."

I turn to look at the chair and then at her, trying to understand where this is headed. Without hesitation, I do as she asked. The leather chair creaks beneath my weight as I lower myself into it. I spread my boots on the floor and pat my lap, already aching to feel her weight against me.

She strides closer, pausing to remove her shoes one at a time, her eyes never wavering from mine. When she gets near enough, I reach for her hips, wanting to push that skirt up around her waist. Wanting her to straddle me. I want my hands on every last inch of her skin, and I want Grant to forget his own address until I'm done with his sister.

But even more than that, I just *want* Alice. I want her easy smile and her generous heart and the way she makes me laugh until my sides ache. I want her unflinching honesty and her faithfulness to those she cares about. Touching her, feeling her body between my hands, it's a way of assuring myself that she's close.

I start to guide her toward me, but she grips my wrists, stilling my movements.

"No," she says softly. Moonlight drifts through the window, illuminating her delicate features, her big blue eyes. "I know what you were going to say at dinner." She opens her mouth, and it takes her a moment to voice the rest, as if she's not entirely certain she's right. "You think you're not good enough for me?"

It comes out like a question, but it shouldn't. Because she's dead right.

Her hand finds my cheek and I press into it, my eyes closing. "You look at me like I'm something you don't deserve. But you are worthy of me, Colt Mitchell." She's silent for a beat. "You are worthy of so much. Much more than you've been handed."

I open my eyes to see Alice sinking to her knees between my thighs. My breath catches as she pushes my shirt up, her warm palms finding my stomach.

"Alice," I say.

She presses her lips to my abs. "You made me feel like I had value for who I was." She kisses me again, lower. "You are impossibly strong, and brave. You're a *soldier*, and I feel safe when you're around." Another kiss, this one directly above my waistline. "You make me feel capable." Kiss. "You make me feel protected." Kiss. "You make me feel unstoppable." Alice grazes her fingers down my abs, stopping at the button of my jeans.

I'm rock hard, straining against my zipper, her words landing like a spark on tinder. I reach for her again, wanting to pull her up, to taste her, to make her feel how she's making me feel. But she gently pushes my hands away.

"Do you not trust my judgement?" Her blue eyes search mine.

"No," I rasp. "I didn't mean to imply—"

"Then let me do this for you. Let me show you how you make me feel. I want to, Colt." She pauses, lips brushing the line of hair disappearing beneath my belt. "Unless you don't want me to."

"I do." The words arrive rough, immediate. "God, Alice, I do."

She presses her hand to my chest and pushes until I'm leaning all the way back. And then, with slow, resolute fingers, she frees me from my jeans. My cock springs out, heavy and aching, the head already slick. Alice wraps her hand around the base—warm, firm—and leans in. Her breath ghosts over me, teasing. And then her lips part, and she takes me into her mouth.

I suck in air between my teeth because the pleasure is instantaneous, and overwhelming. Slowly, deliberately, she slides down until I feel the back of her throat, and then she eases back up with a soft moan that makes my head fall backward against the chair. Her tongue swirls around my cockhead on every pass before pressing flat and firm against the vein underneath. I groan from the sensation, one hand sliding into her hair, feeling the silk strands between my fingers.

"Alice..." Her name comes out wrecked.

She hums around me, the vibration shooting through my body as I claw the armrests. Alice takes me deeper, cheeks hollowing, eyes lifting to meet mine. Her mouth moves in long strokes that rise and fall like the tide, hand twisting gently in time with her lips. I fight to keep my hips still. To let her set the pace. But my thighs are trembling from the restraint of not thrusting upward into her mouth. Pressure forms low and tight, every nerve firing at once.

Alice pulls off just long enough to kiss the underside, tongue tracing from base to tip, then she takes me again, faster now. My fingers tighten in her hair, anchoring myself. "Alice, I'm... Fuck, I'm close."

She doesn't stop. Her eyes stay on mine, determined, telling me without words that this is exactly where she wants to be. The sight of her—lips stretched around me, lashes dark against her cheeks, soft hand pumping my cock —it pushes me over the edge.

I come with a groan torn from my chest, hips jerking. She swallows every pulse, every throb, mouth working me through it until I'm shaking and empty and entirely hers. As the pleasure begins to recede, she eases off, pressing one last kiss to the sensitive head before resting her cheek on my thigh.

I stroke her hair, chest heaving, the world obscenely quiet outside the window. There are no words. Just the two of us, an empty house, and the truth settling into my bones —that I would burn the world to the ground for the woman at my feet.

And that even when Alice Sinclair is on her knees, she fucking owns me.

27
ALICE

MY HEART DOES a little gallop as I click submit. A dozen titles from a small press out of Colorado will soon be en route to my address. I pivot to the giants next—the Big Five—stocking up on bestsellers I know shoppers will ask for and cherish. But the real thrill comes from the industry disruptors, also known as indie authors. I spend twenty minutes agonizing over a debut fantasy novel, eventually ordering five signed copies.

Each time I check out, I'm reminded—this is real. My bookshop is no longer ideas in a sketchbook, it's a ledger of debts and assets. It's inventory management and logistical solutions and future customers leaving my shop with their next favorite read.

I allow my eyes to drift to Colt, who's working on the front porch. His shoulders and biceps flex beneath a sweat-dampened shirt as he builds my ladder. It's a thing of childhood dreams, stemming from countless rewatches of *Beauty and the Beast*.

The ladder will stand eight feet tall and glide along the

brass rail he installed yesterday. Once completed, I will slide back and forth on it, one arm flung open, book held firmly in my grasp. I will most likely do this in my underwear. I will most likely do this in my underwear to the soundtrack of *Beauty and the Beast*.

In the kitchen, the floorboards creak as Grant raids the fridge. It's been three nights since Colt and I had the house to ourselves, and I can't stop thinking about it. How powerful I felt giving Colt a taste of the ecstasy he's given me. Before I'd knelt before him, he'd look at me with self-loathing reverence, as if he weren't worthy of receiving pleasure. Afterward, he'd looked at me like a man on fire.

I wonder what happens if things go south?

Maggie's words rush back to me.

So do Colt's: *I want to sell my mom's place and get the hell out of here.*

I know I should tread lightly where Colt is concerned, but I can't seem to care about anything beyond stealing every second I can with him. At some point, we'll need to discuss what will happen to us after he *does* sell his mom's house, but the thought of that conversation terrifies me. I'm so blindingly happy with Colt that I can't entertain the concept of him not being here.

Colt pushes the front door open, carrying the ladder inside, and I jump up from my chair to help. But when I go to close my laptop, I catch the time. 9:45 AM. "Oh, no."

Colt's eyes dart to mine at once. "What? What's wrong?"

"Oh, nothing." I grab my purse off the makeshift counter. "I'm just late for the festival meeting. But I can help you—"

He jerks his head toward the front door. "I've got it. You go."

I almost ask if he's sure, but it seems Colt is *always* sure. Casting a glance toward the kitchen, I quickly press a silent kiss to Colt's cheek. A heartbeat later, Grant rounds the corner, a powdered doughnut hanging from his mouth.

Risky, risky.

And totally worth it.

"See ya!" I yell, practically diving out the front door.

BLESSINGS BARN IS PACKED by the time I arrive. I whisper repeated *excuse mes* as I navigate the crowded aisle and slide into a seat next to Maggie and June. Roxanne is already at the podium, gripping the sides of the lectern, speaking quickly though I don't catch a word of it. Whatever it is must be bad, because people in the audience are grumbling, visibly agitated.

"What's going on?" I whisper.

"Oaktree poached our vendors," Maggie states flatly. "They offered them double the cut. Corn maze guy and carriage ride company are both out."

My stomach drops. The corn maze and carriage rides are the festival's two biggest draws. The kids love them, and we rely on those kids to beg their parents to bring them to the festival. Without those events, we're down to craft stalls, food stands, and live music. It's not enough. It wasn't enough to begin with or the inn would've been booked solid already.

"Someone suggested a scavenger hunt," June adds,

dispirited. "And Sawyer suggested hayrides using his tractor, but Roxanne says he'd need insurance."

At the front of the room, Roxanne holds up a hand, quieting the room. Her hair, which is usually impeccably pulled back, is falling down around her face. There are circles beneath her eyes and she's wearing—

Oh, my god. Roxanne is wearing athleisure.

This is worse than I suspected.

"Look." Roxanne sighs, the sound amplified by the microphone. "I've called everyone within a fifty-mile radius. Everyone is booked. If we don't have a main attraction, we don't have a draw. And if we don't have a draw, we don't have a festival. Maybe this just isn't our year. I move that we consider canceling the—"

A collective gasp ripples through the barn as panic grips me. I'm relying on the festival. My grand opening coincides with it. I've almost tapped out my loan and already spent every penny I managed to save in college *and* every paycheck I earned at The Buttermilk Cafe. I need festival foot traffic to show that the bookshop can be a profitable venture.

And what about my friends? I glance over to find Maggie tapping manically on her phone and June staring blankly ahead. I have a safety net. If this fails, I can work for my parents' company. I could even crawl back to Frank if he hasn't already filled my shifts. But my friends? They've poured their lives into the community and their businesses, and they've supported me on my own journey. They don't deserve this.

A voice in the back of my mind—a voice that strongly resembles my mother—says to walk out the door. To return to the task at hand. It says that success requires prioritization. That I'm already exhausted and not sleeping enough. It says to let someone else fix this and solution for my own business.

"Well," Roxanne says, exasperated. "If no one has any better ideas, then I don't see that we have much—"

My chair screeches across the floor as I shoot to my feet. "I have one."

The room goes silent, a hundred pairs of eyes swinging toward me.

"Get it, girl," Maggie whispers.

Roxanne waves a weary hand toward the podium, already stepping aside. "By all means."

I walk toward the front of the room, feeling as if I'm wading through water. Why did I speak up? There's no way this idea will be substantial enough to make a difference. And even if it does, who will execute it? Roxanne looks like she's at the end of her rope.

I reach the podium and the microphone releases a piercing squeal of feedback. I flinch, my cheeks heating. "I... uh..." I begin, my voice too quiet, even when amplified. "I had an idea. A while back."

"What is it?" someone calls out.

"Tell 'em, honey," June adds.

The fact that June has no clue what I'm referring to but still believes in me—it straightens my spine. I clear my throat and start again, projecting this time. "We've been running our events with outside vendors. Paying people from other towns to bring in attractions. But we have an alternative, a *better* one, right here, and it runs through every part of this town. It's even in our name. Holly River."

I lean into the mic, gaining confidence, and explain the plan in detail, answering questions as they arise. Maggie snaps at certain moments and June nods along enthusiastically, and around the room, I notice others are listening intently. "We need something that'll play well on social media," I add. "And this will do that."

"Preach," Maggie calls from the back.

"Quiet," Roxanne clips.

"We'll need to do a test run and share photos and videos online. We'll also need volunteers to decorate and others to manage the lines since we won't have temporary staff from outside vendors. It'll be a lot of work because we'll have to manage this attraction along with increased foot traffic at our businesses. But since we won't be splitting event revenue with outside parties, we'll have a bigger budget to work with."

"And who is going to head all of this?" Roxanne asks. "Who's going to coordinate the volunteers and where in the world are we going to get—?"

"I will," I announce. And I mean it, because now that I've laid it all out, I believe in this plan. It could work. It *will* work. We're the only town within three counties that's built directly beside the river. We could turn this into an experience that people from miles around add to their family traditions.

"Okay." My voice trembles slightly as I gaze out at the crowd, because this is the moment of truth. "Raise your hand if you'd be willing to help with decorations."

Maggie and June fire their hands into the air. For a moment, no one else moves. Then, slowly, Ms. Devonshire —my neighbor—raises her hand. Harold raises his own immediately thereafter. Next comes the hardware store owner. Three more follow in quick succession.

"I'm writing down names," June says, pulling a notepad out of her purse.

"And who can help with filming?" I ask. "We'll need to post promos as soon as possible. That means we need to start on decorations, like, yesterday. But we can do this. I know we can. If we work together, we can make this year's Fall Festival better than any before it."

I glance at Roxanne, worried I may have offended her. But instead, I'm met with a grateful smile. She nods and says, "I'll help with filming."

By the time I'm walking home, I'm bursting with ideas, overjoyed. But the closer I get to my not-quite-a bookshop, the adrenaline fades, replaced by a gnawing sense of dread. What have I done? As a kid, I'd sign up for five clubs and three sports and be burned out after a single semester because I couldn't prioritize. Eventually, my parents prioritized for me in the form of a fuzzy little tennis ball.

I feel like I just made the same mistake again, ten years later. I'm supposed to be focusing on opening my business, and now I'm leading the Fall Festival? Did I just sabotage my own dream to save everyone else's?

I turn onto my street, head down, drowning in a to-do list that just got even longer. I'm so entrenched in my own worry that I almost trip over the front steps.

I stop.

I look around.

My porch...it's been transformed.

Pumpkins trail down each step. They line the railings. They cluster in flower beds and spill down the walkway.

They are absolutely everywhere—in various shades of orange and white—in all different shapes and sizes. Against the stark white house, the effect is breathtaking. Lifted from the pages of a fairytale.

And I know exactly who's responsible.

I glance toward Colt's truck and note that the tailgate is down, dirt and broken pumpkin stems littering the bed. A smile sweeps across my face and I shake my head in disbelief. He must have overheard me talking to Maggie and June about this.

I stand there on the porch, the weight on my shoulders notably lighter. I'm sleep-deprived and over-extended, and I'm probably going to have a breakdown by the soft opening. But as I take in the kaleidoscope of pumpkins, I remember that I'm not alone. I have a partner. And for as long as he's in Holly River, I'm going to embrace the woman he believes me to be.

October 2019
Camp Inwood, Texas

Alice,

I'm sorry it's taken me so long to reply. Writing back takes me a while because ~~I'm so tired~~ the words don't come easily, but I wanted to thank you for continuing to send me letters.

It's starting to get a little cooler, huh? I remember how much you love the fall. Have your parents already bought all those pumpkins? It always shocked me how many they'd get. It's funny how ~~much I wish~~ often I imagine being there. I think when I have a home of my own, I'll do the pumpkin thing too.

I can't believe you're playing 18U tennis tournaments already. You say you can't return their serves, but as recruits we're trained to never say "can't." Maybe this mindset could help you too. You aren't returning their serves well YET. But you will. You've always been excited by a challenge. That's why you were always the first to sign up for things at school. Remember that, Alice.

The routine here hasn't changed much. We're up at 0500 for PT, and I spend most of my days at the armory or out on the grinder. I'm working with the M4 and M27 IAR now. You asked what I liked to eat here. We do steak nights sometimes, and that's probably my favorite. There's also a decent dish where they put creamy hamburger meat on toast. I'll spare you the name for it.

Alice, thank you for offering to go see my mom, but PLEASE don't do that. It's not safe, especially not alone. I can get in contact with her ~~if I want to~~ when I need to. That's enough. But it means a lot to me that you offered. Really.

I'm glad to hear that you're happy and that your sophomore year is going well. It's good that you're seeing someone, but please let him know that I picked up my Expert rifle badge last week.

Thank you for your letters. You can send more if you want.

Semper Fi,

Colt

28
COLT

GRANT PUSHES through the screen door and walks out onto the porch, keys clenched in his fist. "You think it's still coming today?" He checks his watch. "I really need to get on the road. I've got clients starting at eight."

Grant comes to stand beside me, staring at the gaping hole in the wall as I check my phone for the umpteenth time. The tracking link still shows the window is out for delivery. But it's been that way for hours now.

I shove the phone back into my pocket, my jaw clenched. "You should go. I'll handle it. I'm sure it'll be here later tonight."

Grant claps me on the shoulder. "I'll see you Saturday, yeah? My parents are excited to see you."

He marches toward his truck as I analyze the empty, rectangular space—a metaphor for my shortcomings on this project. As Grant pulls away, I eye the leftover lumber that I used for new paneling inside the house. I could probably cut down a few pieces and cover the hole with that.

I'm grabbing my tape measure when the sound of

Alice's approaching footsteps reaches me. I don't need to look up to know it's her. Still, I glance over anyway, because I can't stop myself from seeking out her face every chance I get.

Alice grows closer, struggling under the weight of a box she's carrying. She grins over the top of it when our eyes connect.

"Ali." My tone is chastising, but I'm secretly proud of how often she insists on tackling things alone. When I take the box from her, I shoot her a surprised look because it's even heavier than it looked.

"Books from Maggie, June, and Dalton," she explains. "I'm going back for more tomorrow." She follows me up the porch stairs and grabs the door. "My biggest shipment is delayed due to the storms on the east coast, but I'll get a smaller one in tomorrow. I figured I could add these so we look fully stocked this weekend."

These books won't do nearly enough to fill the shelves, but I admire her resourcefulness.

Alice eyes the window. "Still hasn't shown up, huh?"

I set the box on the floor. "No. But I'm sure it'll be here soon."

Alice presses her lips together, and I spot the worry on her face. I'm tempted to rip the window out of a neighboring house to ease her concerns. Travis's home would do just fine, I reckon.

"Grant already left," I add, nervous energy shooting through me at the notion of being alone with Alice. Because the last time that happened, she was on her knees, her mouth wrapped around... I clear my throat. "I'll cover the window for the night. But Alice, I'll need to stay over.

You can't be in this house alone with a boarded-up window."

Alice wets her lips, thinking. The sight of her tongue goes straight to my dick, my arms practically shaking from the need to pull her body closer.

"Cover the window," she agrees. "Then let's touch base."

I nod and get to work, returning inside only after the task is done. After washing my hands and double-checking that the boards are secure, I find Alice in the main room, shelving the books she borrowed. I glance around the room, taking inventory of the situation—in addition to being short the tempered glass, I also need to retile the bathroom, build the checkout counter, and add trim to the windows and doorways.

We're also missing the decorations Alice insists we need and, most importantly, enough books to fill the shelves, which remain seventy percent empty. Everything feels one loose screw away from being finished. And yet, it all hinges on these final few days and things showing up when they're supposed to.

I bend down, helping Alice shelve the novels. The task feels therapeutic. *This* we can do. This small chore to convince ourselves that it'll all come together in the end.

One thing's for sure, the heat between us—the kind that's simmered since the first time we kissed—is still hot enough to ignite this place. Somehow, it feels like everything will shake out as long as that heat keeps burning. Because at this point, we're running on caffeine, pizza, and lust.

Alice's lashes flutter over her cheeks as she digs

through the box, and my hand twitches with the need to touch her. She's so damn gorgeous. So inspiring. Despite the setbacks, she never loses faith. Never wavers. Briefly, I envision her alone in this house while, years ago, I was miles away and her parents were prioritizing Grant's football schedule. She must have felt terribly alone, and then those fuckers at her school teased her, made her feel even more isolated. This last thought infuriates me. Makes me want to tear a hole through the fabric of time and rewrite the memory.

My mouth opens before I fully think through what I'm saying. "You still have that book?"

Her head pops up. "What book?"

"The one from high school," I clarify. "The one he read aloud."

Alice's face goes red in a heartbeat. She laughs and straightens books she's already tended to. "Colt..."

I square my shoulders, determined. "Do you?"

She meets my gaze. Shakes her head just a little, but I spot the lie in her eyes. "Why are you asking?"

I feel a smile form. "Show it to me."

She laughs freely now, blushing in a way that makes me ache with longing, even though she's two feet away. "I told you, I don't have it. I threw it out when—"

"You have the book," I insist.

Alice collapses onto her bottom, narrows her eyes at me and grins. "What makes you so sure?"

I tip my head. "Let me see it."

Alice examines me for a beat, searching my face. When she finds not a single trace of humor there, she sighs and rises to her feet. Moves to the other side of the room, bends down, and slides something off a shelf. Returning to me, she holds the book out stiffly.

"Here," she says.

I turn it over in my hands. It's clearly a romance book, but the cover is on the subtler side—a heart wrapped in chain mail surrounded by rose petals. I flip it open. "What part did that dickhead read aloud?"

"Colt," she repeats.

I meet her gaze. "Show me."

She sighs again, deeper this time, and then takes the book back. Alice turns the pages, goes back a few, and then forward a couple more. For a moment, she reads to herself. Finally, she shoves the book toward me, pointing at a passage. "The end of this chapter. Starting there."

I take the book and sit down, leaning against the shelves, knees up. Turning the book around, I point to where she did, an eyebrow raised.

She nods, amused.

I clear my throat as if preparing for a stage monologue and begin reading aloud. "James had the music playing when she arrived, each pluck of the guitar strings landed like a stroke between her thighs."

I give Alice a questioning look that implies I'm scandalized, and she drops her head into her hand, laughing.

Rising, I cross the room.

"Where are you going?" she asks, leaning forward.

I move to the record player and choose a Vince Gill vinyl. Lifting the needle, I put the record on the turntable and lower it again. *You and You Alone* begins playing a few seconds into the song.

Alice throws her head back, laughter pouring out of her. "Colt, stop."

I lift the book and continue on. "When he asked Angeline if she wanted a glass of wine, it felt like he was asking her permission for something else."

I raise a finger and head to the kitchen.

"No, please," Alice calls out, but she's giggling harder now. The sound reverberates through my chest, filling me with the sense of accomplishment I sought while awaiting the window. I return with a glass half-filled and offer it with a flourish.

Alice considers it, and—after feigning deliberation—accepts it with a smile.

I skip ahead, reading aloud, and hold out my hand to Alice. She takes it, and as I read 'James pulled Angeline against him,' I circle my arm around Alice's waist and tug her close. "He kissed her like he was drowning," I read, my voice dropping an octave, "like she was the air his lungs sought."

I lower my head, and the smile on Alice's face quiets.

Our lips meet, the soft touch of her tongue tearing through me. Breaking the kiss, I ask, forehead pressed to hers, "You want me to stop?"

She shakes her head, and I lift her off her feet, her legs encircling my waist. I kiss her against the wall, just as the characters do in the book, and grind against her, which is a glaring omission from the scene.

I trail kisses down her neck, glancing at the book just long enough to read, "Angeline was laid out before him, an offering he couldn't refuse."

"It sounds like they're in the bedroom," Alice whispers against my ear.

I need no further encouragement. I climb the stairs two at a time, carrying her up, her arms tight around my neck. When we reach her room, I lay her down, then return to the pages. I keep reading, following the characters' lead. Laying the book aside, I do as James did to Angeline—unbuttoning Alice's jeans and guiding them off, one leg at a time, kissing the inside of each ankle. Next, I remove her shirt, watching as her hair spills over her shoulders and down her back.

Alice is left in nothing but her bra and underwear, and I'm left with a decision to make. Grant should be an hour outside of Holly River by now. There's no reason to rush. No one to keep us from crossing certain lines. If we stopped now, we could chalk up everything that's happened between us to just messing around. I don't know what lies on the other side of sleeping with this woman. This woman who's looking at me like I hung the damn moon.

As it is, I can hardly tolerate the ten hours I spend away from her each night at the inn. I toss and turn, a nocturnal animal, desperate to return to Alice. If we sleep together, it'll be over for me. She'll always be The One in my head, regardless of whether she chooses me in return. I'll be ruined for anyone but her.

Alice takes the book from the bed and lifts it, her lips wrapping around the words as she reads. "James undressed hurriedly."

When I don't immediately move, she nudges me with her foot.

"Alice," I say.

"It says hurriedly," she whispers.

I strip my shirt off, my eyes never leaving hers. My jeans come next. I remain in my boxer briefs, my cock impossibly hard. Alice draws in a breath and sits up, running her fingers over my arms, my abs. With one fingernail, she traces the scar on my shoulder before pressing a lingering kiss there.

She hands the book back to me, and I note the slight tremble of her fingers. I wonder if she sees the same in my own.

Swallowing, I read on. "Angelina cried out when his tongue found her eager heat."

I meet her eyes, and she gives the smallest nod. Hooking my fingers in her panties, I drag them down over her hips, her thighs, her ankles. My cock throbs as I pull her toward the edge of the bed. And then I'm sliding her slender legs over my shoulders and kneeling before her. Her pussy is spread out before me, already slick with arousal.

"Fuck, Alice," I growl.

And then I lower my head, unable to wait a second longer. I drag my tongue in one slow, indulgent lick between her folds. The moment I taste her, I groan, gripping her thighs to ground myself. Because now that I've had a sample, I want the whole goddamn meal. I bury my face between her legs, circling her clit, savoring the way her hips buck toward my mouth. Alice's fingers run through my hair as I suck her gently, and then firmer, drinking in the little gasps she makes. She's shaking, legs tightening around my head as I dive my tongue inside her and then follow it with two fingers. My lips form a seal around her clit and I suck in a rhythm that has her coming off the bed.

I can feel how close she's getting.

But I don't let her tip over.

Not yet.

I slide up her body, kissing every inch on the way up. Alice's hand slips down my boxers and wraps around my cock. Her grip is firm as she strokes me. I thrust into her fist once, twice, and bite down lightly on her shoulder to keep from groaning too loudly.

Her voice comes out in a broken pant that makes me throb in her grasp. "What happens next?" she asks quietly. "In the book?"

The book's forgotten somewhere on the mattress. No longer needed because we both know what comes next. She's scared. I can see it all over her beautiful face. I'm scared too, because this woman is the best thing that's ever happened to me. What if I fuck it all up? What if I lose the only thing that's ever felt like family?

Alice cups my face in both hands, pulling me out of my head. "Hey, look at me. We've been working so hard." She nods to show it's true. "We just... We just need to relieve some stress."

I search her face, desperate to believe that's the extent of this. And not like I'm falling from a rappel tower into a feeling I've never known. I nod. Small at first, and then with more conviction. "There's...a lot at stake. It's your dream."

"Exactly." Her fingers stroke my cheek. "And if we don't let off some steam, we'll burn out. Just like you said."

I nod again, entranced by her wide blue eyes. By the taste of her on my lips. "Letting off steam is a good idea."

Alice presses into me, her hands gripping my face a touch tighter. "I want you, Colt. Do you not want me?"

I drop my forehead to her shoulder, trying to exhume the right words. Turning my head, I kiss her neck, her chin, her forehead. My lips brush over her skin as I say, "I want you more than I've ever wanted anything. I *burn* for you, Alice. I dream about touching you every second of every day."

"Then touch me now, Colt," she says, kissing me. "And think of nothing else."

Her soft voice, the stroke of her thumb against my cheek—it blankets every hesitation I have until all that's left is her. I remove my boxers and her bra and then fish a condom out of my wallet, rolling it on as she watches.

Alice's arms wrap around my middle as I settle between her thighs. The head of my cock nudges against her entrance and she draws in a sharp breath. I kiss her neck, dragging my mouth up the column of her throat, knowing there's no going back after this. But I don't care. The only thing I care about now is being inside her.

I push into her.

The tip of my cock slides in, and fuck if she isn't hot and tight and *perfect*. Her body stretches around me, and my own body practically shudders from the feel of her. I hold still, allowing her to adjust, my forearms braced on either side of her head. Another inch, and she moans, her pussy like velvet around my cock. I grit my teeth, fighting the urge to drive deep. But I hold myself back, wanting her to feel every second. Wanting that for both of us.

Her hips tilt up, chasing more, and I oblige at once. I sink another inch, then another, until I'm buried completely. We're locked together, hearts thundering against each other. I stay there, deep inside her, just feeling her around me. The closeness. The *rightness*, despite my earlier worries. Being inside her, I can't believe I ever doubted that this is where I'm supposed to be.

I start to move—long, slow thrusts—savoring every whimper, swallowing every moan that leaves her mouth. Her legs wrap tighter around my hips and I rise up, angling to hit her in just the right spot. Alice's head falls back, her lips parting, and the pleasure on her face is something I'll recall as I take my final breath on earth.

We move like that, slow, savoring the feel of each other, until Alice grows restless, her body writhing, irresistible whimpers leaving her. She nudges my arm until I pull out of her entirely, the absence of her heat maddening. She rolls over onto her stomach, spreading her thighs.

Alice lifts her hips up a few inches in invitation, and I cover her body with mine. Aligning myself, I push back inside of her. Alice moves backward against me, impatient, and I'm there to meet every measure of her need. I wrap a hand around her neck, sensing the energy shifting into something more desperate. The other hand braces my weight as my head drops between her shoulder blades.

"Spread wider for me," I growl against her ear.

She does instantly.

"Good girl," I praise.

The moan she releases tells me everything I need to know about what gets her off, and goddamn it's getting me off too, because I'm *relishing* the sense of control. I jerk her hips up higher, drive into her harder. I can hardly believe this is happening. That I'm fucking Alice Sinclair. But I won't stop. Not a fucking chance.

I can tell from the way she's moaning, pushing backward to meet every thrust greedily, that she's close. I find her clit again, rubbing firmly. "You're going to do exactly as I ask, aren't you, baby?"

She whimpers, nodding frantically as her nails dig into the sheets, twisting them.

I groan, kissing the back of her neck, her shoulder. "You're taking me so well. Being so good for me."

Another frantic nod.

Fuuuck, she is so sexy like this—ass in the air, spread wide open for me, hips rolling toward my cock and fingers. I angle deeper, grinding against that spot inside her that makes her cry out. Lifting Alice's hips a fraction higher, I move faster still. My balls slap against her clit with every thrust, and she lets out a small gasp each time our bodies meet.

"Come for me, Alice," I growl, squeezing her hip. "Come on my cock. Come for me, baby."

I drop down once more, my body engulfing hers. My hand tightens slightly around her throat and my fingers circle her clit, squeezing lightly.

She comes hard, pussy gripping my cock in waves that nearly flatline me. Alice all but screams my name, chasing the pleasure as it rocks through her. I follow her over the edge, spilling into the condom with a groan, hand gripping her hip. The orgasm is a tidal wave of ecstasy, a high that obliterates everything else in existence. My hips jerk through the last pulses, trying to extend the sensation as long as possible, buried as deep as I can get.

Eventually, the pleasure subsides. We come down, gasping, gripping each other. Holding on for dear life because although we told ourselves otherwise, something fundamental has shifted between us. Now that I've been inside Alice, I don't just feel deep affection for her.

I feel protective.

Territorial.

Like there's nothing I wouldn't do to ensure she's safe, cared for. *Happy.* I pull out of her, already mourning the absence of her wrapped around me. Stripping off the condom, I tie it off and throw it away. Then, as quickly as I can get to her, I'm back, wrapping my arms around Alice and pulling her close.

We don't speak as she nuzzles her head beneath my chin.

We just cling to each other.

29
ALICE

MY PONYTAIL BRUSHES the back of my neck as I walk home, Wilson tennis bag slung over my shoulder. It's been three years since I've played, but this morning I answered the court's siren song. As the sun rose over the pines, I tossed to myself, practicing forehands before moving on to backhands. Both were rusty, but I was surprised how quickly I started hitting with topspin.

To anyone who might've been watching, I must have looked like a maniac, smiling the way I was. My muscles worked with a familiar burn, and a sheen of sweat tingled across my skin despite the morning chill. The sport returned to me slowly, hesitantly, wary of how I'd cursed it years prior. But in the light of a new day, with the memory of Colt in my bed, tennis felt different. It felt decidedly *mine.* My parents' stern voices were replaced by Colt's encouraging one.

And then, by the end of the hour, it was my own voice I heard, gently correcting my swing or praising a ball well-placed.

I'm wondering if next time I might bring a hitting partner when I round the corner and find Colt lounging on the porch in—heaven help me—gray sweatpants. When he spots me, he shakes his head and raises a white piece of paper.

"Ms. Sinclair." His voice is a playful rumble. "Do you make a habit of leaving men in your bed with only a note to explain your absence?"

I rush up the stairs and through the front door, cupping the side of my face to hide from his chastising.

"Oh, I don't think so." Colt follows me inside and scoops me around the middle, drawing me flush against him. My tennis bag flops to the floor, already forgotten. He buries his face in the crook of my neck. "You need a shower," he mumbles against my skin. It's an invitation, one I would happily accept if I weren't pressed for time.

I'm relieved that we're touching. That we're playing. After sleeping together, I'd worried things would be awkward between us. I'd woken before the sun was up, nervous energy coursing through me, demanding release, which thankfully I'd achieved on the court.

As Colt finds my ear, biting gently, kissing the sensitive skin there, my mind buzzes right back to last night. Specifically, that authoritative tone he used. A tone so different from the gentleness he typically reserves for me. I know there's a strong, lethal man beneath the kindness, and my god how I liked submitting to it.

And *feeling* it.

"I have another festival meeting." My eyes slip closed under the press of his lips.

"That's a negative, Sinclair." Colt's hands slide down to grip my ass.

My head falls back with laughter, and Colt takes every opportunity of the exposed skin. His lips, his teeth, they trail down my neck. Almost immediately, I am wet, aching between my thighs where I want him, *need* him. But I made a commitment to this town, and I have to see it through.

I manage to squirm out of Colt's grasp and start backing up the stairs, pointing a warning finger in his direction. He slinks after me, eyes predatory, a smirk playing on his lips.

"I thought we were just letting off steam last night." I giggle when he matches every escape step I take.

"I have more steam to give," he says.

He lunges, diving toward me with a mock growl. I squeal and scramble up the remaining stairs to change. Elation rings through me, because I wasn't sure it was possible to be this happy.

~

AN HOUR LATER, this morning's bliss feels like a distant memory. I stand in the Holly River Elementary School cafeteria, facing the volunteers who agreed to decorate our festival attraction.

The space is filled with bench-style tables, currently covered in our crafting materials, and the air smells like—I breathe in—cheeseburgers? Overhead, maple leaves dangle from rafters, painted by children who are eighty-two minutes away from storming our workspace.

"Alice, dear, do you really think we need this many

stringed lights?" Mrs. Devonshire asks, her glasses perched on the tip of her nose. "Because my hands are starting to cramp and maybe we can—"

"Where do we file for reimbursement?" Harold interjects. "Do we submit receipts as we get them, or should we wait until we've purchased everything? Because I had twenty dozen paper lanterns show up at my house, and I've got—"

Another woman, Georgia, saunters over to inquire whether I want her to tie the pumpkins together now, or wait until we're riverside. At the same time, her college freshman son, home for fall break, raises a glittery glass ball and asks, "Like this?"

I look at Maggie and June for help, but Maggie is untangling yet another ball of lights, and June is...

Where is June?

I spot her talking to the lunch staff. She's pointing out trays of ingredients, speaking quickly and wearing an inquisitive expression.

"June," I call out, my voice pleading.

She spins and smiles. "Coming! They have the most fascinating method for batch cooking and—"

"Alice?" Harold presses, waving a stack of receipts.

"I...I'm not sure," I answer honestly, finding it hard to breathe. "I'll have to ask Roxanne."

"Roxanne isn't here," someone pipes up from a bench. "Just tell us what you think."

The questions keep coming as my mind spins—

Should there be more lanterns, or more pumpkins?

Why are we adding glass ornaments if it's a fall festival?

How will we keep all these strands lit, and won't this be a fire hazard?

My head begins to pound and my heart races. I have so much to do back at my bookshop and these questions are making me feel like I should be *here*, every second, until the Fall Festival arrives to ensure it goes smoothly. I'm suddenly in awe of Roxanne. She's carried this weight alone for years. Her mother did the same before that. They're saints, I realize. Both of them.

Despite the chaos, we make solid progress, and by the time the double doors swing open to a stampede of children, we're packing up the final, stray materials. The kids barrel toward the food line, dressed in burnt orange t-shirts that read:

Holly River Elementary Fall Field Day

Several of the kids beam, strutting around with plastic medals draped around their necks. A few even have three or four clinking together.

"Okay, everyone," I announce over the din of sneakers on linoleum. "Thanks for your hard work this morning. Tomorrow, let's meet by the river behind the Hall at seven. We'll install what we've got, film some footage to share online, and then remove it until the big day."

As June, Maggie, and I head for the exit, I spot a little girl sitting alone, not bothering to line up for lunch. Her face is red and splotchy, her bottom lip trembling. I set my bin of craft supplies down and kneel beside her.

"Hey," I say softly. "Are you okay? You want me to grab your teacher?"

The girl looks up, sniffling. "I didn't get any medals,"

she says, tears rolling down her cheeks. "And I tried as hard as I could. I ran *so* fast."

My heart cracks down the middle. I glance up at my friends and see that Maggie has her hand over her chest, frowning.

"Well, that simply won't do." I rummage through the bin and find a sheet of cardstock. Pulling out my scissors, I cut long strips and then staple the ends together. Maggie catches on, reaching into her own bin for a yellow zinnia. She grabs the hot-glue gun, still warm, and attaches the silk flower to the paper necklace I created.

"By the power vested in the Fall Festival Decoration Committee," I smile, looping the makeshift lanyard around her neck. "We award you the spirit medal and declare you Field Day Queen. May you wield your power fairly."

June sneakily offers the girl a monster cookie from her refreshments box. Right before she hands it to her, she asks, "Any allergies, your majesty?"

The girl shakes her head, a radiant smile breaking through the tears.

June hands it over as a boisterous boy stomps toward us. He's a head taller than the girl and wears four shiny medals.

"Hey! That's not fair," he whines, pointing at the girl. "She didn't win anything. Why's *she* getting that?"

Maggie bends at the waist, going eye to eye with the boy. "Get lost, kid." She plucks a tater tot off his tray and pops it into her mouth.

"Maggie," I snort, pulling her away before we're banned from using the cafeteria for life.

AS I WALK BACK through downtown, I'm ticking through what needs to be accomplished before the bookshop's soft opening, a mere four days away. I'm also thinking about what I'm still missing for the festival attraction—specifically, an electric boat—as I pass Clover Patch Market.

The door swings open, and Travis steps out, a bag of groceries tucked under one arm. I hurry my pace, hoping he doesn't see me, but his voice rings out.

"Hey! Alice, wait up." Travis skirts past a group of locals and a mildly terrifying scarecrow mounted outside Magnolia Antiques. Falling into step beside me, he asks, "How's the bookshop coming along?"

A flash of irritation fires through me. This man has the audacity to behave as if we're old friends. He teased me mercilessly in high school, then acted surprised when I broke up with him. He tried to win me back, and when I refused him, he practically encouraged half the school to ostracize me. He's also derailed my construction progress, twice, and here he is—still shooting his shot. I've held my tongue in an attempt to avoid more conflict, but after last night with Colt, I'm done pretending.

I stop short on the sidewalk, turning to face him. "What do you want, Travis?"

Travis blinks, his smile faltering. "Whoa, okay. I think your Mama and Daddy taught you better manners than that, Ali. I'm just asking how you're doing." He actually has the nerve to look hurt, jutting his bottom lip out slightly.

He shifts his groceries to the other arm and reaches for my plastic bin. “Here, let me carry that for you.”

“I’ve got it.”

“Come on.” He reached for the handles. “I’m trying to be a gentleman here.”

He tugs. I hold on. He tugs again, harder this time, and the handle snaps. The bin hits the sidewalk with a clatter. Glue sticks, cardstock, and spools of fishing wire go skittering across the concrete. A jar of orange glitter shatters, sending a shimmering cloud into the October breeze.

“Oh, man.” Travis kneels down, gathering what fell. “I’m sorry, I didn’t mean to... I just know how hard you’ve been working. And I wanted to help.”

I don’t say a word, too afraid that if I start speaking, I won’t be able to stop. My jaw clenches as I snatch the fishing wire before it rolls into the gutter. People are walking past us, coats buttoned against the chill, boots crunching on fallen leaves.

“Maybe I could take you to dinner tonight,” Travis chances, oblivious to my silence. “I was happy to hear you moved back to Holly River, but I feel like I kept missing you all summer. You were always so busy at the cafe, and now with this bookstore thing...”

We’re both still crouched, grabbing the last of the supplies, when Travis takes my hand in his.

That’s it.

I shoot to my feet, clutching the broken bin to my chest.

“Travis. Stop.” My voice is loud enough that a couple of passersby turn to look. “I don’t want to date you. Why would I? You teased me in high school. And when your friends targeted me, you just stood by and watched. It was like you were showing me what happens to a girl who rejects you."

Travis stands, face turning red. "Alice, that was years ago—"

"And you haven't changed!" I continue. "You're trying to get in the way of my bookshop so that my parents end up selling it. You just want more real estate. More power in this town. And for what?"

I take a deep breath, softening my tone. "I know you must be a good man somewhere deep down, Travis. But the way you act...it pushes people away. It pushed *me* away. I'm certain you can behave better than you have been. And once you do, I'm sure someone wonderful will embrace you. But that person won't be me."

"Alice." Travis reaches for my arm, but I jerk away.

"You tried to force me into that bathroom," I hiss, leaning in. "I was yelling for you to stop but you kept—"

Travis holds his hands up. "I wasn't going to do anything, Alice. Jesus. I was sixteen."

"And I was *fifteen*!" I'm shaking, because now that I've said it aloud, I remember it so vividly. How Travis found me after tennis practice, before my parents had arrived to pick me up. The lights in the hallway were dim, and we were alone. I'd seen him and tried to turn in the other direction, but he caught up with me.

Thank god the janitor had appeared.

The words fly out of my mouth before I can stop them. "I'm with Colt now, anyway." I don't know if that's exactly true, but I want it to be. Especially while standing before Travis, remembering that day.

Travis's face scrunches up like what I just said is revolting. "Didn't that dude *live* with you?" he asks. "What, were y'all messing around back then, too?"

"Travis." I shake my head, my body drained from this conversation. "It may have been years ago, but you... You called me a whore. I'll never forget that."

"Yeah, well," Travis says simply, "maybe you were."

I drop my head, his words cutting through me, even though nothing he says should bother me anymore. When I raise my eyes, I say only, "I meant what I said. You could be a good man, if you chose to be."

I start walking. After a few steps, I glance back, worried he might follow me. But he isn't. He's just standing there, fuming. The look on his face sends a shiver down my spine, so I hurry my steps home, clutching the broken bin to my chest.

30
COLT

ALICE IS HOVERING over the cast-iron skillet, frying eggs. Twice, I try to help, to make myself useful, but she shoos me away. As I slide onto a barstool at the counter, I note that her under eyes are lightly shadowed, as if she didn't sleep well last night. She's also got an absolute death grip on that spatula, so clearly something is bothering her.

For two days now, ever since she returned from that festival meeting, she's been on edge. At first, I worried that she regretted sleeping together, but that didn't make sense because she was fine, glowing even, the morning after. So most likely it's just the soft opening that's stressing her out, which tracks. It's only forty-eight hours away and Alice is still missing a crucial book shipment, and the front window remains MIA despite numerous heated phone calls.

Alice slides the eggs onto our plates next to crispy bacon and sliced figs. I insist on pouring our coffee, and after handing Alice her mug, I squeeze her shoulder. "Alice," I say, attempting to connect for the third time, "you gotta tell me what's going on in your head."

She forces a smile, shrugging away the concern. "It's nothing. I'm just...nervous. My parents will be here soon, and I'm worried about what they'll think."

I reach up, carefully untangling a stray hair caught in her diamond stud earring. I was there when she received them at her thirteenth birthday dinner. I'd never seen such luxury. Had marveled how they shone when the box was passed around the table. Moments later, the waiter had asked how I wanted my steak cooked. Yet another mystery to me at the time.

Once the earring is worked free, my hand returns to her shoulder. "Come on. Talk to me. Please."

She sighs, her eyes darting to the kitchen window. I follow her gaze, but all that's out there are three hens scratching through dead leaves. Something flickers across Alice's face—something substantial and meaningful.

She opens her mouth, hesitates, and then blurts out, "I need a boat."

I blink, my hand falling away. "I'm sorry?"

"For the festival," she clarifies, the words tumbling out. "Remember I proposed that we host our own event attraction? I need a boat for it. An electric one, to be precise. Two boats would be even better."

I smile, shaking my head. Because this woman is a damn force of nature. Here she is, two days out from a life-defining moment, and she's worried about the town. Alice might very well succeed even if the Fall Festival flops. But if others sink while she swims, she won't be happy. I'm still not sure that's the entirety of what's bothering her, but it's what she's chosen to share, so I accept it.

I pull out a chair. "Show me this boat you need."

Alice grabs her laptop, and while we eat, she walks me through why this particular boat is crucial. I ask questions, and she answers them, working out details in her head as she speaks. By the time we've finished breakfast, she seems lighter, and I feel a surge of pride that I could help alleviate some of her stress.

Alice is about to open a new tab when there's a sudden knock at the front door. It's not a neighborly knock. It's impatient, aggressive, and it comes again after only a beat of silence. I drop my fork, the metal clattering against the plate, and cross the room to swing the door open.

Travis stands on the other side. My eyes shoot to Alice, and her face pales.

Travis marches inside without an invitation, and my blood boils. Because this isn't just Alice's house. For a time, it was my home too, and I'm fed up with this man throwing his insubstantial weight around it.

"Morning, Colt. Alice." Travis is curt, looking at neither of us. Instead, his eyes roam the space, taking stock of what we've accomplished despite his interference. He's got a device in his hand—a moisture meter. "Had a report. Anonymous, of course. Says there's a leaky pipe and that moisture's been accumulating behind the drywall."

I step into his path. "Travis, you need to get the *fuck* out of here. I'm tired of this shit."

Travis sneers, and I nearly put my fist through his teeth. "Hey, you want me gone?" he says. "Fine. But then the site is shut down. Official stop work order. I'll pull your permit before I even hit the sidewalk."

Alice appears beside me. "Go ahead," she challenges, no longer pacifying him, which pleases me to no end. "Test the walls. There's no moisture. You're only doing this because —" Her teeth snap together. "Just do it and get out."

My eyes dart in her direction, wondering what else she was going to say, but Travis doesn't wait for further encouragement. He starts moving along the perimeter, pressing the meter against the drywall every few feet, looking for a win where there is none.

He gets to the main wall—the one that houses the majority of the floor-to-ceiling bookshelves and Alice's rolling ladder. He presses the tool to the wood, and the device emits a shrill, steady beep.

Travis spins around, a smug grin splitting his face. He holds up the digital screen. "Just as I suspected. High-level moisture trapped right here. The wall will have to come down to address the pipes or you'll have black mold within a month. It's a health hazard to anyone who steps foot in here."

"Bullshit!" My hands curl into fists. "There's a steel support beam and foil-backed insulation in that wall. It's a false positive, and you know it."

"Well, the thing is," Travis says, scratching his head, "I don't know that at all, Colt. What I do know is that I got a report saying there's a leak, and now I've got evidence that they're right. So..." Travis smiles at Alice. "The wall comes down today, or I condemn the building. Which will it be?"

Alice pulls out her phone. "I'm calling City Hall. Harold needs to verify what you're saying."

Travis laughs dryly. "Good luck with that. Harold hasn't been in the office for almost two weeks. The buck stops with me now, Ali."

"I'm not taking that wall down." I step into Travis's

personal space, staring down at where sweat beads on his upper lip. "Get. The Fuck. Out."

Travis glares at me. Then he turns and storms out the front door. For a second, I think he's caved. That he's crawling back into whatever decrepit hole he must sleep in at night. But then I hear his truck door slam for a second time and suddenly he's back, lugging a sledgehammer.

"Are you *kidding* me?" I roar, because if I had any doubt that he was inventing excuses to sink us, I don't anymore. "You just happen to have that with you?"

"If you won't do your job," Travis pants, hauling the heavy tool. "Then I'll do mine as an inspector." He raises the hammer, aiming for the custom shelving.

I lunge, grabbing the handle, muscles locking as I wrest it to the floor. He shoves me, and I shove him back twice as hard.

"Stop it!" Alice squeezes between us, her hands spread, separating us. I tear the hammer away from Travis, afraid to leave him alone with it, especially with Alice nearby. Alice looks at the wall, then at the tool in my hand. Her eyes brim with angry tears, her breath coming in ragged gasps.

Before I can stop her, she yanks the sledgehammer from my grasp. She's small, but she's also fueled by months of suppressed frustration.

I step toward her. "Alice, don't—"

She swings.

The hammer head buries itself into the drywall, right between two hard-carved shelves. She yanks it out and swings again.

"Alice!" I reach for her.

She spins around, hammer head thumping against the

floor. Tears stream down her face, her jaw tight. "The sooner it's down, the sooner we can rebuild it," she snaps.

Alice steps right up to Travis. "You will never stop me, Travis. You will *never* own my family's home. Find an issue, I'll fix it. Find another one, I'll fix that too. You could burn this place to the ground, and I'd rebuild it, brick by brick. So go ahead." She shoves the handle into his stomach. "Take it down."

Travis takes the tool, stunned that Alice actually did what he challenged her to do. He looks at me, looks at the hole. I wave my hand toward the wall like *you heard her*. Travis bites down, determined to save face, and struggles to lift the hammer. He swings, hitting the wall three, maybe four times. Almost immediately, he's winded, sweating through his button-down.

Travis stops, red-faced, and wipes his brow. He leans toward the hole he's made, reaches in, and yanks on a cluster of wires. "Well, look at that," he pants, pointing to the yellow casing. "Non-metallic cable without a conduit. That's a fire code violation."

That's it.

I grab him and slam him against the adjacent wall. My right fist is pulled back, a second away from shattering his jaw.

"Do it," Travis hisses, spittle flying from his mouth. "Hit me."

My heart shotguns in my chest, because I want to. *I will.*

Alice is tugging on my arm, trying to get me to let go. And it's only when I look at her face that I hesitate. Because if I hit Travis, he'll ensure I spend the next day or two in jail. And then who will fix this mess?

It's exactly what he wants, and I'll be damned if I give him the satisfaction.

I stare back at him for a beat longer, and then shove him against the wall once more before stepping back.

Travis stumbles, almost falling. Then he rights himself and releases a shaky laugh. He straightens his shirt, emboldened by the fact that I backed down. "Yeah, that's what I thought," he sneers. "You're a real tough guy, aren't ya, Colt? But you don't want to go to jail, do you?"

A new voice cuts in from the open doorway—

"I don't mind going to jail."

I freeze. Because I know that damn voice.

Standing in the door frame, one arm propped lazily against the wood, is a man who resembles the reflection I see in the mirror every morning. He's wearing a faded denim jacket and an amused expression.

Warren.

I haven't seen my brother since our mother's funeral, and before that, not since I watched his taillights disappear when I was fourteen.

"Who the hell are you?" Travis spits.

My eyes swing toward Alice.

I'm sorry, she mouths.

"This is a restricted site," Travis continues. "You need to leave or I'll—"

Warren flicks his fingers toward Travis. "Quiet, small man." He looks at me. "So? Should I hit him?"

"You won't if you know what's good for you!" Travis yells, already making his way toward the door, seeking an exit path that doesn't involve coming in contact with my brother's willing fist.

Warren blocks the doorway and raises a questioning eyebrow in my direction.

"Colt, I think he's serious," Alice says.

"Yeah." I scrub a hand over my face. "He is. Warren, let him go."

Warren shrugs and steps out of the way, and Travis scurries toward his vehicle, sledgehammer forgotten.

Alice reaches for me. "I was going to tell you. I didn't know if he'd actually come and—"

I hug her, pulling her close against me and kissing the crown of her head. Because I know Alice had the best of intentions when inviting my brother.

Warren gestures between the two of us. "Didn't see that coming."

I release Alice and turn to face Warren. "Wherever the hell you came from," I say, my voice dead serious. "You go right the fuck back."

March 2021
Holly River, Texas

Dear Colt,

Guess what?! You'll never believe what happened today! I started screaming the second I saw the email from Texas A&M University. I got in, Colt! I'm officially going to be an Aggie! Mom and Dad are really excited. Dad keeps telling me the names of agricultural and engineering tycoons who graduated from there. I kind of want to major in Fine Arts, but Mom and Dad say I should get a management degree. That it'll be useful when I work for their company.

I've been thinking about your last letter, Colt. I don't mean to offend you, but you seemed kind of down. I hate that I don't know where you are. Is it beautiful there? Is it like a different world? In your next letter, you should tell me one beautiful thing you see. It doesn't have to give away your location. Just something simple that you like.

Do you remember that time I lost my favorite hoodie? Mom said it was a valuable lesson in being responsible for my belongings, and Dad *refused to buy me a new one. But you went out and retraced my steps, and you found it! Remember that kid had it and you made him give it back? That poor kid was probably scared stiff.*

But that's who you are, Colt. You're a helper. You've always been someone who steps in when people are in trouble, and that's exactly what you're doing in the Marines. You're helping people! You're probably helping people you'll never even meet. How cool is that?

Sometimes I lie in bed at night and think about how you're keeping people safe. It makes me feel secure, like I can do anything just knowing you're out there. You're a hero, Colt. I know you'll probably roll your eyes at that, but I'm serious. You help people. And you keep them safe. That's what heroes do, right?

Remember to send me that one beautiful thing in your next letter. It's okay if you can't write back for a long time. I know you're doing really important things and don't always have time. That's okay! I'll just keep sending you letters unless you ask me to stop. I don't mind at all.

Before you know it, you'll be back in Holly River. The very first thing we'll do is go straight to the river. I've been practicing while you've been gone. I bet I can swing out much further than you now! Or maybe not. You are a Marine after all. And I'm just an Aggie. I'm an Aggie!!!

Stay safe.

Love,
Alice

31
COLT

ALICE'S LAUGHTER rings through the house. I'm still gritting my teeth over what Travis did yesterday, but she's found a way to move on. To focus on the positive. It's funny how caring about someone this much makes me fearful. I keep worrying that Alice is going to fall apart under the weight of her pursuit, but she proves time and again how resilient she is.

She'd make for a hell of a Marine.

I concentrate on the task at hand, drill whining as I sink a screw into the bookshelf, trying to repair what Travis ruined. Through the open windows, I can hear June laughing too. I straighten, stretching my back, and watch as they hang a blanket over the wrecked wall. I'm not sure the blanket will be much of an improvement, but it'll have to do because we're out of time.

"Hand me that level." I stretch my arm behind me.

Dalton reaches into the toolbox and passes it over. He's been here most of the day, acting as a second set of hands. And more importantly, as a buffer between Warren and me.

"When's Grant getting in?" Dalton wipes the sweat from his forehead and leans against my truck.

"Tomorrow night," I grunt, tightening a bracket. "Driving up with his parents."

"They know you're screwing their daughter?" Warren asks from the porch steps.

My grip on the tool tightens, and I have to force myself to breathe. I may understand why Warren took off when I was fourteen, leaving me alone with our alcoholic mother, because I know how chaotic it was living in that house. But that doesn't mean I forgive him. He makes it awfully hard to do so. "If you're going to say shit like that, you need to get the fuck out of here, Warren."

Dalton pauses, a water bottle halfway to his mouth. He looks between us. "Wait...are you and Alice actually...?"

"No," I snap.

"Yes," Warren says at the same time.

I shake my head, my eyes drifting to the window again. Alice hasn't stopped moving since Travis tucked tail. The second he was gone, and I got Warren out of there, she was ordering books online—paying full price to get them here by today—and painting the entire shop. She made so many runs to the hardware store that eventually, I took her keys and insisted I'd handle it, unable to watch as she ran herself into the ground.

We didn't fall asleep last night. We *collapsed*. At around three in the morning, I turned over—watching her sleep, tangled in the sheets, still in her blue jeans—and wondered if this was my fault. Travis is a prick, but my presence in Alice's life is the match that lit his fuse. If I weren't here, maybe she wouldn't be painting around holes in the middle of the night.

Alice appears at the window, hands braced on the frame. I force my face to soften and give her a reassuring smile. *I've got it*, I communicate silently. *Everything's going to be okay.*

"Y'all want tea?" she asks.

"I'll take one." Dalton wiggles his empty water bottle.

"I'll just bring them for everyone." Alice dives her head back inside.

I watch her go, wondering if she's really as unfazed as she seems.

Seeing my concern, Warren scoffs.

I round the worktable and step toward him. "What is your problem, Warren?"

"I ain't got a problem, little brother." He raises his hands in mock surrender.

"Then why the fucking face? Why are you even *here*? Did you come back in town just to fuck with me? Because I've got shit to do. I don't have time to handle you too."

"Jesus, dude." Warren stands up. "I thought you jarheads were supposed to be calm under pressure." He flicks a hand toward the house. "Your *girlfriend* invited me."

"She's not my—" I cut myself off, raking a hand over my buzzed head. "I can't fucking do this."

Dalton steps between us. "Hey. Let's uh...chill, yeah? Maybe we should grab a drink. It's been a long day."

Warren's eyes light up and he claps Dalton on the shoulder. "Now *there's* an idea."

"No fucking way," I say. "You're not gonna get blasted. I'm not taking care of your ass again."

"*You* take care of *me*?" Warren snorts. "Oh, that'd be the day."

I step toward Warren, even as Dalton pushes against my chest, trying to keep distance between us. "What the hell does that mean?" I snap.

The screen door cracks open, and Alice comes out onto the porch. She's carrying a tray with four mason jars of tea, the ice clinking against the glass. Warren straightens, his expression smoothing into something resembling respect.

"Sweetened," Alice clarifies as she offers Dalton a glass, and then one to me. When she gets to Warren, she offers him a warm, inviting smile. "I'm so glad you're here, Warren. I know I've already said this, but it was really nice of you to travel so far to support Colt."

"Course," Warren mutters, taking the tea. "Actually, we were just talking about heading down the Hall to catch up. You and your friend want to join us?" He tilts his head toward the window, glancing at June's silhouette.

Dalton's posture stiffens instantly. He eyes Warren with sudden weariness and steps out from between us, like he might be okay with me throttling him after all.

"No. No, we were *not* talking about that." I glance at Alice, shaking my head because I hate that my brother is adding complexity to an already stressful situation. But she looks at me like it's her who's apologizing, and my god, how that crushes me. Because this woman has only ever cared about me. *Supported* me.

"I'm actually going to take Warren to the inn," I continue.

"Nah," Warren says. "I'm not going back there."

I hold out my hand to him. "Shut the fuck up, Warren."

Alice glances between us, worry etched on her face. "Maggie will be here with the arch soon anyway, and that should pretty much do it for today."

"I can stay and help set it up," Dalton offers quickly. He looks inside to where June is buzzing around the remaining shelves.

Alice smiles gratefully. "That'd be great, thank you."

I grab Warren's arm. "Let's go."

He rips out of my grasp. "The fuck off me. I'm staying at Mom's. You can follow me there if you want."

I go rigid, because I definitely *don't* want that. But I need to get Warren off Alice's property. "Fine," I mutter, slinging open my truck door.

Warren gets into his own truck and starts backing out of the driveway. I follow him, my eyes flicking to the porch where Alice stands. She raises a hand, waving goodbye, and holds it there. I do the same, every bone in my body straining to return to her side. To touch her. To hear her breathy moans in my ear again.

I flip on my headlights, straighten the truck, and take off down the road—following Warren to the last place I want to go.

WARREN WAITS while I unlock the door, though he knows where the spare is hidden. I push it open, motioning for him to go on through. He looks at me for a minute, and then moves inside. I don't know why he wanted to stay here, nor do I care. I only want to ensure he's somewhere other than Alice's house, and that he doesn't leave.

Warren kicks off his boots, same as I did the first time I came back here. I find myself wondering, once again, why we bother. And why we bothered back then. It's not like our parents cared about playing house. Warren picks up a ceramic statue of two boys, a gift from a grandmother we barely knew, and sets it back down.

He saw this place only a few months ago, when we were here for Mom's funeral, but he was plastered then. I wasn't sober myself, but better off than him. He peers into the kitchen, then pauses by the hallway, neck craning as if trying to see into his room. For a moment, I think he'll go back there. But in the end, he just presses his lips together, frowning, and moves to the kitchen table. Yanking out a chair, he drops into it.

I stay near the front door, shoulder leaning against the frame. The tension between us settles in this place. Outside these walls, we're in constant battle with one another. But in here, we're on the same side; a shaky alliance born out of necessity during childhood.

Warren drums his fingers on the table and then gives a short, breathless laugh. "It's fucking weird being back here."

I nod, grateful—despite how he wears on my nerves—to have someone who understands that feeling.

"I know we were here for her funeral, but that was different. I was..." He shakes his head. "Distracted. By everything."

"I know."

Warren slaps his hand on the table and rubs the wood. "Smells different in here."

I can't stop staring at Warren. In the shadows of the fading light, he looks alien. His shoulders are broader, his face weathered by whatever he's been up to over the last thirteen years. When I was younger, Warren was the fucking sun. A boulder of an older brother who once beat the shit out of a kid on the bus for making fun of my backpack. Even now, with our past pressing on his shoulders, there's an immovable gravity to him.

Warren looks up at me suddenly, combativeness falling away. "How can you stand being here, Colt?"

I clear my throat, shifting my weight. "I don't come here that much. I've been staying at the—"

"No," Warren interrupts. "In this town. In this fucking place."

I glance out the window. The sun is gone now, darkness settling over our childhood home like spackle, smoothing the edges and filling the cracks. Making it look like any other home, where grown kids eagerly return, brimming with nostalgia and homesickness.

"It's not always easy," I admit. "But there're some good people here."

"Those people aren't like us." Warren leans back, the chair creaking. His eyes drift to a spot on the wall, and his lips quirk upward. He nods at it, and I find myself smiling too. Even in the dark, I can make out the four small punctures in the drywall. Last time we were in this house together, we'd eaten pie, attempting to get along. After that failed, Warren had hurled his fork across the room. It impaled itself into the drywall like a dart, and we'd roared with laughter. Then we spent a good twenty minutes trying to repeat the feat, because why the hell not? Not like this place would be ours for much longer. And thank god for that.

"You remember that time she left us for almost a week?" Warren asks suddenly, his voice quieter. "I think you were like...seven, maybe?"

I look down at my boots. "I remember."

Warren laughs, the sound full-bodied. "We ate everything in the house, man. We were down to a bottle of ketchup by the time we caved and went to school. Remember we agreed to bring back as much shit as we could from the cafeteria?"

I smile, knowing where this is going.

Warren points at me. "And I brought back steak fingers and pizza wrapped in napkins. And you remember what *you* brought back?"

I start laughing.

"Fucking chocolate milk, Colt!"

"You drank the shit out of it though, didn't you?" I say, finally looking up.

"Hell yeah, I did!" Warren nods. "And we made forts out of the couch cushions. And we barked at the mailman until he finally snapped and started barking back."

"He flipped us off too," I add.

"Did he?"

I nod, still grinning, relieved to recall something from my past prior to the Sinclairs—just one thing—that feels worthy of remembering.

Warren leans back, his eyes going to the ceiling. "Five or six days she was gone."

An uncomfortable silence follows, stretching between us, reminding us why we fight each other. Because we couldn't fight *her*, not with the condition she was in, and we couldn't fight him either, because he was gone before we were old enough to know that fighting was an option.

"At least she came back," I say finally.

Warren's eyes dart to mine. "Was that a shot at me? Or at Dad? Because if you're talking about Dad, then—" He cuts himself off, shaking his head.

"What?" I ask, stepping toward the kitchen, eager for even the smallest morsel about a father I can barely put a face to. "What about Dad?"

Warren glances away, jaw working. "Forget it. Doesn't matter."

I struggle against the urge to press him for more. But exhaustion from the day is catching up to me, and I need to get back to ensure Alice sleeps more than four hours tonight. "I've got to get going," I mutter. "You sure you're good here? I don't mind paying for a room."

"I'm fine, Colt," Warren says, his voice flat, cynical. "Go back to your perfect life."

I open my mouth to fire back. To tell him that my life is far from perfect. But I stop, because he's baiting me and I know what happens when I take it. "I'll see you tomorrow," I say instead. "Just...you need to behave tomorrow night, alright? Alice's parents will be there. It's a big deal for her."

"Can't wait," Warren deadpans, his eyes already drifting back to the shadows.

I stare at him for a moment longer, feeling like I should say something else. Feeling like *he* should. But in the end, I just leave him there. Same as he did me.

32
COLT

I'M ON EDGE. Alice is too. Today should be the culmination of our hard work. A moment for popping champagne, pulling Alice to my side, and whispering against her neck, "We did it, Ali."

Instead, June is setting out pumpkin-shaped cookies and apple cider doughnuts on a folding table instead of a finished checkout counter. And Maggie is centering a vase of orange and black flowers, covered in fake cobwebs, on a coffee table that still needs refinishing.

"Monster Mash" plays over the loudspeakers, complimenting the rubber bats hanging from the ceiling and the Halloween decorations illuminating every corner, all borrowed from June's vast collection. It looks like a haunted house in here, which is closer to the truth.

Dalton offers me a beer, his gaze sweeping over the space through the eyeholes of a Batman mask. "My place looked way worse than this two weeks before opening."

I refuse the drink because I need a clear head tonight. But I still slap Dalton on the back, thanking him for the encouragement, and head outside to find Alice. Her parents will be here any minute, and she hasn't changed into her costume yet.

I step out onto the porch, eyeing the flower arch Maggie and Dalton erected last night. It's extraordinary, it really is. Right now, it's also covered in cobwebs, but come daylight, it'll be a marvel. Exactly as Alice envisioned.

"Hey there," Alice says from a stool. "Had a last-minute idea."

She's got a paintbrush in her hand and is leaning toward the window which, despite resorting to prayer and cursing in equal measure, remains in transit. I step back to get a better look and see that she's painted a faux window over the plywood. She's even painted window boxes at the bottom, overflowing with orange and yellow flowers.

I smile. "It looks good."

Alice stands up, coming over to wrap her arms around me. She peeks through the screen door to ensure no one is watching, and then kisses me. Her mouth is warm against mine, parting when my tongue brushes her lips. My body reacts to her instantly, and I briefly consider whether—if I took her to the side of the house—I could make her come before her parents showed.

"Mmm," she purrs against my mouth. "I'm going to need you to wear that costume tonight."

I harden at the sound of her sultry tone. "You got a thing for lumberjacks?"

She twists the ends of my fake mustache. "I've got a thing for synthetic facial hair."

I laugh, kissing her forehead.

Maggie sticks her head out, and we shoot away from

each other. She grins, glancing back and forth between us. "Uh-huh," she mutters beneath her breath, before adding, "You better get that booty into a costume. Otherwise, my Little Red Riding ass is gonna hop on June's broomstick and fly home."

Alice checks her watch. "Oh, my god!"

Maggie rolls her hand toward the open door, hurrying Alice along. When Alice dives inside, Maggie slaps her rear without taking her eyes off me.

"So," Maggie says as Alice thunders up the stairs. "Heard the firefighter was in town. He coming tonight? Not that I care."

I laugh, preparing to tell her I have no idea where my brother is. And also, that she'd be best served keeping a wide berth. But the sound of an approaching vehicle reaches us, and we turn toward the street.

Alice's parents pull up to the curb, her dad behind the wheel.

My heart pounds in my chest, because I miss them. It's been eight years since I left this house. Eight years since I've seen them. But they still feel like the closest thing to proper guardians I've ever had.

Mrs. Sinclair pushes open the passenger door of the SUV and rushes across the front yard. I jog down the stairs and meet her halfway, lifting her off her feet when she hugs me. "Let me look at you. You've gotten so big! Are you good?" she asks. "Let me see your shoulder."

"Janet, leave the poor boy alone," Mr. Sinclair booms. The man takes me by the shoulders and jerks me into a hug, nearly crushing my ribs. He slaps me on the back twice, knocking the air out of my lungs. "Did you save your money like I said, or spend it at pubs across the globe? I hope it was a bit of both."

"Honey, can we not pry into his finances ten seconds after getting out of the car?" Mrs. Sinclair sighs.

Grant steps past his parents wearing a Hulk Hogan costume, and offers his hand. I clap my palm into his and we bump chests, patting each other on the back. "Why don't I lay him down before y'all both hump him to death."

"Grant!" Mrs. Sinclair cries.

"Entirely uncalled for," Mr. Sinclair adds.

"Alice!" Mrs. Sinclair hurries toward the porch, and I turn to see Alice dressed in a silky black gown, black feathered wings attached to her back. I'm not proud of the thoughts that race through my head with her dad standing a foot away. But here we are.

Alice hugs her mom and dad in turn, and then grabs her mom's hands. "Come on! I want to show you around."

As she heads up the stairs, Maggie withdraws her phone and leans toward Alice, her voice low. "Want me to film... everything?"

She's asking if she should show the unfinished parts of the bookshop too, or strategically edit to make the work look further along.

Alice pauses, mulling it over. "Film it all."

Maggie gives Alice an approving smile and then shakes Alice's parents' hands as they pass her to go inside. When she gets to Grant, she jerks her hand back and flips him the bird. Grant sinks his mouth over her finger.

"Jesus, Grant!" Maggie wipes her finger off on her costume. "You're disgusting."

As Alice walks her parents through the space, I hold my

breath. I can see the adolescence in her as she over-explains why they can see wires through holes in the walls. I can hear how badly she just needs to hear *We're proud of you, baby* as she explains why she hasn't hung any artwork, but will soon.

"Where are all the books?" Alice's mom scans the room.

My eyes shoot to Alice's face, searching for any sign that the question bothers her. But she just smiles and explains that they're en route. That she didn't want to stock them before the front window was replaced because moisture causes books to swell.

Good girl. I know Alice is nervous, but her response is a far cry from the shaky responses she gave her parents as a kid.

Mr. Sinclair lifts the blanket, peering beneath at the damaged wall. "What happened here?"

"Those shelves will be the centerpiece of the entire room," Alice shorthands. "And Mom! Guess what? Colt made a library ladder for them."

Mrs. Sinclair forces a smile onto her face, but I know the woman well enough to recognize that she isn't pleased. Her eyes roam over the space, looking past the lit jack-o'-lanterns and dry ice billowing across the refreshments table. She turns and glances at the stairs, railing wrapped in twinkling orange lights, and frowns as if imagining what's lacking on the second story.

"Y'all want champagne?" I ask in an attempt to lighten the mood. "I think Alice wanted to announce the bookshop's name with everyone here."

"Oh, right!" Alice rushes toward the kitchen, her wings catching on the doorframe. "I'll get it!"

I glance at Alice's parents, whose faces have fallen now that she's out of sight. Frustration burns in my chest, because all they're seeing is what's unfinished, not the insurmountable challenges she's overcome to get it this far. Dalton meanders over, asking Alice's folks how the drive down was, and how they're liking the new Shreveport office.

With them distracted, I take the opportunity to excuse myself and follow after Alice. I find her near the wine fridge, pulling out a sleek gold and black bottle. She digs through the drawers, movements frantic.

I touch her back lightly. "Hey."

Her head snaps up, worry evident on her face. "Do you think they're happy? You think they like it?"

"They should," I say quickly. "You busted your ass, Ali. This place looks like a bookshop now, because it is. It may not be finished, but it sure as hell isn't just a house anymore. You made that happen."

Alice nods as she labors to uncork the champagne. When I note that her hands are shaking, I take the corkscrew from her. For the first time, I wonder if I've underestimated how hard it might've been growing up in this house, where she was expected to excel at all things. To pick a path by age ten and pursue it ruthlessly. To focus only on that which reaps athletic accolades and financial rewards.

To constantly compare herself to two people who attended a Top 20 university as scouted, scholarship athletes before bootstrapping a business to success.

I pop the champagne and fill eight glasses as Alice places them on a tray.

"I think it's time," she says, eyes wide, anxiety rolling off her. She moves out of the kitchen, carrying the tray. When June sees her, she insists on taking it, asking with a witch's cackle if it's poisoned.

"Everyone, if you'd like to accompany me into the main room..." Alice says, her voice raised above the music.

Maggie zooms her phone's camera in on Alice, letting out a little whoop, and June follows close behind as Dalton passes out the champagne. Alice takes her spot near the front of the room, standing beside a makeshift sign that's been covered in a sheet since this morning. A sheet I was instructed not to touch under any circumstance.

Alice waves me to the front, and I come to stand beside her, feeling an unexpected wave of anxiety myself. But when she glances up at me, her smile stretching wide, the unease vanishes.

She faces her parents, her brother, her friends, and raises a glass. "I'm so grateful to have all of you here for the soft opening. We've got more to tackle over the next..." She glances at me again and laughs nervously. "Thirteen days. And I couldn't have gotten this far without Colt, who's been here every step of the way and donated his time to help me fulfill my dream."

"I helped too," Grant calls out.

Maggie rolls her eyes.

"So," Alice continues. "Without further ado, I'd like to officially welcome you to..." Alice steps back, pulling the sheet off the temporary sign. "Birds Bookstore!"

My eyes dart from the sign to her, and I huff a laugh, shaking my head. Because I can't believe she did this. Alice beams back at me, her eyes communicating that this means exactly what I think it does.

The birds. *My* birds. The ones that meant safety when I was deployed.

"Alice—" I begin.

"Who is that?" Maggie interrupts, lowering her phone.

I follow her gaze to the window and see Warren staggering up the porch steps. He grabs onto the railing, balancing himself, and then continues toward the door.

"Fuck," I breathe. "Stay here," I tell Alice before beelining toward the porch.

Maggie beats me there, opening the screen door and stepping toward Warren. She raises a hand, stopping him, like she too can sense that he's wasted. "Hey. You must be the fire—"

"Move," Warren demands.

Maggie's face scrunches. "Ex-cuse me? Okay, why don't we go onto the porch. You look like you've—"

Warren lowers his face to hers. "Get the *hell* out of my way."

I shove Warren backward, putting space between him and Maggie. Over my shoulder, Maggie yells, asking who the hell he thinks he is. I start pushing my brother away from the doorway, but a sound behind me steals my attention.

Spinning, I watch Alice rushing toward the kitchen, pushing through the *employees only* swinging door I installed just this week. I can see instantly that she's upset. Turning back around, I stab a finger into Warren's chest. "Don't move. I mean it! I'll be back."

Maggie crosses her arms, staring down Warren. "Don't worry. I've got him."

I hurry into the kitchen, and when I see Alice's face buried in her hands, I move to her side. "Hey," I say gently. "Alice. Alice, look at me."

She raises her head, and when I spot the tears in her eyes, I jerk my face back like I've been slapped. Seeing her like this—upset, vulnerable—it makes me want to physically hurt someone. I don't think, I just reach for her, pulling her into my arms.

"Alice, what did they say?" I ask.

She shakes her head against me, her tears dampening my flannel shirt.

Jesus, I walked away for two minutes. How could her parents have crushed my girl this quickly? I press a kiss to the crown of her head, knowing I need to get back out there, trying to find the right words to soothe her.

"The hell is going on here?" a voice cuts in.

I release Alice and turn.

Mr. Sinclair stares at us.

Alice steps toward her dad, wiping her face. She takes my hand, grips it tightly. "We're seeing each other, Dad," she announces defiantly. "We have been for a few weeks now."

Mr. Sinclair's face pulls into an expression of disbelief. Or maybe it's disgust. Either way, it cuts me far deeper than I thought possible. "Are you kidding me?" His eyes widen as he glances back and forth between the two of us.

"Dad," Alice says.

Mr. Sinclair points a finger in my direction. "This... It's not right, Colt."

Warren pushes the door open, glancing between us. He laughs humorlessly. "Ah. So you found out Colt's dating your daughter." His eyes slide to mine. "Did he take it well, Colt? Welcome you into the family?"

Mr. Sinclair stiffens. He may be older, but he's a farm boy, born and raised. And even with new money to his name, I don't doubt that he'd accept any challenge Warren threw his way.

"Warren," I bark. "I told you to stay outside."

Warren folds his arms, leaning against the open door. Mrs. Sinclair slips closer, brows furrowed in confusion. Behind her, Maggie, June, Dalton, and Grant laugh about something, oblivious to the escalating tension.

Warren nods toward me, but looks at Mr. Sinclair. "So? Does he have your approval?"

Mr. Sinclair faces him. "I don't know who you are, boy, but—"

"I'm his fucking brother, that's who I am. Who are *you*?"

"Warren!" I yell, stepping between them.

"Let me guess," Warren says, words slurring. "He was good enough to babysit your kid and make sure he got that football scholarship, but not quite good enough to date the daughter, am I right?"

"Enough!" I push him backward.

He staggers a step, and then moves toward Mr. Sinclair again, who's starting to yell back. "You already got outta him what you needed, huh? He's no use to you anymore? Once he finishes working on this place for free, that is."

"That's not—" Alice begins.

But now Grant is grabbing Warren's arm, asking what the hell is going on.

Warren shoves Grant. "Get off me!"

Grant stumbles back a few steps before righting himself.

"You the one who pretended to be Colt's brother while I was gone?" Warren scoffs.

"Fuck you, man," Grant fires back, not missing a beat. "You left him, didn't you? Someone had to be there."

I lunge for Warren, but it's too late.

Warren tackles Grant, and the two crash to the floor.

I'm on Warren in an instant, yanking him off Grant and hurling him to the other side of the room. It's not easy. The guy weighs more than I do, but I have better training. The moment Warren's on his feet, I'm in his face, shoving him once, twice. "What the hell is wrong with you?" I roar.

"Both of you need to get out of here!" Mr. Sinclair booms from the doorway.

I corral Warren toward the front door as he runs his mouth.

"You're on *their* side, Colt?" he hollers. "They used you!"

I keep shoving him until we're off the porch and in the front yard. Everyone piles onto the porch, watching the chaos unfold. I don't care. I don't care about anything other than getting Warren off this lawn and out of my life. "Yes!" I yell. "Yeah, I'm on their side. They took care of me when *you*," I shove him again, "took off."

"Oh, they took care of you," Warren mocks. He flicks his hand toward where Alice's parents stand. "Go on then.

Ask them. Ask if they're okay with you dating their daughter. Since they're your family and all, I'm sure they'll approve."

I hesitate, a cold blast rattling through me.

Warren staggers, catches himself. "Go on."

Alice rushes down the stairs. "Of course they'd approve. Daddy?" she says, turning back to them. "Mama?" When they don't immediately respond, Alice's eyes widen, her voice rising. "Look at everything he's done for me!"

Mr. Sinclair grips the railing, his face like stone. He looks at me like he sees exactly who I am. A boy with an absent father and an alcoholic mother. A man without a college degree, educated on how to hold a rifle but not on how to hold down a job.

This is what I imagine he thinks as he looks at me, but what comes out of his mouth is even worse. "Did something happen when you were living here?"

My mouth falls open in surprise.

"For fuck's sake," Warren mutters.

"She was eleven when you lived here," Mr. Sinclair states flatly, knuckles whitening. "And you were sixteen. She was...*thirteen* when you were eighteen."

Warren charges toward Mr. Sinclair as his wife screams. Mr. Sinclair stumbles backward inside and I rush after Warren, grabbing him around the middle before he can reach Alice's dad. Warren twists, shoving me away from him. We crash into each other, thirteen years of abandonment erupting out of me as we trade blows, smashing into bookshelves, wrestling across the floor.

Grant grabs me and Dalton grabs Warren, and they tear

us apart. We're still kicking at each other, cussing, both of us more enraged about our pasts than each other. But we make for far easier targets.

Warren jerks out of Grant's hold and barrels toward the front door. Dalton releases me and runs after him, stepping in front of June as Warren stumbles down the porch stairs once more.

"Get the fuck out of here!" I yell, pointing after him. "I don't ever want to see you again!"

Warren stops, chest heaving, and turns toward me. Alice is grabbing my hand, trying to pull me toward the house, but my eyes are locked on Warren. His face is bleeding, a deep cut above his eyebrow that I take satisfaction in.

"Our house," Warren says, seeming tired now. "That's who we are, Colt. And this..." He gestures toward the soaring Greek Revival, referencing the pristine paint job and thick white pillars. "This is theirs. They're never gonna accept you. Not if you don't have use to 'em."

"That's not true," Alice insists. Her eyes, nearly manic now, dart between Warren and me. "Colt, that's not true."

Warren points at her, but the hardness has left his voice. "My brother's got real shit he needs to recover from. And you're robbing him of the chance to heal by..." He nods toward the window. "Painting...fucking flowers."

"Shut up, Warren," I force out, but it's suddenly hard to breathe.

"This happy little fucking town ain't for us, Alice," Warren continues. "It's ain't for me. And it ain't for him." He turns abruptly and starts walking toward the street, nearly falling off the curb when he steps off it.

I stare at the ground, the world spinning beneath my feet. "Warren," I yell after him, glancing up. "You need to go to the hospital. Your head."

He waves an arm without slowing, brushing off the concern.

"I think it's best you both leave," Mr. Sinclair says from the porch.

"No!" Alice cries, reaching for me again.

I turn and pull her into a hug, because I can hear how her voice shakes, can see the tears streaming down her face, and my god, the last thing I want to do is hurt her. But her parents just watched two grown men fight in their old home, and they aren't going to leave their daughter alone after that.

"I'll be back in the morning," I whisper urgently in her ear.

"No!" she insists, panicked. "No, I'm going with you. We'll go the inn and—"

"Alice, baby." Her mom walks toward us.

"Let her go if she wants to," June calls after Mrs. Sinclair. "She's a grown woman."

Alice's mom holds a hand out to June, gesturing for her to stay out of it.

"No, Mama," Alice says when her mom approaches.

"First thing in the morning," I repeat, kissing Alice's temple. And then I release her, walking after where I last saw Warren.

Alice calls out after me, begging me to come back. It rips the heart straight out of my chest, because I can hear the pain in her voice. Pain that matches my own. And fear...

that what happened tonight just shattered what we had. Or rather, widened fractures that already existed.

"Colt!" Alice cries one last time.

I glance back once and see Alice's parents standing on either side of her, heads lowered, speaking quickly, urgently. They're talking her out of me. And as I walk away, chasing my past through the dark, I wonder if they're right to do so.

NOVEMBER

33
ALICE

I PRESS my forehead to my knees, pulling my legs tight against my chest. There are a thousand things I need to tend to before opening next Friday, but my body is too heavy to lift, my mind too foggy to think clearly. My parents finally left after a forty-eight hour vigil that made me feel twelve instead of twenty-two. Every fear I harbored that my parents would find this place—and me—lacking came to fruition.

The entire time I was working on this dream, a small voice in my mind whispered that I'd never pull it off. And when it came down to it, I didn't. Because I had a concrete goal to have this place operational by the soft opening, and it wasn't. My parents saw that, and they held a spotlight to the shortcoming the same way they have my whole life.

I am a constant disappointment.

They've called their realtor to get quotes on the house that was never quite a bookstore, and insisted that I'll fulfill my potential in Shreveport. *With us to supervise your every move,* they didn't add, but undoubtedly thought. If I ever had any misconceptions, I now know exactly where I stand in their eyes.

I wish I could say the same about Colt and me.

I tilt my head, pressing my cheek to my knees, and peer out the side window. The sky is an oppressive, wet gray; late afternoon already, and November at long last. A month I've counted down to since the defining moment Colt said, his hand raised in the air, *Let's fucking go, kid.*

I close my eyes, and it's a mistake. Because behind my lids, Saturday night repeats itself. I see my dad and Warren yelling at each other. I see Warren shoving Grant. And I see Colt—*my* Colt, steady as an oak tree—exchanging blows with his own brother.

And then I see him walking away from me in the dark. And while I know it's insecurity talking, it felt like—when Colt left—he was choosing his past, his brother, over any future with me. Like he'd seen who my parents really were and picked those who were familiar, however flawed, over those who'd outright reject him.

After the horrible thing my parents accused him of, I can't blame him for disappearing.

My body jerks at a sharp knock on the door. For a moment, I remain still, boneless. But then I force myself to my feet, body filled with lead, and trudge toward the front door. When I open it and see Colt standing on the porch, a smile flickers on my face, heavy, but there.

He wears a canvas jacket, collar turned up against the damp chill. He looks tired too, his jaw shadowed with stubble, eyes rimmed red in a way that says he hasn't slept any better than I have.

"Hey." His voice is low, almost cautious.

"Hey." I push open the screen door, hinges creaking mournfully. "Come in."

He steps inside but doesn't move far from the threshold. His eyes sweep over the room, but it's not unfinished tasks he's seeking. Instead, it looks like he's searching for physical evidence of he and Warren's altercation.

"Your parents are gone?" he asks, confirming what I texted him earlier.

I wrap my arms around my middle. "Yeah. Left like... thirty minutes ago."

Colt nods, stuffing his hands into his jacket pockets and gazing down at his boots. The silence between us isn't the comfortable kind we share while working on the bookshop. This one feels combustible, like something is about to be said that will undo everything we've built. I want to throw my arms around him. I want to *kiss* him.

No. I want him to do those things to me.

When he doesn't, I say, unable to stand still a moment longer, "I was about to feed the girls." I point toward the back door.

Colt's shoulders drop an inch, relief relaxing his features. He needs a task as badly as I do. Something to do with his hands. "I'll help."

We walk through the kitchen and out the back door without another word. The backyard is spongy from last night's rain, the grass transitioning into a dull, dormant brown. I breathe in the smell of smoke from a neighbor's chimney. It nearly makes me smile, imagining a fire in the bookshop's hearth, stockings and twinkling Christmas lights hung on the mantle.

The hens charge over, legs practically pinwheeling

because they know what we're good for. I toss feed onto the ground and then sprinkle out a few mealworms from the treat bag. Pickles, Mabel, and Dixie peck in a flurry of motion, trying to outeat the other two. Pickles pecks Dixie, scaring her off from the last mealworm.

Leaning down, Colt reaches for Dixie. She flattens her back, feet tap dancing on the ground, and he lifts her into his arms. He holds out his hand, and I sprinkle a couple of dried mealworms into his palm. Dixie pecks at them when he offers them to her.

Colt transitions to petting her, his eyes fixed on the docile hen. "Alice, I can't begin—" He sighs sharply, the air huffing out in a faint cloud. And then he shakes his head. "I'm so sorry, Alice."

My heart pounds in my chest and a tingling sensation shoots across my skin. Is this it? Is this apology a preamble to the end? "For what, exactly?" I ask. And what I mean is —*are you apologizing for what happened between us, or for what happened Saturday night?*

Colt finally looks up at me, his expression grieved. "For all of it. For ruining your party. For upsetting your family and embarrassing you in front of your friends. You worked so hard, and I screwed it all up for you."

I take Dixie from his arms. He lets her go easily, and I set the hen on the grass where she dashes back to the other two. "You didn't mess it up, Colt. There wouldn't have been a party without you." I can feel my voice rising, panic setting in because I don't like how he's looking at me. Like he's decided something, and won't change his mind. "My parents were out of line. And trust me, I told them so."

"They did what any parents would've done." Colt's voice is terrifyingly calm. "They were scared I'd done something to you. And they saw the way Warren behaved and remembered that..." He shrugs here. "That we come from the same place."

"But they *know* you," I snap, anger striking through me. "They had no right to accuse you of...anything. And honestly? Maybe Warren was right. Maybe they only gave you a place to stay because you helped Grant. My brother would've flunked his sophomore year if it weren't for you. So maybe they did have an agenda." I turn my face away, fuming. "I wouldn't put it past them."

Colt grabs my arms, his grip light but reassuring. "Hey. No. Don't turn on them. They're good people doing what they think is right. They shouldn't have left you alone when you were in high school. That pisses me off. But they *did* help me. That happened. Regardless of what their motivations were, they gave me a place to stay. They fed me, clothed me. They treated me like I was...one of their own kids."

Colt releases me and steps back, the sudden absence of his touch jarring. He shifts his weight, folds his arms across his chest, and looks past me toward the horizon, like he's working up the nerve to say something. "I, uh... I got an offer on my mom's place."

The words hit me square in the chest, nearly taking me off my feet. I knew this was coming, but I'd pushed it from my mind. Thinking about it—him selling, him leaving—was far too complicated to dwell on.

I manage a small nod.

"I still want to finish the bookshop," Colt continues

quickly. "If you want me to. The deal on my mom's place won't close for a few weeks anyway."

I turn away, pretending to check the latches on the chicken coop. Tears burn behind my eyes, but I refuse to let them fall. Because crying would mean this is really happening. That he was serious when he said he's only here until his mom's house sells.

I'd allowed myself to believe...

I straighten and turn back, forcing a smile onto my face. "Of course I want you to help finish the bookshop," I say, injecting lightness into my tone. "We started this together. We need to finish it together."

Colt attempts to return the smile. But it's no more convincing than mine is.

"And then," I say, forcing the words out. "And then you'll go back to Inwood. That was your plan, right?"

Colt glances at the hens, his jaw clenched. "That was the plan."

He seems upset. I think he seems upset. But I don't know why. Does he regret us? Does he want more of us? I wish he'd say something!

Anxiety twists my insides. I suddenly envision Birds Bookstore opening. I envision running it alone, with him three hundred miles away. No more waking up to his knock at my front door. No more cold pizza dinners, sawdust in our hair, Brooks & Dunn on the record player. No more stolen moments beside the house. Or in the shower. Or in my bed, his hands on me. My lips on his.

How can I bear losing him after I've learned what it's like to *be* with him?

"Hey," I say, pulse racing. "Let's go to the river."

Colt's brow furrows. "The river? Now?"

I grab his hands, gripping them. They're cold, but I squeeze his fingers anyway, afraid to let go. "Yeah. Right now. Just like we used to. Like we did when you first got back. Let's just go."

Colt's expression softens. "Alice—"

"Come on, Colt." I hear the naked plea in my voice. But I don't care what I sound like. I only care about keeping him. I already lost my parents' approval that I dared hope for. And I might lose this bookshop if it doesn't come together by next weekend. Losing Colt too? It's inconceivable.

"Please," I continue, "I'll just change into my tennis shoes. It'll take two minutes." I shuffle backward toward the house, a smile—practically a real one—stretches across my face. "Say yes."

Colt watches me for a long beat, wearing an expression I can't quite read. Finally, he lets out a breathy laugh and nods. "Okay. Yes."

I rush inside, taking the stairs two at a time. If I stop moving, the reality of everything will catch up to me, pin me to the floor. So I outrun it. I yank on my sneakers in a flash and fly back down the stairs.

Outside, he holds the truck door open for me, and I slide in, a smell I've grown to love greeting me—old leather mixed with the peppermint gum he keeps in the cupholder. Colt climbs into the driver's side and cranks the engine. The truck rumbles to life, and he shifts into reverse, throwing one arm over the back of the seat as he looks through the rear window.

The muscles in his forearm flex, and for a second, I just

watch him, memorizing his face, his mannerisms. My hands move nervously in my lap, twisting and untwisting, as I tell myself over and over again that he hasn't left. He's right here.

And that I won't be left alone.

Again.

34
COLT

ALICE WEARS a bright orange life vest that's too big for her small frame, but it's all they had left so late in the day. Her hair is pulled back into a high ponytail, reminding me of what she used to look like coming home from tennis practice.

"You good?" I check.

She nods, her smile eager in the fading light. "Yep!"

I push her kayak off the muddy bank and it thunks into the water, where she immediately begins paddling toward the middle. Once she's off, I slide my own kayak into the tea-colored water and jump in. The life jacket is a comfort against my body, a ghost of plate carriers I wore for many years.

As I paddle, my eyes drift toward the sky. We've got maybe an hour of light left, then we'll need to pull out. It took longer than expected to get the rentals sorted, but the river is glassy and calm, reflecting the loblolly pines and bald cypress trees that line the bank, and now that we're out here, I'm glad we came.

Alice is a few feet ahead, though I catch up easily enough. She smiles when our boats become parallel. It's too wide, that smile, not quite reaching her eyes. But I smile back, knowing last Saturday impacted her more than she lets on. I'd like to think she's doing what she always does—focusing on the positive—but this feels different. She's fidgety, anxious, and earlier, when she'd opened the door for me, I knew she'd taken her parents' disapproval—of her bookshop, of me—even harder than I'd feared.

I guess I did too. I still find it difficult to breathe when I think about how sideways everything went. She put in so much work, and then it all got fucked up...because of me. I want to hate Warren, and a part of me does. But he's also my brother, and always will be. We came from the same situation, but I joined the Marines. For eight years, I was surrounded by men, many of whom shared a similar background to mine. The Marines offered us a clean slate. A chance to start again. We fought hard, did what we were told, and in the end, more than anything else, we gained self-respect.

We *earned* that.

But Warren never had that transformation. He became a firefighter, but I don't know what he did before that. I don't even know if he's *still* doing that. What I do know is—despite how physically challenging and mentally taxing firefighting must be—it doesn't require the same radical reset that the Corps demands. And so I have to wonder how he's dealing with our past.

Alice stops paddling and looks around. "It's so beautiful out here, don't you think? I always thought Holly River was prettiest in the fall."

I nod to that, pausing my own paddle to hear a bullfrog croaking in the reeds. Up ahead, a Great Blue Heron wades in the water, releasing a dinosaurian cry.

"Only eleven days until the Fall Festival," Alice reminds me. "You're going to love it."

"You think so?" I watch as she trails her fingertips through the water. "And yet you still won't tell me what you're planning. You know, I could help if—"

Alice shakes her head, laughing. "Nope. You'll have to wait. I want it to be a surprise."

I smile because, for a moment, she seems genuinely happy again. "I'm sure I'll love it."

"What's your favorite thing about Holly River?" she asks suddenly.

I shake my head. "What'dya mean?"

"Like, what's your favorite thing about living here?"

I paddle, thinking on her question. I know what Alice is doing, but the truth is I don't have a lot of good memories about this place before I lived with the Sinclairs. The first memory that springs to mind is the summer carnival. Warren and I went every year because it was free to walk around. But we never rode the Tilt-a-Whirl or Zipper. Never had money for candy apples or cotton candy. To me, Holly River wasn't the postcard town Alice knows it as.

"I like how much you like it," I say finally.

Alice returns to rowing, faster than before.

Watching her—her graceful neck, adorned in a simple gold necklace—I find myself thinking about Mr. Sinclair, a man I'd thought of as a father figure. Even after the evolution I experienced in the Marines, returning to Holly River challenged the man I'd become. Reminded me with crystal clarity what I used to be. I was slapped with that reminder when Alice's dad openly opposed me dating his daughter.

But I understood it.

She's his little girl, and he wants the best for her. Though I imagine I'm doing better financially than he realizes, I reckon if he were picking a partner for his daughter, he'd want someone with a college degree. Maybe a future as a doctor, or an attorney, or as the founder of some promising company. Two well-to-do parents who'd make for solid in-laws. The kind of partner whose upbringing and future prospects matched or exceeded her own.

He wouldn't pick an uneducated Marine with a broken-down truck, two problematic parents, and an older brother who wreaks havoc on their home.

And I get that. I think if I had a little girl one day, I might want that for her too. So what does it say about me that, knowing all this, I still want to keep Alice for myself? How could I possibly let someone like her go? Someone who lifts me up and sees the best in the world. Someone with pitifully small hands I love holding, and a way of laughing that makes me feel like a person again instead of a weapon.

If she'd be better off without me, with someone who could give her a better life, shouldn't I try to let her have that?

I have to try.

We paddle for a long while, enjoying the scenery and silence. Then, up ahead, I spot the split in the river. To the left, the water remains calm. To the right, it gets choppy. "We should probably get out here. The light's fading anyway."

Alice doesn't slow. She's staring at the right fork, shoulders tight.

"Alice? Let's head back."

"You know," she says, her voice strangely flat, as if she's in a trance. "Holly River isn't perfect. I know that. But have you ever wondered why we have so many festivals and parties?"

She looks directly at me and smiles. It's a sad smile, and it absolutely shreds me.

"I think it's because people need it. Life is hard...for *everyone*, Colt. Everyone is struggling with things behind closed doors, even if it doesn't look that way on the outside." Her voice cracks, and she pauses. "And I think... I wonder if the people who love towns like Holly River, the ones who call them home, or those who travel to visit them, or even the ones who like to read about them in books... I wonder if those people aren't the ones hurting the most. And maybe they... They just need a place like Holly River to try and feel happy again."

Alice stops smiling suddenly. It's there and gone in an instant, as if she's lowered a mask she's worn for a decade. And when I see the raw pain in her eyes, it slams into me with the force of a battering ram.

I think about being in the Marines, having brothers in arms. I think about having Dalton, and later Grant, in high school and how them being there helped me survive what would've otherwise been unbearable.

I think about Alice alone at an age when having people —when feeling like you *fit in*—is more important than ever. I think about being ignored in hallways. Of sitting alone. Of being whispered about. Laughed about. I think about her turning towards her parents, hoping they'd fill that gaping hole, only to find them gone. Or worse, having them question her achievements.

I think about what that would do to someone.

Always feeling inadequate. Unaccepted.

And forcing yourself to smile through it all.

Alice turns toward the river. "I think I'm going to try it."

My brow furrows. "What?"

I turn and look at what she's fixed her eyes on. When I realize she means the right side of the river, the rapids—split by a giant, mossy rock—I stiffen. "No," I say immediately. "We'd need helmets for those rapids. And it's getting dark."

"They're class two," Alice says without taking her eyes off the split. "It'll be fine."

"No, Alice, there's been rain lately. They'll be closer to a three. You can't—"

"Yes," she snaps. "I *can.*" She starts paddling, digging into the water. "Get out now if you want," she clips. "But I'm doing it."

I know exactly where this is coming from, but there isn't time to dissect those feelings, because she's already less than ten feet from the split, paddling faster, shoulder blades working.

And for one asinine moment, I admire Alice's determination to reclaim a sense of power. I *understand* it.

I paddle hard until I've pulled ahead of her, seconds to spare until there's no going back. "Okay," I call out above the rising rush of water. "But follow my lead. If I signal, paddle for the bank immediately. You hear me?"

She nods, a spark of life flaring behind her eyes. "Got it."

I face forward, shake my head once, adrenaline pumping through my veins. "Alright, then," I yell. "Let's go, kid!"

My muscles scream as I propel my kayak into the fast-moving current. The roar of water grows quickly, drowning out the sound of anything else, demanding attention, respect. The transition is instantaneous. The calm, peaceful surface vanishes, replaced by a churning mass of brown and white.

The first drop is a two-foot ledge. I tuck my chin, hit it straight, cold spray hitting my face. I glance back. Alice hits it a little sideways, her kayak wobbling dangerously, but she recovers, working her paddle with a ferocity I didn't know she possessed.

"Thata' girl!" I yell, though I doubt she can hear me over the thunder of water.

The river narrows, hemmed in by steep limestone banks. The current is a living thing, bucking and twisting beneath the hull. I'm constantly adjusting, bracing against the water, eyes scanning for submerged logs.

I navigate a sharp S-turn, the water boiling into haystacks—standing waves that threaten to swamp the cockpit. The adrenaline soars now, everything else falling away. There is no Warren, no bookshop, no end to a beautiful thing. There is only the water and the next three feet in front of me.

I look back again. Alice is navigating a stretch between two large boulders. And she's crushing it. She looks strong, her arms moving in a blur of motion. In the fading light, I can see her face. She's smiling, laughing. Not the fake, brittle smile from earlier, but something triumphant and alive.

We reach a chute. It's a fifty-yard stretch where the river drops ten feet through a narrow gap. The water is a sheet of seething, unyielding white.

"Follow my line!" I shout.

I head into the center, kayak vibrating as it gains speed. I'm flying. The spray is blinding, the cold water soaking through my clothes. I hit the bottom of the chute, the kayak nose-diving into a wave before popping back up like a cork. I paddle hard to clear the stopper wave and pull into a small eddy behind a rock to wait for her.

I turn, my lungs burning, ready to cheer.

Alice enters the chute. She's perfectly centered, concentration absolute on her face. She's almost through. She's got it. But then something catches the bow. The kayak jerks violently to the left, and in a heartbeat, the craft flips. Alice's eyes widen, her mouth opening in a drowned cry. Her head slams against the limestone shelf with a sickening thud.

And then she's gone.

"Alice!" I roar.

I'm out of my kayak, diving into the freezing water without a thought. My body is instantly swept downstream, tossed like a rag doll. My shoulder hits a rock underwater, pain ripping through me as I reach the surface and gasp for air.

I search for Alice, sputtering water. But there's no sign

of her. Just white foam and a darkening sky. Panic explodes inside my head, jackhammers in my chest as I dive back under. My nose and throat burn as I open my eyes underwater, twisting side to side to look for Alice, but it's too muddy, too dark.

I come up, lungs screaming, and see a splash of orange bobbing twenty yards down. I swim with everything I have, muscles seizing in the cold. When I reach her, I grab the straps of her vest, flipping her over. She's limp. Dead weight.

"Alice," I yell. "Alice, look at me!"

Her eyes are closed, her face a terrifying shade of white. There's a pool of blood spreading from the back of her head and disappearing into the water. Keeping hold of her lifejacket, I swim one-handed toward the muddy bank. The current fights me every inch of the way, trying to pull us back to the center. My boots find purchase in the muck, and I scramble upward, dragging her into the grass.

I collapse beside her, coughing up water. "Alice. Alice!"

I check her pulse, put my ear to her mouth. She's breathing, but it's shallow. I call her name twice more, and when she doesn't answer, I lift her, starting to run. I've carried men twice her size through the desert. Run with a hundred-pound ruck until my feet bled. I run like I did then, with every ounce of my strength, heart on the verge of bursting.

I dive straight through the brush, thorns tearing at my skin, the mud trying to trip me. In minutes, I've reached the road, my breath coming in burning stabs. I lay Alice in the passenger seat of my truck, cranking the heat to full blast.

I drive like a demon, gripping the wheel so hard my knuckles ache.

"We're almost there, Alice. You're gonna be okay." My voice breaks, tears blurring my vision. I turn my head, just for a second, and see her fingers, blue-tinged and motionless.

I screech into the hospital parking lot, tire jumping the curb. I'm out of the door before the engine quiets. Cradling her against my chest, I sprint toward the sliding glass doors to the ER.

"HELP!" I roar, my voice cracking. "I need help!"

The fluorescent lights are blinding, and a few startled faces turn in my direction. An orderly takes three quick steps in my direction, then rushes toward a curtain. A moment later, the orderly reappears with two nurses and a gurney. I lay Alice down, my hands shaking, my pulse pounding.

"Please. She hit her head," I tell them, my words coming too fast. "She was underwater. I don't know how long. Maybe a minute."

Alice's skin is turning blue now, her breathing more labored.

"Sir, you have to stay out here," a third nurse says, placing a hand on my chest.

"No, I'm staying with her!"

"You need to check in at the front desk. We need her—"

I don't hear the rest of what's said. I'm too busy watching them roll the bed toward the back. One of the nurses is bagging her, forcing air into her lungs.

"Oh, my god," I breathe.

I try to follow, frantic, calling her name, but another

nurse joins the first, pushing me back. The last thing I see is Alice's hand hanging limp over the side of the bed, pale and small, swaying with the motion of the gurney as they disappear into the hallway.

The double doors swing shut.

And then she's gone.

December 2023

FPO, AE 09315-1234

Dear Alice,

I'm struggling with how to begin this letter. I guess I want to thank you for writing to me all this time. Has it been five years now? I think that's right. I know I haven't answered ~~as often you~~ lately, and I feel terrible about it. But I wanted to let you know that they mean ~~everything~~ a lot to me. More than I can express.

I'm thrilled to hear that college is going so well for you. I can't believe you're a sophomore already. You mentioned that meeting new friends has been challenging, but you seem really happy, so I bet you've met more people than you let on. I can't imagine someone not liking THE Alice Sinclair.

Alice, it's hard to write this letter. I'm

struggling with every sentence. You're such an optimistic person, and I think that's why I've hesitated to continue responding. Because it felt like I'd have to choose between lying, or dragging you down with me. If I lied, I'd tell you everything was great. That being a Marine is challenging but satisfying work. And that I've gotten to visit some really cool places.

But if I were being honest, I'd tell you that ~~I think I'm depressed~~ I get down sometimes. And that I've seen ~~horrible things that make me question whether people are worth saving~~ some bad things. I'd tell you that I sometimes wonder what I'm doing here ~~and whether any of it makes a difference~~.

~~I'd explain how your letters are often the only thing that keeps me from drowning~~ I miss you, Alice. I miss Grant and your parents. ~~And I miss my brother, and sometimes I even miss my mom.~~ ~~Especially in this place.~~ See? I've scratched out half this shit. And it's because I just want you to keep being happy. I NEED that. ~~Because I'm really scared that I may never be happy again after what I've seen. There was this woman whose child~~ No. I can't possibly tell you that. I can't even send this letter. I think something is wrong with me, kid. Sometimes I just wish

35
ALICE

COLT'S EYES are locked on the mug, ensuring the coffee doesn't spill as he nears my bed. He carefully positions the tray over my lap, and I push myself upright. This morning, he's made two pieces of thick French toast dusted in powdered sugar, a side of bacon, and a bowl of sliced strawberries. I doubt very seriously that he cooks this way for himself.

I catch his hand, squeezing it. "You don't have to keep doing this."

Colt lowers into the chair he placed beside my bed two days ago, right after getting me home from the hospital. He's barely left my side since, despite my protests that I'm fine. His hand moves to my cheek, and he strokes the skin there. There are worry lines around his eyes, an unmistakable fear stretched across his features. The look on his face says he failed me.

But the only person who has failed is me.

I lean into his touch, feeling like I should make a joke to lighten the burden he's wrongly placed on his shoulders.

But I can't summon the energy. Ever since last Saturday night, I've felt heavy. Like it takes too much energy to do anything. And I'm ashamed of that. I should be able to bounce back like I always have. But everything about building this bookshop has been so much harder than I ever expected. And I risked my parents' money and Colt's time along the way. If this dream were meant to be, wouldn't it have been easier than this?

My parents never looked as disappointed in me as they did last Saturday. As if they'd allowed themselves to believe that I might actually come through. And when I'd failed to deliver a finished bookshop, they'd been frustrated that they now had to parent me instead of celebrating my independence. I'd proved, once again, that while I have copious ideas, I am incapable of execution.

And then there was Colt. Wanting him was the easiest thing in the world. That man unraveled me, and made me feel whole. He set me on fire, and then burned beside me. He told me to leap, and then built my dream with his own two hands.

And yet here he was, slipping through my fingers.

"Do you need anything else? More water?" He reaches for the bottle by my bed and shakes it, seeming disappointed that it doesn't need refilling.

"I'm good." I force a smile onto my lips. "Actually, I do need—"

"What?" Colt leans in. "What can I do?"

I tilt my head on the pillow, my heart in my throat. We should talk about us, discuss what happens when he leaves. But all I can manage as my head throbs is, "Kiss me?"

Colt closes the distance between us at once, his mouth

capturing mine. He kisses me with fervor, his hands grasping my face, as if he's afraid I'll suddenly vanish. Our tongues brush, lips moving gently, and then with more urgency. For a moment, I don't think about how Colt leaving will shatter me. I only focus on the feel of his mouth against mine, the way his touch engulfs my mind.

Colt stops, pressing his forehead to mine. "Alice," he says, his voice a rasp. "I can't stop thinking about—"

There's a knock at the front door, and Colt jerks backward, his eyes darting to the window. "I'll be right back," he says. "Eat. Please."

As his footsteps echo on the stairs, I close my eyes, willing my head to stop aching. The dull pain comes and goes, along with bouts of dizziness, especially if I'm on my feet for more than a few minutes. All symptoms that should resolve within a few days, the doctor said. I'd been lucky, according to the nurse, to only need skin glue instead of stitches.

But I don't feel lucky. I feel like an idiot.

I pick up a piece of bacon, but before I can bite into it, there's a thunderous sound and then two women tumbling into the room.

"We're here!" Maggie announces.

June holds up a bag. "And I brought bagels! Oh. You already have food. Did Colt make that?" June leans over my tray, examining his work. "Not bad. This is the color you want on French toast. Though if he wanted, he could—"

"June." Maggie takes hold of June's shoulders. "Concussion."

"Right." June drops down in the chair, placing the bagels on the nightstand.

Maggie sits on the edge of the bed, her hand coming to rest on my leg. "How are you feeling?"

"You mean since you saw me yesterday?" I smile, feeling lighter now that they're here. "Ten feet tall and bulletproof."

"Should we test that theory?" Maggie pokes my stomach like she's making bullet holes.

I grunt, almost laughing, but it dies in my chest. Nodding toward the bag, I say, "Hit me with one of those."

June lights up and dives her arms in, producing a bagel swirled with cinnamon and packed with cranberries. I take a bite because I know it will please her. It's rich and gooey and golden brown, but I find myself struggling to swallow.

"It's incredible," I murmur.

June points at Maggie. "Told you she'd love them."

Maggie rolls her eyes. "So? Has Colt heard from Warren?"

I shake my head and keep my voice low. "Not yet. But I'm not sure if—"

"I still can't believe that guy. *Such* a prick," Maggie continues. "That dude thinks because he's all huge and has that...hair...and those...eyes...that he can just do whatever he wants. That's how guys like that are. And all that aggression? It's honestly really concerning."

June smiles knowingly, but remains quiet.

"What?" Maggie looks back and forth between me and June. "I'm serious. That guy's a walking red flag." She gives a full-body shiver and then pats my knee. "But don't you worry about him. Or about anything else, for that matter."

"Just worry about your bagel," June suggests.

Maggie nods to that.

"Did you bring the route plans?" I ask.

Maggie rolls her eyes and groans. "Woman? What did I just say?" But she produces a folder from her bag anyway and flips it open. "Yes, I brought it. I do as I'm told. But you really don't need to think about this right now. There are *nine* days until the festival."

"Exactly. Nine days is nothing." I spread out the sheets, relieved to be of value after my soft opening flop and an injury that has Colt and my friends waiting on me hand and foot. "You found someone to do pickups?"

"Dalton says he'll handle them," June confirms. "He's going to take them directly from the river to the Hall, which makes sense and will boost his business."

I nod to this. "And they can walk to the nearby shops from there."

"Right," Maggie agrees.

I sort through the pages, asking questions as they come to me until my head starts to throb. When I close my eyes for a brief moment, June touches my shoulder. "Alice, honey, are you sure you don't want us to call your family and tell them what happened?"

"No," I say quietly. "They'll just worry. And I'm fine. Everything is fine." But the words ring hollow, even to me. And when I open my eyes and see Maggie and June's concerned faces, fine is the last thing I feel.

Colt appears in the doorway, nervous fingers tapping the threshold. "Alice, maybe you should rest now. The doctor said to avoid concentrating on anything for too long."

Maggie looks up, her eyes narrowing as she takes him in. "Colt. Have *you* slept?"

When he gives an entirely unconvincing nod, she stands from the bed and moves toward him. Her tone turns hushed but insistent, and she guides him away from the doorway. She must imagine I can't hear her out there, but Grant and I learned as kids that our voices carry in the hallway.

"I'm good," Colt insists. "I have to stay awake to make sure she doesn't—"

"You're no use to her if you don't sleep," Maggie replies.

Colt says something I don't catch, and when Maggie responds, her voice is firm. "I understand you better than you know. Trust me."

My brow furrows at that, and when I glance at June, she looks equally confused as she strokes my hand.

Their voices raise, strained with concern, and I turn my head on the pillow, facing away from June. The movement triggers a pounding at my temples as I listen to their argument. To the sound of two people who care about me so much that it's hurting them.

June squeezes my arm. "They're just worried about you."

I want to tell her that they shouldn't be. That I'm okay. I want to bolt upright and devise a plan that entails charging ahead. Tackling these next nine days with a leader's evangelism to ensure that the bookshop's opening, and the Fall Festival, is a spectacular success.

But instead, I just close my eyes.

36
COLT

I DIP the brush into the paint can, wipe the excess against the rim, and then drag it along the replacement shelves. Seven days. That's all we have left until the Fall Festival. And somehow, it feels like the more I tackle, the more there is to do.

Countless times Alice has come down those stairs, insisting she help. But the doctor was clear—she needs rest. She's still getting headaches, and her spirit... Well, her spirit is injured far worse than her body. I've never seen Alice like this before. Hardly able to smile. The light in her eyes dimmed.

When I think about that moment in the river—

The paintbrush in my hand stills.

My heart pounds.

I'll never forget the sight of her still body in the water. I thought I'd lost her. For a moment, every good thing in my life was gone. To picture a world without Alice in it is unthinkable. Unbearable. She's still here, thank god, but something in her has died all the same.

But that's okay. Because I will do whatever it takes to put a smile back on that woman's face. I've filled the house with flowers from Maggie's shop, cooked all of Alice's favorite meals, and I will finish this bookshop on time if it kills me.

Alice always tries to show me how beautiful life is.

Now I'll remind her of the same thing.

Optimism doesn't come naturally to me. I'm trained to look for the ambush, the IED, the flaw in the plan. But for Alice? I'll learn to believe in the best-case scenario. I'll show her that she was right to believe in this place. And in me.

I've been working on a plan of my own. A plan like Alice once had. And after seeing Alice in that hospital bed, I know I have to finish it.

I stand, checking my phone. The tracking notification for the front window says it's scheduled for delivery tomorrow. Once that glass is in, the shop will stop looking like a boarded-up bunker and start looking like a business.

A sharp knock comes at the front door, and I spin around. At first I think it's Alice, who left a few minutes ago for her first venture out since the accident. She was dead set on going alone to get ingredients for baked apples. And though she won't admit it, I know it's because her mom used to make those when we weren't feeling well.

But it's not Alice out there. Between the gaps in the plywood, I make out a man's frame. He bends down, his shadow growing closer, and I gather that he's trying to peer inside the house.

I rush across the room and gaze through the peephole, finding exactly who I expect on the other side.

Travis.

I spin away from the door and lean flat against the wall, closing my eyes, forcing myself to take calming breaths. Because if I open that door, I'm going to beat the shit out of him. And I can't do that here. Not on Alice's property. That will give him the exact reason he's looking for to have this place closed before it's ever opened.

He knocks again, harder this time. "Colt. I know you're in there. I see your truck."

I stare straight at the kitchen, hands curling into fists. That bastard isn't stepping foot inside. If he does, he'll find more fabricated compliance issues. I'm not sure I can get this place done by next week as it is. If Travis issues another bullshit citation, we're finished.

"Colt," he shouts, pounding on the door. "Are you interfering with city-mandated inspections? Because if you refuse to address the issues I have confirmed reports about, I'll be required to issue a stop work order."

I gaze through the peephole again. The sun is setting, but even in the shadows, I can see that Travis is red-faced, wearing a long-sleeved button-down that's too tight across his soft gut.

"Fine," he sneers, looking right at the peephole. "I'll be back Monday with a formal ordinance and a sheriff's deputy if I have to. You're not opening this hazard to the public. Not on my watch."

He retreats toward the sidewalk, and I wait, statue-still, until the sound of his car fades completely. Then I spring into action. I set the brush in the kitchen sink and grab my keys from the counter. I'm moving on instinct now—a tactical focus that doesn't leave room for second-guessing.

I swing the front door open, heading for my truck, and nearly steamroll June.

"Whoa! Sorry!" she gasps, clutching a book to her chest. "Didn't mean to startle you. I just finished reading this and thought Alice..." June's expression shifts from surprise to concern. "Colt, what's wrong? Is Alice okay?"

My eyes flick to the street. "Travis was just here."

She *tsks* and shakes her head. "Oh, that guy is the worst. Tries to screw over her bookshop and then has the gall to ask her out?"

I flinch, the world tilting on its axis. "He asked her out? *Recently*?"

June's mouth falls open and she winces, realizing Alice didn't tell me. "Yes?" she says cautiously. Then, frowning, she forges ahead. "He was really hassling her, Colt. They were outside the market and he just wouldn't stop and—"

I storm toward my truck, blood roaring in my ears.

"Thank you, June," I call out. "Go on in. Alice will be home soon."

I slam my truck door closed and peel away from the curb, heading for my mom's place.

THE HOUSE SQUATS amidst the pines, my brother's rusted-out Chevy parked in the driveway. I don't bother knocking. I just shove the door open and walk inside. Warren is sitting at the kitchen table, a beer bottle in one hand and a half-eaten sandwich in the other. I want to kick the chair out from beneath him when I remember the defeated look on Alice's face at the soft opening. I want to finish the fight we started at her house and not stop until one of us folds.

Warren sets his sandwich down, looking at me with wary eyes, as if he can't decide whether to meet that energy.

I pace, crossing back and forth across the stained living room rug. "There's this guy," I explain. "This *fucking* guy that keeps interfering with the renovations. He's a city inspector. But only part-time, I think, because he's also into real estate and—" I throw my arms up. "It doesn't matter. He's trying to fuck with Alice."

Warren turns bodily toward me and takes a sip of his beer. He watches me over the bottle, then taps it down onto the table. "So," he says evenly. "Why aren't you doing something about it?"

"Because that'll just give him the ammunition he needs to shut her place down," I snap as Warren bites into his sandwich. "I can't do that to her."

Warren sighs, tossing his sandwich a few inches away. His eyes meet mine. "You forget who we are, baby brother."

I look at him for a long moment.

And then I nod.

"You wanna go?" he asks.

I stare at him, hesitating though I've already made up my mind. Without a word, I turn toward the door.

There's a scrape of chair legs against the floor.

And then there's Warren, following me to my truck.

~

IT'S FULLY DARK out now, and Alice is probably wondering where I am. But all I can think about is protecting her from this asshole who I should've handled the first time he stepped foot in her space.

I roll up to Travis's place. His address has burned a hole in my brain ever since the first time I looked him up. I think I'd always envisioned showing up on his doorstep the same way he does Alice's.

Warren cocks his chin toward Travis.

"That him?"

I nod, watching as Travis loads rental signs into the bed of his truck.

"Go on then," Warren says, already pushing open his door.

June's words fire through my mind: *He was really hassling her, Colt.*

Fuck this guy.

I get out of the truck, rage coursing through me, because now that I've allowed myself to really feel how much this guy pisses me off, I'm boiling. I flip open my toolbox and grab a screwdriver. Start powering toward Travis.

Travis turns, confusion sweeping across his face.

"What the hell are you—?"

I jerk my arm up, screwdriver clenched in my fist. Travis covers his head, falling backward. With every ounce of my strength, I slam the screwdriver into the sidewall of his tire. Then I'm on Travis, shoving him against his truck.

"You ask Alice out?" I snarl.

Travis starts to speak, and I slam him against his truck again. "You come by her fucking place? Try to force her into dating you? Is that what you're *fucking doing*?"

Travis tries to shove me off, then raises his hands.

I slap him, more an insult than anything.

Nearby, I hear my brother laugh.

"What the hell is wrong with you?" Travis roars. "You better get out of here before—"

"Before what?" I sneer. "What are *you* going to do?"

"I'll have your ass tossed in jail!" Travis tries to shake free from my grasp. Tries to kick me off him. "The second you leave, I'll report you—"

"Nope," Warren interrupts, his voice unfazed. He leans against the tailgate, glancing casually in both directions to ensure no one is coming. "I'm afraid you're mistaken. My little brother was with me all night."

Travis starts to yell again, but I grab him by the throat and slam him against the truck, even harder this time. His head bounces off the window, and his eyes glaze over for a second.

I lean in. "You think you'd be the first man I've killed, Travis?"

Travis stops moving.

"People always think soldiers kill with guns. But sometimes, Travis, it's with our hands. They train us how to kill with our hands. Just in case..." I search his face. "Just in case it ever comes to that."

"Colt," Warren says. "I thought you were just going to scare him."

"Changed my mind," I growl, knowing exactly where Warren is going with that comment.

"Goddammit," Warren mutters, shaking his head. "I'm not helping you this time. If you do this, I swear to God..." Warren whispers urgently. "Just let him go."

"No," I bite out, letting Travis see in my eyes the shit I

carry every day. The things I've seen and what it's done to me.

Travis raises his hands in surrender, his entire body trembling. "Okay," he says, voice shaking. "Okay, I'm sorry."

"Too late," I scoff.

"Colt, please!" Travis begs.

"Warren, give me that screwdriver."

"Okay," Warren says.

Travis breaks away from me, running for his front door. I grab him by the shirt and tear him backward toward me. He spins, stumbling, hands raised.

I punch him.

His head snaps backward and he falls to the ground. I wait while he curls into a ball, holding his jaw, moaning. Then I kick his boot with mine.

"Come around Alice again, and I'll put that screwdriver through your neck."

I turn and walk toward my truck, yanking the screwdriver out of his tire as I go. Warren pushes off the tailgate and follows after me. I glance back once and watch as Travis scrambles inside, slamming his door shut behind him.

The second he's out of sight, Warren shoves my shoulder, roaring with laughter. "He really thought you were gonna kill him."

I bat his arm away. "Get the fuck off me," I say.

But I smile, just a little bit.

August 2026
Holly River, Texas

Dear Colt,

I'm back home. Can you believe it? The plan was to live near my family after graduation. But I have an idea and want to give it a shot. The thing is, I'm really struggling to take the first step. I guess I'm doubting that it'll actually work. So, for now, I'm waitressing. Far less glamorous than what you're doing, saving the world and all. You know what's funny? I looked for you when I got back to Holly River. I wasn't expecting to see you here, but I really hoped I would.

Are you still in the Corps? I know you decided on another four years, but those are probably finished by now, right? It's strange that I don't even know if you're in the military. I'm not even sure you're getting these letters anymore. It's been a few years since I last heard from you, and that's okay. I promise I don't mind. The truth is, I think writing to you has helped me far more than it's ever helped you.

Do you ever feel lonely, Colt? Probably not. You

always seemed to make friends easily. You have a quiet, thoughtful way about you that draws people in. But can I tell you something? I've struggled with that. In high school, it wasn't always easy. I thought things would change in college, and to a certain degree, they did. But I never felt particularly close to anyone. I wonder if there's something wrong with me.

I've made a couple of friends here in Holly River. One of them was in your and Grant's grade. It's been wonderful having people to talk to. But I find myself scared, more than anything. Scared that they'll decide they don't like me anymore and will start excluding me. I even have dreams about it. Isn't that childish?

I miss you. Is that even possible? It's been over eight years since you left, and I still miss you. Do you want to hear something really sad, Colt? You'll probably think I'm crazy when I say this, and for once I'm thankful that you're probably not getting these letters. But, well, here's the thing... I think you were the best friend I ever had.

Love,
Alice

37
ALICE

HOLLY RIVER IS alive with the promise of celebration. Stringed lights sweep back and forth between light posts and wrap around pine trees. Pumpkins squatting on haystacks line Main Street, and silk maple leaves encircle the gazebo cupola like an ornate crown atop its head.

My headaches have stopped and the skin glue is gone, leaving only a thin pink line that I cover with my hair. I should feel happy, and *lucky*, that I'm okay, that the Fall Festival is only three days away, and that my final book shipment has arrived.

But instead, I feel exposed, as if I'm walking around skinless, vulnerable to the elements. And it's all because I can't stop thinking about Colt leaving. In three days, the festival will unfold—boisterous and enchanting—and then he will go, his job here complete. I can't believe I allowed myself to imagine he'd stay.

"That went as well as could be expected," Maggie says.

We're walking back from test running the festival attraction. And she's right, if it all falls into place, and it seems like it might, then it'll be even better than I hoped. "It's really something," I agree. "Everyone worked so hard on it."

Maggie bumps my shoulder. "Yeah and, you know, it was *your* idea."

I smile at her. "An idea is nothing without people to execute it."

"Which you *also* did," she reminds me.

My eyes travel from one neighbor's porch to another as we approach my place. It's like they're trying to out-decorate each other, and the overall effect—even if it does come from a place of competition—is breathtaking. I wish it lifted my spirit the way it normally does.

"It's too bad we weren't able to get those boats," I lament.

Maggie doesn't respond to that. Instead, she says, "You getting close on the bookshop? I can't wait to see you flip that sign to *Open*. I'm so proud of what you guys have accomplished, Alice."

I smile, grateful for Maggie's kindness. Colt and I really have given it our all, but there's so much more to tackle before Friday. "Finishing feels like digging a hole in sand," I explain. "Every time we knock out one thing, another pops up."

"Like gophers on a golf course," Maggie says. "Damn, we're killing it with the similes today. Is that right? Similes? Or metaphors?"

"Simile."

"Pssh. What do you know?" She winks. "So, what's left to do?"

I blow out a breath that fogs in the chill. "Everything.

I'm still manually correcting SKUs because the scanner hates books. And that damaged shipment? I've got to photograph every bent cover to get a refund. My middle-grade section looks bare, so I need to put in a rush order. The lightbulbs are emitting different shades of light, the front door sticks, the extension cords need hiding, my receipt printer needs unjamming. Oh, and Google doesn't have our hours listed and we still don't have a permanent sign above the door and— Should I keep going?"

We stop outside my house, and Maggie grabs my shoulders, forcing me to look at her. "You'll get there. I promise you, Alice. I was in the same situation when I opened Pardon My Garden. But you'll cross that finish line or my name isn't Maggie Aphrodite Rockefeller."

I laugh and pull Maggie into a hug, holding on for a beat too long. When I release her, Maggie's eyes move to the front porch, where Colt is crouched down installing new door handle hardware. He glances over his shoulder and waves.

"Hiii!" Maggie sings. Then, under her breath, she mutters, "Lord. You guys need sleep."

"He's been killing himself," I admit.

"He cares about you." Maggie starts walking backward. "Let him." She waves once more and then turns, heading toward her shop to finish her dahlia bouquets, which she'll wrap and sell outside her shop come Friday.

I walk up the sidewalk and Colt stands, wiping his hands on his jeans. Up close, the exhaustion on his face is unmistakable. He looks like he can barely keep his eyes open. And yet, he smiles at me, reaches for me. It's enough to make my throat tighten with emotion.

The last three days, we've worked until the windows went black. But after we fell into bed, utterly spent, we've still come together, lips on skin, hands and mouths drawing pleasure from each other's bodies before he's moving inside me. Few words are exchanged. We're too exhausted for that. Or perhaps it's that we don't know what to say, or what will happen after he leaves.

In the middle of the night, Colt always rises, shifting the mattress as little as possible before returning to the work downstairs. I know, because when I rise the following morning, tasks are completed that weren't the night before.

"Okay, Superman," I say. "It's time for bed."

Colt's eyes drift to the sky. "There's still light. Just need one more—"

"Colt, look at me." My voice is firm but quiet. The porch light catches the lines of fatigue on his face. "You need sleep. I know you've been getting up after we go to bed. Let me handle tonight's list." When he starts to argue, I take the screwdriver from his fingers, setting it on the railing. "Bed. Please."

Something flickers in his eyes—relief, maybe, or surrender. He lets me lead him inside and up the stairs to my bedroom. The house smells like the molasses candle I burned earlier, reminding me that I still need to eat dinner. I guide Colt until his knees hit the bed. He falls face-first onto the mattress, and I smile at the sight. As he buries his face in the pillow, I remove his boots, setting them gently on the floor. Then I cover his strong, wide frame with a quilt.

Before I've even reached the door, his breathing has evened out. I shut the door quietly and stand there, my heart full and aching at once. Padding back downstairs, I stop at the landing to admire how the last of the sunlight spills through the new window, making the book spines appear golden. It's a sheet of uninterrupted glass, that window, taking up almost the entire front wall, and it's exactly how I always envisioned it. For a moment, I feel unbridled satisfaction. The sight is enough to make me push up the sleeves of my sweater and get to work, even as fatigue pulls at my weary body.

Twisting my hair into a bun, I dive in. I start by sanding the front door just enough so that it no longer sticks, and then oil the hinges, ensuring it swings smooth and silent. The lightbulbs come next. I climb the rickety ladder and swap out every white bulb for softer ones so that the entire place glows ethereally.

I place a rush order for middle-grade titles, wincing at the expedited shipping cost, then zip-tie the extension cords and adhere them to the baseboards where, hopefully tomorrow, they'll be concealed by the new rug. As I work, I think about the night Colt arrived at my house after confronting Travis. He spared me the details of their altercation, but assured me that Travis was fine, and also that he won't bother us again. He also insisted that I tell him everything going forward, and I wondered—though I didn't say it aloud—whether he'd be around for me to do so.

After finishing the extension cords, I glance at the clock. It's 2:47 am. My back aches and my eyes burn, but I've made progress. If we had two weeks instead of three days, I'd be feeling entirely optimistic right now. But the clock continues ticking faster than my to-do list.

Stretching, I head toward the stairs. There's one more

thing I'd like to knock out since I'm on a roll, but first I want to ensure that Colt is actually sleeping. Lately, even when he's not working on the shop, he's on his phone, either scrolling or typing notes into an app. What it is he's doing exactly, I don't know. He's being very secretive for a man who insists on transparency.

The bedroom door creaks when I open it. Moonlight spills across the quilt, and Colt stirs, eyes blinking open in the dark. I cross to the bed and sit on the edge, my hand finding his head.

"Hey," I whisper. "Go back to sleep. I was just checking on you."

He's lying on his side, looking up at me. His fingers move to my thigh. In the dark, having just woken, his face is open, unguarded. He searches my expression, and the air in the room suddenly holds a weight it didn't a moment ago. Something profound passes between us—years of letters, months of working on a shared goal, learning each other. *Leaning* on one another. And days of unanswered questions.

"Why did you run from me, Alice?" he asks, his voice rough from sleep. "When you first saw me at the Hall?"

My heart flies into my throat. At first, I don't respond. Because I thought we'd safely sidestepped this conversation. But now, here it was, full-bodied and unavoidable. My hand moves to his cheek, brushing the stubble there. Inside my veins, my pulse thrums, making me feel flighty. But there's no place I'd rather be than here with him. So I summon my courage, and respond with honesty.

"I sent you a letter a few weeks before you got here," I admit. "I was scared you'd read it."

Silence stretches until I can hardly bear it. And then, Colt moves his hand to my wrist, squeezing gently. "I did," he says. "You sounded upset. You'd never sounded like that before."

I glance away, embarrassment flooding my face with heat. "You felt sorry for me?"

"No." Colt sits up, the quilt falling away. His hands cup my face, thumbs sweeping my cheekbones. "I saw you in that letter, Alice. I felt a kind of...kinship...when I read it. For years, I didn't write back because you always seemed so happy. And I didn't want to take that away from you by introducing my own...shit. But I should have. I should've answered every single one." He shakes his head. "I see that now. But that last letter you sent me... Yes, I was worried. But also... It made me feel like maybe you understood me more than I realized. And that we weren't so far apart after all."

Tears burn my eyes. "And so we found each other."

Colt nods emphatically. "Yes, Alice, we found each other."

I start to cry then, unable to silence the question that's burned inside my brain since he said his mom's house sold. "And for what?" I falter. "So I can have my heart broken when you leave?"

He drops his head, and the world holds its breath. I don't dare move. Don't dare speak. Because what he says next determines everything. If he confirms that he's leaving next week, I will crumble right here on this bed—a handful of ashes tossed to the wind.

Colt presses his forehead to mine, breath warm against my lips. "Alice," he says, his eyes closing. "I could never leave you." He kisses me once, soft. "You are my home." Another kiss, deeper. "You are everything I never allowed myself to want."

My heart sings, and laughter—rich with relief—bursts from my chest at his words.

"I want you, Alice," he continues. "Every moment of the day. I want to wake up beside you every morning. I want to go to bed with you every night. Building this dream beside you... It's been the best few months of my life." His mouth finds mine again, slow and sure, tasting of salt from my tears.

"You're not leaving? I whisper against him.

"If you want me to stay—"

"I do," I say fiercely. "Don't leave me."

"Never." The word fires from his mouth. "I will *never* leave you. I would live in your backyard if it meant staying near you. I would sleep in the chicken coop."

I laugh through the tears, and he smiles against my mouth.

"I thought I could go," he admits quietly, rocking his forehead back and forth against mine. "I thought you might have a better life with someone else. But when I saw you get hurt in the river—"

"No." My hands fist in his flannel shirt. "It's only ever been you, my Colt. It can only be you."

Colt grabs my face and kisses me with a longing I feel down to my bones. His fingers find the hem of my sweater, and he peels it up and over my head. The cool air hits my skin, but the warmth of his mouth is right there, kissing the slope of my shoulder and the hollow of my throat.

"You really came back after you got my last letter?" I ask.

"The second I got it." His hands slide down my ribs, pulling me against him. "I wasn't surprised to see you in the Hall that night, Alice," he says. "I was *searching* for you. My whole life, I've been searching for you."

Colt kisses me like he's sealing a vow.

And the heat between us ignites.

"Colt." I breathe his name, euphoria flooding my system.

He looks at me, eyes turning hungry, drinking in the sound of his name in my mouth. He pulls off my jeans and panties, kissing the insides of my thighs, my ankles, as he goes. The fatigue we felt moments ago is forgotten, replaced by the need to show each other how we feel.

"Lie back for me, baby," he murmurs, voice low but commanding. "Let me see you."

I do, spreading my legs. He settles between them, breath hot on my inner thigh, teasing, before ghosting over my pussy. "So perfect," he whispers, tugging me closer toward his impatient mouth. "Are you wet for me, my Ali?"

"Yes," I gasp.

He licks a stripe up my center, tongue warm and flat against my clit. I arch with a gasp and he groans in approval, the vibration shooting straight through me. "You taste so damn good. I could devour you whole." He sucks my clit gently, then harder, two fingers sliding into me. I clench around them, moaning. He pumps slowly, mouth never leaving my clit.

"That's it." He raises his head to watch me writhe beneath his touch. "Look at me, Alice."

My eyes find him at once.

"Watch me work your cunt."

I whimper, my head falling back.

"Baby," he urges. "Watch me."

I force my head up and watch as his forearm flexes, fingers disappearing inside me.

"You're squeezing me so tight already," he growls. "I can't wait to get my cock inside you. On your knees now, Ali," he says abruptly, as if recognizing he can't wait a moment longer. I obey, trembling with desire as Colt undresses, because I worship this side of him. The one that allows me to relinquish control and trust that he'll bring pleasure to us both.

He juts his chin toward the bed. "Hands on the headboard."

I watch for a moment longer as his cock springs free, thick and heavy. He strokes it a few times, then moves toward me. Turning, I grab hold of the headboard, already spreading my legs. Wanting him so badly I'm vibrating with need.

Because Colt is *here*.

And he isn't leaving.

Colt kneels behind me, cock nudging my entrance. He wraps one arm around my waist, holding me in place, then he buries his face in the crook of my neck. "Alice," he breathes as he pushes into me an inch. The emotion in his voice tangles with his lust, making my pussy throb. He leans back a touch, watching his cock disappear the rest of the way inside me. "Look at you," he groans, barely audible. "So beautiful stretched around my cock. And you're mine. All fucking mine."

I moan hearing that word on his tongue—*mine*.

He bottoms out and stills, letting me adjust, one hand gripping my hip, the other reaching around to circle my clit. "Move for me, baby. Show me how bad you need it. Show me that you're mine."

I rock backward, fucking myself on his cock. The words tumble out of my sweet, quiet Colt's mouth as I work myself, using his body for my own pleasure.

"That's my girl," he growls. "Take what you need."

The angle is deep, devastating.

Colt pulls out and moves me onto my back with a gentleness that belies the filth spilling from his lips. Filth I want to swallow whole and beg for more. I will never have enough of this man. Will never get enough of those abs, those biceps. The raw desire in his eyes and the feel of his cock buried inside me.

Colt slides back into me, his body covering mine. "Wrap your legs around me."

I lock my legs around his waist. "Yes, sir."

Colt's head snaps back, his eyes darkening. "Say it again," he growls, pupils blown wide.

A bolt of confidence fires through me at the look on his face. At the memory of him saying he'd do anything to remain by my side. "Yes, sir." I drag the words, biting my bottom lip. "I'm ready to obey your every command, sir."

Colt drops his head to my shoulder. "Fuuuuck me."

"Gladly." I rock against him.

Colt thrusts into me, his movements growing erratic. My hips meet every thrust, my fingers gripping the muscles in his back until he captures both wrists and pins them above my head, driving into me faster, deeper.

He slows, kissing me. Against my lips, he breathes, "Not done with you yet." He pulls out, lies back, and guides me on top of him. "Ride me, Alice," he instructs. "Slow at first. Let me feel every bit of you."

I sink down onto him and he grips my hips, guiding me as I start to move. Every rock drags my clit against him, making my vision dance and my breath quicken.

"Beautiful," he whispers when I sit straight up. His eyes sweep over my body, my face. "You're so beautiful."

He sounds reverent, entranced.

He sounds like a man in love.

I ride him harder, grinding my clit against his pelvis. He sits up suddenly, arms wrapping around my middle, warm mouth on my nipple when I arch backward. And then he's pulling me flat against his chest as I continue taking him. One of his hands slides up to cup the back of my head.

"Tell me you're mine." He moves faster.

"Yours," I say at once.

I'm nearly sobbing with pleasure now, my orgasm hurtling toward me with the force of a tsunami. My nails dig into his back as Colt thrusts upward into me. "Alice," he says again, that same tone as before. Broken. Vulnerable. Desperate. "Alice...I—"

"I know," I whisper, crashing my mouth onto his. "I know."

He kisses me like he's dying. Like this is the last thing he'll get to do on this green earth. His rhythm falters, hips snapping harder. "Come with me, baby," he murmurs, his lips against mine. "Come with me."

We crash over together, his cock pulsing deep inside me, my walls gripping him as ecstasy cracks me open, filling me with him, and him, and *him* until I know nothing but pleasure. Until my heart is so full from joy and our future that I fear I'll die in his arms.

After a minute, our chests still heaving, he eases out of me, pulling me into his arms again as we collapse onto our sides. His heart hammers against my back, his fingers sliding up to gently sweep my hair from my face. He leans forward and presses a lingering kiss between my shoulder blades.

A smile forms on my lips, and though I've worn many smiles in my life, I've never known one like this. "Colt?"

"Mmm," he hums against my skin.

"Maybe instead of sleeping in the chicken coop," I say, "you could sleep here. In this bed."

Colt doesn't respond at first. Then he backs up and pulls my shoulder until I turn to face him. His hand cups the back of my neck and his eyes are unwavering when he replies, "Anywhere you are, Alice Sinclair, that's where I'll be."

I smile at that, even wider than before, letting my head fall to his chest. When at last we succumb to sleep, me drifting off to the sound of his heartbeat steady against my cheek, one single thought shines bright and full of possibility in my mind—

Colt is my forever.

38
COLT

WE'VE GOT fifteen hours until we open this bookshop, and it's abundantly clear we won't be ready. The light fixture above the New Release section is dangling by its wires. Boxes of backstock are waiting to be stored. The chandelier needs to be hung. The accent chair needs assembling. And the window display, which will be a marvel once installed, isn't up.

And that's just what I can see from here.

Yet Alice seems happier than I've ever seen her. Since the moment we woke up, we've been struck dumb with lovesickness. Every time we pass within three feet of each other, we crash into one another, drawn by some invisible but irresistible force. I'll seize her waist, she'll hook her arms around my neck, and we'll spend ten minutes making out.

The exhaustion is there.

But the dopamine is stronger.

I'm high on the fact that I'm not going anywhere. That I'm staying in Holly River, and it's because she *wants* me here. At this point, if Ali asked me to clear every loblolly pine in East Texas with a hand axe, I'd be halfway through the first acre before she finished the sentence.

I'm not sure I ever allowed myself to admit how much I wanted this. Since the first time I kissed her... No, from the first moment I *saw* her when I returned to Holly River—grown, gorgeous, the same woman who never deserted me—I knew I wanted her. But at the time, I didn't believe I deserved happiness, and I wasn't used to life working out the way I wanted it to.

This time, though, it had. And as long as Alice would let me, I'd bring home her favorite pie from June's shop (cherry), and take care of her hens (even Pickles). I'd rub her feet after she'd been on them all day running the bookstore—just to hear those wonderfully erotic moans she makes—and act out every book boyfriend scene she wanted, especially those involving nudity.

I'd decorate for the holidays just the way she liked and take her dancing at the Hall whenever she felt the itch. I'd do all of that and more—anything, really—if it makes Alice happy. Because she's already made me happier than any one man has a right to be.

That's why the bookshop not being ready kills me. Because I want to give this to her and for it to be perfect. We're close, so painfully close. But the fact of the matter is, the shop won't be ready by tomorrow. We'll be able to open, but it won't be as Alice envisioned. At least not for the first week or so. And such is life. When one thing goes well, another falters. But as long as Alice still wanted me? Well, the entire planet could drop out from beneath my feet and I'd still grin.

Alice grabs the stepladder, unfolds it, and starts to climb.

"Not a chance." I hook my arm around her waist and sweep her off the rungs before her feet can clear the second step.

Her laughter rings out as she reaches backward for the ladder.

"What did I say?" My lips find her neck, biting playfully. "No more than six inches off the ground at all times. My heart can't handle another injury."

"You're being ridiculous."

"Can't be too careful."

"You can, actually." Alice points at her rolling library ladder. "What about—?"

"Off limits."

She pulls back, eyes wide with mock horror. "You can't be serious."

I heave her into the air and recatch her, tightening my grip. "In fact, to guarantee your safety, I should carry you everywhere you need to go."

Alice nods toward the fantasy section with a grin. "Well, I need to move that row of books up."

I carry her to the wall. "Proceed."

Alice laughs again, briefly dropping her head against my chest. Then, with a regal expression—as if one really should be carried everywhere in one's own shop—she starts to reorganize the wall. "There," she announces. "Perfect." She beams at me, and then her eyes sweep the room as if deciding what to tackle next. A subtle shadow darkens her features, and she smiles sadly. "I wish everything could be perfect for opening day."

The admission, finally voiced aloud, twists my insides. Though I know Alice places the blame on her own shoulders, this is my failure. I talked her into taking the leap. I promised to help her. I'm the one with the carpentry skills, only half developed, so it was on me to finish the renovations.

I open my mouth to apologize, but am interrupted by a knock at the door. Immediately, I'm on alert, my mind jumping straight to Travis, but surely he doesn't have the balls to show up here again. Setting her down, I hold my hand out, gesturing for Alice to stay put as I move toward the entrance.

When I peer through the peephole, my muscles relax.

I swing the door open.

"Howdy, partner." Maggie raises her arms, a bottle of champagne in one hand and a flower arrangement in the other. "To a fully finished bookshop!"

I push open the screen door. "I don't think that's in the cards, but—"

"Not alone, it's not." Maggie steps aside.

The breath stills in my lungs, because standing in the yard is a small army of people, only some of whom I know. June, Roxanne, and Dalton stand arguing over something while—off to the side—Frank and Grant share a laugh. From across the street, I see Alice's neighbor, Mrs. Devonshire, walking in our direction, Harold at her side.

Alice comes to stand beside me, her eyes wide. Confusion crosses her face at the sight of the half-dozen strangers.

"Oh, them?" Maggie says. "They're followers. And fans! They traveled a day early to be a part of the bookshop's completion."

"Y'all are here to help?" Alice asks, stupefied.

"We can't *wait* to help, honey," June calls from the yard. "We're so excited to have a bookshop in Holly River. We weren't going to let you do this alone."

Alice flies through the door and onto the porch, throwing her arms around Maggie. Then she turns and waves everyone toward the house. "Come in! Please come in! I'll put on some music. I...I can't believe this."

Alice and I shake hands with the strangers—her followers—who even brought their own toolboxes. They introduce themselves, explaining how much her journey meant to them. And then everyone disappears inside.

I remain on the porch for a second, shell-shocked. Somewhere along the way—whether it began in childhood or in the military—I'd decided that people were, at their core, selfish. It made the festivals and gatherings in this town seem like the product of ignorance. People who either didn't realize how troubled the world was, or didn't care.

But as I watch through the window as friends and strangers spring into action to assist us, I can't help but wonder if the truth isn't more complex. That perhaps human beings are capable of both terrible things *and* profound kindness. And that maybe whichever I look for is the one I'll see. My entire perspective, the one I've used to survive since I was a kid, shifts a few inches in a new direction.

"Colt."

I turn to see Alice holding open the screen door, her angelic face glowing.

"Come on, handsome," she says. "We can't do this without you."

I smile and follow her in.

Alice starts the old record player because the new speakers aren't yet wired. Everyone cheers when the needle drops and Dolly Parton's "Working 9 to 5" fills the small space. People scatter, each working on projects that Alice or I assign. June and Mrs. Devonshire take over the coffee station, unpacking mugs and setting up the brewer. The visitors start hauling boxes of backstock to Grant's old bedroom, which serves as a temporary storage solution.

I'm showing Harold where to mount the paper towel dispenser in the bathroom when Roxanne taps my shoulder.

"Colt." She inclines her head. "There's someone at the door for you."

I nod, confused, but thank her and navigate between the bodies toward the porch. When I push open the screen door, I find Warren standing on the other side. He looks uncertain, hands shoved deep into his pockets, posture stiff.

"Hey," he says, looking down at his boots and then at the window to see who's inside. "Alice texted me."

I glance over my shoulder at Alice, who's busy filling the glass jar on the checkout counter with June's chocolate chip cookies. *That woman*, I think, shaking my head fondly. I really need to start hiding my phone from her.

"I can go if you want." Warren meets my eyes. "But I'm not here to cause problems." He lifts his hands in surrender. "I swear."

I consider him for a moment longer, gauging the genuine expression on his face. Remembering that he helped me with Travis the other night, and hasn't said shit about it to anyone. Nor did he make the situation worse, which I half-feared he would.

I sigh and shove the door open wider. "Grab a hammer."

Warren nods and follows me in. He moves toward the toolboxes situated in the middle of the room, and he and Grant lock eyes. Warren abandons reaching for a hammer and straightens. He takes a step toward Grant and a few words are exchanged, none of which I can hear over the music and the sound of people chattering. But I do see Grant nod, though his face remains wary, his gaze watchful.

When Warren walks off, Grant catches my eye and comes over.

"Your brother's a fucking menace," he says, watching as Warren kneels down to address the baseboards.

I nod. "That he is."

"Can't tell if I like him or hate him."

I nod to that too, because I can relate.

Grant slaps my chest. "Hey. Hey."

I look at him. "Don't fuck my sister."

I smile a little.

"Like, I approve and shit. But you guys can never, ever touch intimately."

"Got it."

"And if one day you guys want to have kids or whatever," he continues, "adoption is the answer you're looking for."

"No sex," I confirm.

"Good man." Grant hits my chest once more. "My, uh... My folks will be here tomorrow. They were pricks, alright? But they've had time to think about it, and they know that now. Also, because I've told them repeatedly that they were pricks." Grant pauses. "Maybe give them a chance to redeem themselves? For Alice's sake?"

"Grant?"

"Yeah?"

"Frank is taking money out of the register."

"Yeah. I'm on it."

I follow Grant over, deciding to hang the Employees Only sign on the swinging door that leads to the kitchen. Mostly because it'll allow me to keep an eye on both Frank and my brother.

"I remember you," Frank says when Grant approaches him. "You're the football kid."

"Hey, Frank," Grant responds, taking the cash from Frank and putting it back in the register.

"Oh, I wasn't gonna..." Frank begins, before trailing off and putting his hands on his hips, belly protruding as he examines the room. "This gonna be a bookstore, huh?"

"Nah," Grant replies, shoving the register drawer shut. "A titty bar."

Frank barks a laugh. "See, now that I'd patron."

"Tell me about it," Grant responds.

I shake my head, biting back laughter as I apply Command strips to the sign.

"You know, I went to Dallas once," Frank declares. "Awful city, but they had this place called The Milk Bar. All the cereal you wanted. Different kinds."

"That's dumb," Grant says.

"It is dumb, Grant. It *is* dumb. But I liked one thing alright. The name. *The Milk Bar.*"

Grant nods to this.

"Got me thinking about titty bars."

My head snaps to the side in confusion, but Grant just says, "Yeah."

"I started wondering...what if there was a titty bar that featured older women."

"Older?" Grant asks.

"Yeah." Frank picks up a book, examines it, and promptly puts it back down. "We got plenty of younger titties. What about the older ones? That's where the money's at. Niche business."

Grant cracks open a Dr. Pepper, considering this. "Would people pay to see older tits?"

"Oh, my god," I mutter to myself.

"Hell, yeah, they would!" Frank looks at me like *Who is this kid?* "Older women, they got them seasoned titties. Them *seen the world* titties."

Grant's gaze slides toward the ceiling, and I can see that he's thinking hard. Perhaps for the first time in his life. He opens a hand and arches it over his head like a rainbow. "Seen the world...titties."

Warren pipes in from his place near the floor. "It kind of makes sense."

Frank whistles from the corner of his mouth and points aggressively at Warren, as if he just proved his point. "Alls I know is that as a woman ages, her hips get bigger." Frank opens the glass jar and pulls out a cookie, waving it at Grant before biting into it. "You ever heard a man complain about a woman's hips being too big?"

Grant shakes his head. "No, sir."

"Damn right, no sir!" Frank bellows.

Frank and Grant continue strategizing their strip club,

managing to complete at least some work while they talk, and by midnight, the impossible has happened. The books are shelved. The floor is swept. The POS system is operational. Even the coffee station has been stocked. The shop isn't just complete; it looks like it's been a Holly River staple for thirty years.

Alice stands in the center of the room, looking around with exhausted, teary eyes. She waves a black Sharpie and raises her voice above the cacophony. "Before we hang the sign, I want everyone to sign the back of it."

People file over to sign the large wooden sign leaning against the wall. They scrawl their names as Maggie films, and when Alice notices that Warren doesn't move from his spot in the corner, she strides over and flips a second pen toward him, eyebrow raised playfully.

Warren looks at her, surprise opening his face.

He smiles and takes it, and Alice gives him a playful shove toward the sign.

If I could want that woman anymore than I already do, I would. But I'm afraid that's impossible. So I just walk over and wrap my arms around her, pulling her against me. "Thank you," I whisper in her ear.

Alice gazes up at me, emotion raw in her eyes. "Your turn, cowboy."

I lower my head to kiss her and—from across the room —I hear people cheering.

My head pops up and I spot Alice's followers celebrating the fact that we're kissing. I glance at Alice and she laughs, shrugging as she calls out, "It's true. We're dating!"

They whip their phones out, no doubt posting the

news that every Birds Bookstore follower suspected—or at least hoped for—thanks to Maggie's social media strategy.

As I walk toward the sign, Grant catches my gaze and puts two fingers beneath his eyes and then points at me, like he just saw me kiss his sister. I laugh and sign my name, then toss the pen and hoist the board.

"Alright," I say. "Let's get this baby up."

Grabbing the ladder, I head outside. Alice follows me with the mounting brackets. I position the sign directly above the entrance, and Alice climbs the ladder to hold the other end.

"Six inches," I say under my breath.

Alice laughs, a sound I will never tire of.

I bolt the brackets into the header above the door, then slide the sign into place, locking it down. Everyone streams off the porch and into the front yard. The early morning air is freezing, our breath hitching in white clouds. Maggie hands out champagne flutes and raises her phone to record Alice's moment of triumph.

"Ready?" Alice calls out, her hand on the light switch.

"Wait!" Maggie shouts. She runs back inside, and a second later, the opening chords of Journey's "Don't Stop Believing" blast over the newly installed speakers. She sprints back out, so focused on capturing Alice's achievement that she misses the last step.

She stumbles, arms pinwheeling, a second from face-planting when Warren catches her.

Maggie crashes against his chest, and for a second, neither of them moves. But then Maggie says, "Let *go*," and Warren releases her, an annoyed look on his face that says he wants no part of women right now, and especially not *that* one.

Maggie brushes herself off and turns back to Alice, phone raised. "10, 9, 8..." she begins.

The crowd joins in. "7, 6..."

I lean toward Alice, lips brushing her ear. "Look around, kid. This is your moment."

"...3, 2, 1!"

Alice flips the switch.

The Birds Bookstore sign erupts in light. It's backlit with a warm, golden hue that silhouettes the letters against the white house. The sign shines impossibly bright, throwing an amber glow across the scattered pumpkins, illuminating the faces of those who helped make this possible.

The crowd cheers, and June dabs at her eyes, laughing. Even Frank claps. Alice beams, her face upturned toward the sign, the light reflecting in her eyes like stars. And it's in this moment—with the music swelling and Alice smiling at our friends and family—that I know something pivotal in me has changed. And that before me lies a future paved with good things, if I'm brave enough to believe I deserve them.

If I'm willing to admit that life isn't one thing or another.

It's just that—life.

Hard and ugly, but also beautiful and surprising just when you've counted yourself out. And if you're lucky—if you're really fucking lucky—you can experience all of it, the good bits and the bad too, beside someone who loves you.

Who will hold you and say, *Look there. There's a bit of good right there on the horizon.*

And you'll do the same for them, time and again.

39
ALICE

I TURN IN A SLOW CIRCLE, taking in the moment. Today is the Fall Festival, and I'm standing in the center of my finished bookstore. With so much at stake, my heart should race, my pulse should quicken, but instead I am perfectly calm, like I've been holding my breath my whole life and can finally exhale. I've never been this happy. It's a crystalline joy that could shatter if I speak too loudly, and yet it's moored by the weight of a thousand books.

What used to be the downstairs of my childhood home is a transformation I can't believe we conjured. White oak shelves stretch floor to ceiling—giving the space a bright, airy feel—crowned with elaborate molding. The front window dominates the street-side view, and morning light pours in buttery bright, igniting the gold-leaf book spines and turning the pale blue rug into a shallow, sunlit pool.

Colt leans against the wall, thick arms folded across his chest. He wears blue jeans and a white long-sleeved shirt, pushed up to reveal corded muscle in his forearms. He smiles from the corner of his mouth, watching me soak in the moment with a look that's half pride, half hunger. I return his smile, chest tugging at the sight of him there, standing amidst what we built.

Behind Colt is the blue and white landscape wallpaper I chose. It covers the stairwell wall and embraces the front window. Above us hangs the crystal chandelier that took ten weeks to arrive, an explosion of frozen raindrops that catch the light. My fingers trail along the shelves, brushing softly over the rolling ladder, brass wheels gleaming against the rail. I glance back at Colt with a mischievous tilt of my head. He lifts his eyebrow in warning before the playful sternness melts into a devastating grin.

After everyone left last night, I hardly slept. I lay in the dark, vibrating with excitement, my future singing through the floorboards beneath my bed. Outside, the town is waking up for the Fall Festival. Soon, sidewalks will fill with tourists and my door will be thrown open, ready to welcome our first customers. But right now, in this final, quiet moment, I stand on a bridge—one that stretches between the girl who dreamed this, and the woman who did it.

For years, I battled the idea that I didn't have the fortitude to follow through on a dream until the very end. But it turns out, even though it was far more challenging than I ever could have imagined, I had it in me all along.

I continue my lover's caress of the bookstore. *My* bookstore. My fingertips reach the checkout counter. It's a long, inviting slab of wood, with plenty of space for customers to set down their books. A glass jar housing June's cookies perches on one end, Maggie's flowers on the other. Behind the counter, floating shelves wait patiently, ready to collect pickup orders.

And then there's the framed chalkboard.

In careful calligraphy, I've written out this week's book recommendations. By next week, the list will consist of customer favorites along with a hidden gem, all featured like rotating ice cream flavors at a parlor.

Leather armchairs sit in a spill of light from the staircase window, appearing well-loved though they're new, and against the far wall, a sapphire-blue couch is joined by more leather chairs and a coffee table. Through the archways, what used to be the downstairs guest room and office are now additional library nooks. Their ceilings are adorned in shimmery blue wallpaper and miniature chandeliers, and each room has its own leather chair and matching side table. The seating, sprinkled throughout my shop, is an invitation to linger, to disappear into a book and forget the time.

I've returned to the front window, gazing outside when I hear Colt moving behind me. The pumpkins that dress my porch steps catch my eye, and I smile at them as his strong arms wrap around me, pulling me close. My bookshop—and every last miraculous detail of it—recedes into the background when I turn and face him.

Colt leans down, lips grazing my ear. "Are you ready, Alice?"

"I'm so happy, Colt," I admit, my eyes slipping closed. And I am, but I also find that I'm rattled. Because I almost didn't do this. In another life, I didn't take the leap, and I'm not standing in the bookstore that I dreamed of, fought for, and cried over for months. In another life, I don't realize just how much the hard work pays off. And that thought—far more anything else—is what's terrifying.

Because here's what I've learned—

Chasing a dream is messy, the progress nonlinear, the self-doubt merciless. And the end result is rarely what you envisioned. But the end is still an end. And you can hold it to the light, turning it this way and that, saying quietly to yourself, *Look. Look at what I created. It was very hard and very messy. But here it is.*

He pulls back just enough to soak in my expression, and then he kisses me. His lips are eager, his hands sliding up my back. Our tongues touch, a slick heat that has me bunching the fabric of his shirt and whimpering into his mouth. Desire pools between my thighs, and already I imagine the things we will do when this day is over. Colt breaks the kiss, but keeps our foreheads pressed together.

"Open your bookstore, Alice," he encourages me. "Show the world what my girl did."

"What *we* did," I clarify.

He gives me one last squeeze, a silent acknowledgement, and steps back. I walk toward the door, so giddy with excitement that my hand trembles. What if no one comes? What if they do, but I don't get enough sales to prove the shop's viability? I glance over my shoulder at Colt and see the unwavering belief in his eyes.

My hesitation vanishes.

I flip the sign from *Closed* to *Open* and let out a squeal of exhilaration.

FIVE HOURS LATER, the sanctuary of this morning is long gone. And so are any doubts I held. Because the shop is a symphony of sound and motion, and the door hasn't stopped chiming since nine o'clock. It's a success so absolute that the last iota of uncertainty I carried lifts from my shoulders, floating away.

People meander through the room, sinking into chairs and pointing out the rolling ladder and raindrop chandelier. A woman pauses under Maggie's flower arch to capture a photo, and another patron rocks on the front porch swing, engrossed in the book she bought while her son devours one of June's cookies.

Behind the counter, I ring up purchase after purchase. Not just for books, but for river attraction tickets too, something Maggie insisted upon. And she was brilliant for doing so, because it's lured in customers who might not have otherwise visited.

"These flowers are incredible," a customer sighs, leaning in to smell Maggie's arrangement. He turns to his husband while I ring up his books. "I saw a woman selling flowers on the sidewalk. Let's get some for our room." The man's husband nods and, even though I'd decided on one free cookie per transaction, I slip the happy couple an extra one when I notice them eyeing the jar. Then, before they go, I explain how to get to Maggie's street setup from here.

In the middle of the rush, June slips through the door, her dress dusted with flour. She weaves through the crowd and pulls me into a rib-crushing hug. "Alice, look at this!" she cries. "It's a raging success. I told you, didn't I?"

"You did tell me." I squeeze her back. "And the cookies are a hit! People are going crazy over them."

"I know that too," she grins. "I've already had a half-dozen customers come in asking for more." Her eyes dart around the shop, landing on a figure in the romance section. "Is that Mrs. Devonshire?"

I lower my voice. "She's been there an hour."

June waggles her eyebrows suggestively. "Mrs. Devonshire is freaky. I like it."

At that exact moment, a group of teenagers meanders too close to Mrs. Devonshire and, though she looked as if she might actually make it to the register this time, she quickly reshelves the book. Then she ducks her head, smooths her sensible coat, and scurries out the door.

"Damn," June says. "Almost had her."

A moment later, the door chimes again, and Harold stomps in. He pulls his cap low over his eyes, ignoring the crowd, and marches straight to the counter. "Loretta come in yet?"

I exchange a knowing look with June. "You just missed her. She left not two minutes ago."

Harold's face falls. "She said she was gonna come by around two."

"She did," I explain. "She was browsing for a while, but I think the crowd scared her off."

Harold's bushy eyebrows rise hopefully. "She buy any books?"

"No," I lean against the counter for the first time all day, grateful to give my feet a break. "But it looked like she wanted to."

I point out the romance section to him, gesturing to the particularly steamy shelf where Mrs. Devonshire spent the most time. Harold plucks a title off the shelf and starts flipping through it.

June and I stand shoulder-to-shoulder, lips pressed together to keep from laughing. Harold's eyes slowly widen, brows migrating toward his hairline. "You sure it was these?"

"Hmm, hmm." I nod.

Harold grunts, examining the shelf a beat longer. Then, with two hands, he seizes the length of books, removing the entire row, and sets them on the counter. I ring him up, unable to halt the smile on my face, and catch Colt's attention so he can restock the empty shelf. When Colt sees who's buying what, he tips an imaginary hat in Harold's direction.

"Oh, take this too." I bag one of June's cookies and hand it to Harold. "On the house."

Without another word, Harold leaves, two bags of romance novels swinging from his fists. He beelines for Mrs. Devonshire's house, stepping past Maggie as she slides inside the bookshop.

"What are we looking at?" Maggie asks, joining us by the front window.

"Harold bought Mrs. Devonshire some slutty books," June explains.

The three of us practically press our noses to the glass, watching as Harold knocks on Mrs. Devonshire's door. She swings it open, and we hold our breath. They talk, he shows her the books, and Mrs. Devonshire's face breaks into a slow smile.

"Yeah," Maggie mutters as Harold goes inside. "Get ya some."

I pull my friends away from the window, laughing, and rush back to the counter when I spot a customer. After I scan their books, I add a bookmark and a sleeved cookie to the customer's bag, thanking them before turning back to my friends. "What are y'all doing here?"

"We came to relieve you." Maggie steals a cookie from the jar. "You're going to miss the entire river thing, which *you* came up with."

"But I can't leave the store," I argue.

Maggie looks at June. "Are we useless?"

"Do we not have arms?" June adds.

Maggie glances back at me. "You think we haven't run a register before? Or restocked shelves?" Maggie rounds the counter and takes my shoulders, guiding me away from the register. "We can cover you for an hour. Unlike you, we have part-time employees, which I strongly suggest you hire. Now go!"

I laugh, asking if they're sure, but June is already handing me my sweater and waving down Colt to go with me. I barely manage another protest before they've effectively evicted me from my own shop.

"I guess we're going to the river." I smile and give Colt a helpless shrug.

Colt takes my hand and raises it to his lips, kissing my knuckles. It's the first second we've had to connect since customers started pouring in, and I suddenly find myself longing to hug him. To *kiss* him. To maybe even spend the free hour in our bedroom instead of...

Colt releases my hand, his smile vanishing.

I spin around, following his gaze, and see my parents standing on the sidewalk. They're watching people flow through the bookshop, their faces open with surprise. When they catch sight of me, their expressions morph into something cautious, but warm.

My parents walk toward Colt and me, and I note that my brother is with them. He stayed at the inn last night, saying he wasn't about to overhear *something* and be forced to put his head through a window.

"Alice." My mom looks at the shop, then at me and Colt, her eyes bright with wonder. "It's...it's *beautiful.* I can't believe what you've accomplished since we were last here."

"Told you," Grant says.

"Colt." My dad takes a small step forward. "I wanted to... *We* wanted to apologize for what was said at the soft opening. I was out of line." His cheeks flush with embarrassment.

Colt starts to say something, but my dad forges onward as if he needs to get this out.

"We've had the pleasure of getting to know you very well, and when we slowed down to actually remember that, we realized that... Well, we should be so lucky to have Alice date a young man like you. If that's what you both want."

I take Colt's hand, lacing my fingers through his. "It is."

My dad looks at our joined hands and then nods. He reaches out his own hand and, after a heartbeat of hesitation, Colt shakes it. My dad smiles a little, shoulders dropping in relief. Then his eyes trail to the bookshop. "We underestimated you, Alice. It appears you're the dark horse of the family and a real visionary. Look at this place."

We all turn for a moment and admire the hand-carved

sign, the flower arch, the carefully crafted bookshelves and buzzing customers visible through the window.

"Will you show us around?" My mom looks at me with such hope in her eyes that I feel myself soften.

"We have to run right now," I tell them. "But y'all should go inside and check it out. Maybe we can meet up for dinner."

I glance at Colt to gauge his reaction, and he smiles down at me. "I'll book a table at Hillstone," he offers.

My mom hugs me, holding on far tighter than necessary. Her hug says more than I know she's capable of. And while I know my parents aren't perfect, standing outside my new bookshop and their old home, I feel an unexpected wave of gratitude. Because Colt encouraged me to chase my dream, but all my life, they've pushed me to remain focused and to follow through.

And this time, I did exactly that.

~

COLT and I walk toward the water's edge, admiring Holly River in all its festive glory. Music plays in the streets, children chase one another around street lamps, and the smell of fried dough fills the air. As people stroll, they bite into sticky candy apples and hold hands and duck in and out of storefronts, bringing much-needed commerce to our businesses. There are more festival attendees than we dared hope for, and all of Holly River owes Maggie and her social media savviness a debt of gratitude.

I glance up at Colt. "You sure you're okay with meeting my parents for dinner tonight?"

"For sure." Colt stops suddenly, squeezing my hand. "Alice, they're kind of my family too, remember? I get to be mad at them also. And forgive them."

Emotion tightens my chest as certain words fight to leave my mouth. Three words, in fact, that would perfectly encapsulate how much I care about Colt.

Colt's eyes drift toward the river, and he spots the crowd. "Am I finally going to see this secret of yours?"

"I'll show you mine if you show me yours."

He growls at the innuendo and loops his arm around my waist. "Very soon, my girl."

Dalton waves when he sees us, and we head toward him.

"We can wait in line, Dalton," I say as we approach.

"Nonsense," he responds, eyes alight with something I must be missing. "You created this. And besides, we have a special boat waiting just for the two of you."

"Kayak," I specify. "Though I suppose it's—"

I stop cold when we reach the dock. Tucked away from the cluster of kayaks are two electric picnic boats, exactly like the ones I showed Colt. They are low-slung, elegant vessels with a helm bench toward the back and, near the front, a circular seating area surrounding a built-in picnic table. Both boats have been decorated in fall garland and shimmer in the dappled sunlight.

My hands fly to my mouth. "Who did this?"

Colt smiles down at the ground, rubbing the back of his neck. Dalton's grin and pointed stare at Colt gives it away.

"I can't believe it." I gaze up at Colt in shock.

He shrugs. "Your dad told me to save and invest, and to take a financial risk only when I found an idea that made sense." He meets my bewildered stare. "I can't think of a single thing that makes more sense than you, Alice."

"But what if it doesn't work?" My heart races. "What if you lose your money and—"

Colt juts his chin toward the lines. There's a shorter one for people awaiting kayaks, but the one for the picnic boats stretches nearly to the Hall. "The only concern I have right now is whether to add a third boat."

I shake my head at him, smiling like the lovesick woman I am as he leads me into our private vessel. The picnic table holds thick wedges of cheese, ripe pear slices, sugar-dusted cider doughnuts, and tarts filled with caramelized onions and goat cheese. In the center, nestled in a bucket of ice, is a bottle of champagne. The immaculate spread has June's name written all over it.

Dalton jumps behind the wheel. "Pretend I'm not here." He winks and starts the whisperlike motor.

The boat glides away from the dock, the movement so smooth it's like we're floating on air. Colt pours two glasses of champagne and hands one to me. We sit huddled together on the padded bench, and I drape the wool blanket over our shoulders.

As we round the river bend, the world transforms into an autumnal wonderland. The arching trees lining the banks have been wrapped in thousands of tiny orange lights, creating a glowing tunnel. White lanterns hang from branches like low-hanging moons, and glowing pumpkins dangle from invisible wires. Just overhead, chains of marigolds sweep back and forth, so close that when I reach up, my fingers graze the soft, silken petals.

Colt glances at me, awe stretched across his face.

I kiss him, quick, wanting to bottle the look in his eyes. Wanting to keep it by my bed and revisit it time and again. Shake it with both hands and watch flecks of gold dance around his expression like a snow globe.

From the boat's speakers, jazz plays softly—a soulful saxophone that dances the same way the lights do across the water's reflection. The gentle lap against the hull is the only other sound. A few kayaks float nearby, the people inside looking up at the lights with the same quiet reverence Colt wears. The same one I feel inside. Because it's like we've been transported from my bookshop straight into a living fairytale. One I never want to leave.

Colt draws me closer against him. "Look at what you created."

I lean my head against his shoulder, the champagne and the music and the magic of the moment making me feel weightless. "Look at what *we* created," I say. "You and me and everyone else in this town."

We drift in silence for a long time, the boat carrying us through the heart of the fire-lit woods. The jazz swells, a melody seemingly written for this exact moment. And suddenly, the decor shifts, just as I envisioned. The orange lights give way to white, the pumpkins replaced by strings of glittering silver and gold ornaments. As the boat continues its silent commute, people around us smile and laugh, watching as we leave autumn behind and float into the mouth of winter.

Colt shifts, turning to watch my face in the glow of the white lights. He studies me for so long that I laugh and bring a hand to his cheek.

"What is it?" I ask.

"I've been working on something," Colt admits in a near whisper.

I smile. "I know."

Colt scrubs his head, as if summoning the courage to divulge this plan of his. His hand finds my thigh, and he meets my eyes. "I bought these boats because you wanted them, but also because I can rent them out between festivals. And *during* festivals, like this one, I can rent them to the city."

"It's a good idea," I agree.

"And I'm going... I'm gonna be a contractor. When I reached my EAS and got out of the Marines, I'd thought I'd be a carpenter, like my dad. But I've been acting as a contractor these last few months, orchestrating plumbers and electricians and overseeing the entire operation. So I think I can do it."

"Of *course* you can," I encourage, because if Colt said he planned to grow wings and fly to the moon, I'd believe him.

"I figured..." He shifts again. "I don't have to sell my mom's place. If we wanted, if *you* wanted, I could build a proper house on the land. Or we could get a place in town."

"Colt." I turn to face him more fully. "That sounds like a dream, and I would be happy living with you anywhere. But we already have a home. The bookshop is our home, if you want it to be. We created it together."

Colt reaches into his pocket, withdrawing papers and unfolding them. "I thought you might say that. So I sketched plans for an exterior staircase so you can reach the second story without entering through the shop. And here." He points out a second blueprint. "A private interior staircase that leads to the kitchen. For when you want a day off and..."

Colt glances away, frowning, like he's worried he's blowing this. I gather his hands in mine, encouraging him to continue, and he looks back at me, his face a mask of determination. "I want to take care of us," he explains softly. "Like your parents did. I want to give you that life, Ali."

My ribs open. My breath stills. Because suddenly, I understand.

"Colt." I place my hands flat on his chest. "I don't want my parents' life. I want *our* life. I want *you*. As you are now. And as you will be. That's what I want. Just you, with me."

Colt drops his head, breathing hard, and when he finally looks up, he doesn't speak. He just searches my face, and my belly flips, because I can sense the words gathering courage in his mouth, the same way they've done mine. And I know, one beautiful heartbeat before he says it, what he's about to voice aloud.

But nothing prepares me for how it'll feel.

"I love you, Alice Sinclair."

The lights. The music. The people.

They vanish.

And then there is only Colt. He's fifteen years old again, standing outside his mother's house, shame in his eyes, his mother's harsh words rolling over him as he runs toward our idling car. And there's me—gripped with empathy so deep I can't breathe past it—wanting to *do* something. Wanting Colt to feel safe, and loved.

Wanting to save him, but not knowing how.

Tears prick my eyes, blurring the lights into streaks of

gold, and I say the easiest words I've ever known. "I love you too, Colt. I'll love you 'til the day I die."

He kisses me then, his grip on me growing tighter and tighter, as if he's afraid I'll suddenly vanish. Then his lips press to my temple, and to my ear. And he whispers, "Forever, then."

I close my eyes, breathing in the smell of the crisp fall air, and the river, and this man sitting beside me. This man I love with every part of me. And the boat keeps going, sailing beneath an ocean of lights, leading us someplace spectacular.

Someplace where dreams come true.

THANKS FOR READIN'

I really hope you enjoyed spending time with Alice and Colt! It would mean the world to me if you'd consider **leaving a review** on a bookseller platform and/or on social media. Please tag me on socials so I can show my appreciation for ya.

@HEYTORIFORD

Don't miss the second book
in the Holly River series

BURNIN' TIDES

COMING MARCH 2027

BONUS CONTENT

December 2026
Holly River, Texas

My Darling Colt,

I'm writing you this letter from Birds Bookstore, and I'll never get tired of saying that. How are things at Camp Inwood? Is it strange being back there? I'm delighted to hear that Sergeant Taylor favors me, but I can't possibly believe that he likes you "like a hole in the head." After all, he agreed to continue teaching you what he knows about carpentry, and I'm sure he's a busy man. Though not nearly as busy as you'll soon be.

Guess what showed up at the house today?! Your LLC paperwork! You're officially a business owner, you handsome, delectable man. Soon, all of Holly River, and then all of East Texas and beyond will learn what those hands can do. Though I imagine they'd be scandalized if they knew what those hands do to ME.

Yes, darling, I got all seven of your letters. How did you even manage that? You've only been gone four days. I laugh every time I think about Sergeant Taylor waking you up at 0500, as you put it. How dare he imply that my man is lazy? Does he know you built an entire bookshop with only pizza, coffee, and hot sex?

Speaking of hot sex, I bought something while you were gone. It's red, velvet, and trimmed in white fur. I'm sorry to say that it's far too short. And dips far too low up top. In fact, I look like a horny Mrs. Claus in it. Shall I return it, my darling? Or shall I wear it for you when you return? I'm told you've been a very naughty boy.

I can't wait to spend our first Christmas together! I feel like I'm still stuffed from Thanksgiving, and I fear June will go even more overboard for Christmas dinner. Do you think Warren might come? I tried to visit him yesterday, but he wouldn't open the door. I can't believe he's still at your mom's house and that the sale fell through. I thought I might invite him to lunch with me and Maggie, though I could tell Maggie didn't like the idea. It's odd, because she's usually more forgiving than this. I think there's something complicated there, but I won't press.

Roxanne is doing great at the bookshop and seems thrilled to be there. She created these surprise book bundles, wrapped in holiday paper, and added June's chocolate peppermint bark to each one. We've already sold a half dozen of them.

And she's rented out your boats twice since you've been gone! Maggie was absolutely right about hiring part-time help.

Two more days, and you'll be home. Remember, you promised we could visit the Holiday Market. It looks so beautiful. White twinkling lights everywhere, the smell of gingerbread in the air, and those rustic little huts offering everything from handmade ornaments to candied pecans. Every shop in Holly River is playing Christmas music, and you know I started doing that well before Thanksgiving. It's such a peaceful, magical time of year, isn't it, Colt? And I can't wait to spend it with you. So hurry back, my builder of dreams. My chicken nugget thief. My bird lover and quiet protector.

I miss you, and I love you.

I LOVE you.

Forever,
Your Alice

I'M MIGHTY GRATEFUL

You guys, self-publishing a book is *wild*. Coming from the world of traditional publishing, I had no idea what I was getting myself into. Somehow, despite the loss of sleep and sanity, I crossed the finish line. But I certainly couldn't have done it without the following rock stars.

Enormous thank you to my cover magicians, Austin Drake and Jet Purdie, and to my audiobook narrators, Kallestra Spencer and Ryan Barber. Take a bow, dream team!

To my editor, Katie Seaman, who helped this story become everything it could be—*thank you* is not enough. I'm saving you a seat at The Buttermilk Cafe.

A round of cold ones is owed to Reed Timmermann, the whitewater pro who helped me nail down those river scenes, to Andy Bradford, the Marine who lent his expertise to Colt's military background, and to Gustavo Girao, the tennis pro who ensured Alice sounded like an authentic (Brazilian!) court rat. All remaining inaccuracies are my own.

Thank you to Garnet Gilbreath, my assistant and right-hand woman—I'd be lost in a sea of emails without you. And to dear friends Dustin Lancaster, Kevin Wade, Irina Genyuk, and Jacquelyn Kung, all of whom offered input on everything from pen names to plot points. Also, thank you to Dr. Glover, who talked me down when I accidentally shipped blank books.

A standing ovation to book influencers who shared the cover, read ARCs, posted reviews, and cheered on *Fallin' Tides*. You guys make this job *fun* and provide indie authors a shot at success. Pardon My Garden bouquets for everyone!

My gratitude to Humble Pie for supplying criminally addictive cherry pie. Your sugar fueled this sweet romance, so naturally I put your name in the book. And to Bird's Bookstore, my local bookshop that wove itself into the heart of this story. Thanks for feeding my TBR!

To my mom, dad, sister, and brother, thank you for loving me despite my many flaws, and to my niece, Faith Wittmann, who has demanded early access to my books since age ten (now twenty-three).

Thank you—always and forever—to my husband, Ryan, who never, *ever* doubts me. Who would quite possibly bankrupt us out of sheer belief in my writing. And to my daughter, Luci, thank you for telling me (countless times) that this story is good. That *I* am good. Gilmore Girls for life, my little lemon!

HOWDY, Y'ALL

Tori Ford is the author of the Holly River series. She also authored nine young adult novels under the name Victoria Scott. Her books have received starred reviews from Publishers Weekly and Kirkus, and have been translated and sold in over a dozen countries. Tori's bestselling title, *Fire & Flood*, is currently an Amazon Teacher's Pick. Her work has been featured by *USA Today*, BuzzFeed, and Good Morning Texas. The author lives in Dallas and loves hearing from readers. Find her on Instagram, TikTok, and Meta at @heytoriford.

Y'ALL STAY IN TOUCH NOW

Join **Team Ford** and subscribe to Tori's newsletter, where you'll get sneak peeks at upcoming Holly River books, first looks at cover reveals, and news about book signings and special edition releases.

Subscribe to Newsletter:
heytoriford.com

Follow Tori:
@heytoriford

www.ingramcontent.com/pod-product-compliance
Lightning Source LLC
Chambersburg PA
CBHW030012100926
51243CB00021B/137

* 9 7 9 8 9 9 5 8 3 7 2 0 6 *